WINTER WARRIORS

Stuart Slade

Dedication

*This book is respectfully dedicated to the memory of
Marshal of the Soviet Union Georgy Konstantinovich Zhukov*

Acknowledgements

*Winter Warriors could not have been written without the very generous
help of a large number of people who contributed their time, input and
efforts into confirming the technical details of the story. Some of these
generous souls I know personally and we discussed the conduct and
probable results of the actions described in this novel in depth. Others
I know only via the internet as the collective membership of the History,
Politics and Current Affairs Forum yet their communal wisdom and
vast store of knowledge, freely contributed, has been truly
irreplaceable.*

*I must also express a particular debt of gratitude to my wife Josefa for
without her kind forbearance, patient support and unstintingly
generous assistance, this novel would have remained nothing more
than a vague idea floating in the back of my mind.*

Caveat

*Winter Warriors is a work of fiction, set in an alternate universe. All
the characters appearing in this book are fictional and any
resemblance to any person, living or dead is purely coincidental.
Although some names of historical characters appear, they do not
necessarily represent the same people we know in our reality.*

Copyright Notice

Contents

Previous Books In This Series
Available From Lulu Press

Winter Warriors	(1945)
The Big One	(1947)
Anvil of Necessity	(1948)
The Great Game	(1959)
Crusade	(1965)
Ride of The Valkyries	(1972)

Coming Shortly

Lion Resurgent	(1982)

CHAPTER ONE
RED SKY IN THE MORNING

1st Platoon, Ski Group, 78th Siberian Infantry Division, First Kola Front, November 1945

"It is time to kill some fascists, Bratishka." Lieutenant Stanislav Knyaginichev let the bolt of his SKS rifle slam forward, chambering a round, ready to fire.

"It is always a good day to kill fascists, Tovarish Lieutenant. This day is yet young." Sergeant Pietr Ivanovitch Batov spoke with grim satisfaction. As he did so, he looked on his young Lieutenant with care that was almost fatherly. 'Knyaz,' as the men in the unit called him was a good officer. In fact, he had the makings of an excellent commander; assuming he survived. He started his career as one of Mekhlis's zampolits, the political officers, so many of whom had done so much to harm the Russian Army in 1941. Knyaz had not been one of those. Instead, he had been a good zampolit, using his powers to aid rather than hinder. As 1941 had ground on in days of fire and death, he had become loved by his men as much as he had been respected by his officers. When, in November 1942, Stalin had died and unitary command was restored, he had been one of the zampolits selected to be trained as a real officer. Six months later, he had been assigned to the 78th and there he had lead his men well.

Then, he had gone down with pneumonia. His men mourned him for they knew that pneumonia meant death. This time, it did not; fate had once again saved Knyaz. He'd been taken back to the hospital the Americans had set up at Murmansk and given some of the new wonder drug they had there. Pensin, or something like that, Batov didn't know the name, but it had saved their Lieutenant. Now, once again, he commanded the Ski Group formed from the 78th.

This year, winter had come down early and very hard upon the Kola Peninsula. It froze the ground, covered it with thick snow and turned everything to ice. Already, the front line that had marked the furthest extent of the German advance was immobilized. The units that held it had gone into winter quarters. Cantonments provided some semblance of warmth and protection from the bitter cold and howling winds. The spaces between the camps were patrolled by ski troops. On the German side, they were Gebirgsjaegers, specialized divisions of mountain troops. They were specially equipped and trained to fight in the snows. Like all specialist troops they were very hard to replace. That made bleeding them worthwhile.

The Russians did things differently. Every one of their units had been expected to form its own ski patrols. That was no problem for the 78th Siberian Infantry Division. Siberians had been born on skis. To them, the cold of the Kola Peninsula was a mild thing compared with the frozen tundra of their home. Once the whole division had been Siberians. In 1941, they had been brought from the east and thrown against the Germans standing at Tula, on the very doorstep of Moscow. They had hurled the Germans back and hounded them through the blinding snowstorms, sparing none. That had been four years ago; few men from those days survived. Enough did to provide a cadre for the unit and to give the recruits a sense of being in an elite unit.

Knyaz checked the positions; the ambush was set. The snowmobiles that had brought them were parked several kilometers back. They had been tucked away where they were unlikely to be seen. Even if they were, their position was deceptive. It looked as if they were laagered just on the Russian side of the lines, not as if their ski troops had penetrated into German-held territory. *Maskirovka*, Knyaz thought, *maskirovka, always maskirovka. Mislead, deceive, conceal. Never do the obvious, never do the simple. Always mislead and deceive.* The Germans didn't practice that art with the same grim

6

determination as the Russians and now they were going to pay the price. The Germans were very good but they got into bad habits. Like using the same patrol routes too often.

"You ready, drug?" Knyaz spoke to the youngest of his new recruits. Kabanov was a true Siberian but one who had only joined the unit a week before. He'd never seen combat so he was still a lowly 'drug,' a friend, but not one raised to the comradely fellowship of the 'brats'. He would be, soon, if he survived. The boy nodded, pretending to concentrate on his SKS but wouldn't speak because his mouth was dry with fear. *No shame in that, but the boy wouldn't understand, not yet.*

"They're coming!" The growl of engines could be heard. It was amazing how far it carried over the frozen snow. The Germans didn't use snowmobiles for their ski troops. Instead, they had a strange vehicle called the kettenkrad, a motorcycle with a sidecar but tracks instead of wheels at the rear. The patrol approaching had six of them, in two columns of three. Each pulled four ski-jaegers. *Tough troops,* Knyaz thought, *well trained, well-acclimatized to this frozen wasteland.* The ski-jaegers didn't blunder around in the cold the way the German infantry did. *A pity only a half-platoon was approaching.* He'd wanted to bag a whole platoon. Still, a half platoon, two squads, a prize worth taking.

His two DP-28 machine guns would open the game. The two crews were already be tracking their targets. Two Kettenkrads were out in front, forming the point element of the patrol. The machine gunners would let those pass, if they could, and catch the following four in the L-shaped killing ground. He carefully swept his eyes around again; not a sign of his men waiting motionless in the snow. Their rippled white and light gray camouflage suits blended perfectly with the snow that hid them.

The point element of the patrol swept past. The four vehicles of the main body followed them right into the killing ground. Their engines sounded small and weak against the immensity of the snow; yet the sound carried so well that Knyaz believed he could hear each individual pop of the engines. The engine sounds were drowned out by the snarl of the DP-28s. The fire walked across the snow, tearing into the kettenkrads at the front of each column. The nearest driver was hurled from his seat. His blood sprayed dark and agreeably red against the whiteness all around. His kettenkrad tumbled as it lost its driver, dragging the four ski-jaegers behind it into a chaotic, confused heap.

Knyaz sighted and fired his SKS, squeezing the trigger of the semi-automatic rifle again and again. Gone were the old days of fumbling with the bolt of the Moisin-Nagant, fighting the stickiness caused by lacquer from cartridges building up in the chamber. His rifle cracked again and again, ten rounds rapid fire. One of the fascists in the chaos below tried to move to get under cover but his body jerked and stopped. *Who had hit him? Did I? Who cared, the fascist was dead.* His rifle was open, the last round gone. A new stripper clip, push down, five rounds into the magazine, another clip, five more. Bolt forward and ready to go again.

Out in the killing zone, one of the ski-jaegers was pointing at the long arm of the ambush, where the muzzle blast of the SKS rifles threw up a cloud of snow. Then, his head jerked and he crumpled. Noble Sniper Irina Trufanova had done her work. Her spotter identified the leader and the telescopic-sighted Moisin-Nagant had sent him to his grave. Now, the team would be moving to a new location. When the ski group fought, Trufanova and her spotter worked independently. They knew their job and nobody dared to advise them otherwise.

The second kettenkrad was burning. Armor-piercing incendiaries from the DP-28s had ruptured its petrol tank and ignited the contents. More figures scattered around. Few of the ski-jaegers towed by the vehicles the machine gunners had hit first managed to survive. That left the eight men and the two kettenkrads at the rear of the patrol and the two at the front that had already passed out of the killing ground. They'd be turning already, coming back to aid the main body. This was the critical bit. If it went wrong now, Knyaz knew his unit would be trapped between the two forces.

A roar of rifle fire from the StG-44 'banana guns.' They were the fully-automatic rifles arming the ski-jaegers. The men carrying them had gone to ground and were hosing fire at the ambush position above them. Their machine guns had gone; they'd been on the two destroyed kettenkrads. Even without their support, those automatic rifles put out a fearful volume of fire. The Germans were trying to pin the ambushers down so they could be isolated and picked off. That had been anticipated; most of the Siberians had already slipped away from their original positions. The fascist ski-jaegers had fewer machine guns than the regular line infantry but they carried more ammunition and they had the banana guns. Knyaz watched a group of four fascists run forward a few meters, taking advantage of the lull in the Russian fire caused by the blast from the StG-44s. They'd take up new positions and provide covering fire for the other group of four. Soon, they'd be in grenade range. Or so they thought.

A new sound, something indescribable. The PPS-45 machine carbine didn't snarl or roar, the sound was more like paper being ripped. It fired a version of the 7.62x25mm pistol round that had been "improved." The Americans had done it. They'd taken the original cartridge and reloaded it with new propellant, pushing the chamber pressure up through the roof. A new, longer, heavier bullet took advantage of the extra energy. The new cartridge had its tip painted green because anybody who tried to fire it from a Tokarev TT-33 or an older PPsH-41 would lose his hand when the chamber burst open.

The tried and tested PPSH-41 had been redesigned with a 41cm barrel and a new foregrip. The result was a weapon half way between a submachine gun and the SKS. It still had the light bolt of the PPSH, so its rate of fire was phenomenal. Still, it did have its 71 round drum magazine to feed it. There was something else about it as well, the PPS-45 was built in one of the new American-supplied factories at Khabarovsk. Any part from a PPS-45 fitted any other PPS-45. If something needed replacing, the spare part would fit, right away, no need to file it down or select the best from a pile. It would fit. A magazine, any magazine, taken at random from a pile would fit any PPS-45. Amazing.

Knyaz knew what was happening. The two point kettenkrads had turned around and were towing their ski-jaegers to attack the ambush; the men held the tow lines with one hand and fired their banana guns from the hip with the other. Only, Knyaz had foreseen that and he had four of his six PPS-45 men in a skirmish line waiting for the move. *An ambush within an ambush, maskirovka, always maskirovka.*

The PPS-45 men waited until the range was point-blank and they sprayed the approaching fascists with long, long bursts. If it went right, they would sweep the fascists from their seats and tumble the ski-jaegers into the snow. The fascists wouldn't be fighting back. At that close range, the greentips made huge gaping wounds in their victims as the bullet tumbled and broke up in their bodies.

Another surge forward from the fascists in the killing zone. Almost instantly one spun and fell into the blood-soaked snow. *Another score for Noble Sniper Trufanova.* Explosions. The fascists had thrown stick grenades, the long handle giving them extra reach. One DP-28 opened up and two more of the running men went down, the last diving for cover again. *One DP-28? Had the other crew already died? When?*

The five survivors of the fascist unit were pinned down in a ditch-like depression. The DP-28 was snapping out short bursts, keeping the fascists pinned, making sure any fire from them was wild and unaimed. Meanwhile, two more men with PPS-45s and two men with grenades, moved around their flank. Knyaz knew that Trufanova had watched the fascists go to ground and was already moving to somewhere that would give her a clear shot. He thought he saw a movement in the trees, off to the fascists' right. They saw it too. They tried to turn and fire but two black objects arced out of cover, into their pit. The explosions were muffled by the snow but they still hurled the fascists back, stunning them. Then the four skiers burst out of the trees. The two men with PPS-45s hosed the fascist position with a long continuous burst; the snow fountained red and white around the occupants. The two grenadiers fired their SKS's from the hip as they rode in. It was over, the last of the ski-jaegers were dead.

What happened next was a well-ordered drill. One part of the Russian group skied out. They first checked the bodies of the fascists lying sprawled around the kettenkrads, then the little vehicles themselves. They picked up the StG-44s, and stripped the bodies of ammunition, documents, anything of value. Letters especially, for no matter how careful the writer was, they always let something slip in a letter to a loved one. Binoculars, radios, everything. Nobody said anything but sometimes be a groan from a wounded fascist was silenced by a quick thrust from a knife. It wasn't practical to take prisoners; even if they could, they wouldn't. Unless they were needed for intelligence, nobody took prisoners on the Russian Front, not any more. Not even the Americans and Canadians, who were ridiculously sentimental and squeamish about realities, took prisoners any more. Not in winter, not on the Kola Peninsula.

Up on the slope, Knyaz looked at the rest of his ambush force. As he feared, he'd lost a machine gun crew to a stick grenade. Three of his riflemen had been killed by fire from the banana guns. Three other men had wounds; one bad, the other two not so much so. The badly wounded man could ride on a captured kettenkrad. The rest could ski. Then he saw the boy who had been the unit drug. He was standing on the slope, looking down and shaking with delayed shock and fear. Knyaz went over to him and clapped him on the back. "Remember, bratishka, you have to be alive to be cold!" Knyaz was very careful to misunderstand the shaking.

Kabanov looked at him. His eyes lit up as the meaning of his lieutenant's words sunk in. He'd seen action; he had fired his rifle at an enemy. He was a proud brat now, not a humble drug. Behind him, Sergeant Batov dipped his fingers in the pool of blood that surrounded a dead fascist, blood already freezing in the bitter cold. He dabbed it on the boy's forehead and cheeks. The old hunter's ritual. Batov called out in a voice that carried across the ambush site. "Tovarish, we have a new Brat today." A quick cheer; very quick for the unit needed to get moving. They picked up their dead, made their wounded man as comfortable as they could on one of the two captured kettenkrads then set off on the long traverse back to their snowmobiles.

Captain's Cabin, CV-33 USS Kearsarge, *Churchill, Nova Scotia, Canada*

"Something old, something new, something borrowed, all of it midnight blue."

Captain Karl Newman chuckled as his CAG, Commander Pearson, dropped into a seat. "We have our new airgroup then. What we got?"

Pearson flipped through his clipboard. "Eighty eight birds; five squadrons of 16. Two fighter squadrons. One with FV-3 Flivvers, the other with F4U-7 Corsairs. Two light strike squadrons with F4U-4 Corsairs, one heavy strike squadron with AD-1 Skyraiders. Difference between fighter and light strike is a bit academic really. They're both trained for either role. In addition, we've got a detachment of four F4U-4N night-fighters and another four Adies equipped with APS-20 search radars."

"FV-3s? We got a new version of the Flivver?"

"They're the new bit, along with the F4U-7s. The FV-3 is similar to the Air Force's F-80B Shooting Star, only it's got a hook and folding wings." Pearson spoke with satisfaction. The older FV-1 and

FV-2 had fixed wings and they'd caused handling problems on the deck. The jet fighter was far faster than anything else in the fleet; hence the nickname 'flivver' after the 1920s sports car. "They'll do 557 on the deck, 580 higher up. Rate of climb is 4,870 feet per minute. That's forty, fifty miles per hour faster than the 262 and it climbs almost 1,000 feet per minute faster. 'bout the same edge over the 162. The U-7s aren't so shabby either. Can't compete with the jets, well, it's about as fast as the 162 on the deck where it matters so I guess it can."

"And I guess the U-4s are the old. So, what's the borrowed?"

"Our heavy bomb squadron was Mames, but I talked to the CAG on the *Evil Eye*. They've got two heavy bomb squadrons, were going to be one of Mames and one of Adies. So we agreed to swap our Mames for their Adies. We're switching everything that goes with them now. Better for both of us; we get Adies, they have two squadrons of the same type."

Newman nodded. The Martin AM-1 Mauler could lift heavier loads than the AD-1 Skyraider and was a touch faster, but the Adie had an awesome reputation for toughness and reliability despite some worrying instability problems. But then, both aircraft had been rushed into service. The deal to swap squadrons made sense to him; the skipper of CV-11 *Intrepid* must have thought the same.

"Loadout?"

Pearson flipped another page on his clipboard. "The usual. Rockets, five inch high-velocity aircraft rockets and 12 inch Tiny Tims. Thousand and two thousand pounders, rocket-boosted sixteen hundred pounders. Some five hundreds. Napalm of course. Mines and torpedoes, more than usual. Rumor is we're running cover on a convoy, a big one. To Murmansk. Guess the powers that be want to get as much supply through as they can before winter really sets in. Expect we've got the torpedoes in case the Kraut fleet comes out."

"If only." Newman's voice was loaded with longing. "Nobody's ever put a battleship at sea down with airstrikes before. Good time to be the first." The German fleet was still orientated around its battleships. They only had three carriers, and one of those had been captured from the British. Third Fleet had twenty Essex class carriers with more than 1,950 aircraft, including those on the *Gettysburg*. Five more of the big CVBs were on the way, three would join the fleet before spring next year. "Anything else I should know about?"

"Notice anything about our airgroup Captain?"

Newman looked down the list. "All single-seaters."

"That's right. It's the same right across the fleet. All the multi-crew birds have gone. The Beasts went a long time ago and nobody misses them, but the Avengers have gone as well. Even on the last cruise, when a couple of the carriers still had them, they were short of crews. Now, they're all gone. No flight engineers, no navigators, no gunners, nobody. All single seaters, just pilots. Odd that. I'd have expected it to be the other way around: plenty of aircrew, shortage of pilots. I hear the ASW hunting groups still get their crews but the rest of us are running mighty short."

"I guess the Air Bridge must be draining off the aircrew. Running that must take a lot of manpower. Still, it is odd that it's hitting us this hard. It's not just you CAG. We're having difficulty getting aircraft mechanics and hangar deck crewmen. Bear that in mind. We're short-handed on the decks; it's going to take us longer to turn birds around and a lot longer to repair cripples. Anything else?"

"No, Skipper, not unless you count some more Foo Fighter sightings."

The two burst out laughing at the thought. Every so often a ship reported some highly anomalous radar contacts. Very high altitude, relatively slow moving, usually inland over Canada but sometimes over the sea. Always on the edge of radar coverage and peculiarly hard to get a hold on. As if the radar pulses kept slipping off them. The Foo Fighters led to all sorts of weird explanations, the usual clutch of secret weapons and (from the pulp magazine devotees) space aliens. The scientists had explained it. There was a thing called the Jet Stream, a very high-speed current of air that circled the globe. The B-29s had found it when they'd started their ill-fated career and a lot of problems it had caused them. Apparently, every so often, a pocket of moist air got caught up in the jetstream and floated around in it until it dispersed. Those pockets were remarkably stable and could last for hours. While they did so they gave a solid radar return. That made sense. Radar shadowing from moist air pockets down at sea level were a constant problem, so why shouldn't the ones high up be the same? No, the Foo Fighters were nothing to be concerned about. Just a natural phenomenon of no great consequence.

No importance at all.

Battery Anton, 71st Infantry Division, Army Group Vistula, Kola Peninsula

"That damned fool will kill us all." Sergeant Heim swore, fluently but quietly. After all, nobody knew who was listening these days. It was true though, that damned Captain from the staff, that perfect perfumed prince from Berlin, seemed perfectly determined to kill them all.

The convoy wasn't a big one. A half-track with a quadruple 20mm gun at the front, another with a squad of infantry, then two big Henschels towing the first pair of 15 cm sFH 18s. Then, another half-track with infantry, one mounting a 37mm anti-aircraft gun and two more Henschel 10 tonners with the other pair of sFH 18s. A second half-track with a 37mm gun then four British-built AECs carrying ammunition. Another quad twenty on a half-track and one more half-track with the rest of the infantry bringing up the rear. Almost more escorts than escorted in this convoy. That made it like every supply convoy on the Kola Peninsula. Russian Partisans and Ami Jabos saw to that. And, right in the middle of the convoy rode the thing Heim considered more dangerous than either, a staff officer desperate to break the pristine, decoration-less monotony of his uniform with a medal or two.

"We must get the guns into place by evening." he had said. "The Jabos will not fly in winter," he'd claimed. So now this artillery battery, *his artillery battery more the pity*, was moving in broad daylight. Something no sane person did when Ami Jabos were on the prowl. Even moving at night was getting dangerous, the Ami Night Witches saw to that. *A country so rich it could put radar sets on ground attack aircraft,* Heim shuddered at the thought. The Night Witch struck from the darkness and never gave any warning of its approach. Perhaps moving in daylight was better.

Heim's eye was caught by a flash in the sky up ahead. *The sun reflecting off a cockpit perhaps?* There was a chance, a slim one, it was a Luftwaffe fighter but the odds weren't in their favor. He scanned the area with his binoculars; they were good ones, taken from a dead officer. There were lots of those over the years. At first he saw nothing. When the truck lurched a little he caught a glimpse. Two engines, a nose that stuck far, far out in front. *Damn it*, he thought, *Grizzlies, just what we needed. Probably four of them, carrying rockets, a couple thousand kilos of bombs or, horror of horrors, jellygas.* Six .50 machine guns and a 75mm gun that stuck out of the nose like the unicorn's horn gave the aircraft its distinctive appearance in the recognition books. The Beechcraft A-38D Grizzly to give it its full and proper name. *Where would they be coming from?*

Heim scanned around fast, over to the left, a low ridge. *The Grizzlies will dive down, use the hill as cover, then slash across us.* Different tactics from different air forces, the Russian Sturmoviks would circle their prey, each diving on it in turn. The Americans made straight strafing runs across the target area. Difficult to say which was worse. He looked around his truck.

"Jabos coming. Get your snowshoes on. When I give the word, bail out and run like the wind, to the left."

That was a painful lesson, learned at grim cost. Run away from the Ami jabos and they'd give chase, treat killing the men on the ground as a game. Run towards them and one might, might, get under the attack, escape that way. Whatever one did, get away from the vehicles. For vehicles drew jellygas.

Heim was right. Four Grizzlies erupted over the ridgeline, heading straight for the convoy. The vehicles lurched and swayed as they came to a halt, the anti-aircraft gunners swung their weapons to bear. Those who couldn't fight the jabos were already running for the snowbanks on either side of the road. The perfect perfumed prince stood in the back of his kubelwagen, shouting something. *Probably exhorting his men to stand and fight. He would learn. Learn and burn.*

Tracer screamed across the sky towards the racing jabos, the noses of the aircraft vanished behind the orange fireballs as they fired back at the flak guns. Nobody had ever accused the Amis of being inventive; they found the best way of slaughtering their enemies and stuck with it. This was the first act. They would concentrate fire on the flak guns and take them out. *The guns will probably die, but if they can maul the Grizzlies, they might not go through with killing the rest of us.* Heim couldn't see the flak gunners serving their guns behind him, he was too busy running across the hardened crust on top of the snow, for the soft, deep banks where he could hide, but he knew they'd be steadily, efficiently, serving their guns.

He couldn't see but he sensed the fountains of snow erupting around the half-tracks. The guns on the Grizzlies outranged the flak pieces, so they'd be hoping to get at least some of them before the range closed. He heard the clang as an armor piercing round hit the side of one of the vehicles, heard the explosion as the ammunition in the half-track exploded, felt the heat from the ball of flame as the 37mm gun and its crew died. The viciously cold air was burning his lungs as he ran. He saw some snow banks and hurled himself into them as the Grizzlies swept overhead. The rockets screamed from under their wings and he heard the explosions. The mass of secondary explosions meant he didn't need to look to know that the trucks brought all the way from England had just blown up.

He did sneak a look anyway. Pyres of black smoke were rising from where both the 37mm guns and one of the quadruple 20mms had gone. The AECs weren't just burning, they were an inferno of exploding ammunition and fuel. The infantry, the convoy's guard against partisan attack had spread out into defensive positions, away from the guns but near enough to protect them from any partisans closing in on the scene. Joint attacks between Ami jabos and partisans weren't unknown but they weren't common either. More often the partisans stayed in the background and called in the air attacks.

Up above, the four Grizzlies were turning away. One was streaming thick black smoke from its starboard wing. Heim watched it turn away still further and head north slowly losing height. One of the other jabos was leaving with it. Another difference between the Amis and Ivans. A crippled Russian aircraft was on its own, left to get back to base as best it could. The Americans detached aircraft to escort the cripple. If it crash-landed, they'd land to pick up the crew. They'd risk men to save men. In their eyes, expending treasure, machines, resources to rescue their men just didn't enter into the equation. If their men were down, they'd do what it took to get them back. May the good Lord help anybody who got in the way.

The Grizzlies vanished behind the trees again. Heim guessed what was coming next. It wasn't an accident that the 20mm quad at the front of the convoy had been knocked out in the first pass. He and his men took the opportunity to get still further from the trucks on the road. They had little time and it ran out as the two remaining Grizzlies broke over the treeline. Their 75mm guns belched out the familiar orange ball of flame. They were joined by the flat hammering of the .50 machine guns. Heim saw the lead ten tonner explode. A 75mm round had plowed through the front and it shattered the vehicle into blazing fragments. There were only a handful of shots, the range was short and the Grizzlies had better things on their mind. Better for them that was.

Heim watched the two stubby tanks detach from the bomb racks on the jabos. They wobbled down, turning end over end as they fell. An inaccurate weapon but it didn't matter. It was the dreaded jellygas, the foul thing the Amis had created by mixing gasoline with stuff that made it burn hot and slow. Stuff that made it stick to whatever it touched. Stuff that nothing could put it out.

The first pair hit the ground just short of the wrecked 20mm half-track. They bounded high and erupted into a roaring mass of orange and black flame. It boiled skywards as the bouncing tanks spewed the hellish jellygas back along the lines of stalled vehicles. The second pair hit just behind the middle point of the convoy and repeated the inferno that was consumed what was left of the convoy. Roaring and screaming, the black smoke and orange flames blotted out the sky above the convoy. The black cloud of smoke turning the sun blood red. Heim's face blistered as the heat from the nightmarish holocaust rolled across the snow. He felt the hard-packed whiteness soften and saw it turned black with soot from the fires.

The two Grizzlies swept over the inferno below them. The orange glare of the fires reflected off their glossy white-and gray camouflage paint. Then they were gone, heading north. *Probably for more ammunition, more fuel, more jellygas.* Heim got up and waited for the roaring conflagration to die down. Then, he went back to the cooling remnants of the convoy. Around him, the survivors did the same, slowly, shocked by the ferocity of the assault. The vehicles were gone. Some had been hit by gunfire and rockets, others incinerated by the jellygas. Most cases it was hard to tell which was which. *Burned, blasted, who knew?*

Only one vehicle had survived, the little kubelwagen right in the middle. It must have been just far enough back to miss the first pair of jellygas tanks and too far forward to catch the second. Around it, the wreckage on the convoy burned. Scattered around it were the blackened, carbonized husks that had once been soldiers.

The perfect perfumed prince stood immaculate, in the middle of the destruction, neither burned nor asphyxiated. Mentally, Heim raised his eyes in despair. He had long since ceased to believe in God; this was just another example of the injustice that made up his world. The survival of the perfect perfumed prince responsible for this nightmare confirmed his disbelief in any form of divine providence. "Sir, I shall assemble the survivors. We should head back to the depot."

The depot was a safe cantonment heavily guarded against attack. They had to get back there by dusk; the Partisans were closing in. They'd have seen the smoke and heard the explosions. They knew what was happening. Most of the Partisan bands had radios now. It was a fair bet that they'd been told of the strike, to find any survivors the Grizzlies had left and kill them.

"Our orders are to reach the 71st Division base area as soon as possible. We will go on."

"With respect, sir, reaching the base area is no longer possible. We are barely a third of the way there. Even if we are left undisturbed, we will not make it by nightfall. We will be hard put to get back to the depot by then. It is cold now; when dusk comes it will be much, much worse. We can't make it. Even if we could, the wounded couldn't. We must go back."

The perfect perfumed prince stared at the shabby, grizzled sergeant. Slowly Captain Wilhelm Lang realized the truth that lay behind the words he had heard. The stink of the burning vehicles and incinerated men drifted across him and with great annoyance he realized his spotless white scarf was in danger of being stained black by the soot from the fires.

"Very well Sergeant, we will head back for the depot area. With the guns gone, there is no point in carrying on anyway. For the sake of the wounded, we must return to the depot."

Top Floor, Bank de Commerce et Industrie, Geneva, Switzerland.

"I've got the latest production figures from Germany, Loki. Third quarter, 1945. And the transportation requirements for military and civil resource allocations."

Loki was leaning back in his high leather chair, looking out over Geneva, the wet roofs glistening in the morning sun. "Thank you, Branwen. Anything interesting?"

"I've only had a brief look but it looks like much the same as before. Steel, coal, nitrates; all have increased a bit but not much. Armored vehicle and aircraft production are holding steady. It looks like Speer's reforms have finally finished working through the system. Production totals have been steady for two quarters now. I expect they'll drop a bit in the fourth quarter as coal production gets diverted from industrial production to heating. If one goes up, the other goes down, there's no slack left in the German economy any more. Everything they do these days is a zero-sum game, as one thing goes up, another goes down."

Loki took the two-inch thick file and started to skip through the pages. "You know, this would all make a lot more sense if we had the American and Russian figures by way of comparison. We've no idea how much of the American economy is mobilized."

Branwen snorted. "I had Manannan take a look of the American economy; more or less from what we can see they've produced and guesswork at the rest. He reckons the Americans have mobilized about half their productive capacity. To put that into perspective, they're producing around two thirds of the world's aircraft engines."

"About half? I wonder why they haven't mobilized the rest. German's running, what eighty, ninety plus percent mobilized? And the Russians?"

"Germans at least that. Russia? No means of knowing. Most of their industrial infrastructure was in the area now occupied by the Germans. The Russians evacuated a lot and destroyed the rest but how much and what did they have to begin with? We don't know. How much of what they evacuated has been returned to use? We don't know. We do know the Americans have been building factories and resource recovery facilities in Siberia but their output? We just don't know. Loki. It's maddening. We know far, far more about the Germans than about the people we're supposed to be working with."

"With Stuyvesant over there at the heart of things, does this surprise you? I'm astonished he's even told us there's a war on. Ask

Manannan mac Lir to drop up and see me this afternoon will you? I need to talk with him about the Americans and Russians."

Branwen made a note on her pad. Manannan had some odd theories about the American war effort. He believed that something about it didn't quite make sense. As if anything in the madness that was tearing the world apart made any kind of sense.

Loki started thumbing through the thick file again wondering if those who got the data understood where it came from. *Masses of numbers from all over Germany. Mostly from little people who didn't like what Nazi Germany stood for but were too afraid, either for themselves or their families, to do much about it.* That, Loki could understand, he had seen the brutality of the Nazi regime for himself. *But, a few economic figures, how many rifle bolts they had produced, how many trains went through a station, what the consist on those trains was, surely that didn't matter?* Loki snorted to himself. *Individually, none of it did but put together by talented economists it meant a lot. Not just raw economic data either.*

Loki's spy ring, his Red Orchestra, had assembled a complete performance and design specification dossier on the Type XXI U-boat and got it through to the Americans. It had arrived in time for them to have a test boat, modified from a British S-class submarine, at sea before the first German Type XXI was in service. The Battle of the Atlantic might have looked quite different if it hadn't been for that coup. "Natural oil production seems steady as well. The Russians did a good job in blowing up their oil fields. Mostly this comes from Romania. Synthetic fuel production is up but not enough, Germany is still running at a net deficit in fuel." Loki found that satisfying.

"Consumption's slackened off a bit. The end of the B-29 raids has reduced the amount of fuel the home defenses burned, and that's been reallocated to the Russian Front. Also the submarine operations have been cut right back in the second and third quarters. You can see how much less fuel is going to the U-boat bases."

Loki nodded. Fuel was the one German weakness, their one over-riding constraint. They were short of all types of fuel, bunker oil for ships, gasoline for aircraft engines, diesel fuel for armored vehicles, kerosene for jets. They just didn't have enough. They spent their time shifting what supplies they had around, trying to make do with what they had. That's what made the distribution of fuel supplies such a marvelous indicator of future operations.

Loki turned to the pages of railway transport data. *So simple to obtain, just needed one man to count the wagons in a consist and drop the list in a dead letter box somewhere.* Meaningless numbers. One of those who collected the train data had been caught by the Gestapo, but had talked his way out of the arrest. He had claimed that the numbers were his orders for black market goods, so many grams of sugar, so many of sausage. They'd believed him. Who would confess to being a black marketeer when interrogated by the Gestapo unless he was one? They'd beaten him senseless and dumped him in the street as a warning to other black marketeers - and the lists had kept coming.

Loki looked sharply at the train consists again and then at the summary. "Branwen, did you see this?"

"Hmm?"

"The consists of the trains heading east. The fuel shipments going through Kaunas are up 20 percent in the third quarter; those through Minsk and points south are down by the same amount. Kaunas is the rail nexus that supplies the northern end of the front. Especially the area from Petrograd to Archangel. Last time we saw that was second quarter, 1944."

Branwen flipped through her own file, turning to the trend lines. "First quarter. There was a jump in second quarter as well, but first quarter was the big one. Right before the great Northern offensive, the one that broke through to the White Sea."

Loki sucked through his teeth. Those had been grim days, the most recent great breakthrough on the Russian Front, the Russian Army sent reeling backwards. Petrograd and the whole Kola Peninsula cut off, Archangel besieged. Archangel still was under siege, still fighting grimly. *Were the Germans planning to finish off Archangel?* Something wasn't right. to strip the areas further south of fuel to bring that siege to an end, it seemed disproportionate somehow. *Were there other areas being reinforced?*

"Branwen, you've got the area summaries. Where else is the oil going?"

"Gasoline, kerosene and diesel, are running through Kaunas as you say. . . . " Branwen hesitated for a moment. "Now, that's odd. Bunker oil for ships, production was up in the second quarter. We noted that but we thought it was just an adjustment to earlier production deficiencies. It's up this quarter as well. And a lot of it, a whole lot of it, is going to Kiel."

"German naval base Kiel?" It was, just barely, a question.

"Where else, Loki? Where else would that much bunker oil be going?"

"Power stations?" Loki was playing devil's advocate and they both knew it. Asking questions they both knew the answers to, just in case.

"Not a chance. Germany generates electricity from coal-fired stations, mostly brown coal from open-cast mines, and hydro from those dams along the Ruhr. Not from oil. The few power stations that used oil converted to coal a long time ago.

"It has to be the ships then. Has to be. With that much bunker oil moving, the Germans have to be planning a major naval movement. Surface navy with these quantities, not submarines."

"Linked to the northern front?"

"Don't ask me, I'm a futures trader remember? I'm not the great all-seeing strategist." Loki was bitter and spiteful, his long-standing hatred of Phillip Stuyvesant dominating his voice. "We've got a major shift in fuel supplies to the extreme northern end of the Russian Front and indications of an equally major naval operation impending. Let's get it all off to Washington. Stuyvesant can make sense of it. We've done our job; let him do his for a change."

Admiral's Cabin, KMS Derfflinger, *Flagship, High Seas Fleet, Kiel, Germany*

His ships had more fuel in their tanks now than at any time since 1939. Further shipments arrived every day. After years of existing on fuel delivered by an eyedropper, they now had as much as they needed and more. That made Admiral Ernst Lindemann a very

22

happy man. For the first time since it had adopted that honored name in 1944, the High Seas Fleet was actually capable of putting to sea.

In numbers, this High Seas Fleet didn't compare, with the battle fleet of World War One. In fighting power, that was hard to say. Certainly the old fleet had nothing to compare with the four 55,000 ton battleships of the First Division. The 40.6 centimeter gunned *Derfflinger, von der Tann, Seydlitz* and *Moltke* were the most powerful battleships in the world. Not even the American Iowas could compare with them. Their main guns had given the First Division its nickname, "the Forties", just as the Second Division had been given its nickname, 'the Thirty-Eights" from its 38-centimeter main guns. *Scharnhorst, Gneisenau, Bismarck* and *Tirpitz* were very much the second division. Their status was not helped by the fact that *Scharnhorst* and *Gneisenau* had only six guns each. The eight battleships still represented an awesome force, even if they had yet to fire their gun against an enemy ship. Well, technically, the *Scharnhorst* and *Gneisenau* had, but that was before they had been rearmed with their new 38 centimeter guns.

Lindemann knew that the Americans believed the day of the battleship was done; that the lumbering gun-ships couldn't stand up to the concentrated aircraft striking power of fleet carriers. That was why they had ended their production of battleships with the Iowas. Now, they were building carriers as fast as their yards could turn them out, and that was terrifyingly fast. The Americans had already built twenty four Essex class carriers, each with a hundred aircraft. There were rumors of an even bigger class joining the fleet.

Lindemann believed they had made a catastrophic blunder in listening to their air power advocates. Aircraft were all very well, but they couldn't replace the sheer battering power of a ship's heavy guns. Aircraft couldn't fly in very bad weather and bad weather in the North Atlantic was the rule rather than the exception. Lindemann looked forward to the day when he could get the American carriers under the guns of his battleships, just like *Scharnhorst* and *Gneisenau* had once got the British carrier *Glorious* under their guns.

He desperately hoped the Americans had got it wrong. If they hadn't, Germany had and the new High Seas Fleet was an obsolete anachronism. It had only three carriers; none were close to the size and capability of the American ships. *Graf Zeppelin* and *Oswald Boelcke* were German-built, weird, ungainly designs with a heavy, useless, low-angle gun armament. *Graf Zeppelin* had 32 aircraft, *Oswald Boelcke* a mere 20. The third was the *Werner Voss*. On paper she was a better carrier, certainly she looked better. Appearances were deceiving, for the *Werner Voss* had started life as HMS *Implacable*. She'd already been launched when the British Fleet ran away to Canada. Too incomplete to join them, she'd been scuttled at her shipyard. Her sister ship, HMS *Indefatigable,* had still been on her building slip and the British had done a very thorough job of blowing her up.

Still, between the two wrecks, there had been enough salvaged to complete the *Implacable* a few months ago. On paper. In fact, everything imaginable was wrong with the ship and the British shipyard workers had managed to devise 'construction errors' that no sane person could have dreamed up. There wasn't a watertight door on the ship that fitted properly; they were all twisted just that little bit out of true. The cable runs led through the "watertight" bulkheads and the "seals" were constantly dripping. The gearing for the main turbines created dreadful vibration at cruising speed, enough to break glass and cause the engine room gauges to become unreadable. The officer's latrines, now they were a masterpiece. They worked fine as long as the hatch was left open but if somebody absently-mindedly closed it, the unfortunate occupant couldn't get out until somebody rescued him. The mess decks were beyond description. It wasn't just the smell although the stench of rotting herring permeated the entire ship. It was that even the paint scheme seemed deliberately designed to induce nausea and heartburn.

Three carriers, between them had 106 aircraft. Barely more than a single Essex class. Their aircraft, they were a hasty adaptation of whatever could be found for them Their fighters weren't too bad, Ta-152Fs, hurried modifications of the Ta-152C. A lot better than the converted Me-109s originally planned. The *Zeppelin* had twelve, the *Boelcke* ten, the *Voss* had twenty four. It was the strike aircraft that were the problem. Despite frantic efforts, nobody had found anything better that could fly off a carrier than the aged Ju-87Es. They served as both dive and torpedo bombers, the *Zeppelin* carried twenty, the *Boelcke* ten and the *Voss* thirty. When the fleet put to sea, Lindemann intended to use them primarily as scouts. The Ta-152s would serve as fighter cover for the battleships. Still, the old High Seas Fleet hadn't had any aircraft carriers at all, so he was ahead of them there.

There was worse trouble in the smaller units of the fleet. The High Seas Fleet had one heavy cruiser squadron, with three ships. Two, *Admiral Scheer* and *Lutzow* were awkward hybrids. Their six 28 centimeter guns made them too big for cruisers, too small for battleships. One of the class had already been lost, the British had sunk the *Graf Spee* down in South America. Lindemann fumed at the memory. *Three of their cruisers had shot her up, then that spineless coward Langsdorff had run for port and blown his ship up rather than fight it out. Turning the German Navy into a laughing stock in the process.* Both the surviving Panzerschiffe bore the humiliation of that fiasco.

The other heavy cruisers had even worse luck. On paper, they were good, 14,000 tons with eight 20.3guns, but the class had been cursed with ill luck. *Blucher* had been sunk by a Norwegian coastal defense battery, *Prinz Eugen* had gone down in the Kattegat after a submarine put four torpedoes into her. One had been sold to the Russians and was now a floating battery at Petrograd, firing on the German troops south of the city. *Seydlitz* had been converted into the *Boelcke.* That just left the *Hipper*, a ship that had become a by-word for mechanical unreliability.

And, if his heavy cruiser force was weak, his light cruisers were even worse. He had three: *Koln, Leipzig* and *Nurnburg.* Nine 15-centimeter guns each. Weak ships, poorly designed but there was nothing better. His destroyers? Lindemann snorted in disgust. The best were also the oldest, the ten survivors of 22 Z-1 class ships. The British had destroyed the other twelve in the Norway campaign. That had been a nightmare. At Narvik, the new German Navy had faced the British in combat for the first time. The destroyers had taken the brunt of the onslaught as the British had gone through them like a buzz-saw through butter.

Those destroyers had five 12.7 centimeter guns and eight torpedo tubes each. On balance Lindemann felt that made them as good as the American destroyers. The other twenty of his destroyers, well, some fool had armed them with 15 centimeter guns, leaving them over-armed and poor seaboats. They were all right inshore and in the Baltic. Take them out in the North Atlantic and they'd be hard put to stay upright, let alone do any fighting. Lindemann had made repeated requests to have them rearmed with 12.7 centimeter guns but he'd been turned down.

Lindemann put down his status report file. The major fleet units were all right; it was the smaller stuff that was so lacking. That was logical. It took time to build the big ships, the Forties had taken five years, and the last two had never even been started. The idea had been that the smaller ships could be built quickly when the need arose but that wasn't the case. By the time the need arose, the demand for tanks on the Russian Front was over-riding everything else and the small ships had never been built.

Until now that was. The High Seas Fleet had orders. The Americans were expected to send a huge convoy through to Murmansk and Archangel. It would be a mixture of Canadian and American ships bring supplies for the troops on the Kola Peninsula and besieged in Archangel. It would be heavily escorted, at least two battleships, probably more, cruisers and destroyers. An American aircraft carrier group would be providing distant cover. But, the new American battleships were with the carriers and the not-so new ones were out in the Pacific. The only battleships left for the Atlantic convoys were the very old *Pennsylvania, Nevada, Arizona,* and *Oklahoma.* There were reports that the even older *Arkansas, Texas* and *New York* had already been sent back to the States for scrapping.

So, at most four old battleships, all ready to be destroyed by his guns. Then the convoy was to be annihilated. It didn't take much insight to see what the plan was. His ships would destroy the convoy, leaving the Kola and Archangel troops desperately short of supplies. Then, the army would attack and overrun both northern ports. It wouldn't win the war but it would be a break in the grinding deadlock.

"Lutjens!" Lindemann called his chief of staff. Once Lutjens had been the senior, a full Admiral to Lindemann's mere Captain but Lutjens had mysteriously fallen out of favor. Just as mysteriously, Lindemann had gained a place in the sun. It was, perhaps, a measure of the man's character that he'd never displayed resentment or ill-will from that turn of events. "Lutjens, we are going to sea as soon as the tankers are filled up. We have a mission worthy of us at last."

Headquarters, No. 9 Counter-Intelligence Corps Detachment, Canadian Intelligence Corps, Kola Peninsula, Russia

"So what are we up against?"

"In global terms, sir, the German armed forces deploy a total of three hundred and thirty three divisions and forty three independent brigades, of which sixty six divisions and thirteen independent brigades are drawn from their 'allies'. That force totals some six and a half million men. Their major effort remains facing the Russians and the Americans along the Volga. There, the Germans deploy 258 divisions and 16 independent brigades totaling just over five million men.

"Against them, the Russians have deployed three hundred and ninety one divisions with an aggregate of six point one million men and, now that SUSAGIR has entered the line, the Americans deploy 72 divisions with a total of one and a half million men."

"SUSAGIR?"

"Second United States Army Group In Russia Sir. It and FUSAGIR are much more powerful than their numbers suggest. Every one of those divisions is fully mechanized, by the standards of the Russian Front they're armored divisions. And they have tactical air power coming out of their ears."

General John M Rockingham grunted. "And very nice for them it is I'm sure. What I need to know is what do we face here?"

"On the Finnish Front Sir, the Finns have deployed a total of sixteen standard infantry divisions and one mountain infantry division plus an independent armored brigade. They're backed up by two German mountain divisions and four German infantry divisions together with two independent armored brigades. We, First Canadian Army, face that force with two corps, with a total of five divisions. Six once your Sixth Infantry Division comes into the line. Three infantry divisions, four as soon as the Sixth arrives, and two armored divisions.

"The odds aren't as bad as they seem. The Finns have 250,000 men at most, the Germans about 100,000. We have 120,000 men. The catch is aircraft. The Finns have about 200, the Germans less than a hundred. Here in Kola, we have 300 planes, the Americans have 350 and the Russians 950. So we rule the air pretty much unchallenged. As long as we have avgas, of course. If that runs out, we're in a world of hurt.

"To complete the picture, at a right angle to our deployment is the Petrograd Front. The Russians have fourteen infantry divisions, one mechanized corps and two tank corps down there plus about forty independent battalions, most of them in Petrograd itself. They face Army Group Vistula under the command of Field Marshal Erwin Rommel."

"Vistula? How did it get that name? The river Vistula runs through the middle of Poland." Rockingham was amazed at the out-of-place name.

"The Germans only change the name of their Army Groups when they get seriously defeated or are split. They started the war here in Russia with three, Army Group North, Center and South. Near the end of '41, Army Group North split with Army Group Vistula being formed to mop up the Baltic states and Petrograd. The rest remained Army Group North and headed east. I guess the Vistula was the nearest big river back then and there's been no reason to change it. Down south, Army Group Don is still in business as well. Anyway, Vistula has two armies, Ninth and 11th SS Panzer. Total of 17 infantry divisions, one mountain division, two SS Panzer divisions and three SS Panzergrenadier divisions. Ninth is pretty poorly equipped, but 11th SS? Well, they're SS divisions, if its good, they've got it."

"If they outnumber us that much, why don't they attack?" The balance of forces he faced appalled Rockingham.

"It must be very tempting Sir. The Germans have seventy five divisions and twenty seven independent brigades not deployed on the Volga Front. Of those, a total of thirty five divisions and three independent brigades are deployed here on Kola. That's not quite half their uncommitted forces but it's pretty close to it. It must be frightfully tempting for them to attack, roll us up and seize Kola. Once that's done, they could free up, probably, the whole of the German contingent and leave most of the occupation work to the Finns. Thirty more divisions on the Volga front, well, it won't win the war for the Germans but it'll swing the deadlock there in their favor.

"Look at it this way Sir. The Germans are tapped out; like us, they can't support any more than they already have. They've got pitifully few troops outside Russia. Most of their occupation forces are those 'allied' divisions. Romanians and Slovakians mostly. Those German units that are elsewhere are reconstituting after being torn up in Russia."

For a second Colonel Charles Lampier looked very tired. "Europe's bleeding to death Sir, the whole continent is just bleeding to death."

There was a grim silence. Running through both men's minds was a terrible question that neither would admit to even thinking. *Had Halifax been right? Was striking a deal better than this endless slaughter? Canada is stretched as far as we can go in supporting First Canadian Army. We're being bled white by the casualties we're suffering.*

"So why don't they?"

"Three reasons Sir. Two are military, one is political. The first military reason is that the terrain here is some of the finest defensive ground in the world. It's a maze of lakes, rivers, ridges, swamps. You name it, we've got it. The weather is frightful; you saw how bad flying down here. That isn't the worst of it; you wait until we get white-out conditions. The sky fills with windblown snow and nobody can see where the sky ends and the ground begins. Too dangerous even to try and fly.

"This whole area is a defending force's paradise. Even a high correlation of forces in favor of the attacker doesn't help much. The attack is channeled into a series of narrow thrusts and the additional troops just stack up behind the lead elements. A company can hold a division for days, weeks if necessary, and when it's finally destroyed, the next defending company has moved in behind it.

"That brings us to the second military reason: air power. The Americans in particular; they shoot up everything that moves. And I do mean everything. If your division has vehicles on the move, make sure they display the recognition panels and pray intensely. All the Yank fighter-bombers are trigger-happy but the Grizzlies are the worst. They have a 75mm right in the nose and it's accurate so they tend to shoot from long range. Let's just say they aren't too careful sometimes.

"But, once all those troops stack up in front of a defensive position, the aircraft get to work and they reduce those forces to a shambles. You should have seen the roads west of here a few weeks ago. The Germans tried a local advance to straighten their line before winter. There's a lot of that going on, everybody tries to seize the best shelter for their own people and to deny it to the enemy. Anyway, the front was about the width of a main road. A couple of SU-100 tank destroyers and an infantry platoon blocked it then the fighter-bombers got to work. Mostly Thunderstorms and Grizzlies but even some of our

Williwaws got in on the act. By the time they'd finished, the road was a tangled mass of burned out wreckage.

"Anyway, put together, those two things mean that attacking here is slow and expensive. Applies to us as much as the enemy of course but we don't plan to go anywhere though. The Germans don't know that of course; they can see that if we broke out of here, we could cut off their whole northern flank. Isn't going to happen, but they have forces pinned here in case. The ground their side isn't so defensible so they need more troops to hold it.

"The third reason is political. The Finns want to survive this war as an independent state and the way they've screwed the political side of things to date puts a big question mark against that. The Russians and us are doing a good-cop, bad-op act on them. The Russians make noises that, when the allies have won, Finland is going to be occupied and reduced to a Russian province and any Finns that don't like it can seek new lifestyle opportunities in Siberia. We tell the Finns, we can argue the Russians out of that but how effective our arguments are depends on how active a part they take in the war. The more operations Finland engages in against us, the less will be left unoccupied post-war.

"Of course, the Finns have the Germans telling them that they're going to win and if Finland wants to survive post-war and get a share of the goodies, it had better be an active German ally. So they're dancing a tightrope. Frankly I doubt if anybody here has any sympathy for them. We all had when we arrived, Winter War, gallant little Finland and all that, but it didn't last.

"The problem is that we need to keep this front quiet, that's our prime driver. We need to keep the activity, and thus casualties, down to a minimum. You know how stretched manpower is back home. We're keeping units up to ToE at the moment but if the casualty rate spikes, that'll end and we'll drop behind the curve. Once that happens, we'll never catch up. It's not as if we could draw on any of the Free British units. They're all being reserved and trained for the invasion of the UK. If that ever happens."

"You don't think it will?"

"I have my doubts. Oh, sure, the Yanks are going through the motions. They've trained and equipped a Marine Corps, six divisions of it, and are planning a landing in France. They've got the Royal Marines and various other units doing beach reconnaissance and all those good things and they're training and equipping the Free British units for a landing in the UK but there's something missing. Either they're not serious about it or they're heading for the worst amphibious foul-up since Gallipoli.

"Six divisions sounds really good and, as we've seen, there isn't that much to oppose them, not at first. But the Germans are on interior lines; they can move troops around. We just can't get at their core railway system, so they can shift forces west without much interference. If they moved, for example, 11th SS Panzer Army west, they'd go through the Marines on the beach like shit through a goose. And they're talking of landing in France? Why would they do that? The UK is the fortress that guards Europe from the west; that's been true since the time of the Barbary pirates. Retaking it has got to come first. Surely they'd do that with one landing, at full strength, not two spread out over half Europe?

"No, sorry General, but I think they're bluffing. They're not really planning to land in the west; they're just trying, not too successfully, to keep German troops pinned down in France and the UK. The issue's going to be decided here, in Russia. And we won't see Free British troops out here.

"So, I'm sorry to have to tell you this but at least half your job is political. We've got to keep the Finns scared enough so they stay quiet but not so scared they decide they have nothing to lose. Anyway, another thing running for us. Our Intel is good, very good indeed. Don't ask me how, but we get warning of every major German move, when and where. In effect, the Germans are telegraphing every punch and that gives us a huge edge. I believe a lot of stuff comes in from the Norwegian resistance and I think we get more from the Swedes."

"I thought the Swedes were tight with the Germans?"

"They are, or so we thought, but the intelligence thing makes it look different. It's really weird. There are Swedish volunteer units fighting with the Germans. One of the SS panzergrenadier divisions is a third Swedish, yet I'm pretty certain we're getting all this good intel out of Stockholm. Another thing that doesn't make sense. Looks like the Swedes are playing a really deep double game and the Germans are not pleased about it.

"In terms of equipment, one of our two armored divisions have got late-model M-4 Shermans. They have HVSS suspension, wide tracks and 90mm guns. The other has M-27 Sheridans; same gun but a bit more armor. Between them, they'll handle most things except the German heavies. There's a few of those, mostly Royal Tigers down around Petrograd. The Russians have JS-IIIs down there and seeing those two go at it is a real treat. This isn't really tank country though. Armor is a help but it's a supporting weapon, not a decisive maneuver arm.

"Our infantry is outgunned. The Germans have those banana guns, StG-44s. We still use bolt action No.4s. We've got Capsten sub-machine guns though; they fire the hot greentip Tokarev 7.62s. Machine guns, its mostly our Brens vs their Spandaus but we've got the Vickers and those water-cooled machine guns are worth their weight in gold. They'll fire forever in the cold and snow. One thing, make sure all your sub-commanders check their ammunition supplies. We're shipping both our .303 and Russian 7.62 three-line ammunition through Murmansk and the two rounds are alike enough to get mixed up. Happened already, it'll happen again. You don't want one of our battalions to find out it's got three-line ammunition just as it goes into action."

CHAPTER TWO
A CHILL IN THE AIR

Curly, *Battery B, US Navy 5th Artillery Battalion, Kola Peninsula.*

From above, the railway tracks looked like three snakes sliding side-by-side in the snow. If the observer above looked closer he'd see that there was another kind of snake down there, three trains, side by side on the rails. A long way between them, almost half a mile, but still there. Trains that were 14 carriages long. A very astute observer might realize there was something very strange about the fourth carriage in the train.

It was the long barrel that gave the game away. The train was a railway gun and its entourage; the wagons that held the massive 2,700 pound projectiles, the bags of charges, living accommodation for the crew, cranes to lift the loads and anti-aircraft guns to protect the whole assembly. The curves on the tracks allowed the gun to be trained at any point within a wide arc. Together, the three supercharged 16-inch 50-caliber guns could put down a devastating barrage of fire on a target up to 40 miles away.

Here and now, on the Kola Peninsula as winter drew in, railway guns had suddenly regained the importance they had lost when aircraft had taken over the role of long-range artillery. Most times during a Kola peninsula winter, the weather was too bad for aircraft. Even if they could get up, it was too bad for them to strike accurately. Weather didn't affect the big guns. If they knew the position of their target, they could strike at it. When they did, their power was devastating.

The allies had learned that in the winter of 1942-43, the first full Russian winter the American troops had experienced. They'd suffered at the hands of the German railway guns, so they'd brought their own. Four 14-inch L50 railway guns at the Washington Navy Yard had been hastily converted to Russian railway gauge and shipped to Murmansk. They'd been followed, a year later, by six 16-inch L50s; guns that had been in store ever since the battlecruisers they'd been designed for had died under the Washington Treaty axe. The 14 inchers and three of the sixteens were down at Petrograd, at the western end of the Kola Front. The other three 16s were here, at the eastern end.

Commander James Perdue's reverie was broken by the sound of a siren going off. It was the alert that a shoot was about to take place. He'd barely had time to register the noise and start to act before the train lurched and began to move. *Forward, that would mean the gun was training to the right. If the target had been to their left, they'd have been moving backwards.* Their gun, affectionately known as *Curly* was too large to have a turntable mounting, instead it was moved along the curved tracks. There were marks at regular intervals along the curve, each marking the increments by which the barrel was swinging. When the fire control system gave them the deflection needed, the engine would move the forward wheel of the gun-carriage so it was level with one of those marks. All that the gun crew needed to do was elevate to the specified degree and make a fine adjustment to the bearing.

The train shuddered and stopped. Then Curly rocked gently as a fine adjustment was made. Perdue was already heading back, down the accommodation car to his gun. He knew what was happening. The crane had lifted a 2,700 pound semi-armor piercing projectile from the stack on the flatcar and loaded it onto the conveyor. Now it was being run to the gun where it would be rammed into the breech. Behind it, the magazine cars had opened and powder bags were being brought forward. The number was determined by the range to the target. *Curly* had originally been designed to take eight bags but had been modified to accommodate up to ten. That level of supercharge would wear out

34

the barrel but it wasn't a problem. When that happened, they'd get *Curly* rebarrelled.

"How many charges?"

"Full load Sir." This was going to be good. *Curly's* barrel was already arcing upwards as the hydraulics drove it into the fire position. A crash seemed to shake the whole frozen landscape and a brilliant ball of fire lit up the sky. *Curly* sent its projectile off towards whatever target it was that had caused the commotion. A split second later, far off to the right, *Larry* sent its shell on its way to the same target. Perdue assumed it was the same; they usually were. Over on the left, the third gun, *Moe* fired its shell. The last one off, *Moe's* crew would get their legs pulled about that. *Curly's* barrel was already dropping as the gun returned to the load position and the railway engine pushed the gun train back to the mark.

The German railway gunners could get off one round every six minutes; the American navy men fired twice that. *Larry* must have done slightly better because the 16-incher got its shell off a split second before *Curly*. *Moe* brought up the rear again. Four shells each later, the guns ceased fire and their locomotives pulled them back to the rest position. Perdue hoped the target, whatever it was, had been duly grateful for the effort made on its behalf.

Headquarters, 71st Infantry Division, Kola Front

"So you are the idiot who destroyed my heavy artillery battery." Major-General Marcks spoke thoughtfully. Outside, his aide quietly crept away. When 'Old Lenin,' as he was known behind his back, spoke thoughtfully, being somewhere else was a very good idea.

Captain Wilhelm Lang knew how to deal with this situation. It was necessary to take action, to show initiative. This was one of those cases where bending the rules was actually a good thing. It showed a concentration on fulfilling the objective, of gaining the required results, a good thing. "Sir, yes sir. But I have been on the long-distance radio link to a friend of mine in Army Group headquarters. He's fixed everything. We will have new heavy guns here to replace them in a week or less. Well before we are required to bounce off."

Lang looked at his General with what came perilously near to a smirk. It faded when he saw the irascible general going white.

"You used the long-range radio? How long ago?"

"I just came off it, just before I came in here, I was using it for five minutes, perhaps ten."

Marcks grabbed the telephone on his desk. "Emergency evacuation now! Everybody out! Clear the area, as far as possible." Then he pushed past Lang and headed for the door. Outside sirens wailed.

The headquarters area was a madhouse. Corporal Krause was already running the engine of Marck's kubelwagen. He started to roll as soon as the General was in the back. Lang pulled himself in as the little vehicle sped off down the road plowed through the snow. Around them vehicles were moving. Each took as many of the headquarters staff as they could scoop up. Krause threaded his kubelwagen through the throng, heading as far away from the camp area as possible.

They made it. Krause drove the kubelwagen straight at a tree sticking out of the snow, hit the brakes and spun it around. As he did, Marcks leapt out and looked down on the HQ area nestling at the foot of the ridge. Lang had waited until the vehicle had stopped and left more circumspectly. "Best driver in the division Krause is." Marcks was still watching the base.

"I don't understand. . . ."

"Have you never heard of radio intercepts?"

"Of course, I've read the manuals. I wrote some of the more important ones myself." Lang was almost-smirking again. "But there was high ground between the transmission site and the Ivans."

"Not the Ivans you have to worry about. . ." Marcks was interrupted by an escalating roar. Beside him Lang could swear that he saw a black streak race down across the sky and hit the center of the now-deserted headquarters. There was a white puff. For a split second, he thought the shell was a dud. Then the whole center of the camp bulged, looking for all the world like a saucepan of milk boiling over. It inflated and rose upwards, impossibly large before bursting open to

36

send a shotgun hail of frozen mud, snow and ice into the air. The two officers dropped flat as it scattered down around them. Even before it had landed, a second shell had slammed into the area, a little to the south of the main camp area. A third landed to the west of the camp. The ground rolled and shook, punching Marcks and Lang with body blows from the repeated concussion of the shockwaves.

It went on and on, shell after shell slamming into the camp. The semi-armor piercing shells penetrated deep into the frozen earth before exploding. The boiling milk of the ground threshed and contorted under the remorseless hammering. As the ground wave from the last shell passed away, it collapsed as if the heat had been taken from under the pan. What was left of the HQ area was utterly devastated. Not a single building left standing. The ground itself was destroyed, snow and mud stirred and shaken into a blended, featureless nothingness.

"As I was saying, it's not the Ivans you have to worry about. It's the Amis. You see, Lang, the Amis are rich. They fight their wars with machines. When we fly a Tante Ju transport up here, everybody fights for centimeters of space, for every kilogram of load, because we do not know when the aircraft will be available again. When a mother in Arkansas wants to send her little boy some cookies, if there is no space on the aircraft, *the Amis build another one*.

"Some of those transport aircraft are stuffed with radio intercept equipment. For some reason the Amis call them Rivets. They orbit safely behind their lines and listen for somebody foolish enough to use their radio links. When they find one, they triangulate for his position. Aircraft are good at that; they can establish a long baseline quickly. So, they get a quick, accurate fix and send it in. In this case to a railway gun battery north of here. Your call was a gift to them. A long call like that, they had every chance to get hold of it and fix the position exactly.

"Then that railway gun battery fired on us. You saw those shells? They weigh 1,300 kilograms each and they penetrated thirty, perhaps forty meters into the ground before exploding. The ground down there is like quicksand. It's been shattered, powdered. We can't go back there until it freezes solid again. Lang, so far today you've destroyed one of my artillery batteries and my headquarters. Could I ask if you have any plans for the rest of the day?"

Lang shook his head dumbly, still shaken by the immensity of the explosions that had destroyed the base. He'd never thought of railway guns, had no idea of their terrifying power and accuracy. It was a lesson he knew he would never forget.

There was a lot Marcks wanted to say but Lang was on first-name terms with more important people than he could easily count. For the moment, Lang was untouchable. Sarcasm would have to substitute for the more direct action he longed to take. "Well, if I may be permitted to make a suggestion. Have you considered serving the Fatherland by transferring to the Russian Army?"

Washington International Airport, Washington D.C. USA.

"How was the flight?" The question meant more than it sounded. 'The flight' was a long trip for the Pan American Constellation. It was a civilian airliner in name only. It had military-style seating and equipment; its Pan American paint job was a gesture towards the countries on its route. The first leg on the outward journey, Washington to Lajes in the Azores, was trouble-free enough, both were American territory, although the ever-cynical Achillea had her doubts about Washington. The second leg, Lajes to Casablanca, was where the fun kicked in.

Casablanca was technically Vichy French but it was actually run by the Free French. To be more precise, the faction of the Free French lead by Admiral Darlan. So, there was a constant underground war going on between the various groups and the resulting level of intrigue and conspiracy was surpassed only by Cairo. The third leg, Casablanca to Rome was even more interesting. There that the civilian cover of the Constellation was essential. Italy was a neutral in the war. Its economy was booming as a result and Mussolini had every intention of keeping it that way. So, the airliner had to be civilian. The final leg of the journey was the train trip from Rome to Geneva where Igrat, Achillea and Henry McCarty would meet up with Loki and pick up the monthly economic intelligence data. It was a regular trip and the question had actually been 'did you get the data?'

"Pretty good. We got the stuff. Had a little trouble in Casablanca on the way out though."

"Germans?"

38

"Nah, OSS." McCarty leaned back in the limousine seat. Let me tell you about it."

Gusoyn grinned to himself. McCarty was an excellent story-teller and this promised to be good.

Cafe Sahara, Casablanca, 36 hours earlier

"Special operations are for skilled professionals, not amateurs." The local OSS man leaned back in his seat, radiating scorn for his company. Behind him, Igrat looked around the Cafe, it was empty, even the staff had made themselves scarce. In Casablanca, everybody knew when shady stuff was going down and those not involved took off in any convenient direction. It wasn't that they were afraid of the authorities. It was well known that the Vichy police only arrested the innocent as a last resort. It was just smarter not to be involved.

Frank Barnes was emboldened by the lack of response to his comment. "And look at you. You're supposed to be couriers for some important documents. An old man and two women. Weak, undisciplined civilians. You need to be in peak condition and have specialized training for this sort of thing. I've a good mind to make a report to Washington on this. What would happen if Nazi agents attacked you? Huh? Suppose a Nazi came at you with a knife?" Barnes pointed at Achillea. "What would you do? Huh?"

"I'd take it out of his hand."

"This isn't funny. A Nazi could take that case away from you right now. Look, let me teach you what to do." Barnes reached into a pocket and pushed a pencil across the table. "Pretend that's a knife and come at me with it and I'll show you the tricks."

Achillea looked down at the pencil. "No need to pretend. Uhhh, wait a minute." She got up and walked across to the counter where a selection of chef's knives hung on the wall. She inspected them for a minute before selecting one, not quite the longest but one with a broad, strong blade. Then she touched the edge with her thumb and pushed her lower lip out in disgust. *Blunt as a spoon.* She disappeared through the service hatch and a few seconds later the sound of a knife being drawn across a sharpening steel rang through the empty cafe.

Frank Barnes started sweating slightly. "I'm only trying to help you know. This is a dangerous business, too dangerous for amateurs. You should leave it to us." Igrat smiled at him; in the other corner, Henry just stared

"Madam, you can't come in here. Staff only." The cafe manager's voice was smooth and cultured, although muffled by the closed service door.

"Hand please." Achillea's voice was abrupt. A split second later there was an outraged squeal followed by an irritated "still blunt." The sounds of a knife being sharpened grew in energy.

"Uh, I just hope my old war wound won't interfere with this." Barnes was sweating heavily now and glancing around. The cafe was still empty. Then the service door swung open and Achillea stepped through. Her eyes fixed on Barnes and she dropped into her habitual crouch, knife in her right hand, down low, point aimed unerringly at Barnes' groin.

"Err, good Lord, is that the time? I have to make my scheduled call to headquarters." Barnes tried to rise, but his foot got caught in something and he half-tripped. Igrat steadied him and helped him to his feet. "Perhaps we can schedule this another day." He was backing towards the door now, colliding with it, trying to open it the wrong way before finally getting out. He climbed into a passing taxi and was swept away.

"I wonder where he's going." McCarty sounded vaguely amused. Achillea sighed with disappointment and put the knife back in its rack.

"I don't know, but he's in for an interesting time when he gets there." Igrat sounded smug as she reached inside her blouse. "I've got his wallet."

Washington International Airport, Washington D.C. USA.

Gusoyn's snort of laughter almost caused him to crash the car as he backed out of the parking spot. "When did you give it back to him?"

"Give it back? Moi?" Igrat's eyebrows arched. "It's going to his boss as soon as we're in the office. That fool could have messed up the delivery with his grandstanding."

McCarty nodded, for all the incident's funny side, it could have been a serious breach that endangered the information pipeline and they were all aware that the information they carried was literally priceless. Then he frowned. "Iggie? Wasn't there some money in there?"

"There was." Igrat confirmed. One of McCarty's eyebrows lifted. "New hat. And the cutest little switchblade for Achillea. It was mine by right of conquest after all. To the victor the spoils and all that."

United States Strategic Bombardment Commission, Blair House, Washington D.C. USA.

The eerie wailing of the sirens sounded the all-clear and the room relaxed. A few seconds later the telephone rang and Phillip Stuyvesant picked it up. He listened, absent-mindedly nodding as if the person on the other end could see him them acknowledged the message briefly.

"Three missiles Sir. One shot down, the other two hit south of here, down around Alexandria. Both exploded in open country, no casualties this time. My guess is they were trying for the torpedo factory."

"Not a damned chance, not with those things. If they were aiming for anything specific it was for the East Coast and they did well to hit that." President Thomas E. Dewey sounded relieved. The wild inaccuracy of the Fi-103 'Doodlebug' didn't mean that they couldn't do a lot of damage.

"Coastal have backtracked the missiles and we've got a good fix on the sub that launched them. Navy PBJs and a hunter-killer group are prosecuting it now. They won't get away."

That was a bit hopeful, Stuyvesant thought. *The casualty rate for submarines launching missile attacks on the East Coast is around 50 percent. A bit safer for them than attacking convoys but not that much more.* Outside, Washington was shrouded in darkness. Anybody breaking the blackout would be on the receiving end of a shouted "Put

41

out that light!" and a stiff fine. That was the lucky outcome. It was not unknown for people careless with their lights to be accused of signaling to submarines off shore. Their neighbors took a dim view of that supposed act. As a matter of fact, the FBI had been unable to substantiate a single accusation of signaling to German submarines, but the very fact the accusations were being made was a symptom of a deeper problem.

"So, Seer, progress on Downfall?"

"We're getting started Sir. For all its faults, JANSP-23 provides us with a base to start from. It's given us the magnitude of the task we have to undertake even if it overstates the measures needed to execute the mission." Stuyvesant, already better known in military planning circles as 'The Seer' after his USSBC code-name, paused for a second. The Joint Army-Navy Strategic Plan No.23 had enormously overstated the number of atomic devices needed to destroy German war-making potential. It wasn't that they'd overstated the task; they had underestimated the sheer destructive power of the new weapons. It was easy to say 'equivalent to 20,000 tons of TNT' but another thing entirely to appreciate the incredible destruction that implied. Only when one saw the mushroom cloud boiling upwards, felt the ground shuddering under one's feet, heard that all-encompassing, crushing roar did the reality sink home. But then, nobody had, until Trinity back in August. Stuyvesant had been there and he had realized then that 'destroying German war-making potential' with these weapons actually meant totally destroying the country.

It quite surprised him that the realization was taking so long to sink in. *Didn't people realize that the moment the doctrine of strategic bombardment was accepted, it axiomatically meant the complete destruction of the target country? Because it was impossible to draw the line between where the war-making potential of a country ended and the purely civilian began?* Years before, when Mitchell and his supporters had proposed Strategic Bombardment as a 'humane' alternative to the slaughter of the Western Front in World War Two, Stuyvesant had seen where it would lead. As the doctrine had gained strength and its supporters had seen it become an accepted doctrine worldwide, his worst fears had been confirmed. Technology was advancing so fast that it had outrun the ability of people to understand or control it.

"We're convinced it has to be The Big One?"

42

"Yes indeed Sir. It has to be. What we have is a one-shot deal. We have two complementary military secrets of equal importance, nuclear weapons and the ability of the B-36 to overfly enemy defenses. If either is prematurely compromised, the whole thing falls apart. The first blow has to be cataclysmic, so appalling in its power that the enemy cannot continue the war. Anything less just doesn't have the necessary impact. I think even General Groves is coming around to that opinion now."

"He put up a good fight." Dewey chuckled. The long duel between General Groves and General LeMay had been a spectacle to behold. "When can we go?"

Stuyvesant thought carefully. "Assuming that projected B-36 and nuclear weapon production stay on schedule, sometime during the first six months of 1947. We're shifting device production to the Mark 3 now; they'll be entering the depots early next year and we've got six Bomb Groups equipped with B-36Ds either operational or working up."

Dewey was horrified and his voice showed it. "Seer, mid-1947? In eighteen months time? My God man, do you understand we are losing 800 men a day on the Russian Front? And you want us to wait another 18 months? Do you realize that means almost half a million men are going to die out there while we wait for the bombers to be completed?"

The Seer suddenly looked very old and very, very tired. "438,000 to be precise, Mister President and yes, we all do understand that. The Big One is the only chance of ending this war quickly. Say again, the only chance. If it goes off half-cocked, if we try half measures, it will fail and this war could go on for years, decades even. Our death toll then will make a half million seem very small.

"Mister President, when we throw The Big One, it'll do two things, quite independent of the attack itself. One is that it will tell the world that nuclear weapons are possible and give pretty much everybody a few good clues on how to build them. The other is that it will tell everybody that high-flying bombers are very hard to intercept and give them clues on how to build them as well. How long after a failed Big One, Mister President, will it take Germany to build its own long-range, high-altitude bombers and the nuclear weapons to arm

43

them? Months? A year? Won't be much more than that. Or how long will it be before the doodlebugs coming over have nuclear tips? And what about Japan? We have to wait Mister President, we must. It's the hardest thing of all, to have a deadly, war-winning weapon and to wait until the time to use it is right, but it is also the only thing we can do. Any other way lies disaster."

Dewey nodded. In his head, he could see the inevitable, undeniable logic; his mind's eye also saw the lines of graves, lines that lengthened inexorably with every day that passed. "Can we hang on? Can the Russians hang on?"

"The people are getting tired, Mister President. Tired of the casualties, tired of the wartime shortages and rationing, tired of the blackout, tired of the deadlock. We need a victory, a big one. The German breakthrough last year was a bad shock for morale but this endless stalemate is worse. The Russians will fight on. Without us, their ability to do so effectively is questionable. The Russian military industry has lost most of its coal supplies and more than half its energy resources. Virtually every industrial complex they have, including the ones we've built, is short of fuel, power and metals. Now, there is some good news. Our oil industry people have been to their Siberian oil fields. The Russians had very poor extraction technology and those fields can produce, and are producing now, much more than they got out of them in the 1930s. Even better, our oil people say we haven't even found the king and queen fields yet, let alone the emperor field."

"King, queen, emperor? Doesn't sound very egalitarian to me?" Dewey's voice had its usual dry humor back.

"Sir, oil fields come in a hierarchy. From the smallest up, Squire, Duke, Queen, King, Emperor. The structure of an oil-producing area is an Emperor field, surrounded by two or more King and Queen fields and they're surrounded by Duke and Squire fields. All existing Siberian production is coming from Duke and Squire fields. The undiscovered oil wealth that's potentially there is enormous. Until recently, we were shipping Siberian crude to US refineries and then shipping products back but we've started building refineries in Russia itself. We have tuned up their metals mining facilities, coal recovery. Thank God the Russians have no objections to strip-mining, but they're still short of everything, from people to fertilizer. Without us, their ability to hold is arguable at best. And we need a victory, a big, decisive one."

"Is there hope of one? Or do we have to wait until 1947?"

"Sir, this morning I would have said no and yes respectively. That's changed. We've just got the latest intelligence digests through. Triple source confirmed." Dewey shook his head slightly; he didn't want to know the sources. The Seer wished he didn't know either sometimes. The data came from three separate routes. The Geneva spy ring called the Red Orchestra, run by Loki, a second spy net nobody could quite identify called Lucy and an ultra-secret code-cracking operation called Ultra. Between them, they gave a brilliant insight into German strategic plans.

"Mister President, shortly we will be running out big pre-winter convoys through to Murmansk and Archangel. A huge supply convoy, more than 250 ships, that will carry enough munitions, fuel etc. to keep the Kola Peninsula going until spring."

"A convoy that big? There's a saying about eggs and baskets."

"I know, but in this case it doesn't apply. A given submarine attack can only sink a given number of ships regardless of the number in the convoy. So, a big convoy has proportionally fewer losses than a small one. Also, a big convoy isn't significantly easier to find than a small one so one big convoy is less likely to be found than the equivalent number of ships in a series of small groups. Mathematically, we're much better off with big convoys. We've got to get this convoy through before winter really sets in. That's when the ice boundary moves south and pushes us too close to occupied Norway for comfort.

"Anyway, with the main convoy will be a smaller but an equally important one, a troop convoy carrying the Canadian Sixth Infantry Division to Murmansk. We know that the German fleet plans to overwhelm the escorts for those two convoys and destroy them. Simultaneously, they plan to launch a land offensive that will take advantage of the supply crisis caused by the destruction of the convoys to take the Kola Peninsula. With Murmansk gone, Archangel and Petrograd will fall, and the Canadian Army in Kola will be destroyed. That will free up a mass of German resources for the main front.

"Sir, we had planned to cover those convoys with a single carrier group, while the rest pounded northern Scotland. In view of this information, I suggest we use all of the groups to set up an ambush and sucker-punch the German fleet as it heads north. The Germans don't really understand naval warfare." *Nor do I,* thought Stuyvesant, *but I know a lot of people who do.* "The initiative is with us, we decide when to send the convoys out, we decide when and where the battle will be fought. We wait for good weather, give our carriers every edge we can, and then we turn them loose on the German battleships. We can wipe their fleet out. That's a pretty valuable goal in its own right, but it's also the victory I think people need."

"And how long do we have to wait for the weather we need? Months?"

"The Gods are smiling on us, Sir. We had a rough fall up there, but the weather magicians tell us we're in for a spell of fine weather. By North Atlantic standards anyway. We can go as soon as possible. Now if we wish."

"And the land battle?"

"On Kola? If the supplies get through, we can win that as well. Or at least make sure the German offensive goes nowhere."

Dewey nodded. It made political and military sense. That was a rarity, usually the two demands opposed and contradicted. "Very good, Seer. We'll make it happen." Then his face fell again as the image of the ever-lengthening lines of white crosses in the snows of Russia returned to haunt him. "You're right, we've got to win something, somewhere."

Short-Range Hunter-Killer Group "Oak", Off the Virginia Coast.

"Pickets in place Sir. We've got four PBJs overhead. They're dropping sonobuoys now."

Captain Albert Sturmer nodded. That made twelve hunting platforms gathered around the position of the Type XXID that had launched its missiles at Washington. Eight were modified Gleaves class destroyers. They had been stripped of their anti-aircraft guns and three of their five-inchers after they had been phased out of service with the carrier groups. Now, they had three Hedgehogs, a big trainable launcher in place of B gun and two smaller fixed weapons amidships. Between them, the three launchers could put down a devastating barrage of charges. They also carried an array of depth charge throwers aft and big, one-ton depth charges in their torpedo tubes.

If this had been a long-range hunter-killer group, they'd have had at least one jeep carrier with them, a CVE stuffed with Avengers and Bearcats. Instead, the PBJs overhead were the Navy's version of the Air Force's B-25J Mitchell. They had sonobuoys and an ASV radar, plus homing torpedoes in their bellies and rockets under their wings. For the endgame, they had their noses stuffed with machine guns; eight in the nose itself, four in packages on the aircraft side. Just in case the Germans decided not to go down with their ship.

The Type XXID had two choices. It could run as fast as it could, and the Type XXI was fast underwater. By doing so, it could clear the area and make the search area much larger. The problem with running at high speed for any length of time was that doing so depleted its batteries. Within an hour or so, it would have to charge them. Even using its snort, that would make the job of finding it easier. Worse still, running at high speed meant it was generating flow noise and that also made finding it easier. That was why the PBJs were dropping their sonobuoys. One of the things the Navy had learned from the experiments with the modified British S-boats in Bermuda was what frequencies to listen for. That and the experience of the first wave of Type XXI attacks during late 1944 and early 1945.

The other choice facing the Type XXID down there was to go slow and try to creep away. That had the advantages of extending battery endurance, to days if necessary, and cutting noise to a minimum. That would make it hard to detect. The disadvantage was that going slow meant going very slow indeed; four knots, barely more than walking pace. The missiles fired at Washington an hour ago had come from here. If the Type XXID that had fired them was going slow, it was still somewhere here, alive and well and with plenty of battery charge. If it had gone fast to clear datum, it was somewhere within a radius of 16 miles with dead batteries.

"Anything from the PBJs?" Sturmer snapped out the request.

"Nothing on the buoys, Sir."

"OK, Sweep the area, active search." Two destroyers were sitting out on the flanks of the formation, ready to lash the water with their active sonars. The old sonars had been "searchlight" systems with a single beam. They had been fine for tracking the old, slow Type VII and Type IX U-boats but the Type XXI was fast enough to run between the sweep of the tracking beam. The current sonars had been modified and used three beams in an overlapping fan. It wasn't perfect, but it was a good enough solution until the new generation of scanning sonars left the laboratories and joined the fleet. Whenever that was.

Still, the new sonars gave the Type XXI down there another set of choices. It could accelerate and run between the net of tracking beams but that would deplete battery life and make noise that would be detected by the passive sonobuoys from the PBJs. Or, it could keep going and try to sneak away. A third choice was to try and get to the bottom and sit there. Sturmer paced the bridge waiting for the hunting systems to tell him which choice the U-boat skipper had made.

"Contact Sir. *Grayson* has picked up something on the bottom." *Option Three, then*, Sturmer thought. *Gone to ground.*

"Set up a line attack." The waiting six destroyers were already formed into a line and they curved around to the location from their left-hand picket destroyer. They were accelerating to attack speed, a speed that left their own sonars blind. It didn't matter. They were being coached in by the two pickets that lashed their contact with all the sonar power they had available. *Earle* shuddered as her Hedgehogs fired. The big bow launcher put down an eight-shaped barrage of the small charges, the two waist Hedgehogs added their circles, overlapping the center of the eight. The other five destroyers in the line laid down their own patterns. The result was a maze of intersecting circles that gave the submarine underneath little chance of escape. Even a XXI couldn't outrun the carefully planned web that was dropping on it. The same attack pattern had driven old Type VIIs and Type IXs from the sea.

On board *Earle* the crew waited. Hedgehog rounds only exploded if they hit something hard enough to activate the fuze. The mud of the sea bottom wouldn't do it. Opinions were divided about that. Some people preferred the heavy Squids carried on the Canadian destroyers, their charges exploded at pre-set depths and gave a satisfying mass of explosions. On the convoys to Russia, American and Canadian destroyers worked together; Hedgehog and Squid complemented each other. That was why not many German submarines survived to make a second voyage and very few made a third cruise.

Two explosions sent columns of water skywards. The destroyers turned to bring their depth charge throwers into action. The ten-charge patterns went over the side, covering the area marked by the Hedgehog round explosions, then *Earle* lurched again as her torpedo tubes fired a one-ton depth charge square over the position of the contact.

Now, they had to wait while the water cleared from effects of the explosions. Sturmer resumed pacing the bridge again.

"It's still down there!" The voice from the sonar room was the epitome of frustration. There was no way a bottomed submarine could have survived the hammering that had just been handed out.

"Damn. Order *Grayson* and *Mayo* to drop a pair of one-tonners each on it. That should blow the damned sub apart." *Earle* had the picket role now; she painted the contact with her sonar and coached the other destroyers in. Then, even her sonar picture vanished as the water was roiled by the massive explosions of the big depth charges. There was an anguished wait while the trace cleared and a sigh of disappointment. The submarine was still there.

"Sir, I've got an uneasy feeling about this."

"What's up, Nav?"

"Sir, we're not that far from where *Porter* went down a couple of years ago. It's possible, more than possible, that's her wreck. There's a lot of sunken ships around here, but she's the best candidate."

Sturmer nodded; it made sense. No submarine could take the pounding that had just been handed out. It had to be a wreck on the bottom. And that meant their real target had had that much time to get clear. In fact, the German skipper had probably chosen this point for his launch for just that reason. It was time to start over.

Starting over didn't do any good. The destroyers and aircraft crossed and recrossed the search area; one that was expanding with every minute that passed, and found nothing. As the night went on, the hunting group was slowly forced to accept that the Type XXID had got clean away.

At dawn, Sturmer went back to his cabin. The Germans had used their best technology and every skill at their command and blown up a few trees and possibly the odd skunk. The Americans had used their best technology and skills and pounded a sunken wreck. All that effort, all that skill wasted, all that expenditure for nothing. It struck Sturmer that the night hunt had been a pretty good metaphor for the war as a whole.

1st Platoon, Ski Group, 78th Siberian Infantry Division, First Kola Front

"The sentries are out Tovarish Lieutenant. I have a rota set up. They will be relieved at 20 minute intervals. The storm out there is getting worse."

The arctic storm hit hard and without warning. The winds picked up, the skies clouded over then the snow started coming down. The wind blending the fall with the loose covering already on the ground to create a white-out that reduced visibility to near zero. Outside was just a white mass. There was no way of knowing what was ground, what was sky, what was solid, anything. In the white-out, a man could walk into a tree never having seen it.

The Siberians knew these conditions well. They'd grown up with them, and they'd seen the storm coming. They'd parked their snowmobiles and the three captured Kettenkrads in a hollow where they'd be sheltered from the biting wind. Then they had built themselves a "Zemlyanka," a ground-house. They'd dug a cave in the deep snow, then continued to dig for another 2 meters into the ground. Fortunately, on Kola, the ground wasn't permafrost so it could be dug out easily. They'd covered the pit in the snow with wooden sticks broken off from nearby woods, put more snow over it, leaving just a small entrance. They'd taken care to see that entrance looked no more than a simple dark hole under a rotten tree. They'd even built a dummy zemlyanka close to their vehicles, maskirovka, always maskirovka.

Sergeant Pietr Ivanovitch Batov had arranged the sentry roster with care. A man who spent more than twenty minutes outside would freeze to death. He'd arranged for them to be relieved before that could happen. The men had been divided into three teams of six. Every twenty minutes, two men would come in and spend the rest of the hour warming up again while two more went out to keep watch. Each team of six men would rotate that way, 20 minutes on duty and 40 minutes warming up, for three hours before another team of six relieved them. There were 18 men in the unit; each group of six would have six whole hours to rest. The storm could last at least that long.

Lieutenant Stanislav Knyaginichev looked around the zemlyanka. It was cramped, not from necessity although that had played a part, but from design. Men grouped together shared warmth, those apart wasted it. Warmth was the key to life. There was another reason as well, morale. Keeping men's spirits up was as important as food and warmth in surviving the arctic. Knyaz had something to help him with that.

"Bratya listen. So, you want to hear some new stuff from the papers?"

"Yeah, sure." The voice from the back of the zemlyanka was only marginally interested.

Another voice cut in. "Anything new from Tovarish Ehrenburg?"

"As a matter of fact, yes." Knyaz reached into a pocket. "I have his latest speech. This is one called 'Kill'." That did it, there was a stir of interest and approval. Ehrenburg knew what the Frontniki thought and his pamphlets found ready acceptance with them. "Now listen. Here it is." Knyaz shone his dim torch on the dog-eared paper and started to read.

"Germany is dying slowly and miserably without pathos or dignity. Let us remember the pompous parades, the Sportsplast in Berlin where Hitler used to roar that he would conquer the world. There, he showed us the truth. Germany does not exist, there is only a colossal gang of murdering rapists. The Germans are not human beings. From now on the word German means to use the most terrible oath. From now on the word German strikes us to the quick. We shall not speak any more. We shall not get excited. We shall kill. If you have not killed at least one German a day, you have wasted that day. If you cannot kill your German with a bullet, kill him with your bayonet. If there is calm on your part of the front, or if you are waiting for the fighting, kill a German in the meantime. If you leave a German alive, the German will

51

hang a Russian man and rape a Russian woman. If you kill one German, then kill another -- there is nothing more amusing for us than a heap of German corpses. Do not count days, do not count kilometers. Count only the number of Germans killed by you. Kill the German -- that is your grandmother's plea. Kill the German -- that is your wife's demand. Kill the German -- that is your child's prayer. Kill the German -- that is your motherland's loud request. Do not miss. Do not let through. Kill.

There was a mutter of approval around the crowded snow house. Knyaz could sense the men nodding. "But not everybody feels this way. In Pravda, Tovarish Georgy Aleksandrov replies to 'Kill' with an article entitled 'Tovarish Ehrenburg Oversimplifies'. I have not got the full text here, but Grazhdanin Aleksandrov says that the fact the Gestapo hunt for opponents of the regime and appeal to Germans to denounce them proves that all Germans are not the same. He says it is the Nazi Government that has brought about this calamity in the name of national unity and that very act proves how little unity there is. He says that we should punish the enemy correctly for all his evil deeds and that the slogan of 'kill them all' oversimplifies. What do you think."

"Grazhdanin Ilya doesn't oversimplify!' The voice was belligerent and the outburst met with another mutter of approval.

"Tovarish Aleksandrov needs to spend a few weeks out here. Then we'd hear him speak of 'oversimplifying.'" Another voice, another mutter of approval.

Knyaz smiled slightly in the gloom of the zemlyanka. There had been a time when an article in Pravda had been the epitome of truth; that was after all what Pravda meant. Woe betide anybody who argued with it. Those days had gone at last. "So bratya, we capture some Fascists." There was a chuckle of grim, cynical laughter at that idea. "Hypothetically speaking of course. One of them produces his Communist party card and claims to have been a Member since 1920. What should we do with him?"

There was a pause while the soldiers thought it over. Then their new brat, Kabanov, spoke up, hesitantly. He was still uncertain of his new-found status and whether it gave him the right to speak up. Before being conscripted, Kabanov had won prizes for dialectic in his school and had been picked to go to one of the Moscow universities.

After the war of course. He didn't want the men around him to think he was posturing or trying to curry favor with their officer. He knew he'd won a little respect in the ambush a few days before and he was afraid they'd think it had gone to his head. "The others we kill straight away. That one, we should beat him before we kill him."

"And why should we do that bratishka?"

"Because he should have known better. When a wolf takes a baby from its cradle it is not because the wolf is evil, it is because he is a wolf. It is his nature to prey upon the helpless. We kill him for his act but that is all. When an evil man does evil things it is because it is in his nature and he knows no better. But we expect better of a communist. He should know that these things are evil and refuse to take part. If he knows better but takes part anyway, then his blame is all the greater. Tovarish Aleksandrov forgets that. He is right, there may be good Germans, but if there are, then their blame is all the greater. They deserve death; not less, but more. For they knew good and evil and chose the evil."

There was a swell of appreciation and Knyaz heard somebody give Kabanov an approving swat on the back. *Now, the tricky bit.* "But, bratischkas, bad things happened in the Rodina as well. What do we make of that?"

That caused a silence. There had been a time when Knyaz would have disappeared for making a statement like that. Also, many of the younger soldiers had a positive image of Stalin and thought that he was a great politician. They'd remembered him for his small period of pre-war urban welfare and the idea that he might not be perfect was troubling for some of them. Even in this shadowy zemlyanka, force of habit made people measure their words. Then, a voice spoke carefully from one of the gloomiest parts of the shelter.

"But it has been put right yes? Perhaps bad things were done in past years, Tovarish Stalin had bad advisors who deceived him but those who did that have gone. They have been replaced." *By us* was the unspoken addition. Nobody quite knew what had happened at the end of 1942; they knew everything had changed since then. The NKVD had been broken up between various armed services and the intelligence branch had been re-named back to CheKa. The spy problem had been too serious to allow counterintelligence would vanish completely from the frontlines. Knyaz remembered how Germany easily obtained the Soviet offense or defense plans in 1941-1942. That hadn't been done without the help of massive infiltration. In his heart, Knyaz knew what had happened. When one needed working structures but also had to change their "image" so to speak, purging several key perpetrators could work wonders.

"Tovarish Stalin died a hero in Moskva. We all know that. And anyway, whatever problems we had happened here, we did not force them on others."

"Right, bratishka. We saw that bad things had happened and we put them right. Where are those in Germany, the ones who should have put things right? Of course there are none. If we can change things, why do not the Germans? This is what Tovarish Aleksandrov forgets. The blame of the good is all the greater if they do not resist evil. And let us never forget that the Fascists are here, in our Rodina."

"So are the Americans?" This voice was very hesitant. Everybody knew that it was the Americans with their wonders who had saved their beloved Lieutenant.

"But we invited them to come and they came as guests, with gifts and friendship. And they fight beside us, to drive out the Fascists. Remember what Gospodin Zhukov says. 'It does not matter whether a man fights under the Red Star or the White Star as long as he kills Fascists.'"

The approval was more than a murmur; it was a subdued roar. In the eyes of these soldiers, the Americans had their faults, a tendency to softness and mercy being one. But, they had one great redeeming virtue. They had invented napalm. Anyway, Stalin's propaganda had rarely touched the United States with the fervor it had used to pummel states like the Reich, France and the British Empire. So the soldiers were a bit more open to the idea of the Americans as their allies, all in the spirit of proletarian internationalism.

In the background, Batov tapped two men on the shoulder and they went outside to relieve the sentries. A few seconds later, the two men who had been relieved joined the zemlyanka. There was a quiet muttering as they were brought up the date on the discussion. Knyaz passed his flashlight and the pamphlet over so the men could read it. *A good meeting* he thought, *one that had fortified the men's spirits and intensified their resolution. And all thanks to Tovarish Ehrenburg.*

RB-29C Bad Brew II *3rd Photographic Group, 22,500 feet over The North Sea*

Photographic was a bad joke. *Bad Brew II* did everything except take photographs. Communications intercepts, radar intelligence data, collecting radar images of the coastline in general and of coastal towns in particular. The latter could, just, be defined as photographic. Sort of. *Bad Brew II* didn't even have a bomb bay any more. It was sealed shut and converted into an electronic intelligence gathering center. That didn't matter too much; nobody in their right mind would send a bomber over Germany again. *Bad Brew II's* crew were only too well aware of that.

The Third Photographic Group had once been the Third Bomb Group and they had taken part in the Ploesti Massacre. To be more honest, they'd been one of the four groups that had provided victims for the Ploesti Massacre. The Third had sent 27 B-29As on that raid. *Bad Brew I* had been the only survivor. Two engines shot out, their wings and tail riddled with bullets and shell holes, a quarter of the crew dead and half the survivors wounded; they'd survived because they'd turned back early. The lonely flight back had been an epic struggle to survive. Their B-29 had got them home, how nobody could work out. Rationally, there was no reason why the aircraft should have kept flying, but it had. They'd made it back to base. The undercarriage had collapsed on landing and the aircraft had been written off, a constructive total loss.

The Third had been pulled out of Russia, reorganized as a Photographic Reconnaissance group with RB-29s and then sent to Iceland. Their new assignment, photographic reconnaissance sounded safe enough, but it wasn't. The RB-29Cs operated alone, under cover of darkness; gathering their data as they penetrated closer and closer to hostile territory. Their casualty rate was around ten percent. That was low by the standard of the Russian-based bombing campaign but it was still cripplingly high by rational analysis. Statistically, a ten percent loss rate meant a given crew had a seven percent chance of surviving a tour of duty.

The rewards were worth it. A completed tour of duty meant the crew went back to the continental United States and were then reassigned to the Pacific. Deterring the Japanese by spending hot days on Pacific Island beaches, relaxing and drinking beer, spending warm nights relaxing with affectionate maidens from the Pacific Islands.

Some of the crews had made it, left the Third and went home. Then they vanished. Too busy relaxing with island maidens to write letters was the standard guess. Recently one whole Photo Group, the 305th, had been withdrawn from Keflavik and vanished as well. Another reinforcement for the Pacific; another reason for the Japanese to keep quiet and not annoy the American Eagle. The Germans might be able to stop the B-29. It was a very good bet that the Japanese would have a much harder time trying.

"How's it going?" Captain Jan Niemczyk wanted out of the North Sea at the earliest possible time. As soon as they'd got their radar pictures of the coast and, especially, Hamburg. That meant a long penetration into hostile airspace. An airspace that held night-fighters.

"We've got the pictures command wanted. You reckon the Navy pukes from the carriers are coming down this way?"

"Gotta be. I've heard they're planning to bring their carriers further in. No other reason for us to be this far inside enemy-controlled airspace. Any emissions?"

"Coastal radars only. They're probably tracking us; signal strength is well over threshold. Command says the Germans are too short on gas to send fighters out for a single aircraft."

"Yeah, right." Niemczyk's voice was loaded with cynicism. "Anybody asked them about the birds that don't come back? All eaten by wolves, perhaps?"

There was a bark of laughter around the flight deck. The command line was simple. The aircraft that came back made no reports about being intercepted by night-fighters. Ergo, the Germans didn't send night-fighters out after single aircraft. Much like the nature-lovers claimed there were no reports of people being eaten by wolves. The fault in the logic was the same in both cases. People who were eaten by wolves didn't live to make reports. Nor did RB-29s intercepted by night-fighters.

"Hamburg coming up on the radar screen now, boss." The mapping radar under the belly gave good pictures, particularly where there was water and ground to give vivid contrast. Built-up areas showed up well also; bright white on the dark background. "We're taping the images now."

56

"Good. Let's get the hell out of here."

"Right. Boss, uh-oh."

In the cockpit, Niemczyk decided that the words he hated most in the English language were 'uh-oh.'

"What's the problem?"

"Airborne emissions boss. Fug-220 Liechtenstein. A night-fighter. Signal is above threshold; he's after us."

"Time to go home." Liechtenstein probably meant a He-219. A thoroughly nasty beast; fast and heavily-armed. Radar wasn't that good, not up to the standard of the American fighters, but the German night-fighter crews knew their business. *Bad Brew II* was in trouble. "Engines full emergency power. Where is he coming from?"

The RB-29C had four radar receivers; one in the nose, another in the tail, one in each wingtip. A skilled operator could use those to get a rough directional cut on the radar source. *Bad Brew II* had a very good operator indeed. "He's behind us, Sir, off to port."

"How far out?"

"From echo strength, I'd say 15 to 20 miles. Perhaps 25. Want me to jam him boss?"

"No. Keep the tricks for later. Tell me when he's dead astern. We'll make him work for his dinner."

At this altitude, the RB-29C could manage 390 miles per hour, subject to the engines overheating. If the books were right, the He-219 could manage 416. That gave it a 26 miles per hour speed advantage. The night-fighter wouldn't catch the fleeing reconnaissance aircraft for 35 minutes at worst, 45 minutes at best. The battle would take place anywhere between 250 and 300 miles north of here. The same books said He-219 had a range of 960 miles. The question was, where had he come from? Just how much fuel did he have left?

"Cloud level is at 20,000, Jan."

"OK, we'll head for it. How thick?"

"Weather braniacs said a 5,000 foot layer. There's a hell of a storm system running through. It's not too bad here, but Kola is getting really pounded."

"That gives us some room to breathe." Niemczyk put *Bad Brew IIs* nose down and watched the speed build up. 395mph. That put the Heinkel behind them between 40 and 55 minutes away from closing to gun range. Anywhere between 260 and 360 miles north of their present position. There was another catch. *Bad Brew II* carried a lot more fuel than the fighter behind her, but supplies weren't limitless. If she ran at full power too long, she would run out of fuel also.

It was a strange sensation. The individual minutes seemed to drag by, yet every time Niemczyk looked at the instrument panel clock, the hands seemed to have jumped forward. "Where is he?"

"Dead behind us. Estimated two, perhaps three miles; no more than that. May be less." They were already in the cloud layer, the gray-white shroud clung to them. The enemy radar could still see them, but the crew on the fighter would be searching for the dark shadow of the bomber. The RB-29C had an edge there. Its bright silver finish didn't have much of a shadow. In the air, it tended to be shadows people saw, as dark patches on a light background. Contrary to myth, matte black was a very bad color for a night-fighter.

"Everybody to an observation panel. Watch for the slightest shadow." Originally the B-29 had had multiple remote controlled turrets with their gunners in blisters. The RB-29C had discarded them and the blisters had been replaced by flat, transparent observation panels. "Mickey, you're the most likely to see him first. Yell out at the slightest hint. Just don't fire." The twin .50 caliber tail guns were *Bad Brew IIs* only armament. There was a big argument about ammunition for them. Some crews carried heavy tracer loads in the hope that streams of fire would scare off a night-fighter. Niemczyk thought that was insane; tracer pointed both ways and revealed the bomber's position as clearly as a neon signpost. *Bad Brew II* carried not a single round of tracer.

"Shadow, behind us." It was Donovan in the tail turret.

"Drop chaff. Jam that radar now." Niemczyk waited until the chaff cloud deployed and the jammer in what had once been the bomb bay was pumping out energy. Then he hauled *Bad Brew II* around, breaking left as hard as the airframe would allow. Behind them, the faint shadow in the mist passed their tail. Niemczyk was already reversing the turn, putting Bad Brew II on a parallel course to the fighter, falling behind it. Then, he saw something weird and unexpected. Streams of light headed up from the ghostly shadow in the cloud. *Tracers? Upwards?*

"You see that Jan? He's got cannon firing upwards. What the devil is he playing at?"

"That's new. Logical though. Cannon like that will gut a bomber. The braniacs need to know about them. They were probably firing on an estimated position when they lost us." In front of them, the shadow faded into the mist. Niemczyk thought carefully. *He must know we aren't in front of him, that means we must have turned. So he's going to turn as well, right or left? Did he think we turned right or left? We went left, will he guess that?* Mentally, Niemczyk flipped a coin, then broke right. The longer he could keep the fighter from picking him up again, the better. On instinct, he pulled the stick back and started a slow climb. The speed dropped. The laboring engines drifted even closer to the red danger zones on the temperature gauges. The R-3350 was not the most reliable engine ever built. *Just how long could they take this abuse?*

"No sign of emissions. He hasn't picked us up yet. Wait, I'm getting sidelobes. No main pulse, just sidelobes."

"Feed jamming energy into them. Try and make him think we're heading northeast and diving." In fact, they were heading northwest and climbing. Once again the minutes were ticking past. *Bad Brew II* broke out of the cloud layer, allowing her silver skin to shine in the feeble light of the new moon. Niemczyk cut the engine power back to cruise allowing the needles on the temperature gauges to drop a little away from the danger zone. Their speed dropped to 250 miles per hour as a result. In his mind, Niemczyk saw the night-fighter maneuvering, circling to try and pick up its target again, diving in the belief that the target had dived away from him, trying to gain separation. Then, he'd have come out the cloud layer below and realized he'd been fooled. That would put him at 15,000 feet and *Bad Brew II* was at 22,500. The He-219 was underpowered. It had a climb rate of around 1,800 feet per minute. The fighter would take four and a half minutes to regain altitude. By the time it got out of the clouds, it would be another 20 miles behind them. If they were lucky.

"There it is!" The waist observer had seen the dark shadow of the night-fighter, silhouetted against the white of the cloud layer. "Behind us, 235 degrees. At least eight, nine miles away. Not as good as Niemczyk had hoped, the night-fighter pilot must have realized early what had happened and made a good guess on his target's course. Still, *Bad Brew II*s engines had cooled down a little and that allowed him to go back to full power. Behind them, the He-219 started to follow, then broke off and curved away, heading south east for home. Niemczyk breathed a heartfelt sigh of relief and turned northeast, for Iceland and his home base. He had a long, long story to tell to the debriefers who hadn't believed that the Germans sent night-fighters out after single bombers.

CHAPTER THREE
COLD WIND RISING

United States Strategic Bombardment Commission, Blair House, Washington D.C. USA.

"You've gone brown."

Inanna looked up, rather apprehensively. "How does it look Nammie?"

Naamah inspected Inanna's dyed hair with an authoritative eye. There had been a time when she'd made hair colorings from plant extracts but those days were long gone. "Your eyes don't match, but there's nothing you can do about that. I should know." Naamah's eyes were a dead, slime-green, frightening to the point of being repulsive. "For the rest, only your hairdresser will know."

Inanna giggled at the reference to the advertising slogan used by Clairol for their range of home-coloring products. The company held a national competition to select an advertising slogan for their new product. 'Only your hairdresser will know' had been the alleged winner. On paper, it was a reference to the quality of the product that could match salon hair products. In reality, a veiled reference to the fact that it offered blonde women a way to look less German. Looking

German was neither sensible nor safe. The newspaper on Inanna's desk proved that. "You heard Tommy Lynch sent in an entry to that competition?"

"Oh no, what did he say this time?"

"It read 'mix up a double batch and give yourself a matching snatch'. It won too, only the company management vetoed it despite the fact it would have doubled their sales. Does it really look good? Coloring jobs in salons are getting too expensive these days; this way is a little less costly. I thought I'd try it out first and if it works fine, we'll make sure all the blondes in our family get supplies. We'll dip into the reserves for it."

"That bad, Inanna? I knew there was trouble up in Boston and New York but I thought it was confined to there?"

"What do you think?" Inanna flipped a copy of the *Boston Globe* over to Naamah. The front page picture was a sagging figure, tied to a streetlight post, the head and upper body covered with tar and feathers. "They ripped her coat and blouse off, hacked up her hair and then did that. Nobody bothered to call the police, she was there for twenty minutes in this weather before the cops found her. She's in hospital; emergency ward. Pneumonia and burns to her face and head. What sort of animals are these people?"

"Frightened, angry, frustrated ones." Naamah very carefully kept the anger out of her voice. "I'll bet you any money you like; in normal times, the people who did that would have risked their lives to help a woman in distress. But now, they're trapped in a situation they can't understand or control. They want to slaughter the people who are killing our boys over in Russia but they can't. So they displace that anger onto a scapegoat." Naamah's mouth twisted in disgust. "The normal scapegoats are blacks, Jews, any minority. Even having that thought makes people see themselves as being what they hate, being too close to the Nazis. So they pick on somebody else. In this case women with blonde hair. I'll bet if the FBI picks up the group who did this, they'll find in the background somebody who had a grudge against this particular victim and got everybody else worked up. Not all brutal sadists are German. They're everywhere, here as well; you know that. Over the years, we've seen them often enough in more than enough places."

"That's the line the *Globe* are following. That the woman was the innocent victim of a personal vendetta and the people who were did it were no better than Nazis themselves. Problem is, look at the other story on the front page. More massacres in Ireland, entire villages in County Limerick just gone. Everybody. Men, women, children, animals, crops, everything. Boston is an Irish-American city. A lot of people had folk back 'in the auld country' and they want to hit back any way they can. This country is getting ugly. Nammie, it's in the big cities now, but it's spreading. We need to protect our family."

Naamah nodded. "OK, I'll talk to Lillith and Nefertiti, they'll work out how much we need." She grinned; the picture on the newspaper made it forced and unnatural. "It's lucky we invested in the aircraft and electronics industries a few years back, isn't it." She looked at the picture again and even the forced grin faded. If she ever found the people responsible for that atrocity, she'd take them out for a drink. A very final drink.

Bridge, KMS Derfflinger, *Flagship, High Seas Fleet, At Sea, North Atlantic*

Even the big Forties were rolling in the seas. Huge waves; long, swelling ones that rocked the battleship. Every so often there would be intense vibration as the waves exposed the screws aft and caused them to race before plunging into the deep again. Lindemann looked behind him. The second in line, immediately behind *Derfflinger*, was *Moltke*. Lindemann watched her drive her bows in, taking green water up to Turret Anton. All eight battleships had the "Atlantic bow," raked and flared to improve bad weather performance. It was a great improvement on the flat, vertical Taylor bow the German designers had preferred earlier. It wasn't helping *Scharnhorst* and *Gneisenau* though. They were badly overweight, sat much lower in the water than planned and they wallowed badly. *Moltke* was taking water over her bows, but the two light battleships at the end of the port column never seemed to get their bows out of the green swells. Turret Anton was awash more often than not. As if to hide the two ships' distress, the rain closed in again, shrouding them from view.

Lindemann sighed and went back to the chart table. According to the weather people, once this storm front was past, the weather should be a lot better. By North Atlantic standards anyway. They'd be close enough by then to close on the big convoy and overwhelm it and its escorts. Then, they'd turn on the carrier group and overwhelm that.

After all, nobody had ever sunk a battleship on the high seas with aircraft. As long as the battleships could maneuver, they could avoid the airstrikes. Once the carriers had shot their bolt, it would be all over. Some were even cautiously talking about the rest of the American fleet, probably pounding England or France, coming to the rescue and being added to the pot. Too much to hope for of course. But they would get the big supply convoy and there was word of another smaller convoy, a fast troop convoy. That would be worth the risk of adding to the bag.

The rain squall eased off a little and the visibility improved again. Lindemann looked out the starboard bridge wings, towards the destroyer screen. He could see *Hipper* running ahead of the formation. *Z-23* was steaming just behind and to starboard of her while *Z-24* was clearly in sight, sailing almost parallel with *Derfflinger*. Behind her, *Z-25* was having a much easier time of handling the heavy waves. She should, the designers had finally admitted the heavy twin turret forward on *Z-23* and *Z-24* was a bad idea and replaced it with a single shielded mount. Four 15cm guns, not five and all the better for that. Lindemann swung his binoculars back towards *Z-24*. Another one of those great swells was approaching and he watched the destroyer dig her bows in before she was hidden by the mountain of green water. He watched, waiting for her to reappear, waiting to see her fight her way clear of the wave. To his mounting horror she never did. *Z-24* had vanished.

Lindemann was frozen, watching the scene through the ghostly shroud of mist, spray and rain. *A three and a half thousand ton destroyer couldn't just vanish.* In the background he heard the message from the radio room arrive. 'Destroyer *Z-24* has foundered. No survivors.' Eventually he forced his voice to work. "How?"

"If I may Sir." One of the young lieutenants was speaking very tentatively. "I was training to be a naval architect before I was for . . . . signed into the Navy. There were many doubts about the *Z-23* class even then. That big turret forward is a lot of weight; too much for the structure of the bows. Worse, there is a large compartment underneath the turret. That makes the whole bow structure extremely stressed. Finally, the trunk for the turret is too close to the hull sides. Gunnery was told, Sir, but they insisted on that twin turret forward. I think when *Z-24* dug her bows in, the weight of the wave pressing down combined with the bow rising up was too much for the structure. I think her bows just tore off forward of her bridge. A battleship or cruiser, they might survive that Sir, but a destroyer won't. Her own engines will drive her under and there is nothing to stop the flooding. Nothing at all; she probably sank in less than 20 seconds."

Lindemann stared at the young officer who flushed and turned bright red. "I'm sorry, Sir."

The Admiral slowly shook his head. "There is no need for apology. You had information I needed and gave it to me as was your duty. Communications, send a message to all the destroyers. They are to abandon efforts to hold station and maneuver as necessary to avoid damage." Lindemann raised his binoculars to his eyes again and looked at the patch of sea that had claimed *Z-24* with so little warning. For the first time, he had a very bad feeling about this operation.

Goofers Gallery, CV-33 USS Kearsarge, *Task Group 58.2, At Sea, South of Nova Scotia, North Atlantic*

"The German fleet is out." The young torpedo-bomber pilot made the remark with complete confidence.

"How do you know, George? The German High Command in your pocket? Giving you tips?" The other pilots on the gallery were jeering. The Adie pilot had an air of smug, condescending confidence that set people's teeth on edge. Coming from a family with money could do that.

"That's the fifth pallet of torpedoes that's come aboard in the last half hour. There's five-inch rockets and 12-inch Tiny Tims coming aboard from the aft station. We're offloading 500 and thousand pounder HEs and taking on sixteen hundred and two thousand-pound armor piercing. We had a lot to start; now we've got more. We're going to be taking on other ships for once, heavily armored ones. So, that's the German fleet. They've got be coming out."

Although the other pilots hated to admit it, he had to be right. They watched as *Kearsarge* swung another pallet of the massive Tiny Tim rockets on board. At the same time, a pack of 22.4 inch torpedoes was being hoisted over to *Intrepid*. Between the two carriers, the ammunition ship *Firedrake* was working to keep the stream of anti-ship munitions flowing. A day earlier, it would have been impossible; the storm had still been at full force. Now, it had passed in the night and the weather was fine, as good as it was ever likely to be in the North Atlantic in November.

Not far away, the aircraft carriers *Reprisal* and *Oriskany* were bombing up from the ammunition ship *Great Sitkin*. The carriers were helpless, their decks were cleared, their aircraft struck below or parked forward, out of the way. Riding guard was the fifth carrier in the group, the light carrier *Cowpens*. She was the guard carrier, responsible for providing air patrols over the group with her three squadrons of F4U-7s. Five carriers with over 400 aircraft in this task group alone, and there were four more groups just like it. Well, not quite like it, Task Group 58.1 had the new CVB *Gettysburg* in place of a light carrier. That gave the group more than 500 aircraft. No wonder "Wild Bill" Halsey had made that group his flag.

Lieutenant George Herbert Walker Bush looked away from the flat-tops, towards the other shapes in the weak, gray sunshine. The biggest of them were the battleships *New Jersey* and *Wisconsin*, then the heavy cruisers *Albany* and *Rochester*. There had been three but *Oregon City* had suffered bad storm damage and been forced to head back. There were bad whispers about the 'Orrible Titty.' Some said she'd been built wrong, her spine twisted. Four light cruisers, *Fargo, Huntingdon, Santa Fe* and *Miami*. Eighteen destroyers filled out the group. They were DDKs, Gearing class ships whose job was to hunt and kill submarines. Protecting the carriers was the job of all those other ships. They shielded the carriers while the carriers smashed everything they took a dislike to.

And there were four more carrier task groups just like this one. Then there was the battle line, the support groups, the munitions groups. The ASW hunter-killer groups. All intended to keep the carriers safe and fighting.

Below them, another pallet of torpedoes swung onto the flight deck. The munitions men down there swarmed over it, striking the extra torpedoes down to the magazines. Up on the Goofers Gallery, the other pilots had to admit Bush was right; this many torpedoes, this many rockets, this many armor-piercing bombs meant they were going after the big ships of the German Fleet.

"I'll tell you this guys. When we find the Huns, I'm going to get me a battleship."

It was too much. With one accord the pilots started beating the young Lieutenant over the head with their caps. Eventually they paused for breath and the ring-leader of the attack pushed his battered cap back on. "Yeah right, George. And one day you'll get to be President, won't you?"

USS Stalingrad, *Hunter-Killer Group "Sitka" in the North Atlantic, north of the UK.*

"Ready for launch." Lieutenant Pace braced himself for the slam in the back of a catapult launch. The *Stalingrad* had two F8F-1 Bearcats ready to go. Not far away, her sistership, the USS *Moskva* had two more. They'd fly as two pairs towards the contact one of their picket destroyers had spotted. If the analysis of the target's flight pattern was right, Hunter-Killer Group Sitka had hit golden paydirt. For today, anyway.

"Target is cruising at Angels 26, speed 200. Bearing 135 degrees. Range 165 miles" The situation report was as complete as possible to cut down radio transmissions after the fighters were launched. If this was one of Germany's few remaining Me-264s, they wanted to give it as little warning as possible.

Ahead of him, one of the deck crew made a winding-up motion with his hands. Pace pushed the throttle forward; the R-2800 engine picked up power, making the Bearcat shake. There came the expected thump and he was hurtling down the deck as the catapult fired. He cleared the *Stalingrad's* bows and pushed the nose down. One always traded altitude for speed; no matter how little of the former one had, the latter was worth more. Underneath him, the undercarriage doors thumped closed. He sank below deck level, then he soared upwards. The Bearcat was in its element again.

The cruise out took a little under an hour; time for the target to move roughly 200 miles in any direction. Fortunately, the German pilot was doing the north-to-south leg of a sweep. Probably checking to see what was following the storm front. It was an open question if he'd seen Hunter-Killer Group Sitka. Probably not; German radar wasn't that good and surface search conditions were still pretty bad. He hadn't deviated from his course yet. He, almost certainly, didn't know the Bearcats were coming.

"You're on top of him." The fighter controller's voice from *Stalingrad* was cold, unemotional. The pair of Bearcats from *Moskva* had already peeled away, they'd gone to full power and moved to get between the Me-264 and its base. "There are RB-29s operating. Make sure of target identification before opening fire." With its smooth glazed nose and four radial engines, the Me-264 looked a lot like a RB-29. It was whispered that there had already been some unfortunate accidents.

Pace spotted their target below them. The large twin tailplanes were clearly visible even though the aircraft's dappled light and dark gray paint job blended with the sea far below. Time to open the dance. "Confirm, Me-264. Take him."

The two Bearcats accelerated into a long dive. Unlike the midnight blue aircraft on the fleet carriers, escort carrier group planes were painted light gray with a gloss-white belly. It cut the shadows down making it much less likely that an alert gunner would spot them. Pace was coming in from high seven o'clock; his wingman from high-five. The Me-264 had a single 20mm gun in a turret above its rear fuselage. It could fire at one attacking aircraft, not two widely-separated ones. Suddenly, the German aircraft accelerated and black smoke trailed from its engines. They'd been spotted; and the pilot had cut in his GM-1 boost. For five minutes, the bomber would be almost as fast as the fighters chasing it.

Between dodging the stream of tracer 20mm shells from the rear turret and the GM-1 boosted engines powering the bomber, the two diving Bearcats were hardly closing the gap. It didn't matter. *Moskva's* Bearcats soared up and fired. They hit the Me-264 with long bursts of .50 caliber gunfire, from below and to the right and left. The thin black stream of smoke from the inboard port engine was suddenly transformed into a billowing cloud of black flame and dense smoke. The Me-264 abruptly slowed. The two Bearcats behind were able to close the range at last. Pace took careful aim. His .50s lashed the aft fuselage of the bomber. The 20mm tracers stopped abruptly. Gunner killed.

The Me-264 still had a 13.2 mm machine gun in the forward upper turret, a 20mm gun firing under the belly, two more 13.2mms, one in each waist hatch and a fixed 13.2 firing forward. For all that, the loss of the 20mm gunner was critical. It meant the German aircraft was virtually defenseless against attacks from above and behind. That's where Pace and his wingman made their next runs, raking the bomber's aft fuselage, walking their bursts along the structure into the wings. The gray beast below them was threshing, trying to defend itself but its fangs were being methodically drawn by the four fighters. *Moskva's* two planes made another pass, this time for above and on the beam. Their streams of .50 fire raked the forward fuselage. That left the other upper turret silent. The aircraft was defenseless.

Pace was reminded of a history lesson he had once listened to, of a game when times were harder. A pack of dogs would be let loose on a blinded bear and the crowd would place bets on how long the bear would survive and how many of the dogs it could kill. This was different of course. It was possible, normal, to feel sorry for the bear. Nobody would feel sorry for the bomber below.

Pace swept in again, his aim undisturbed by defensive fire. His .50s streamed tracer, raking into the wing roots and walking sideways towards the engines. The starboard inner engine erupted into flames as his gunfire shredded its nacelle and the Me-264 angled downwards. As Pace's aircraft pulled away, *Moskva's* team made another pass. It was the killer. One of the long wings crumpled just inboard of a burning engine and the 264 went into a helpless spin. It fell from the sky and crashed into the sea. There, it exploded; its death watched dispassionately by the gun cameras on the Bearcats.

"We need bigger guns." Pace's voice was unemotional.

"They're coming. The new 'Cats will have 20mms, according to the scuttlebutt."

"Hope they work a bit better than the last ones." The Navy's previous attempt at a 20mm gun had been a fiasco. The weapons usually jammed after a round or two. "Let's go home."

An hour later, the Bearcats were sitting on the hangar deck being rearmed and refueled. Their gun camera film had been taken and was being flown back to Washington. There, the kill would be confirmed. Inanna would take a file from her cabinet and delete another Me-264 from Germany's shrinking maritime reconnaissance aircraft fleet.

Every reduction in the Luftwaffe's small maritime reconnaissance fleet meant the fast carriers operating out in the Atlantic were that much safer. Without the aircraft to steer them to their targets, U-boats, even the Type XXIs, were virtually useless against the fast carriers. They would have to rely on luck to be in the right place at the right time. In the North Atlantic, that just didn't cut it.

69

"We have a problem." Major-General Klaus Marcks was not given to stating the obvious but there were times when a situation merited it.

"Captain Wilhelm Lang." Colonel Heinrich Asbach also thought this was one of the times when stating the obvious was entirely justifiable. "The question is, how do we get rid of him? And should we?"

"We can't, Heinie." Marcks had a small group of officers who had been with him since the heady days in France, five years ago. The number was growing smaller as the Russian Front whittled them away, but he still depended on the survivors for advice and insight. Only a fool trusted his own feelings when there were other, better sources available. "The man has served on probably everybody's staff over the years. He has powerful friends, the sort who could be very dangerous for this whole unit. He got us six brand new, fresh from the factory, self-propelled 150mm howitzers with a single telephone call. Do you want to take the chance that another call would send us to Archangel'sk? While he was assigned to a new post in the opposite direction?"

Asbach shook his head. It was not a chance worth taking. Even the name Archangel'sk had a horror associated with it, something quite unlike anything else on the Russian Front. There was a legend in the German Army. Archangel'sk didn't actually exist anymore; ithad become a gateway to Hell. That the units sent there just marched into the mist covering the city and vanished as if they had never been. It was pretty close to the truth. Being ordered to Archangel'sk was the nearest thing to a mass death sentence that could be given without actually ordering up the mobile gas chambers. He reached out and took another slug of brandy. His family owned one of Germany's oldest brandy producers and he managed to keep the officer's mess well stocked.

"Anyway, he isn't actually a bad officer, Klaus." Marcks lifted an eyebrow at that. "He knows the regulations inside out. He knows his duties and performs them well. It's just that he has absolutely no experience at all. I guess that back in '38 we were just like him. Only, we spent all our time out here learning the reality of the war we're stuck in. He spent that time in comfortable headquarters units, writing regulations and sending memos. He doesn't know when the rules and regulations apply and when they do not. And he doesn't really understand how the veterans think or listen to their experience. You heard the story about his nickname?"

"No?"

"He started off as being the 'Perfectly Perfumed Prince' and it got abbreviated to 'Prince.' When he heard about it, he assumed it was a term of respect, 'Prince amongst men' or something like that. A normal officer would know when to turn a blind eye. Not our Captain Lang. It was against regulations, so he forbade its use."

"What do they call him now?" Marcks was genuinely fascinated.

"Well, the men started calling him 'The Officer Formerly Known As Prince' but that was too clumsy for general use so now they call him 'Still' because he's still a Perfectly Perfumed Prince."

Marcks barked out a laugh and shook his head. "Well, that's all very fine but it doesn't solve our problem. We're kicking off as soon as this storm is over. It's clearing from the west which is apparently very significant for some reason or another. The engineers have been checking the ice. The lakes and rivers are frozen hard enough to take the strain of our lighter vehicles. The heavy traffic will have to thread its way through as best it can. That includes the artillery, both the towed stuff and our newly-acquired self-propelled guns. Can we be sure than Lang won't get carried away and drive them into a lake or something?"

Both men sighed and inspected their brandies. As they had both suspected, the levels in the glasses were inadequate to permit deep contemplation. Asbach topped them up again.

"I don't think we have much choice, Klaus. If we move him out, who gets the battery instead of him? His lieutenant has even less experience and nowhere near the same level of knowledge. I think we're going to have to leave Lang in place and just watch him carefully." Asbach thought for a second. "There is one possibility of course."

"Do tell."

"My part of the attack is pretty close to a raid. An armored infantry column going in to try and seize those big railway guns north of here. Preferably capture them. If that's not possible, destroy them. We've built the raiding group out of the recon battalion; used its half-tracks and reinforced its infantry component. It's short on tank killing power though, its armored cars have only 75s or long 50mm guns, and artillery. Only, we now have some self-propelled artillery we can take along. So if we attach Lang and his self-propelled guns to that force, it does two things. Beefs up the raid to the point where we can do useful things and put Lang in a position where he's both under a group of experienced officers and in a prime position to get some battle-lore of his own under his belt."

"You're happy to take such an inexperienced man along?"

"Happy is the wrong word, Klaus, but I think it's the best solution."

"Agreed. I'll issue the orders. After we've finished supporting your family business."

Oval Office, The White House, Washington D.C.

"Your ten o'clock Mister President. Senator Stuart Symington." President Dewey's secretary spoke quietly on the intercom.

"Thank you. Send him straight in please." There were those whose services merited immediate access and those who deserved a long, long wait in the Presidential anteroom. Symington was one of the former.

"Senator. Pleased to see you. How goes work on the Air Material Production Subcommittee?"

"Thank you for seeing me so promptly, Mister President. It's one aspect of our work I wish to see you about. Particularly one aircraft, the C-99. On the face of it, the aircraft appears to be a scandalous waste of resources. I wanted to discuss the matter with you before the subcommittee investigates the program. In case there is a reason behind this program that I and my committee are not aware of."

"You have doubts about this aircraft Senator? If you could enlarge on them, perhaps I can set your mind at rest."

"Sir, put at its most basic level, the aircraft seems to perform poorly and demand excessive amounts of support. It is slow. It flies at around 200mph. That makes it appear to be even slower than a C-47 and much slower than a C-54. It is restricted in altitude. My understanding is that it cruises at around 10,000 feet. We have reports that it can't climb above bad weather, so it is often grounded. Worst of all, it uses six of the R-4360 engines that are in such short supply. The Navy is crying out for F2G Super-Corsairs and the Air Force desperately needs F-72 Thunderstorms to replace the old F-47s. Yet the production of both is restricted by the shortage of engines. If we cancel the C-99, we could free up engines for those aircraft."

"Senator, put like that, you make a strong case. If I might show you some pictures, they might put a different light on the matter." Dewey had been anticipating a problem like this and he had the files waiting in his office. Symington's Air Material Production Subcommittee dealt mostly with the components for aircraft; engines, weapons, most recently radar and other electronic systems. His point had been a good one. It was just he didn't, couldn't, mustn't know the whole picture. The President opened the file and handed some 10 x 18-inch prints over to Symington.

The Senator gasped. The pictures, obviously taken from a high-flying RB-29, were of a port. From the size and scale, he guessed they must have been taken from almost 30,000 feet. The port showed clearly. What was even clearer was the mass of shipping that surrounded it. Symington was irresistibly reminded of ants swarming around a leaf. A mass of shipping that engulfed the port, obviously swamping its facilities.

"That's Vladivostok Senator. Of all the supplies that go to Russia, 25 percent goes via the northern convoy route to Murmansk and Archangel. Another 25 percent uses the southern route, via Iran and the Afghan Railway. The other half, all of it, goes via the western route to Vladivostok. And you can see the result. The congestion off the Russian port is terrifying. I'm told Admiral King has woken up screaming in the night when he imagines enemy submarines or surface ships getting loose into that mass of shipping."

Symington nodded. In his mind he could see the exploding ships; enemy warships running through the tightly-packed merchantmen and the burned bodies of seamen washing up on the cold shores. Just like they had back in the bad days of 1942. It could not be allowed to happen again.

Dewey was still speaking. "Of course, we're doing what we can to solve the problem. We've got engineers expanding the facilities at Vladivostok. They've doubled the capacity of the port since 1943. We've moved a whole new prefabricated port over there, called a Mulberry, and that helps. We're even unloading cargoes directly over the beach where we can. They're all only marginal solutions. We've achieved a lot more by building support factories in Russia. There's iron ore, copper, nickel, lead there, oil as well, a lot of it. We used to ship crude oil back to California, then ship refined products back. That blocked the port twice per cargo. Now, we have refineries in Siberia and that saves us a lot of shipping. Only, it's still a marginal solution.

"It's not just Vladivostok. The backlog of shipping is causing congestion in all the ports down the West Coast. Rail yards are full because the trains can't unload until they have a ship to unload them into. The ship can't take the cargo because it's still waiting to unload the previous lot at Vladivostok. Then, we've got the railway problem in Siberia itself. We're double-tracking the railway and building relief lines as fast as we can but we still can't get the job done fast enough. For all that, the equipment needed to enlarge the railways comes by sea, and the ships are backed up all over the place.

"One final thing. Take a look at the map. Look how close that shipping thrombosis is to Japan. Bombers in the Japanese home islands could take off, bomb the stacked up cargo ships and return home without ever leaving sight of their bases. Do you know what it's costing us to persuade the Japanese not to interfere with that lifeline? A free hand in China's just the start of it."

Dewey sighed again. "Look, Senator, I'm sorry if I'm ranting at you, but this shipping problem is keeping everybody awake. The C-99 is the solution to the whole problem. It may fly low and it may fly slow but it has the range to take off from anywhere in the western United States and fly to an airbase in eastern Russia. It can carry 400 men, or 100,000 pounds of cargo per flight. The C-54 carries 50 men or 10,000 pounds of cargo. That means that a single C-99 can carry the human payload of eight C-54s and the cargo payload of ten. It can do all that while flying three times as far. And it doesn't stop there. The C-54 and the C-69 are basically passenger transports. They have small doors and that gives them problems handling bulky cargoes. The C-99B onwards have clamshell doors in the nose that are big enough to handle whole vehicles. We could *fly* tanks to Russia if we had to, and deliver them directly from the factories in Detroit to the troops waiting on the Volga. And they can back-load troops from the Volga to the United States. Think on it, Senator, because of the C-99, a soldier with a five day pass can come home and see his family instead of drinking too much in a 'rest camp.'

"Senator, don't think of the C-99 as a slow, low-flying aircraft. Think of it as a very fast, amphibious, high-sailing merchant ship. In the time a Victory Ship takes to get from the West Coast to Vladivostok, unload, and come back, the C-99 can lift the same weight of cargo and bypass the ports completely. All it needs is an airstrip and we are building those by the score. It bypasses the ports, bypasses the rail system and means we can route supplies far away from Japan. We'll still need merchant ships. There are some bulk cargoes that even a C-99 can't handle but, for the rest, the C-99 is it."

Symington thought over the whole situation, his eyes fixed on the picture of the mass of shipping piled up outside Vladivostok. It would be easy to create a scandal over the C-99. It was a big, expensive aircraft and its performance figures didn't look good. But, what he had just been told made sense. It left him with a choice between making political capital for his party by embarrassing the Government or supporting the interests of the country. He was a Democrat, a holdover from the Roosevelt administration. To a party political man this was a gift. But, to Symington, that wasn't a choice. No honorable man would put his party before his country.

"Thank you Mister President. The situation is quite clear to me now and my initial impressions were quite wrong. I must ask your forgiveness for wasting your time. My committee will say nothing about the C-99."

"Senator, may I ask a kindness of you? Obviously the problems we are having with port congestion must remain completely secret but it would do much good for public morale if the capabilities of the C-99 were publicized. The good with the bad, low speed: low ceiling but great range and payload. Perhaps some color pictures might be released. I understand the orange and silver color scheme used by the Air Bridge aircraft photographs very well. I think the people would be encouraged and cheered by the news that your Committee has expedited the aircraft that brings their boys home on leave. There's nothing secret about the C-99 itself. We could even have some newsreels made."

Symington smiled broadly in response. This was true politics, two men resolving their differences and coming to an agreement that benefitted both. "I think that is an excellent idea, Mister President."

After Symington left, Dewey relaxed in his chair. The case made for the C-99 was a powerful one. It was true, but it was only part of the picture. It was also important that people be taught to see any six-engined aircraft with orange markings as just another transport from the Air Bridge. That brought another thought to mind. Senator Symington was an honest man and an honorable man. This meeting had proved that. He was a good candidate to be informed of the real secret that lay behind the C-99. When the time was right, of course.

C-99B Arctic Express *Seattle Airport, Washington*

"Well, that was unexpected." Captain Bob Dedmon closed the cockpit canopy panels and settled comfortably into his seat. The cargo manifest was on a clipboard in front of him. Ten spare R-4360 engines for an F-72 group and a mass of spare parts, propellers, tires and electronic gear. Plus ammunition and drums of lubricants. Enough to keep the group going for a week or more. A total manifest of 35 tons.

Outside, a cinema newsreel crew had been filming the apparently endless column of trucks bringing up equipment that vanished through the giant clamshell doors in the nose and into the belly of the C-99B. She was a new bird. This would be her first flight to Russia and that was the apparent subject of the newsreel. It had been a well-made piece. The news crew had wound up the tension as the weather reports came in. Would it be possible for the C-99B to make the flight? The plane was too slow and didn't have the ceiling to climb above bad weather so a good forecast was critical. Then, the message had come in from Anadyr in Russia. All clear, good weather all the way. The flight was on.

Dedmon had never expected to be the subject of a newsreel; privately, he'd thought the interview he'd given was a disaster. He'd tried to explain what flying the big transport was like. How the huge double-deck fuselage acted like a sail and caught every hint of a crosswind. How flying it felt like steering a house from its front porch. But also what the flights achieved; tonnage delivered directly to the people who needed it, troops brought back for the short leave with their families that they had all so richly earned. He'd tried to say how much getting the supplies through and bringing the people back meant to the pilots on the Air Bridge, but he'd made a complete stumbling mess of it. He didn't realize that the emotional, semi-articulate explanation of how the C-99 crews thought and felt had the ring of truth that a polished, professional, effort would have lacked.

"Never thought we would be movie stars. Engineering, ready to go. Full power engines three, four, two, five, one and six in that order. Nose doors closed. Check cargo secured." Dedmon glanced out at the transport. The C-99A had its cockpit buried in the contours of the nose and the pilot couldn't see much of his aircraft. Modifying the design to include the nose loading doors had meant the cockpit had to be moved to a bubble on top of the fuselage. From there, he could see the whole aircraft. *Arctic Express* was bright silver except for the outer wing panels and tail surfaces. They were orange-crimson, a high-visibility color in case the bird went down in the snow. *It is one pretty color scheme* Dedmon thought.

"All engines full power. Ready to taxi out."

The big transport moved slowly onto the taxiway and waddled down towards the runway. Sitting so high off the ground gave the crew a tremendous sense of power; they overlooked everything. It was as if they were watching the working of the airfield from a moving control tower. Dedmon glanced down. There was a little C-94 in front of them. It was a small utility bird, the military version of the Cessna Skymaster. He could hardly see it. That was a safety problem worth bearing in mind. "Navigator, got the flight plan?"

"Sure thing Captain. North to Alaska, over the Bering Straits to Anadyr then inland to Khabarovsk. Flight time, estimated 20 hours. Assuming we don't open her up properly." The C-99 was quite a bit faster than the published data suggested although there were strict orders against revealing that fact. The explanation was that the unrevealed extra speed was their ace in the hole, to get away from fighters annoying them.

"Radio message sir, from the C-94 in front. He asks what our plans are."

Dedmon snorted. Viewed from the perspective of the tiny utility aircraft, the C-99 must look like a massive monster towering high in the sky. The thought gave him an idea. "Cargo deck, start opening the clamshell doors. Radio, patch me though to the C-94. Dedmon waited until the connection was made and the rumble of the nose doors showed they were opening. Then he spoke to the C-94 pilot, "I am going to eat you!"

C-66D Dragon Rapide Matilda, *Kola Peninsula*

The blinding snowstorm that had grounded pretty nearly everything north of Petrograd had eased off a little but the white stuff was still coming down hard. It was a matter of great personal satisfaction to Flight Lieutenant George Brumby that his little detachment of antiquated biplanes, the only Australian aircraft operating this far north, were flying while the sophisticated Canadian and American aircraft were grounded. Not that it surprised him. He had come to the conclusion that the Americans couldn't fly unless they were surrounded by every technical luxury known to man. The Canadians were being dangerously contaminated by their close proximity to the Septics. Brumby sighed. *Poor Canada, so far from civilization, so close to America.*

He leaned forward, bringing his nose closer to the glass paneling that made up the nose of his Dragon Rapide. It didn't really help him see better through the falling snow; but it gave him a comforting illusion that he was. In any case, he was flying largely by instruments. Looking through the snow was an effort to warn him of trees and other obstructions. He quickly spared a thought for the four Russians sitting in the passenger compartment behind him. They were squeezed in with a load of supplies and ammunition. A Russian ski patrol, a bunch of Siberians, had hit problems and lost some men. They'd also been caught by the storm and had to hole up, so they were short of food. A few hours earlier, they'd got a message through. They hadn't asked for help but simply reported their situation. Brumby had been asked to take his *Matilda* down, deliver the supplies and replacements, pick up a wounded man and bring him back. It was what the little Dragon Rapides did all the time.

According to the map, he was nearing the target coordinates now. It was hard to know for sure. The snow flattened out the landscape and destroyed the contours that would have helped him find his way. Brumby wasn't that worried. He'd been a bush pilot for years before he'd volunteered for the Royal Australian Air Force. In that time, he'd done everything from flying cargo to taking part in the Flying Doctor Service. He had one of the new navigation gizmos the Septics had come up with. Gee, it was called. A master transmitter and two slave transmitters created a grid on a cathode ray tube in his cockpit. It allowed him to plot his position within two or three miles; that was far better than anything he'd had before. With a little luck, the troops on the ground would hear his engines. It was hard to believe but sound carried well in the snow. They would signal him in.

Brumby strained his eyes and peered harder through the snow. Was that a flashing light? *Matilda* was barely a hundred feet up and doing less than a hundred miles an hour so the weak flash seen through the whiteness was more than adequate warning. With the aid of experience and Gee, he was practically dead on. He cut the two engines on his wings back still further and allowed the Dragon Rapide's skis to touch the snow in a perfect landing. The little transport kissed the snow, bounded slightly and then came to a stop.

"Everybody Out! And take the cargo with you!" The four Russians didn't understand the words but they understood the gestures and the urgency in the words. Around *Matilda*, figures on skis had loomed out of the whiteness and surrounded the aircraft. Brumby clambered out and picked out a figure who seemed to be in charge. He was the one who was telling the four new arrivals what to do and where to go.

"G'day, mate. Got a wounded man for me?"

The figure looked at Brumby in confusion. "Please. Officer come."

Another figure joined the group. "Tovarish Lieutenant. I am Stanislav Knyaginichev. Lieutenant also. Please, call me Knyaz." Knyaz looked at the Dragon Rapide in amazement. It seemed such a flimsy aircraft to be flying in this foul weather. But the biplanes had established an incredible record for doing the impossible. This one was painted gloss white except for a rippling of very pale gray and even paler blue. Even the circular markings were vague and indistinct; just a slightly darker shade of the pale gray. Or was it blue? It was hard to tell. The colors seemed to run into each other.

"Thanks mate. You got a wounded man for me to take out?"

"Yes. We bring him now. He is badly hurt and needs help very much. And we have some papers and documents we captured from the same ambush." Knyaz looked at the aircraft again. This was something that had come with the Americans, the determination to get the wounded out and to the best treatment they could provide. There were those who said the Russian Army didn't care about its wounded. That wasn't true; they'd always done the best they could. The truth was that a poor army with massive casualties didn't have much it could do. Then the Americans with their wealth of equipment and treasure had arrived. It was overwhelming. Knyaz almost resented it, but he reminded himself that, when he had gone down with pneumonia, he'd been flown out on an aircraft just like this one.

"Right mate, put him in. Need to get out fast."

Knyaz nodded. His sergeant barked out a string of orders. To one side, Kabanov watched with satisfaction. Now, the ski group had four new Drugs. Even though he was the lowliest of the Brats, their presence meant that he wouldn't be doing the humblest and most unpleasant details any more. Then he saw something quite unexpected. Under the cockpit of the C-66 was a dark gray maltese cross. *A kill mark? In this aircraft?* Knyaz had noted it as well.

"Tovarish, you have killed a fascist aircraft?" In *this* was the unspoken part of the question.

"Aye, my friend. About three weeks ago. *Tilly* and I were doing a delivery to a Partisan unit when we got hit by this Fokker. Well, the Hun tried to do us in, but we turned inside him and headed for the deck. Anyway, that Fokker followed us down, right down to the deck. I slowed *Tilly* right down. We were doing about sixty and that gave the Fokker real problems. Every time he tried to hit us, he overshot. We were thirty, perhaps forty feet up when we saw a valley and went down it. That Fokker, he was a real determined bastard. He wanted us dead, no mistake about that. He kept trying and we kept swinging out of the way. *Tilly* here drove that Fokker mad I can tell you. Couple of minutes into the valley, there was this line of pines, the tall ones. We flew straight at it. The Fokker saw his chance and came

80

barreling in. Last moment, *Tilly* stood on her wingtip and turned out of the way. That Fokker, he couldn't match the turn and he plowed straight into the trees. Brass back up top are still arguing about whether it was a kill or not. But *Tilly* and I are here and that Fokker isn't, so I know who won."

Knyaz had lost track of the bulk of the story but he got the essentials. "He was a Fokker D.XXI? That would be an Finnish aircraft then. To kill one of those treacherous fascists is very good."

Brumby laughed and clapped the Russian lieutenant on the back. "That is as may be, me old mate. But that Fokker was a Messerschmitt."

Bridge, KMS Graf Zeppelin, *Flagship, First Scouting Group, High Seas Fleet, North Atlantic*

The weather was changing. The howling wind that had driven the rain in blinding sheets had dropped and with it the seas that had rolled the *Graf Zeppelin* dangerously close to her inadequate stability limits. That was the good news. The bad news was that the temperature had dropped as well as the wind. That combined, with the movement of the ship north, changed what had been rain to a mixture of rain and slush. It froze into a sheet of ice when it touched anything. Overhead, the gray masts and yards were turning white with ice. Ice was heavy, it weighed tons, and it added weight in the worst possible place. High up, it reduced *Graf Zeppelin's* already precarious stability reserve.

The weather expert said that this was a temporary stage, a transient condition that marked the trailing edge of the storm. Already, they were crossing the boundary between the storm system itself and the clearer weather that followed it. Captain Erich Dietrich hoped the weather forecast was right. If it wasn't *Graf Zeppelin* would be in trouble.

"Captain, when can we launch?" Admiral Ernst Brinkmann snapped the question out. It was one that needed an immediate answer. The Scouting Group was supposed to find the convoys that were the objective of this whole mission. The battlefleet was following a few hours behind them to the south and east. They were still laboring through the full force of the storm. When they emerged, not so far in the future, Admiral Lindemann would want to know where his targets were. He was not a man to wait patiently for the information. As if in partial answer, the sun broke through the thin clouds overhead. A weak, watery, indistinct sun, but the sun none the less. Dietrich took this as an omen.

"We can start bringing the aircraft up to the flight deck right away, Sir. They have to be loaded and armed on the hangar deck, and they have to warm their engines up here. That should not take long. I can have a deckload ready to go in." Dietrich paused, calculating the times needed. "For a scout mission? I can have twelve Ju-87s on the deck, each with a 250 kilogram bomb and two 200 liter drop tanks, ready to fly in 45 minutes."

"Very good. Communications. Order the *Werner Voss* to ready a force of 18 aircraft to launch at the same time. Same load. Also to have their remaining twelve Stukas loaded with a 1,000 kilogram bomb for anti-shipping strike. Have them ready six Ta-152s as escort. The *Boelcke* will prepare eight of her Ta-152s for immediate launch as our combat air patrol. Then she will prepare six Ju-87s and two Ta-152s as her contribution to our strike force. Got that? Transmit it. Captain Dietrich, you will ready an anti-shipping strike of your remaining eight Stukas and four of your Ta-152s. That will give us twenty six anti-ship configured bombers escorted by twelve Ta-152s as a strike while thirty of our Stukas look for the enemy."

"An anti-shipping strike Sir." The question wasn't even hinted at in Dietrich's tone but the Admiral knew it was there.

"The Amis are out there with carriers. They always have a carrier group covering their big convoys and this one will be no exception. So we need to be able to strike at them before they find us. Carriers are weak, vulnerable. What matters most is getting in the first blow. If we have our strike ready to launch, then we have the edge. We will still have twenty six fighters and four bombers left in reserve. The Scouting Group will adjust course to 270. We need to get clear of this ice as quickly as we can."

Brinkmann watched from the bridge as the aircraft carrier started to boil with action. Despite the change in course, she was still rolling badly. Up ahead, the *Werner Voss* was making much easier passage through the seas. On paper, Brinkmann would have preferred her as his flagship. She was larger, more powerful and had much better flag facilities than the *Graf Zeppelin,* but he couldn't stand the stink that seemed to permeate every niche of the ship and the infuriating faults in her construction drove him mad. So, he'd made Germany's first carrier his flagship and put up with her deficiencies instead.

His thoughts were interrupted by the whine as the aft elevator brought the first of the reconnaissance Ju-87s to the flight deck. Its wings were folded; he watched, the flight deck crew started to winch them down. Once, it had been proposed that electrically-folding wings should be installed but that scheme had been dropped along with so many others. It weighed too much and the performance of the Ju-87 was critically inadequate anyway. Still, it was better than the only alternative, a Fiesler biplane. On the deck, one of the wings on the lead aircraft had jammed; something was stopping the hinged joint from working. Brinkmann watched a deck crewman jump up; he grabbed the wing and jerked it down into place. It worked; whatever had been obstructing the movement gave way and the outer wing panel slammed down.

It dropped into place so hard that the enterprising deck crewman lost his grip on the wing and was deposited, abruptly and unceremoniously on his rear. Brinkmann could almost hear the laughter from his comrades as they saw his inglorious reward. The laugh was very quickly choked off for the *Graf Zeppelin* was rolling and she had started one of her sways to starboard just as the unfortunate crewman hit the ice- and slush-covered deck. Brinkmann had no doubt about hearing the result, the crewman screamed in raw terror as he started sliding towards the deck edge. Two of his fellows tried to grab him; their only reward was to lose their footing and fall also. They were only saved for the same fate by those nearby grabbing them. The stricken crewman was scrabbling, hopelessly, uselessly for a grip as he made his inexorable slide towards the deck edge. Then he was gone, over the side into the gray water below.

"Communications. Man overboard. Order *Z-20* to break position and pick him up." Brinkmann snapped out the orders. *Z-16 and Z-20 were the two trailing destroyers, one of them could surely pick the man up?*

"Message from *Z-20,* Sir. He's already passed. Are they to turn, stop and lower a boat?"

Dietrich spoke quietly. "It's no good, Sir. That will take them at least five minutes. The water temperature, it's below one degree.

That man will be dead by the time they get to him. If he isn't dead already. The fall might have killed him, or the sheer shock of hitting water that cold. By the time *Z-20* has picked up his body, they'll be far behind. It'll take an hour or more for them to catch up."

Brinkmann nodded. It was a hard decision but a necessary one "Order *Z-20* to belay the previous order and hold position. There will be no rescue."

He went out onto the bridge wing and took the great pair of high-power binoculars, the ones used by the lookouts. He could see the body floating motionless in the wake of the two destroyers bringing up the rear. Seagulls were already gathering to feast on it. They knew that anything floating motionless in the icy water wasn't living any more. It was just food for gulls. Already the more adventurous gulls were diving down to snatch the choicest morsels from the unexpected meal.

Brinkmann sighed and went back inside the bridge. Work on the flightdeck was going on, more of the Ju-87s being brought up and prepared for launch. Then, he was shaken by a white blot that appeared on the glass. *Not more snow, surely?* No, it wasn't. It was a tear-drop shaped, whitish blob with a green-brown center. *Seagull droppings.* Brinkmann looked up, the gulls were circling *Graf Zeppelin* as well.

AD-2W Skyraider "Eye's A'Poppin" North Atlantic

It was a nuisance not being part of the formal carrier airgroup. The detachments, night fighters, radar search aircraft, utility birds, tended to come last on the priority lists. They fitted in after everybody else had grabbed the places and positions they wanted. But, once in a while, the detachments were supremely important. This was one of those times. There was a line of AD-2W Skyraiders spaced out across the sea. Each was dozens of miles from the next. Their job was to find the enemy and report on their position. Then, they were to continue to track that enemy, reporting so the strike aircraft didn't waste fuel hunting for their targets. Every pound of fuel they saved meant more warload, more fuel saved for the trip home in what could easily be a critically damaged aircraft. Of course, the problem was that the enemy group would realize the significance of the thin line of Adies and send out fighters for them. Just as the American fleet was watching for the equivalent enemy scouting force and send out fighters to deal with them.

Unlike the AD-1s, the AD-2Ws were two-seaters. Superficially, they didn't look like it. The pilot sat under a bubble canopy identical to the AD-1s. The immediately obvious difference was the mushroom-shaped bulge under the aircraft's belly. That was the search radar, the latest variant in a family whose development had started back in 1942. Then, the intention had been to spot U-boats running on the surface. Over the years, the function had evolved. First to pick out the snorkel heads of a submarine charging batteries while submerged. Then, more added functions, searching for surface ships and monitoring aircraft movements. The radar operator sat inside the AD-2Ws cavernous fuselage, without windows to distract him from his radar screen or to let in light that would dim the displays.

On *Eye's A'Poppin*, the screens showed the picture the searching Adies were looking for. Over to the east, a jumbled mass of chaotic returns marked the position of the storm that had swept across the Atlantic. Now they concealed whatever was still within it. As it had cleared to the east, another contact had emerged. A hard, distinct contact whose slow movement revealed it to be a formation of ships. Around it were some faint, yet still clear marks; ones moving in an arc that ran from due north of the enemy formation to south west. It was the German's own picket line. The Germans didn't have surface search radar, not on carrier aircraft. Only the big maritime reconnaissance birds, the Me-264s and the Ju-390s carried them. Whittling those down had been a Navy priority for a long, long time. The enemy search would be visual.

"We got them boss." Sergeant Kudrich passed the word up to his pilot. "Surface units, medium sized formation, with air activity. It's the carriers." It was the golden strike, the jackpot. Battleships were obsolete, floating targets; it was carrier aircraft that were the center of an enemy fleet. Destroy them and the battle was over. "I'm radioing in the position now." That was another bit of doctrine. The American carriers were running blacked out; not a light showing, not a radio transmission made. All the communications were to them, never from them.

"Any sign of enemy fighters coming out?"

Kudrich shook his head, then remembered nobody could see him in this black pit. "Search aircraft only. No sign of interceptors. Uh, Boss, there's a hunter-killer group south of us, they're in the search arc of the enemy aircraft. Better give them a head's up?"

"Call Wild Bill on *Gettysburg* first, then let the hunter-killer group know what's heading they're way. Threat says the Kraut carriers have only Ju-87s for search; they're not fast enough for a threat to develop that quickly. You know Wild Bill; he gets really upset if he's the last person to find out what's going on.

Admiral's Bridge, USS Gettysburg *CVB-43, Flagship Task Force 58*

"Sir, message from the scouts. Enemy warship group spotted, 220 nautical miles east south east of our position, Medium sized group with air activity. Scouts believe it is the enemy carriers Sir."

"Confirmation?" Admiral William "Wild Bill" Halsey was not a trusting soul at the best of times.

"Multiple Sir. Three of the Adies out there got solid radar hits. They've spotted the enemy scouting aircraft fanning out. They're monitoring the enemy formation, undisturbed as yet."

"Anything else?"

"Sir, a Rivet Joint, an EC-69 out of Keflavik has been picking up a lot of communications. The Krauts are using TBS radio pretty freely. Probably think they can't be picked up if we're over the horizon. There's chatter between the ships in the group the Adies spotted and another location still within the storm line. Traffic analysis and some intel Washington sent us confirms it; the Hun battleships are out."

"Battleships. Ain't that just like the Krauts. Bringing their fists to a gunfight. Right. Signal *Biloxi* to launch a seaplane to TF58.5. They'll take the enemy carrier group down. They've got the moxie to do it by themselves. That way, the Hun main force will think it's just the group we normally have screening a convoy. The rest of us will get bombed up and ready to go as soon as the battlewagons stick their nose out of that storm. Strike waves will launch at 15 minute intervals from lights-on."

Halsey knew well how the maths ran. Five carrier groups, two deckload strikes per group, a total of ten waves. The last wave would be on its way two hours and thirty minutes after TF58 switched its radios and radars on and started to launch aircraft. An hour out, 15 - 20 minutes for the strike an hour back and then a few minutes to recover.

It meant that the first wave would be returning just as the last wave of the strike would be on its way. Half an hour to rearm and refuel the survivors of that first wave, push the aircraft too badly damaged to reuse over the side and the whole process would start again. A continuous stream of attack aircraft that would swarm all over the enemy fleet until nothing was left. Once, when Wild Bill had been a child (something his staff refused to admit as a possibility), he had put the stream of water from a hose on a pile of dirt and watched the mound crumple and washed away under the unrelenting jet of water. Now, he was going to do the same thing again; only this time with the dark blue fighter-bombers on his carriers.

At least the weather had cleared. The met guys said the storm would pass to the east and that there would be relatively mild seas in its wake. They'd been right. Aircraft operating weather about as good as it was going to get for the North Atlantic this time of year. *Gettysburg* was still making heavy weather of it though. She was pitching badly due to her extra length and taking a lot of water over her bows and amidships. Halsey had heard that the second group of CVBs would have a their bows redesigned with the hull plating carried up to the flight deck. It was supposed to be a big improvement.

"Send a courier to Task Force 50." That was the support group of escort carriers bringing up the rear. Their melancholy job was to supply replacement aircraft and crews to offset the losses from enemy fighters and anti-aircraft guns. "Warm up the replacements. Priority will be Adies, then Mames, then Corsairs. We'll have to eat our Flivver losses."

"One more thing Sir. There's a hunter-killer group, Sitka, south of us. They're in the enemy search arc. The Adies have tipped them off. They'll be launching Bearcats to get the enemy scouts."

Halsey nodded. "Add a warning to all messages. There'll be gray and white Bearcats around; make sure of target identification before shooting them down. Try to make sure the Corsair drivers realize not everything with straight gray wings is a Ta-152."

Bridge, USS Shangri-La *CV-38, Flagship TG58.5.*

"Got it!" The comms Lieutenant was exultant. They'd seen the seaplane land and be recovered by the USS *Montpelier*. It had been a few minutes before the signal lamp had started to flash and the message it had transmitted had been a long one. "It's the enemy carrier group. Roughly 180 miles out, bearing 129 true. There's a wave of Kraut search planes coming this way."

"Right. Order *San Jacinto* to launch her dash-sevens to intercept any that annoy us, and any others that they run into of course. She is to get her dash-fours ready for combat air patrol. *Boxer* and *Macedonian* are to ready their Flivver squadron and an Adie squadron each for the first wave, *Valley Forge*, their Flivver Squadron and a dash-4 squadron, we'll do the same. Second wave. Two squadrons of dash-fours from *Boxer* and *Macedonian*. *Valley Forge* will send both her Adie squadrons; we'll send both our Mames. That'll leave us with a squadron of dash-sevens each for CAP and one squadron to asssit Sitka. Clear?" Admiral Peter Knudson knew it was a rhetorical question. This was a well-rehearsed drill. The first wave, the Flivvers to sweep any enemy combat air patrol out of the way plus a light strike of fighter-bombers and some Adies to soften up the target. Second wave the heavy strike with fighter-bombers to suppress flak and a heavy punch of Adies and Mames with torpedoes. More than 250 aircraft in total.

"Orders going out by signal lamp now, Sir."

"Very good." Knudson waited for the 'message received and understood' acknowledgments then gave the order he'd been waiting all his professional life to give. "To all ships. Battle stations."

CHAPTER FOUR
FIRST SNOWFALL

F8F-1 Bearcat Eleanor *Over the North Atlantic.*

He was hunting reconnaissance aircraft again. This time his prey was a very different type of scout bird with a different mission. The Me-264 he'd taken part in killing earlier had been a maritime patrol aircraft out searching the Atlantic for whatever was out there. Now, he was hunting scout planes from a carrier; launched to find his floating airbase for a follow-up strike. He and the other Bearcat pilots were being steered in by radio from the scouts of Task Force 58 to the north. A professional courtesy, really. Given the number of fighters TF58 had available, a few scout planes were hardly anything for them to worry about. For Hunter-Killer Group Sitka, with a total air group of 32 Bearcats and 22 Avengers split between the two CVEs, even a small strike was a significant threat. More than half those Bearcats were up now, trying to bring down the German scouts.

One scout was below *Eleanor*. A Ju-87, cruised below the clouds, looking for an enemy task group. It was a reasonable certainty that it was hunting bigger game than a pair of CVEs and a handful of destroyers but that wouldn't matter too much. Even experienced naval pilots had a hard time telling the difference between one class of a ship and another. There were too many stories of cases of mistaken identity, some amusing, others tragic. The German pilots were skilled and well-trained, but they weren't naval pilots. To them, one aircraft carrier would look much like another and there would be precious little difference between a destroyer and a battleship. The little jeep carriers and their destroyers would look like much bigger game. So, the Ju-87s had to go.

Pace took his Bearcat down in a long sweeping dive. The Ju-87 crew were scanning the sea below for the tell-tale wakes of the formation. They never saw the threat coming from above until it was almost too late. The rear gunner woke up to the two fighters closing in on him and grabbed his twin machine guns in a hurry. The first streams of tracer went wild, more of a threat to the gunner's own aircraft than anything else. The second burst was much better aimed. It licked around the two diving Bearcats; tracers passed beside and between them. Pace aligned his pipper carefully, just ahead of the German aircraft's nose, and squeezed off a burst. To his frustration, just as he fired, the Ju-87 slid to one side and appeared to drop out of the air. It was still as a dive bomber; diving was something it did well. Pace's burst of fire went wild. A split second later, his wingman laced the air with his .50 calibers as well, equally unsuccessfully. That left only one option.

The Bearcats followed the Ju-87 down. It pulled away from them in the wild dive but no matter how skilled the pilot, there was an absolute limit to how long an aircraft could dive. The German pilot left his pull-out as late as he dared and his plane skimmed the sea surface when he was in level flight. That was the idea of course, to get as low as possible so that the American fighters couldn't get at him from below and behind. Pace was less reckless about how late he left his pull-out. Since he was going to be coming in from above again, there was no point in cutting things fine. Once again, he lined the pipper in his gunsight ahead of the Ju-87s nose. It was different now, the German aircraft was wallowing in the aftermath of its dive. His tracers stitched into the target's nose and then Pace walked them along the fuselage, first shattering the glasshouse cockpit, then marching back towards the tail. The Ju-87 didn't have far to go, the sea was only a few feet below.

The ditching was good. The fixed undercarriage broke off on impact and the plane came to a halt bobbing on the waves. Pace and his wingman swept past then arched up and away, coming around for a strafing pass. They held their fire, there was no sign of movement from the settling aircraft. Before they overflew it, the aircraft rolled to port, one crooked wing lifting in a last gesture of defiance before the Ju-87 sank.

"Sitka-One. This is Eagle-Three. Bandit is splashed. Say again, bandit is splashed."

"Acknowledged Eagle-Three. Return immediately to rearm and refuel." Pace's eyebrows went up at the message. Hunter-Killer Group Sitka was transmitting. That meant lights-on had been given and the group was radiating. Radar, radio, whatever was needed. Including the homing beacons which was a relief. However, lights-on meant the group had been spotted. That was very definitely not a relief. *Stalingrad*, aka Sitka-One, was calling her fighters home to face an expected attack. That was more than a lack of a relief; that was downright disturbing.

Bridge, KMS Graf Zeppelin, *Flagship, Scouting Group, High Seas Fleet, North Atlantic*

"Sir, we've lost contact with six of the scout aircraft. The ones covering the arc 240 to 312 degrees."

"That gives us a rough fix. They didn't spot anything I assume?" Admiral Ernst Brinkmann didn't have much hope of that. All too often, the rough fix given by their destruction was the only information a recon aircraft gained. That's why it was called a flaming datum.

"Sir, Metox reports enemy radar transmissions. Airborne radars; a lot of them. Same frequency as their search radar, the one the U-boatmen hate."

Brinkmann winced inside. That was news he didn't want to hear. Back in'43, the snorkel had been the great hope of the submarine fleet. It would allow the U-boats to run submerged all the time and avoid the air patrols that had decimated them. Then, the Americans had brought in a new radar; one that could pick up a snorkel head at ranges of dozens of kilometers. Of course, that meant it could pick up larger targets at much longer ranges. There had been whispers that American scout planes had the same radar so they wouldn't have to close with an enemy formation and die the way the German scout aircraft were dying.

Brinkmann damned the Americans. *Ever since they had entered the war, things had changed. They had an avalanche of material: tanks, guns, planes, ships. Everything needed to fight in such profusion it didn't matter how much was destroyed. A division of tanks gone? Call up Detroit and double production for next month. Need a radar for every scout aircraft? No problem, call the factory and tell them to get moving. There isn't a factory? No problem, build another one.* Brinkmann had heard that Eastern Siberia was being filled with American-built factories; whole towns and cities created out of the open steppes, peopled by the refugees from the west. *It was so unfair. We went to war with Russia knowing that Russian industrial might was in the west. Destroy or capture it and the war would be over. How were we to know that the Russians would move it? Or that the Americans would replace what had been lost ten times over.*

The Americans had even done the impossible; they'd rammed a railway through Afghanistan to feed munitions directly to the Russian troops fighting in the South. Oh, Brinkmann knew that the newsreels had shown the Afghan railway being built by the Indians alone. They'd shown tens of thousands of Indian laborers digging their way along the rivers and through the passes to build the tracks but he didn't believe it. An engineering feat like that had to be the Americans; the Indians just didn't have that ability. An uneasy thought stirred in his mind. *If the Indians had built the Afghan Railway by themselves, if they did have that ability, then what did that say about Germany's claim to Aryan supremacy?* He squashed the thought down, even having such ideas was dangerous.

"They've seen us. Get the strike off now. Tell the pilots to head out on course 270, find the enemy and attack. Once the strike is off and our decks are clear, get the reserve fighters up and off."

"Sir, we don't have time. If the enemy have spotted us, they must be launching now. They'll be with us within the hour. By the time we've launched our strike, got the fighters up on deck, warmed up their engines, and started to launch, they'll be right on top of us. If we're caught with armed and fuelled aircraft on our decks. . . . ." There was no need for Dietrich to complete the thought. Fire was the great fear of every aircraft carrier. German newsreels had been full of the U-boat's greatest score. The American aircraft carrier *Enterprise* had been torpedoed almost within New York harbor itself. The pyre of smoke from her death-blaze had towered over the city. Great propaganda but also a terrible lesson. Fire killed carriers.

"Then launch them cold."

Dietrich's face froze. Launching the aircraft with cold engines meant that some wouldn't make it. They'd lose power at the wrong moment, go into the sea and be run down by the carrier they'd just left. The order to launch the aircraft with cold engines meant condemning some of their pilots to death. "But Sir. . . . . . "

"Not buts. Launch them cold." Brinkmann softened; he knew what he was asking. "There is an Ami task group out there. Four carriers, almost 400 aircraft. We have to get our blow in first. We also have to have every fighter we can up. If our fighters are not up in time, they will be destroyed in their hangars. Launch them, Erich. We must have them up in time to meet the Americans. Whatever it costs.

HMCS "Ontario" Flagship, Troop Convoy WS-18 en route from Churchill to Murmansk

"What are the plans if it all goes wrong Admiral?"

Captain Charles Povey had every reason to be concerned. There was no pretence about the situation out here. Troop Convoy WS-18, Winston's Special 18, was bait. Only part of the bait, that was true. The main portion was supply convoy PQ-17, no less than 250 merchant ships packed into a box 16 ships wide by 16 deep. Not all the ships in that box were merchantmen. There were two battleships in there, *Arizona* and *Nevada*. PQ-17 was a slow convoy; it could afford to have the battleships along. WS-18 was a fast convoy, very fast by merchant ship standards. The five liners, carrying the 40,000 Canadian soldiers that were the whole reason for the convoy, were holding a steady speed of 25 knots. That was fast enough to give even the German Type XXIs a very hard time. Only, that meant no battleships as escorts, only cruisers and destroyers.

"We scatter the convoy of course. The liners will run for it, they're faster than the battleships anyway. Then, we take *Quebec* and the destroyers to attack the German fleet. Buy the liners time to get clear. God willing, it won't come to that. Not with all the carriers and planes the Yanks have waiting."

It sounded hopeful; it was a reasonable hope. The Americans had their entire carrier striking force moving into assault the German fleet. If nothing went wrong, if the strikes found their target, the German ships would never see either of the two convoys. Even if they didn't, the Germans would run into PQ-17 and its battleships first. Not that those two ancient battlewagons would stand much of a chance against the German monsters. They'd die fighting, just like WS-18's escort would die fighting, if they had to.

Ontario had a score to settle. She'd started life as HMS *Kenya* and had run for Canada as part of the Great Escape. There had been two sister-ships for the Canadian Navy building in British yards, neither complete enough to make the run. The original *Ontario* had still been on the slips at Harland and Wolff: she'd been very thoroughly blown up. The original *Quebec* had a more unusual fate. She'd been fitting-out at Vickers-Armstrong's Tyneside yard when the Germans seized her. They'd fussed around her for a few days while the dockies carried on with their work.

Then, the Germans had ordered them all off; apparently intending to tow her to Germany for completion. She'd left under tow. A few hours later, she foundered, sinking beyond any possible recovery given the resources available. Nobody knew officially what had happened. She'd been in the hands of a prize crew who had supposedly secured her for sea. There had been courts-martial over that. The rumor was that the rivets fastening the hull plating under her engine rooms had been drilled out, replaced by soap and painted over. As the ship moved, the pain peeled away, the soap dissolved and a large section of the bottom of the hull had dropped off. It was only a rumor of course.

Anyway, the Royal Navy had offered the Canadian Navy *Kenya* and *Fiji* to replace the lost ships. The Canadians had accepted; the Royals had too few men to provide them with crews. But there was a strange air about *Kenya* that her Canadian crew had noticed as soon as they had taken her over. The ship had an atmosphere of bitterness; as if she knew of tasks left undone. *Ontario* was a good ship. She seemed pleased to put to sea, reluctant to return to port. Povey just hoped he wouldn't have to take his ship in to fight the whole German battlefleet. Finishing off a few destroyers, or pounding a German cruiser to scrap, that would be good. Perhaps it would make *Ontario* feel better.

Admiral Vian looked at the five stately liners plowing through the waves behind him. If everything did go wrong, he would have to come up with a battleplan that gave two light cruisers and a dozen ASW destroyers a fighting chance against the whole German Navy. That was a interesting professional challenge.

Over the Scouting Group, High Seas Fleet, North Atlantic.

The last of the German fighters never really made it into the battle. They were still climbing after launch, their cold engines laboring with the effort, when the American FV-2s slashed into their formations. The American pilots had already firewalled their throttles. In terms of initial position, they had the speed and height advantage. The price they paid was that they were fighting with one eye on their fuel gauges. The gas-guzzling jets had nothing like the endurance of the piston-engined birds. The Shooting Stars were designed to carry wingtip tanks, the FV-1 had small ones that actually made a slight improvement on the performance of the aircraft in addition to the fuel they carried so the pilots had kept them on when dogfights started. Range was still too short though; so when the FV-2 had arrived, the smaller tanks had been discarded in favor of an improvised "Thule Tank." Those had twice the fuel capacity but its length and weight over-stressed the wings. So the American aircraft had dropped their tanks as they approached the German ships. That left them short on fuel compared with the Corsairs but there were plenty of those bent-wing, piston-engined birds following behind. They'd finish the job if the Flivvers left anything behind them.

The German CAP had 32 aircraft up. Two had been lost when their engines had faltered on takeoff. One pilot had drowned under the *Voss* as she plowed over the sinking Ta-152. The other had better luck. He'd managed to swerve to one side and the destroyer *Z-16* picked him up. Those 32 aircraft were hit by twice that number of FV-2s. Protecting the ships underneath was quickly forgotten as the German pilots fought to survive.

The odds against them, bad to start with, were escalating fast. The FV-2s picked off the weakest and most vulnerable of their foes. The days of chivalry, of a seeking a 'fair fight,' had long gone. The Navy pilots in their dark blue Flivvers did what all skilled fighter pilots did; they picked out the most vulnerable of the possible targets, separated him, then swept in and scored the kill. Twelve of the Ta-152s died that way, their aircraft ripped up by the concentrated firepower of the six .50 machine guns closely grouped in the Shooting Star's nose.

FV-2 Shooting Star Flicka

The fighters that hit the climbing Ta-152s had scored big, but their dive had taken them out of the battle. It would take the more than two dozen FV-2s time to climb back up and rejoin the dogfight. In the meantime, the remaining American fighters were on their own. Lieutenant James Talen was painfully aware of that. His section of FV-2s had picked out a group of four Ta-152s and tried to bounce them but they'd been spotted on the way in. The German pilots had hit their throttles and kicked in the GM-1 and MW-50 boost that made up for some of the performance deficit inherent in trying to fight jets with piston-engined aircraft. Ahead of him, the section of Ta-152s had split, trying to scissor the attacking FV-2s. *Well, there was an answer to that.* Talen dipped his speed brake causing the jet to slow sharply. Then he yanked his bird around in a sharp, savage turn that made his vision start to gray out. The gray went red as he reversed his turn and through the changing colors he saw a Ta-152 drift across his nose.

The German fighters were going for the lead section of FV-2s and had already scored, their heavy cannon armament tore two of the lead FV-2s apart in mid-air. Talen's section evened the score on the spot. His own machine guns shredded a Ta-152s from nose to tail as it flashed past. His wing man scored a less spectacular but equally deadly kill. His burst was short and sharp and it scored exactly where it mattered most. The enemy cockpit disintegrated in shower of shattered Perspex and ripped metal. Somewhere in that mess, the German pilot died with his aircraft.

Talen heaved back the stick and poured on as much power as he had, climbing out of the dogfight. Nobody hung around in a furball, none who wanted to live anyway. The smart guys got in, scored their kills and got out. That's what Talen did. His FV-2 outclimbed the Ta-152s by almost 1,000 feet per minute and they were left behind. His section was out and clear. Time to look for another victim.

Ta-152F Blue-Three

Jets were fast, but they had a problem. Their speed and their wing loading meant they were less agile than the Ta-152s. Lieutenant Meissen was well aware of that. He also knew that the surging power from his engine wasn't going to last much longer. He had five minutes worth of GM-1 boost and about twice as much MW-50. Once that was gone, his Ta-152 would be weighed down by the empty tanks and now-useless boost equipment. Most skilled German pilots preferred the older FW-190D-9 to the Ta-152. When both aircraft were without the engine boost, the Dora-nine was a lot more agile. The problem was there were so few skilled German pilots left. The experten, Hartmann, Marseille, Molders, were all gone, swallowed up by the Russian Front. So, the novices and the average pilots who were left, they flew the Ta-152 and hoped its engine boost would let them survive. The boost also wrecked the engines but Meissen had a shrewd suspicion that wasn't going to matter too much.

Some of the dark blue Ami jets had set off after a group of Ta-152s that were coming in from the west. In doing so they'd lost track of Meissen's group. He couldn't chase them. Even with GM-1 his fighter as too slow for that. He could arrange a near-head on match. There, his cannon would tell. He had four 20mm guns in the nose and wings and a 30mm firing through his engine block. He saw the FV-2 racing towards him, allowed for deflection and squeezed the trigger just so. The Shooting Star blew up, turning from an aircraft into a ball of fire, spewing parts and fragments. The Amis walked into the ambush beautifully, the section had been torn apart by the heavy guns of the Ta-152s. Four down, no loss. The aircraft from the *Voss* and *Graffie* were in the fight. What was left of them anyway.

FV-2 Shooting Star Starbright

Jim Nichols was trapped. His FV-2 was in the middle of a group of German fighters that had boxed him in. He was unable to climb out of the formation and unable to break clear without giving the lethal cannon on the Ta-152 a clean shot. That left him fighting to survive. Nichols barrel-rolled his aircraft then flipped away; a wingover that lead to a steep dive. That was a mistake, the Ta-152 was aerodynamically clean and its low drag meant that it picked up speed fast in a dive. Too fast, an inexperienced pilot could stall his aircraft out. Then, that low drag meant it picked up speed so fast in the post-stall dive that it hit compressibility. At that point, its controls locked and it dived straight into the ground. The pilot was no more than a helpless spectator.

That didn't happen here. The German pilot was good; he allowed his aircraft to build up enough speed to close the range on the diving FV-2 and no more. Nichols saw the Ta-152 sweep in behind. Its nose and wings started to flash just before the blows of the cannon shells started destroying his aircraft. *Starbright* burned as it spun out of control, Nichols felt the searing agony as the cockpit filled with fire. Then the jet exploded in mid-air.

Ta-152F Green-Five

Out of the corner of his eye, Hans Braun saw the Shooting Star explode. He swept around to try and emulate the feat. It was hard, terribly hard. The FV-2s were all over the German fighters; slashing at them, ripping with their fast-firing .50s. As soon as he got into position to take a shot, another pair of FV-2s would dive on him. They forced him to turn and leave his prey. Agility was all very well but only the Ami novices were hanging around to dogfight with the German fighters. The experienced pilots made slashing passes through the formation. They picked their men and shot them out of the sky. Braun had no idea what the losses were like. All he could see was the skies filled with the midnight blue jets. Glimpses of Luftwaffe gray were getting rarer.

Another FV-2 was heading away from the fight, trailing black smoke from the fuselage. *A cripple waiting to be killed. Even better it is below me.* Braun racked his Ta-152 around and started to dive on the damaged fighter. Then he cursed. A section of four Ami fighters had seen him and streaked in to protect their crippled mate. Braun hung on for a few seconds, hoping to finish the cripple off. The Ami jets were too fast. They reached out to him with their tracers. He had to turn, to escape the flashing lights that surrounded his aircraft. It was no good. There were too many Ami fighters. Braun realized the days of attacking were over. Now, he was desperately trying to survive.

FV-2 Shooting Star Flicka

Clear of the swirling furball below, Talen breathed a sigh of relief. He was wringing wet, sweat running down his face, puddling in his G-suit. *At least, I hope it is sweat.* He wasn't sure. He'd found the slaughtering match with the Germans so terrifying that he had an honest feel that he'd lost control of his bladder sometime during the wild gyrations. Still, he had escaped and had a split second or so to think. It suddenly occurred to him that he hadn't done that before. He'd been flying by instinct; reacting to the maneuvers without conscious thought. He realized something else. Somehow, he knew exactly where every aircraft in the wild furball was, both absolutely and in relation to his own aircraft. He dismissed it as a freak, as something he needed not worry about Talen didn't understand that the two characteristics together made him a natural fighter pilot.

Below him, a Ta-152 had tried to pursue a damaged Flivver but been forced to turn away as a quartet of FV-2s closed in on him. *The pilot is watching the new threat, not the hawks poised overhead for the kill. A chance, a vulnerable enemy.* He pushed his nose down and started the streaking dive towards the twisting German fighter. Talen carefully lined up his guns. Then, he squeezed off a long burst. He saw his wingman did the same, and as if in slow motion, he saw the streams of bullets intersected with the doomed Ta-152.

Ta-152F Green-Five

Braun twisted away from the FV-2s behind him. Jets or not, they couldn't match his ability to turn. *He had a chance. They are committed to their dives, they can't match or respond to my turns. All I have to do was reverse mine and the Ami would go straight past my nose.* With his battery of heavy cannon, that mistake would be fatal. Braun started to reverse his turn. Then flashes started to appear all around him. His fighter echoed with the drum-like roll of bullets smacking into the airframe. Above and to one side, two FV-2s were diving on him, closing the range terrifyingly fast. Braun realized his mistake, a novices mistake. *I was so concentrated on pulling my ambush that I've become the hunted. Now I'm was paying for it.* Then, he felt heavier, more painful thumps. Somehow the sky seemed to turn red.

A dead pilot at its controls, Green-Five flipped on its back and dived straight into the sea.

Ta-152F Blue-Three

Meissen knew it was over. He was dizzy from the constant maneuvering and frustrated from his inability to line up for a shot. All he could see were the dark blue Ami fighters swirling round him. As soon as he tried to line up on one, three more swept down on him and forced him to break away. He'd survived this long because they were afraid of hitting each other in the chaotic scramble. His GM-1 boost had run out. His MW-50 would do the same any moment. Once that happened, he would be easy prey. His cannon ammunition had to be running out as well. The fighter didn't carry that much to start with. Big shells and a small airframe meant it couldn't. He'd been firing almost constantly. Any second now, he'd press the firing buttons and be rewarded by the "clunk" of empty guns. With almost fatalistic despair he swung after an FV-2. With resignation saw it accelerate and separate from him. What he didn't see were the two formations of FV-2s diving on him from behind. He, quite literally, never knew what had hit him. The hail of bullets from more than two dozen .50 caliber machine guns caused his Ta-152 to explode in mid air.

FV-2 Shooting Star Flicka

It was over. Try as he might, all Talen could see were the dark blue Flivvers forming up. No light gray German aircraft anywhere. Over the radio, pilots were calling in status. Their relief at surviving was obvious. Some voices were shaky. Talen counted them all; twenty Flivvers never answered. Eight more were heading home with damage so bad it was doubtful they could make it back to the carriers.

"Do we strafe the carriers boss?" Talen didn't know who had asked the question, he was rather afraid it might have been him.

"Negative. All hawks return to the carriers. We're on Bingo fuel already. Leave the strike to the Corsairs and Adies. We've done our job."

Bridge, KMS Graf Zeppelin, Flagship, Scouting Group, High Seas Fleet, North Atlantic

Had it been a mistake to get the strike off? It had delayed the launch of the fighter reserve and the last dozen off the carrier had been shot out of the sky without standing much of a chance. *Had those casualties made the difference between the slaughter of the fighter cover and staging reasonable defense?* Brinkmann was uneasily aware that his orders had been specific, use his fighters for cover, use his dive bombers for scouting. He'd disobeyed them to set up his strike. If he hadn't, he'd have had 48 fighters up ready to intercept the Ami fighter sweep, it would have given his fighter pilots a fighting chance at worst. But his way, he'd at least got a punch in at the Ami carriers, that had to count for something.

"Admiral, Sir, another wave of Ami aircraft approaching. They'll be starting their runs in minutes. I can't raise any of our

100

fighters." *Was there a note of accusation in that report?* "Admiral, Sir, another wave of aircraft behind this one, a big wave. I'd estimate it at least another hundred aircraft, probably more. As large as the first two waves put together."

Brinkmann nodded as he digested the information. *It made sense, the American Task Group probably had five carriers, well, I'm absorbing their air groups here. My fighters had mauled the jets that had conducted the fighter sweep, now my aircraft can hit the Ami carriers. While they do that, my anti-aircraft guns will chew up the inbound strikers. We will hand over a nicely weakened enemy to the battleships.*

"Contact Admiral Lindemann, tell him that we've found the enemy, they're on bearing 270. We are engaging their aircraft now and our divebombers are attempting to attack the Ami carriers. Get that off, highest priority."

Flight Deck USS Stalingrad, *Hunter-Killer Group Sitka*

There were three types of CVE. There were the ones built on a freighter hull, the ones designed by Kaiser from the ground up as jeep carriers and there were the ones built on oil tanker hulls.. Only the oiler conversions were really satisfactory for the North Atlantic. The first group bounced around too much and the Kaiser class were too small. The converted oilers had the advantage that they still had great fuel capacity and could refuel the destroyers that worked with them. The other advantage they had was that their flight decks were much larger. Today, every square foot of deck was needed.

It wasn't because the *Stalingrad* was retrieving damaged aircraft. She'd done that often enough. There had been a time when the U-boats had been seized with the notion that staying on the surface to fight it out with attacking aircraft was a good idea. That delusion hadn't lasted long but while it had, the U-boats had gone down, taking an honor guard of Wildcats and Avengers with them. The cripples had come back and found the larger flight deck a savior in times of desperate need.

But that was then, this was now. The big flight deck was useful today because the Bearcats were being rearmed and refueled on the deck as they landed. The pilots weren't even shutting their engines down. They just let their R-2800s idle while the deck crews frantically poured fuel into the waiting tanks and fed new ammunition belts into the guns. It was against every regulation in the book, but the radar screens were an absolute answer to that criticism. They showed a German raid coming in. It was still 45 minutes out, but threatening nonetheless. The fighters didn't just have to get up. They had to climb to meet the inbound attack and do so far enough from the carriers to protect them. There were 16 Bearcats up to meet that raid. The 16 more on the decks of *Stalingrad* and *Moskva* were needed as soon as they could be launched.

Lieutenant Pace saw another example of regulations being broken as he made his final approach. His was the last Bearcat in. The batsman gave him the "chop" signal just as another Bearcat started its take-off run. The two aircraft missed each other, somehow, Pace's aircraft snagging a wire to come to an abrupt halt just as the other Bearcat accelerated out of the way. The grapes in their purple shirts were over his aircraft before it had stopped moving. They had it down to a fine art. They opened the bays in the wings, hooked the end of the old belt to a new one and fed the ammunition back into the tanks. Pace felt his aircraft rock as the fuelling crew pumped gasoline into his tanks. It seemed only to take a few seconds before there was a bang in the fuselage as a crew chief slapped it with his hand.

"GO!" Pace gave him a thumbs-up and slammed his bubble cockpit shut. Then throttles forward, brakes off and his *Eleanor* ran down the flight deck. She picked up speed and rotated with tens of feet to spare. Just eight minutes after he'd touched down, Pace pulled his undercarriage up and formed up with another late-comer from *Moskva*. The two jeep carriers had thrown everything they had into the fight. Now, they would see if they had enough air defense assets to survive.

Combat Information Center USS Stalingrad, *Hunter-Killer Group "Sitka"*

"Sitrep?" The question was a grunt. The truth was that Captain Alameda was getting worried. The little jeep carriers had somehow got themselves mixed up in the middle of a fleet action and they hadn't been designed for that.

"Inbounds are 35 minutes out Sir. We estimate between forty and fifty aircraft. I'm vectoring the fighters we have up to take on their escort. The one's we've just rearmed and launched can take on the bombers. Oh, I've advised COMFIFTHFLEET of our situation.

TG58.5 is sending a squadron of Corsairs down to help us out. They're burning sky to get down here in time but it's a toss-up whether they'll make it or not."

"One squadron? I'd have thought Wild Bill could have spared a few more than that."

"I guess he's tied up Sir, TG58.5 is engaging the enemy carrier group and the Kraut main force will be sticking its nose out of the weather any minute now. Anyway, the Corsairs will be dealing with the rest of the scouts. They're converging on us as well. That'll add another twenty of so Stukas to the raid but they'll be arriving in ones and twos. Those that survive that is.

Alameda nodded and gazed at the plot again. It was almost like a lightening flash. In the middle were the enemy carrier group and Hunter Killer Group Sitka, about a hundred and sixty miles apart. To the south and east of the enemy carrier group, forty to fifty miles further out was the enemy main body, the High Seas Fleet. And to the north and west, the long line of five American carrier task groups, TG58.1 through to TG58.5. That long line of carrier groups was the formation known throughout the Navy as "Murderer's Row."

F4U-4 Corsair Switchblade *Over the Scouting Group, North Atlantic.*

The 32 Corsairs from *Valley Forge* and *Shangri-La* had moved ahead of the Adies. That was the plan. The job of the F4U-4s was to suppress anti-aircraft fire and soften up the German defenses. That process was about to start. The Corsairs were cruising at medium altitude. The ships below were small lines at the end of the white streaks of their wakes. As formation leader of one of the eight four-plane sections making up the wave of fighter-bombers, it was the job of Lieutenant Calvin James to give the signal. He rocked his wings, then rolled his F4U into its long dive. As he did so, the sky erupted into a maze of black flowers. The anti-aircraft guns on the ships had opened fire.

It was a pretty mediocre display by U.S. Navy standards. The Navy philosophy was to fill the sky with so many shells that if they didn't hit the inbound aircraft, the inbound aircraft would hit them. The German barrage was thin by those standards but it could still be deadly. James watched one of the Corsairs from *Valley Forge* develop a thin stream of black smoke. It thickened and spread until it had swallowed the whole rear of the aircraft. Then, it tumbled and fell from the sky. Another Corsair lost a wing. The aircraft seemed to fold up on itself, the aircraft's remaining wing wrapped around its fuselage. Then it came apart in mid-air. There may have been more, James guessed there were, but now he had other things to do.

The F4U-4 wasn't a dive bomber. It couldn't manage the screaming, near-vertical dives of the old SBD. James was bringing his aircraft down in a 45 degree dive, still steep enough by any standards. It made his wings tremble with the onset of the dreaded compressibility. He'd picked his target already. His dive had been left a little late for a destroyer, but there was a larger target off to his left. As it grew in his sights, he took in the details. *Two triple turrets aft, one forward, a light cruiser.* There was something odd about her, the aft turrets weren't center-lined, they seemed pushed out to the ship's side. Most of the heavy anti-aircraft fire was came from the area just in front of them so James ran the red dot of his sight to coincide with the area. Then, he gently squeezed one of the firing buttons on his joystick.

Six five inch rockets streaked out ahead of him, leaving the Corsair standing still in the sky. Out of the corner of his eye he saw one of his wingmen firing almost simultaneously. The rockets headed down leaving trails of black smoke that wreathed the dark blue Corsair. The rockets wobbled and weaved as they closed the gap between the F4Us and the cruiser underneath. Nobody would ever accuse the American five inch rocket of being accurate. James saw his six vanish in orange flashes and clouds of smoke. At least two had hit the ship, the rest had either hit or gone off alongside. A split second later, the cruiser's bridge vanished under more orange flashes and clouds of black smoke.

James' fingers moved slightly. He squeezed the firing button for his .50 caliber machine guns. All six roared. The brilliant streams of tracer lashed at the center-section of the cruiser. Now was the dangerous bit. Pulling out. All too many pilots got so intent on lashing their targets with gunfire and rockets that they forgot to pull out. Not James. He timed his pass to perfection. By the time he was in level flight, he was skimming barely a hundred or so feet above the sea. Behind him, the cruiser was covered in smoke, some from the rocket hits, more from its own guns. There were bigger flashes on her as well. James guessed that some of the Corsairs that had followed him in had dropped their 1,000 pound bombs on her. If so, she would be hard put to survive. Early in the war, before Halifax had pulled his treasonous coup, a group of British dive-bombers had sent a German light cruiser down with just three 500 pound bombs. *How many thousand pounders had hit the one behind? Two? Four? Plus all the rockets of course.*

James looked ahead. The sheer sides of an aircraft carrier were approaching frighteningly fast. Anti-aircraft lashed out from the gun positions down her sides but they were manually-swung weapons. They were hard put to track the racing Corsair. James stared at his bombsight intensely, his fingers shifting again on the control column. *This would take timing but if it worked, the effects would be deadly.* His machine guns fired again, raking the anti-aircraft positions. More black smoke trails from rockets shot past. Some of his wingmen must have held their rocket fire on the cruiser in order to drop bombs on her instead. Now those rockets tore into the carrier's anti-aircraft guns amidships. The streams of fire slacked as the gun crews were cut down.

Any second now. James held his breath and pressed the bomb release. Two one thousand-pound high explosive bombs arced down towards the sea below. James guessed the Germans might be sighing with relief at that point. The bombs were falling short, they'd hit the sea not the carrier. He hauled the stick back, leapfrogging over the deck of the ship. His machine guns burst back into life, peppering the bridge with fire. Then he felt the blast of his two bombs. They'd hit the sea all right but had bounced off it and slammed into the ship's side. Skip bombing, the way all good fighter-bomber pilots attacked ships. He saw the explosions rising behind him. It wasn't mortal damage but that wasn't the point. The two bombs had landed in the anti-aircraft mounts that lined the port side of the carrier.

There was another carrier, off to his right. Its guns pumped out fire at the Corsairs that were raking the formation with their bombs and rockets. James felt his aircraft lurch as something struck home, with a dull ringing noise. Whatever it was, it wasn't lethal, *Switchblade* was still flying, carving her way through the German ships towards a destroyer. Off to his left, another Corsair suddenly erupted into flames. It rolled over onto its back and was still rolling when it hit the water and vanished into a cloud of spray.

James thumbed the button that controlled his machine guns again. The tracers floated out and lashed the platform between the funnels. *If the pictures they'd trained on were right, that's where the quadruple 20mm guns were.* The Germans had two light anti-aircraft guns. The 37mm was pathetic, a slow firing, short ranged, weapon. It was nowhere near the lethality of the American Bofors guns. The other was a 20mm. It was bad as a single mount and hideously dangerous when installed as a quadruple, as most of them were.

The enemy ships were behind him at last. He'd made his pass across the formation and it was time to take stock. As James climbed out from the attack he could see the German formation scattering. It was breaking under the sledgehammer blows of the fighter-bombers' strafing passes. James laughed quietly to himself. *If the Krauts think that was bad, they should see what the Adies can do. They won't have to wait long.*

German Destroyer Z-7, High Seas Fleet Scouting Group, North Atlantic.

It came as a complete epiphany to Commander Micael Rieder. His ship, his *Z-7*, was obsolete. The logic was quite inescapable. His main guns were useless. They could only elevate to 30 degrees and couldn't even begin to fire on the bent-wing demons diving on him. His 20mm quadruple mounts amidships and aft couldn't bear on them either. The Ami jabos were coming in from ahead. All he had to defend himself was a single 20mm gun that had been mounted in the bridge wings. Its fire was pathetic in reply to the murderous hail of heavy machine gun fire from the Ami carrier planes. Four of them had picked *Z-7* and were diving on her. Their machine guns lined their wings with fire. His lovely *Z-7* was nothing more than a target, a loose end waiting to be tied.

Riedel's position was suitable for an epiphany. He was sprawled on the deck of his bridge in a desperate attempt to escape the hail of bullets that were scything down his crew. Anybody not behind armor was doomed by the blast of bullets. That included his anti-aircraft gun crews. For some inexplicable reason, the flak mounts didn't have shields or splinter protection. The murderous strafing had slaughtered his crews as they fought their guns.

The hail of fire seemed to slacken slightly. *Had one of the Ami fighters been shot down?* He chanced a quick look over the edge of his bridge plating. Ahead of him, *Z-6* was surrounded by towers of water and explosions. The cruiser *Koln* was in far worse state, belching black smoke and already listing hard. She was slowing down too, losing her position in the formation. Riedel winced at the sight. *That will be fatal, her pitiful state will draw the Ami jabos the same way a crippled stag draws in the wolves.* Then, a hand grabbed him and hauled him down again. It was just in time. *Z-7* rocked and threshed viciously as a quartet of explosions added to the deafening noise of gunfire, high-powered aircraft engines, gunfire and the demented screams of the rockets.

The explosions left *Z-7* feeling wrong, a soft, squirming sensation in the water. The sounds faded away as the formation of jabos swept past to give the *Oswald Boelcke* the benefits of their fiendish attentions. There was a smoking mass in the water off to one side of *Z-7. Obviously one of the jabos had been shot down but who had done it?* Riedel guessed that nobody would ever really know. Then he looked back at his ship. The midships section was a tangled mass of wreckage, strafed, rocketed and bombed. It looked wrong as well as felt wrong but Riedel couldn't work out why. Then it sunk in on him; the stern was moving separately from the bows. Not much but it was definitely shifting from side to side.

"Sir, Sir, we must abandon ship!"

"How dare you! Order damage control crews to work immediately. Abandon ship indeed."

"Sir, it's no use. We took a single direct hit on the aft funnel but that isn't what has killed us. There were three near misses, very close but alongside. One to port, two to starboard. Right beside the engine rooms. The welding is failing. The ship's back has broken. Can't you see how we're losing speed? In a few minutes we will break in half and nothing can stop it. Can't you feel it?"

The tone was insubordinate but Riedel knew the speaker was correct. He could see the ship was sagging in the middle; the bow and stern rising as the center section flooded and sank. He knew what would happen next. The motion and sagging would increase until the stress levels in the metal passed critical levels and the structure failed. Then, his *Z-7* would indeed break in half and go down, probably very fast.

"Sir." Another officer was speaking. "We can't abandon ship. The strafing has destroyed the life rafts and ship's boats. The water is so cold, the men will only last a few minutes if they go in it. If somebody can't take us off, we'll all . ."

The thought was unfinished but Riedel knew how it would end. *The water is too cold to allow us to survive. The ship's life rafts have been destroyed. Even if they weren't, they are no guarantee of survival. U-boat crews report that American aircraft will strafe life rafts in the water if they can.*

Once, there had been talk of how the Americans were weak and soft, how they couldn't stand the horrors of war. Perhaps that talk had been in the mind of the fool who had machine-gunned the crew of a torpedoed Coast Guard cutter. Then, at the Battle of the Kolkhoz Pass, the Army, or the SS, nobody knew whom, had massacred a large group of American soldiers who had been taken prisoner. Rumor was that it was an SS commander, who had wanted to stop any of his men surrendering to the Americans. Whatever the reason, that act and many more like it, had finally added cold hatred to rage. The old expression 'reaping what one had sowed' passed through Riedel's mind. *Why had nobody understood that somebody else could watch German displays of Schrecklichkeit and turn the doctrine on its creators?*

If his crew stayed on board, they would drown. If they abandoned ship they would freeze. The only option left was for another ship to come along side and take the survivors from Z-7. Riedel looked out to port. Racing in above the waves was another formation of forty or so Ami aircraft. Larger ones, coming in with the low steady pass that branded them as torpedo bombers. *No, no Captain will hazard his ship by slowing down in the middle of a torpedo bomber attack.* Z-7's crew had only one chance. Their ship had to hold together long enough for the torpedo attack to pass and that another destroyer would come back for them. *If that didn't happen*, Riedel thought, *then the Ami jabos would have killed them all.*

AD-1 Skyraider Clementine *Over the Scouting Group, North Atlantic.*

"Oh my darling, oh my darling, oh my darling Clementine."

Lieutenant (JG) Marko Dash had a personal tradition of singing to his aircraft as he made his run towards the line of enemy ships. He did now. The Corsairs had busted the enemy formation wide open. The cohesiveness of the anti-aircraft fire was gone. As the Krauts had swerved to avoid the bombs and rockets, they'd straggled all over the sea. By sheer chance, the eight Skyraiders of his flight were approaching a perfectly placed pair of ships. A destroyer with a carrier behind it. The orders were to take the destroyer with rockets and then torpedo the carrier. They had the equipment to do it, each Adie carried four Tiny Tims, two under each wing, and a 22.4 inch torpedo under the belly. That slowed them down, but the punch was awe-inspiring.

The Tiny Tims might have the hitting power of a 500 pound semi-armor piercing bomb but accuracy wasn't their strong point. The destroyer had increased to maximum speed and was turning frantically to avoid the oncoming onslaught. The Adies responded and pushed in to point blank range. Perhaps because of the ship's maneuvers, the flak coming up was going wild. All the Adies had made it through. *Clementine* lurched as the rockets dropped clear but the flare that took place when they fired up was spectacular. That's why they had to be dropped first; fire them from the wing racks and they'd incinerate the whole wing. They streaked ahead, snaking and dipping but more or less heading for the hapless destroyer in front of them. The explosions seemed to blanket her but they all seemed to be the white columns of near misses, not the black and orange eruptions of direct hits.

Then Dash saw the four black-red explosions as the rockets plowed into their target and exploded deep inside her. Dash watched a forward gun hurled into the air by the explosion of a rocket that had struck just behind it. Another blast ripped through the three aft turrets. A third hit the waterline between the funnels. The last hit the aft funnel itself, blasting it into a wreck. What had once been a trim fighting destroyer had been transformed into a shambles. Her superstructure was twisted and blackened. Fires from blast and burning rocket propellant were already taking hold.

Dash had no time to think about his handiwork. The eight Adies were already lining up for a torpedo run on the carrier. Her automatic guns were firing. Alongside Dash, an Adie suddenly lurched and went into the sea in a long sliding splash. A quadruple twenty, *there was no mistaking that storm of tracer*, got another one. Suddenly Dash, who had started as number six nicely in the middle of the group, was now the extreme left. Then he saw something else. The carrier was already swinging, knowing the torpedoes were coming and trying to comb their tracks. Almost by instinct, he threw his *Clementine* into a tight left hand curve and parted from the group at an angle of almost 45 degrees.

"Get back in formation, you yellow rat!" Dash's flight commander screamed in rage as he thought he saw Dash break away.

Dash ignored him and held his angled course for a few seconds. Then he threw his bird back over in an equally tight right turn. As he did, he could see his guess had been right. The carrier had turned to comb the torpedo tracks. Dash could see three. *Had two more broken up on impact with the water?* It didn't matter. His turns had put him dead ahead of the carrier and it was committed to its portside turn.

Dash made sure his wings were level, his speed right, and he dropped. The carrier was looming larger by the second. He thumbed the switch, raking the bridge with the 20mm cannon in his wings. Behind him, he saw what he had been praying for; the massive column of water. A torpedo, his torpedo, had torn into the aircraft carrier. Just where the flight deck structure met the hull sides, about a hundred feet back from the bows.

"Well done Dashy." The flight commander's voice was contrite now. He'd seen what Dash had seen and understood what Dash had done about it. An important lesson, one that needed to be got back to the fleet as quickly as possible. The doctrine of dropping torpedoes in large tight groups wasn't as effective as it should be; better to split into two smaller groups and hit the target from two different angles. Still, they'd got a hit on the carrier and they'd know better next time.

The Adies skimmed the seas between the ships. Tracers from the anti-aircraft guns licked round them. It was a sure bet some of those shells were hitting other German ships, cutting their gun crews down. *With a little luck, a 4.1 inch crew will get careless and smack one of their shells into a ship that could really get hurt by them. Stranger things had happened after all.*

Another destroyer was ahead. The six surviving Adies had fired off their heavy weapons but they still had their cannon. Their tracers laced the target, sparks of hits flashing all over its dull gray paint. Then they were out and clear. Unlike the Corsairs, they wouldn't be going back in. The bent-wing beasts would continue their strafing passes until the last of the heavy bombers was clear. They'd make their passes even if they were out of ammunition; because anti aircraft guns firing at them, weren't shooting at the Adies. *That's why the Corsair pilots got paid the big bucks.* Dash repeated the time-honored cliché to himself as he swung *Clementine* around for the trip home.

Aircraft Carrier Oswald Boelcke, *Scouting Group, High Seas Fleet, North Atlantic*

Oswald Boelcke had always been unlucky. In many respects she'd been cursed since the day she had been laid down as a heavy cruiser. Her construction had been slowed by the outbreak of the war. Then, when 95 percent complete, orders had been given for her to be converted into an aircraft carrier. That had been an insane decision. It would have been quicker and cheaper to build a new ship rather than rip apart a virtually complete cruiser. But, the orders had come from above and those orders were not to be ignored. So torn apart and rebuilt she had been.

It was bad luck that had placed her as the portside member of the triangle of three carriers in the Scouting Group on a day when the waves of Ami aircraft had come from the west. *Oswald Boelcke* had been the first carrier they had seen and eight of their torpedo bombers had concentrated on her. She'd shot down two and dodged the torpedoes of five. One had hit her and oh, how that torpedo had hurt.

Oswald Boelcke was a converted ship, her internal arrangements were far from optimal. In fact, they were very, very bad. The designers had done the best they could but it had been impossible to do better. They'd been aware of the dangers presented by the storage of aviation gasoline and had elected to use the magazines of Bruno and Caesar turrets as the gasoline storage. These were situated where the hull was wider so there was more space to absorb any explosions. Anton and Dora magazines had been adapted for munitions storage. It was judged that their contents were less subject to exploding so situating them where the hull was narrower was acceptable. Perfectly correct, perfectly logical decisions; the sort any competent design team would have made.

What beat them was *Oswald Boelcke's* thoroughly rotten luck. Marko Dash's torpedo hit directly abreast Bruno magazine. Worse, *Oswald Boelcke* was turning sharply to port when the torpedo struck. That turn, combined with her excessive topweight to cause her to roll severely to port. This had lifted the starboard side of her hull high. Instead of striking the ship's side and exploding on the armor and torpedo protection system, the 22.4 inch torpedo ran under the turn of the bilge and struck the underside of the hull some 20 feet inwards from the side. The hit bypassed the torpedo defense system completely and exploded directly under Bruno magazine.

It was a tribute to the ship's engineers that the blast didn't cause an immediate fire or explosion. The problem that had faced the designers had been to fit the fuel storage and delivery system into the space normally allocated to a 8 inch magazine. Getting the components in had left the fuel delivery system severely compromised. It was contorted; full of bends and misalignments. These had already caused problems. Fuel couldn't be pumped to the aircraft as quickly as the capacity of the pumps indicated. Given the maze of piping, that level of pressure would cause bursts. The piping wasn't shock-insulated either. The blast waves from the torpedo hit shattered the maze, burst the pipes and ruptured the walls of the tanks. *Oswald Boelcke* had used only a small proportion of her aviation fuel. The rest was pouring out of the tanks in Bruno magazine and into the ship's bilges. It was only a few minutes before the crew in the forward part of the hull started to smell the stench of gasoline.

On the bridge, Ensign Zipstein picked up the ship's intercommunication system. The strafing from the Corsairs and Skyraiders caused havoc amongst the ship's officers. Many were dead; more wounded. The Chief Damage Control officer was one of the dead. His deputy had taken an armor-piercing incendiary .50 caliber bullet in the stomach. He wasn't dead; if he came around from the morphine that had been pumped into him, he'd wish he was. That left Zipstein in charge of damage control when the phone had rung and a Petty Officer had told him of the spreading smell of gasoline.

Zipstein was young and inexperienced; he really shouldn't have been where he was. However, he was intelligent and quick enough to associate the smell with the torpedo hit forward. Also, he was quick to realize what had happened. He knew that the danger of gasoline vapor was many, many times worse than that of liquid gasoline and a smell that was spreading meant the fuel-air explosion risk was high. That vapor had to be got rid of fast. Zipstein made his decision and ordered the ship's ventilation fans turned on full power.

Bridge, KMS Graf Zeppelin, Flagship, Scouting Group, High Seas Fleet, North Atlantic

"It could have been worse. A lot worse, Admiral." Dietrich was trying to put a brave face on it. The Ami strike was over, leaving more than a dozen stains on the sea surface where their aircraft had been shot down. The cost had been high; not yet critical, but high. *Z-7* had broken in half and sunk. Her sisters *Z-6* and *Z-8* were burning

112

pyres of smoke and orange flame. It was obvious neither could survive. *Z-16* and *Z-20* were moving alongside to take off survivors. The light cruiser *Koln* had been bombed, rocketed and torpedoed. She was a burning shattered wreck, sinking fast. *Nurnberg* had been hit by rockets from the Corsairs. She had fires but was in good shape overall. Most of the other ships had got off relatively lightly. The strafing had caused serious casualties to their crews but they were otherwise sound enough. It was the carriers that had been hit.

Oswald Boelcke had been torpedoed forward; she'd been slowed and was down by the bows. *Graf Zeppelin* also taken a single torpedo hit amidships but the torpedo defense system had taken care of it. An engine room had flooded but that was all. The *Graffie* was a fast ship, the damage wasn't that worrying. She had a five degree list but, then, her design meant she always had. Now she had a good excuse for it. *Werner Voss* was in a different category completely. She'd taken at least six heavy bomb hits, dozens of rockets, including some of the big ones fired by the torpedo bombers, and two torpedo hits. She was listing badly; the reports from the damage control crews showed hints of desperation.

Brinkmann drummed his fingers. *It wasn't too bad* he told himself. The key factor was the state of the *Oswald Boelcke*. He picked up the short-range radio, called over and demanded to speak to the damage control officer. Zipstein answered, and called down to the damage control teams forward for the latest reports. As Brinkmann listened to the call being made he had a strange mental picture, a ship's internal telephone system making the connection, and emitting few minor sparks as it did. In an atmosphere that contained a lethal percentage of gasoline vapor.

Brinkmann didn't hear the explosion. He saw the shock wave of the fuel-air explosion form into a ball and race outwards. Pieces of steel were hurled hundreds of feet into the air. Others scythed out laterally, lashing at the other German ships. He heard the dreadful hammering as some of those pieces sprayed *Graf Zeppelin* and decimated her gun crews more thoroughly than the Ami strafing. By the time his senses had recovered from the awesome blast, the shock wave had gone. It had left the *Oswald Boelcke* no longer recognizable. Above the waterline, she had been reduced to a pitiful shambles of tortured steel. Her plating had been thrown around so that they resembled the scrambled remains of a destroyed city. The damage below the waterline must have been equally bad. Brinkmann guessed that the blast had ripped huge holes in her bottom. She was going fast, rolling over so quickly that even the fires weren't getting a chance to take hold. It took less than a couple of minutes for what was left of the 13,000 ton carrier to slip beneath the waves. Al that remained was just three figures struggling in the water.

"Another wave of American aircraft approaching fast Admiral."

Admiral's Bridge, USS Gettysburg *CVB-43, Flagship Task Force 58*

The Admiral's Bridge was crowded for *Gettysburg* was the Flagship of Task Force 58 as well as Task Group 58.1. She was also the flagship of the Fifth Fleet but, today, that was just an added inconvenience. This was the fast carrier's battle. Even so, in addition to Admiral Halsey and his staff, Admiral Marc Mitscher and his personnel were vying for the facilities of the bridge. It was fortunate *Gettysburg* was a big carrier. In fact, the two staffs worked very well together, a legacy of prewar service and more recently the first carrier raids on France and the UK. When Spruance had the Fast Carrier Force. it became part of Third Fleet as Task Force 38. He preferred to command from a battleship. Halsey preferred to be with his carriers.

"First wave report in, Admiral. The pilots are claiming seven destroyers, four cruisers and two carriers sunk; five more destroyers, two more cruisers and two carriers damaged. Eighty enemy aircraft shot down."

Halsey grunted. "That's more ships that the Krauts started with. We'll wait to the camera gun film's ready. Losses?"

"Twenty Flivvers shot down in the air battle with the CAP Admiral, they're recovering at 58.5 now. Four more were too damaged to make it home. Knudsen says eight Flivvers are on the hangar decks, too damaged for immediate use. Corsairs, eight down; we don't know yet how many won't make it back to the carriers or how many are damaged. Adies, nine down, same comment. Total 41 lost; probably closer to fifty by the time the cripples ditch. Out of 128."

Halsey winced. *That is getting close to fifty percent casualties. The redeeming feature was that the bulk of the losses were due to the German fighters and they'd gone. The butcher's bill should be less from now on.*

114

Or would it be? The plot showed the German attack on Hunter-Killer Group Sitka was getting close and the fighters he'd sent down to reinforce the jeep carriers were still heading down. There was potential there for another bloody bill.

"Admiral, 58.5's heavy strike should be hitting the German carriers any minute now." Halsey nodded absently; his mind still with the two CVEs to the south.

East of Hunter-Killer Group "Sitka" in the North Atlantic, north of the UK.

The 12 Ta-152F fighter escorts and the 16 Bearcats hit almost head-on in what was almost the traditional opening to an air battle. The Bearcat pilots were at a distinct disadvantage. They'd spent their careers hunting submarines and lumbering maritime reconnaissance. Aircraft. The pilots in the Ta-152s had always been fighter pilots who had some experience, even if it was very little by fighter standards. Half the Bearcat force was already fighting for survival, skidding all over the sky in an effort to avoid the heavy guns of the German fighters. Four of them didn't make it. They'd left their evasions too late; the five cannon on the Ta-152s took them out. The odds were evened though, One section of four Ta-152s was so intent on hunting the Bearcats that they failed to notice a second section slotting in behind them. Within the first few second of the battle starting, eight fighters had gone from the fight.

This was the sort of war that only a white man could come up with. Formations of fighters hurled head on at each other with no regard for subtlety or finesse. Given his choice Lieutenant Simon Darkshade would be out on his own, hunting the enemy through stealth and ambush as his nation had always done, not this wild, furball where collision was as much a danger as anything else. He'd only just escaped the hammering of the German guns a few seconds earlier. Now he pulled the stick back and pulled a vertical bunt, leaving the Ta-152F behind. The Ta-152 was fast and agile when its boost was running. Even then, it couldn't outclimb a Bearcat.

Darkshade rolled at the top of his climb, pushed the nose down and dropped. He plummeted in the way the eagles and buzzards on the reservation had shown him. The Ta-152 was still below him, he hadn't reacted fast enough to the bunt. Darkshade swept his gunsight along the enemy fuselage. When it coincided with the enemy cockpit, he squeezed the trigger. His gunfire ripped the enemy pilot apart. The Ta-152 spun out of control and headed down.

Across from his kill, four more Bearcats pulled the same ambush on the last remaining Ta-152s. Four stubby little F8Fs had climbed out, positioning themselves over the battlefield. Four more had stayed down below. They engaged the German fighters, then extending so the Ta-152s followed them. That was the cue for the Bearcats above to plummet down and rake their enemy with bullets. A few seconds of slaughter and the fight between CAP and escort was finished. The Bearcats called in. Six of the original 16 were gone. The rest set off after the Ju-87s. Would they would catch up in time? It was debatable, the dogfight with the Ta-152s had caused them to drop far behind.

The Ju-87s closed up for mutual protection. The aft gunner's twin 7.92mm machine guns might not be that effective individually, but the close formation allowed the gunners to mass their fire. That did the trick. The second group of Bearcats swept in to meet massed machine gun fire that sprayed their ranks. Two of the gray and white fighters spun out of control, and headed for the seas below. Two more broke off, their engines belching black smoke. The twelve survivors relearned the infuriating experience Lieutenant Pace had suffered before. The ability of the Ju-87 to slip sideways made it a difficult target to kill. With their first pass, the twelve Bearcats scored only four kills. One was Pace's. He'd learned his lesson, he'd come up from underneath where the Ju-87 crew couldn't see him, and killed them before they could dodge. The other pilots watched and noted. In their second pass at the formation, most of them tried the same trick. Eight more of the accursedly-evasive dive-bombers spun out or exploded as the .50 caliber machine guns picked them off.

Pace knew that the problem was; they were running out of time. There were still 14 dive-bombers left and they were approaching the anti-aircraft zone of Hunter-Killer Group Sitka. He also knew there was another formation of around twenty Ju-87s approached from the North. They were the survivors of the scouting line and they converged on the target they obviously thought was the American carrier group. Even while the thought ran through his mind, Pace swung around, hunting another Ju-87. Again, a pass from underneath. An eruption of black smoke signaled another Ju-87 dying. His third for this battle. *Added to the one I shot down earlier that gives me four kills. Just one more and I'm an ace.* Over the radio, orders called the Bearcats off, sending them to intercept the new formation that was coming in from the north.

Pace's formation joined up with the survivors of the dogfight with the Ta-152s. He hit full throttle to try and engage the second formation of bombers. On paper, it was a one-to-one match but the Bearcats were running low on ammunition. *Two passes*, Pace guessed, *that's all*. The accursed defensive fire from the bombers didn't help. The gunners sent two more fighters out of the battle before it was even joined. The first pass was a complete bust. The two formations of Bearcats got in each others way, causing near collisions and lost sight pictures. Pace cursed. He'd had a beautiful shot at a Ju-87 but a Bearcat had lurched in front of him and blocked his line of fire. Chastened, the Bearcat pilots sorted themselves out and tried again. This time they got it right. The Ju-87 formation shattered. Twelve of the dive-bombers went down, either exploding, burning or just falling apart in mid air.

Pace wasn't concerned with that. He'd got his fifth kill. He was officially an ace with the gun camera footage to prove it. He'd exploited the blind spot under the tail again and killed his man with style and finesse. The problem was that his burst had ended early as his guns ran out of ammunition. By the way the other Bearcats were behaving, he wasn't the only one. Eight of the twenty dive bombers had got through. Pace guessed that wasn't good. Then he looked up and saw a formation of 16 Corsairs diving out of the sun on the remaining Ju-87s. *That would do it.* Then Pace looked again. *One group is behaving oddly; it's as if they are coming straight at me.*

Lieutenant Commander Frederick Kellen brought his 16 Corsairs down at maximum speed. That had burned inordinate amounts of fuel to get to the battle and his fighters were in critical condition. He took a glance at the formation below him. *A small group of Ju-87s, eight by the look at it, surrounded by fighters. Straight wings, gray paint, radial engines, bubble canopy, Ta-152s. The strike must have had a heavier escort than we thought and they'd beaten off the defending fighters.* He did a wingover and lead the long dive that hit the unsuspecting fighters, achieving almost complete tactical surprise. The targets didn't even try and evade as the Corsairs screamed down on them and the concentrated blasts of .50 caliber machinegun fire shredded them in mid air. Six spun out and started the long fall towards the sea. Amongst them was *Eleanor*, her pilot dead at the controls. Lieutenant Pace had been an ace for less than 15 seconds.

117

Ju-87R-5 Blue-Six, Over Hunter-Killer Group "Sitka" in the North Atlantic, north of the UK.

The American blunder had been a miracle. Captain Joseph Brandt believed the game was up when the wave of dark blue Corsairs had arrived. He had watched in incredulous amazement as they attacked the Bearcats. By the time the Americans had got themselves sorted out, the Stukas were approaching their target and about to go into their dives. Below them, the two carriers were clearly visible, surrounded by a ring of eight destroyers. For a moment he'd thought the ships were already on fire. They seemed ringed with orange flame, then he realized they were firing. Photographs that had escaped censorship showed the sides of the carriers were lined with anti-aircraft guns and it was rumored the battleships were even worse.

The Ami anti-aircraft fire wasn't just intense. It was deadly accurate. *Somehow, their shells always seem to explode at just the right time.* Soon the approach of the dive bombers was marked by the trails of smoke as the bombers had been hit. Three aircraft in Brandt's formation went down before they even got into position for their runs. Four more had gone down from the other group. The way the Stukas had approached the formation meant that they split naturally into two groups, one taking each carrier. *Two carriers?* He'd thought there were supposed to be five in an Ami carrier task group. Mentally Brandt shook his head and blessed the fact that the reports were wrong. *If two ships could put up this hailstorm of flak, what would five do?*

The anti-aircraft fire was deadly. Of the five surviving dive bombers that attacked the carrier below, only Brandt's survived. The others all died; hit by the heavy and medium anti-aircraft guns that poured fire at him. Brandt saw the deck of the carrier getting larger and larger. It was painted light gray, with the number 107 painted in darker gray. Brandt had only a 250 kilogram bomb on board. It had never been intended to turn a recon mission into a part of a strike but this battle was escalating out of all control. He had to place that bomb exactly where it would do the most damage. The forward lift that filled his bombsight looked good. Brandt squeezed the release, then jerked the stick back in the savage pull-out that ruined a dive bomber pilot's health. Behind him, he saw the ball of fire rise from the deck of the carrier.

The formation attacking the other carrier had better luck. Two of the eight aircraft survived to release their 1,000 kilogram bombs.

Perhaps because of the anti-aircraft fire, perhaps it was the evasive maneuvers of the ships that caused both bombs to go wide. They straddling the carrier but not actually hitting her. The carriers point defense guns opened up. The rows of 20mm weapons sawed both of the Ju-87s out of the sky. In point of fact, they'd have done better if they hadn't bothered. One Ju-87 was hit as it pulled out. The blazing aircraft cleared the deck by feet before crashing in the sea just over the side of the carrier. The second was hit earlier, before it had started its pull-out. It crashed into the carrier dead amidships.

Out to sea and running clear, Brandt started to climb so he could radio a report. It was succinct and to-the-point. The American carrier task force had been heavily defended by fighters and his was the only aircraft to have survived. But, the critical part of the message was that the rising clouds of black smoke showed that both carriers had been hit hard.

USS Stalingrad, *Hunter-Killer Group "Sitka" in the North Atlantic, north of the UK.*

The sirens were blasting. Damage control crews poured across the decks to the scene of the hit. The 550 pound bomb had scored a direct hit on the forward elevator. It had penetrated through it and exploded in the elevator well. The elevator itself had been blown into the air by the blast leaving the well itself as an inferno. The accumulated of oil and grease fed the flames but the rest of the hangar deck was sealed down and the fuel lines inerted. The Avengers were all unloaded and had been parked aft. It was never good to be hit by a bomb but this one had done less damage than it could have done; less damage by far.

Across the way, *Moskva* was in a different situation. *Stalingrad's* fires were subsiding as the damage control teams isolated the blaze and poured foam and water fog onto it. Captain Alameda saw the ball of fire rise where the dive bomber had plowed into *Moskva*. She was still burning. Three of the destroyers came alongside to pour water from their own pumps into her. Her damage control crews faced a nightmare;, a crashed aircraft on the hangar deck with the fuel from the tanks feeding the blaze. Thinking about it, Alameda came to the nasty conclusion that the aircraft was actually a more dangerous weapon than the bomb it carried. He shuddered at the thought. *That way lay madness.*

"Damage control here, Captain. Fire in the forward lift well is contained and controlled. We're dumping foam to smother it and the crews are pouring water on the bulkheads around it to cool them off. We've got teams up to, patching the hole where the lift was, the flight deck will be operational, sort of, in thirty minutes."

Alameda nodded. "Can we land planes now? We've got crippled birds need to come in, four Bearcats at least, and the orphans from *Moskva*. She won't be landing anybody soon."

Below Lieutenant Holcombe looked across at *Moskva*, belching black smoke from her amidships section. She most certainly wouldn't be landing anybody any time soon. "We can land them, Sir. Make sure the pilots know they have to catch a wire the first time or they'll be on the hangar deck faster than they expected."

Alameda made up his mind. "CAG, how many birds to come in?"

"Eighteen, Sir. Eight of them damaged, two very badly."

"Right, get the intact birds down first, then the less damaged ones. If the shot-up aircraft can't wait to last, they're to ditch by the plane guard destroyer. She'll pick up the pilot." *If he survives* was the unspoken add-on.

"Sir?" The question mark was very audible.

Technically as Captain, Alameda's word was law. In reality, on a carrier, Captain and CAG were a partnership. "We must get the intact birds down first, Joe. If anybody is going to crash and block the deck, it'll be one of the cripples. So they have to wait." It was a hard decision and Alameda didn't like it. He made it anyway.

The two men stood and watched as the Bearcats started landing. They had the net stretched across the deck to stop any that lost the wires but the fighters managed their landing neatly. The fifth of the damaged birds didn't. The pilot either lost it at the last second or his controls failed. Whatever the reason, he touched down on one wheel, cartwheeled and lodged firmly in the gallery that ran alongside the deck. There was a dull whump noise as the fuel left in the Bearcat's tanks ignited. They could see the pilot in his seat struggling to get free

120

as the aircraft started to burn, but his harness had jammed or something.

Then, a man ran out from the gallery. He passed the tail that stuck out of the fire, and jumped onto the burning wing. Oblivious to the flames, he reached through the shattered bubble canopy and slashed at the harness. Whatever he did, it must have worked because he dragged the pilot out, through the flames licking around the wings and onto the deck. Other crewmen were waiting with extinguishers and fire-fighting kit. The two men staggered clear of the fire, their flight suits and coveralls already burning. The deck crew sprayed them both with foam. Then, the medics carried them down to the sickbay. If they were lucky, their suits would have protected them; they'd get away with minor burns. If they weren't. . . . .

"CAG, get me that crewman's name." Alameda's voice had a catch in it. "If he doesn't get a Bronze Star for that, I'll order a strike on the Navy Department." Below them, a jeep rammed the burning Bearcat and tipped it over the side.

"A *Bronze Star,* Captain?" In CAG's mind, a higher decoration was merited. The thought was interrupted by an orphaned cripple from *Moskva* landing. He recognized it; the Indian Chief nose art was very distinctive. "That's Darkshade's aircraft. One of the planes shot up by the F4Us. You know, I wouldn't care to be a Corsair pilot on an Apache reservation any time in the next twenty years."

Hangar Deck, USS Moskva, *Hunter-Killer Group "Sitka" in the North Atlantic, north of the UK.*

There was a gaping hole overhead, ripped clean through the flight deck. That wasn't altogether a bad thing. The bad part was that it allowed a constant supply of air to the fires from the crashed Ju-87. The good part was that it also allowed the heat and smoke to escape. That made the jobs of the firefighting crews much easier. Another good thing was that the damage was contained within and above the hangar deck. The tough tanker design of the Commencement Bay class had stood *Moskva* in good stead. The bad news was that the hit was much further aft than on *Stalingrad* among the parked Avengers. Most were destroyed or so badly damaged that they were fit only to be pushed over the side. Men had been working on those aircraft, getting them defueled and sealed down. They'd almost succeeded and their efforts made the fire much less catastrophic than it could have been. More than fifty of those men had paid the price. They'd been caught in the explosion and fires as the wreckage of the Ju-87 had crashed down on top of them.

Chaplain Frank Westover was working his way through the chaos. He was helping where he could, keeping out of the way where he couldn't. Mostly he was keeping out of the way because the area of the fire was reserved for those with the right gear. Westover concentrated his work far forward, away from the heat of the fires, where the casualty evacuation station had been set up. Most of the men caught in the explosion and fire were dead. They'd died quickly but agonizingly as they had been soaked in blazing gasoline. Any Chaplain who'd served on a carrier knew the terrible burns caused by raw gasoline. These were as bad as any he's seen.

Two medics were working on a hideously burned man. They'd pumped him full of morphine and were trying and keep him alive even though it was obviously hopeless. Westover saw them losing the battle and he slipped in to administer the last rites. He had no idea who the man was, which religion he belonged to or anything else about him. The burns were far too bad for that. He knew that the words would be a comfort to the dying man no matter who he was and the just and merciful God that Westover believed in wouldn't refuse a man absolution because the words weren't quite the right ones. As Westover finished, the man gave his last sigh, a little puff of smoke coming from his mouth.

"Any more mortally wounded?" Westover asked quietly.

"No, we've got the ones who have a chance down in sickbay and the rest didn't make it. I'm not sure how to say this Father, but you might have a word with Smitty. He's over there, by the bow 40mm quad. His friend bought it and he's taking it real bad. You know why."

Westover nodded. He made his way forward, where the hangar deck led out to the quadruple 40mm mount on the bow. The dead had been moved there, out of the way of the battle against the fires further aft. In one corner a sailor was knelt over a burned corpse, the charred head cradled in his lap while the man prayed over him.

"Mind if I pray with you, sailor?" Westover spoke quietly.

The man, Smith, started at the voice. Westover looked down at the burned body and marveled at the love that could lead one friend to tolerate the hideous sight of what had once been another. "Sorry, I didn't mean to disturb you, but I'd like to pray with you, if you don't mind."

"He was my friend Father. Now he's gone." It could have come out wrong, a rejection of either Westover or the truth but it didn't. It came out as what it was, an anguished plea for help and understanding.

"And your love honors him. And us." Westover knelt quietly beside the body, made the sign of the cross and started to pray quietly.

"You don't understand, Father. Nobody does. He was my *special* friend." There was almost defiance in the word *special*.

"I know. Smitty, everybody knows. Just because nobody said anything doesn't mean they didn't know. And your shipmates care enough about you to make sure I came over to help you in your time of grief."

Westover left it there; more words would have been meaningless. There were many things he could have said, many that he would not; it was neither the time nor the place. Instead he quietly started to repeat the Lord's Prayer, hearing Smitty pick up the words and join him. The prayer might be a comfort; it might not. At least Smitty knew now that he hadn't been left alone, that he was part of a crew who looked out for him.

Engine Room, KMS Werner Voss *Scouting Group, High Seas Fleet, North Atlantic*

Only the pumps were keeping the *Voss* afloat. The damage control crews did everything they could but the situation had been dire even before the last strike had put three more torpedoes into the *Werner Voss*. Rockets and bombs had added damage but it was the torpedoes that were doing for her. To be more precise, the ship's appalling construction hindered all attempts to control the flooding that had finished her.

Lieutenant Commander Siegfried Ehrhardt felt for the damage control crews. He'd seen their frustration as they closed and dogged the "watertight" hatches, only to see water leaking around the supposed seals or spraying through cracks where the hatch didn't fit its frame properly. As a result, flooding spread constantly. Nowhere in any great amounts; just enough to slowly and surely eat away at the ship's stability. Even worse, all the torpedo hits had been on the same side. She'd taken at least five torpedoes; only one had been amidships where it directly threatened the engine rooms. That torpedo had struck the cemented armor of the lower strake of the ship's side protection. The armor had been brittle; it had had fractured under the stress of the heavy explosion. Pieces of plating were blasted right through the torpedo protection system and into the portside boiler room. Needless to say, the room was flooding. The spread into the machinery spaces was proving impossible to stop.

Two more hits had been up by the bows; the remaining pair dead aft. The ship's stern and screws were gone; now a tangled mass of wreckage, her shafts bent and twisted beyond repair. The Good Lord alone knew how much damage they'd done before their rotation could be stopped. From the way the ship was settling by the stern, a lot. A bent shaft could rip a ship's guts out. Ehrhardt had an uneasy feeling they had.

"List has reached 30 degrees, Sir." The talker in the engine rooms gave the message but his voice was shaking. A 30 degree list meant a sinking ship. Ships might make transient rolls to greater degrees than that, but a set list that great meant that the game was up. As if in answer to his thoughts, the internal phone rang again. Ehrhardt answered it then put the phone carefully back in its slot.

"The order to abandon ship is to be given. Internal communications have broken down. One of the officers called us in case we did not get the word when the order is made. We are to secure down here, set the scuttling charges, and then make our way out."

"The pumps, Sir?" With the screws gone, the pumps and generators were the only things left of value.

"Forget them, the *Vossie* is done for."

"How are we going to get out?" The stoker's voice had an air of panic in it; discipline in the engineering spaces was breaking down fast. There was a reason for the question. Water was already seeping through the overhead hatches and down the bulkheads. That meant there was flooding above them. Ehrhardt could guess what was happening. The uptakes from the port and center boiler rooms ran across the ship to the funnel on the starboard side. As the *Werner Voss* settled and rolled, water flooded those uptakes and then poured down into the machinery spaces. At a guess, rockets and bombs from the Ami jabos had lacerated the sections above them and that flooding was spreading uncontrollably. Still, there was an answer.

"We will use the trunked access. Open the hatch." The British had built the *Werner Voss* with trunked access to all her machinery and magazine spaces. An armored tube ran upwards, unpierced and uninterrupted, to an upper deck so the men down below had a chance to escape a sinking ship. The trunking was even lagged with asbestos so it could be used when the decks above were burning.

The access hatch to the escape trunk took only a second to release. Ehrhardt was mildly surprised by that. The *Voss* had so many sly defects in her construction, he'd half expected the hatch to be jammed. But, the dockyard workers who had built the carrier were men of the sea as well. They wouldn't deprive a fellow seaman of his last chance to escape from drowning. They wouldn't leave him trapped deep inside a sinking ship.

"Charges set? Delay five minutes. Everybody follow me." The charges would blow the valves off the seacocks and open the engine rooms to the sea. The *Voss* would go down fast after that. There were rungs set in the steel oval that formed the trunked access tube. It would be a long, exhausting climb, but better that the alternative. Ehrhardt took a deep breath and started to climb the trunk that bypassed all the decks in between and eventually would end on the main deck. The escape route.

Half way up, Ehrhardt heard the dull thud of the charges going off. It was strange how the trunked access funneled all the noise upwards. That included the roar of water entering the machinery spaces and starting to flood the trunking. He'd ordered the bottom hatch closed by the last man in, but there wasn't a watertight hatch on the *Voss* and he didn't see why that one should be any different. The upper hatch was in reach now. Ehrhardt grabbed the wheel and spun it, undogging the hatch. Then, he pushed up.

The hatch opened a few centimeters. Three, perhaps four, no more than that. Then it jammed. Ehrhardt banged at it desperately but it would not move. Then, he got up close and peered through the crack. There was a metal block welded just so. It prevented the dogs on the hatch from opening properly. There wasn't much holding the hatch shut, just a centimeter or so of steel, but it might as well have welded the whole hatch closed. He'd been right. The dockyard workers had been men of the sea; they'd known just what to do. A tiny modification, so small that it could hardly be noted, but one superbly designed to punish the men who had taken this ship away from its rightful owners. Ehrhardt was trapped in the trunked access, his men strung out beneath him. They were doomed to die one at a time as the waters rose and drowned them. And he would be last, having had to listen to them die. Ehrhardt wept in frustration and despair. Just for a moment, somewhere tucked away in a buried part of his mind, he thought he could hear a peal of laughter echo through the steel structure of the ship.

Bridge, KMS Graf Zeppelin, *Flagship, Scouting Group, High Seas Fleet, North Atlantic*

The first wave had been bad enough. The second had been hideous. Just as many of the bent-winged jabo-devils as before, but three times as many of the big torpedo planes. Some of them were a new type, one nobody had seen before. They carried an even deadlier load. Two torpedoes each and of the first eight that had attacked *Graf Zeppelin*, one had put both of its eels into her. They'd hit so close together that the holes they had blasted in her hull had merged into one. The torpedo defense system had failed; and the aft turbine rooms had flooded, bringing the *Graf Zeppelin* to a shuddering halt. That had done the inevitable. It had attracted the rest of the group and they'd swarmed her the way flies swarmed honey; leaving their attack on poor, shattered *Leipzig* to turn on the crippled *Graffie*. Another sixteen torpedoes dropped. This time the *Graffie* had lost the speed and agility that had helped her survive the previous attacks. Seven hit her, three right aft, three amidships, one in the extreme bow. Two of those torpedoes ruptured the aviation spirit stores and the carrier was turning into an inferno.

Brinkmann looked around at the shattered bridge. Dietrich was dead; most of the bridge crew were dead. The strafing had been ruthless, relentless. Once the jabos had dropped their bombs and fired their rockets, they'd come back to lash the ships with their machine guns and cannon. Even the men trying to abandon ship hadn't been spared. The jabos hosed them with bullets and shells just the same.

By the end, it had been pure slaughter. The ships' gun crews were dead; the ships themselves battered and broken by the relentless attack. *Voss* was going down fast. *Leipzig,* gutted by bombs and rockets, had already slipped beneath the waves. *Nurnberg* would follow her soon. Sixteen of the older torpedo planes had concentrated on her and scored two hits. One had blown the bows off; the other opened her engine rooms. Four more of them had dropped bombs on her. *Big ones, thousand kilos? At least that. They'd stoved her sides in.* Brinkmann was reminded of a street riot back in Dortmund many years before. He and his fellows had cornered a communist. After they'd knocked him down, they'd kicked his ribs in. Now he'd watched the Amis do the same to one of his cruisers. *I wonder if Nurnberg cried for its mother while it died, the way that communist had when we left him bleeding to death in the gutter?*

The destroyers had suffered badly as well. Rockets had done for them, mostly the big ones from the torpedo planes. *Z-10, Z-14* and *Z-15* had been hit hard and early. The bent-wing jabos hammered them with 500 kilo bombs and rockets, then the torpedo planes finished them off. *Z-16* had been torpedoed. Brinkmann wasn't certain whether it had been intended for her or whether she'd just caught a stray.It didn't really matter which, it had broken her in half and sent her down in less than four minutes. He hadn't seen what had happened to *Z-4* and *Z-5;* they'd been up front but now they were gone. Only *Z-20* was left. By a miracle she'd survived with severe topside damage but her hull and machinery were untouched. She was coming alongside to pick up the survivors from the *Zeppelin.*

Brinkmann looked around again. *Sinking ships. Burning ships. Shattered ships. All doomed. The Ami airstrikes were ferocious beyond belief, beyond anything we had conceived. They'd never stopped. They'd just hammered us over and over, with every weapon they had; no mercy, no hesitation. While they'd had ammunition, they'd used it.* Then, he picked himself up from the deck where he had fallen. The mine stowage aft must have exploded. He was surprised it hadn't gone earlier. It had been surrounded by fire from the ruptured aft aviation spirit tanks. *Odd, I can't remember the explosion or being thrown down.* It had been the last straw though, the *Graffie* was sinking fast by the stern. *Z-20* was coming alongside now, it was time to leave.

Overhead, the seagulls circled the dying ships.

Curly *Battery B, US Navy 5th Artillery Battalion, Kola Peninsula.*

This was the time that the railway guns came into their own. For days, the snowstorm had grounded all the tactical aircraft. The big guns, the U.S. Navy's 14 and 16-inch weapons, the Russian 12-inch and the German 11-inch took up the burden of supporting the troops. Not that there was much direct support to be done. The same foul weather that grounded the air forces also pretty much froze the ground troops in place. Froze was the operative word, literally and metaphorically. Only the ski patrols had been out, but when the storm was at its height, even those had hunkered down to wait it out. The big units, regiments, divisions, had retreated into their cantonments and stayed put. Perfectly sensible; any sort of serious military operations had been impossible.

"Supporting the ground troops" really meant firing harassment and interdiction missions. A couple of times, they'd been lucky and they'd had a fix on a major enemy position. Then, the three great guns had fired dozens of rounds at the location. Mostly, though, they'd fired single rounds at predicted enemy positions. In other words, wasted ammunition. The German Army wasn't stupid. They knew what looked like a good cantonment position on the map, knew that the enemy could read maps as well, and avoided likely targets. The same foul weather that grounded the tactical aircraft had also grounded the Rivet Rider communications intercept planes. Mostly they were converted C-47s and their all-weather ability was very limited. That left, *Larry, Curly* and *Moe* firing almost blind. Frustrating.

Still, the worst of the storm had passed; the howling blizzard of snow had settled back to a steady fall. The teams who had been trying to keep the railway tracks clear for the guns were on top of the task at last. All was well with the world, or would be sooner or later. Commander James Perdue shuddered slightly at the thought of how long the task might take. He surveyed the mess on his plate. According to the label on the can, it was Dinty Moore's beef and vegetable stew. Perdue had eaten so much of this particular stew that he was beginning to take a strong dislike to Mister Moore. More particularly, he was taking an even stronger dislike, bordering on hatred, to Mister Moore's beef stew. The worst part of it was he couldn't just throw it away. Since the German breakthrough to the White Sea last year, every scrap of food for the armies in the Kola Peninsula was being brought in by convoy from Canada. Wasting food was a court martial offense.

Commander James Perdue had already decided that when he got home, he was going to devote the rest of his life to eating chicken.

He'd washed out his mess kit; with all this snow around, water wasn't in short supply. He was making his way forward to his gun when the alarms went off. That was a measure of just how much the weather had improved. When the storm had been at its height, the radars around the artillery battalion had been useless. This time, they'd picked up the inbound artillery fire. The crews were already trying to locate the guns that were firing. They had to be Schwere Dora, the German 11 inch railway guns. To the west, they were known to the American crews as *Petrograd Pete*. Long ranged and deadly accurate, they made up for their smaller shells with precision. Perdue dropped all other thoughts and sprinted through the carriages towards the fire control center. He knew he wouldn't make it, he could hear the express train roar of the inbound shells through the steel of the carriages.

"INBOUND!" The warning yells were all around him. People struggling to get the three guns of the 5th into firing position. To Perdue's relief, the shells passed overhead. Their explosions were muffled by the ridge behind him. The train shook slightly with the distant impacts, then violently as the locomotive started to move them forward. By the time he reached the fire control center, *Curly* was moving into its fire position. The tracking radars had already come up with a crude position for the enemy guns. The fire control team had plotted the circle on a map and compared it with the known railway lines in the area. Not many, unless the Germans had built more sidings.

"What have we got?" Perdue snapped the question out.

"Two shells, Sir. They hit somewhere behind us. The Germans overshot us by miles. Two shells, two guns. *Petrograd Pete* has arrived, no doubt about it."

Perdue looked at the map and tapped a portion of railway line with his finger. "Here? Range and angle is right?"

"That's our guess Sir." The telephone rang and Perdue answered it. "Battalion agrees as well. Hit it."

Perdue felt the train creak slightly as men alongside the wheels made tiny adjustments in position. There were more creaks and groans as the traverse of the gun was finely adjusted. In the fire control center, Perdue couldn't hear the crashing as one of the great shells was pushed forward followed by the bags of powder. This would be a supercharge shot, no doubt about it, *Curly* could only just match *Petrograd Pete* for range. The way the train lurched back on the rails confirmed that impression. A split second after the concussion of *Curly's* shot, *Larry* and *Moe* added their shells to the return fire.

The sirens on the trains went off again, five minutes after the first pair of shells had arrived. The German gunners were getting better, Perdue braced himself for the impact, only to hear the train like roar, again passing safely overhead. It hadn't faded before it was drown out by the crash and shock of *Curly* firing. The German Army gunners might have improved but they still had a lot to learn from the American Navy artillerymen. Then, the telephone rang and Perdue took down another string of numbers. The tracking radar had back-tracked the last pair of shells and provided a new set of coordinates and error circle. He transferred the figures to the plot. The new circle mostly overlapped the old but not quite. There was an area common to both and that area was significantly smaller than the circles on their own. The suspect rail line was right in the middle of the shared area.

"Same again." Ten minutes after the alarm signal, *Curly* hurled its third shell towards the German lines. The train had hardly returned to its original position when the alarms sounded for the next pair of German shells. Another set of overs. To Perdue's practiced ear it sounded as if they were heading over on an almost identical trajectory. That worried him. The German railway gunners were good, it wasn't like them to make mistakes like that.

"Error in positioning?" Warrant Officer Phillips was obviously thinking the same thing. A positioning error was the great fear of all railway gunners. It didn't take much to throw the aim hopelessly off. Perdue was saved from answering by the telephone. Another string of numbers; another fix; another circle. This one made a cloverleaf with the first pair and the shared area was much smaller. There was only a single candidate railway stretch in it, not the one they had been firing on. Perdue telephoned in the change. It was confirmed and that meant *Curly* had to be moved slightly.

"We can fire at will." Perdue passed the order through.

"Why, whatever did Will do to us?" An old joke; but the fire control center laughed anyway. Underneath their feet the train shifted forward to make the firing correction. The fine adjustment crews swung the barrel a little further. Then, there was another crash and lurch as *Curly* hurled a projectile at the new target area. Once again, the responding German shells hurtled overhead to explode somewhere in the hills behind the American guns.

Perdue reflected that the duel between railway guns was a slow-motion affair. The exchanges of blows took so long they almost seemed like separate events. The American gun crews were tiring; their rate of fire had dropped to four minutes between rounds, then to five. The German gunners seemed to be holding theirs at one pair of rounds every six minutes; their shots still screamed far overhead, into the hills. After nearly an hour, the German salvoes dropped to single rounds. *Had one of their guns been hit? Or malfunctioned?* Their 15th salvo was the last. After it had roared overhead, there was silence. The three American guns fired a last salvo and then they too fell quiet.

Warrant Officer Phillips added up the figures on the log. "27 rounds inbound Sir. 12 double salvoes and three single rounds. We fired 21 rounds Sir." Perdue nodded and telephoned in the information. "*Larry* fired 20 and *Moe* 18, making it 59 rounds total went out. I wonder if we got *Petrograd Pete?*"

Perdue shook his head. "Doubt it. Long range duel like that, we'd have to be damned lucky to get him."

The telephone rang again and Perdue picked it up. He listened for a few minutes then put the receiver down. "That was the battalion command. We've got a problem. Those rounds we thought were overs? Well, they've smashed up the railway line and a bridge behind us. The Russians are getting a work team on the tracks right away but the bridge is looking pretty sick. They doubt if it can take the weight of the trains, not without a lot of work. So, we're cut off for the time being."

Phillips shrugged. "It's not as if we're going anywhere, Sir. And we're well stocked up with food. A supply train brought in a load just a few days ago. Mostly canned beef stew but that isn't so bad."

Phillips paused and looked at his officer. Just for a moment he'd thought Commander Perdue had whimpered.

1st Platoon, Ski Group, 78th Siberian Infantry Division, First Kola Front

"The fascists are moving already, Tovarish Lieutenant?" Sergeant Batov sounded doubtful. The storm had lessened greatly and was now no more that a minor background irritation for the Siberians but the Germans weren't so used to the wind and snow. Even now, going into their fifth winter in the Rodina, the Germans had still not adapted to the rigors of the Russian weather. Yet, this time they were moving before the storm had cleared.

The firefight had been brief and vicious. Neither side had been expecting to make contact. The Germans weren't expecting to find a Russian unit so far behind their nominal front line while the Russians hadn't anticipated that the Germans would be on the move so soon. It had been a classic meeting engagement. The two groups of skiers had emerged from the snow; for a moment, both had been frozen, partly with disbelief at the meeting, partly with confusion. *Who were these people? Friend or enemy?* They all wore white uniforms, had skis, carried guns. It was the sight picture that had done it. The curved magazines on the German rifles were just that bit more recognizable than the Russian rifles and submachine guns.

That had given the Russians the tiniest edge, an almost invisible edge in the pause that had lasted for brief seconds before the fastest-reacting soldiers on either side had opened fire. When using automatic weapons at point-blank range, even an advantage so small it couldn't be measured was enough to make a vital difference. All four Germans and two Russians had gone down in the brief blast of gunfire. The PPS-45s had scored again; their phenomenal rate of fire literally cutting the Germans in half. It had been over so fast that the men carrying SKS rifles hadn't had a chance to open fire.

One of the four Drugs that had been brought by the transport earlier had carried a PPS-45. He'd emptied a 71-round drum at the Germans and now wore the blood-marks of a Brat on his forehead and cheeks. Two of the four looked at him with envy. They were carrying SKS rifles and had missed their chance. The last of them had also carried an SKS but hadn't missed his chance. He'd been killed in the savage exchange of fire. His body was already being stripped of weapons and identification. The ski group couldn't bring his remains back, so they had to make sure they held nothing of value. Other members of the group were stripping the German bodies.

132

"Bratishka?" Stanislav Knyaginichev had been looking at his map and trying to work out what was going on.

"The fascists, Tovarish Lieutenant. It is very early for them to be moving."

"I have been thinking the same thing. And such a small unit as well. When did we ever run into a detachment of just four men?"

"Only when they were the flank guard for a larger unit. Oh." Batov saw what the Lieutenant was driving at.

"Exactly. I have been looking at the map. We are here, just under this ridgeline. It looks to me as if those four were paralleling the road down here. Perhaps looking for a patrol like ours. They left early to catch us before we could move in but forgot we are Siberians, not pampered Leningraders or soft, feeble Ukrainians. We caught them, not them us. So what is moving on this road that requires flank guards?"

"A supply column?"

"Perhaps, but I have a sense it is something more important. We should check that road, see what it has to tell us. I will take a group of four men down, you stay here with the rest of the men. Get ready to cover us if we need it.

Knyaz picked his four men and skied down the hill to the road that lay half-buried in the fresh snow. Half-buried perhaps, but the tracks there told him everything he wanted to know. The area was still quiet when he rejoined the rest of his unit.

"Bratischkas, we must move back quickly. There is information we must relay to our headquarters.

"Not supplies than." Batov's observation was almost superfluous.

"Not supplies. Tanks and armored infantry carriers. I would say in at least battalion strength. Half tracks certainly, the tanks are Panzer IVKs I think. With Ostketten."

Batov nodded. The fascist Panzer Vs, the Panthers, had the reputation but the Panzer IVs were still the backbone of the fascist tank units. Especially here on Kola, where the heavier tanks had grave difficulty moving. Fitted with the specially-designed Ostketten wide tracks, the IVKs were almost as agile as the T-34s, A lot more so than the heavier fascist tanks. Their interleaved suspension usually clogged with mud and snow, then froze solid. If German armor was on the move, that was something their headquarters needed to know fast.

That was when Knyaz heard something he hadn't for months. Not since Nikolay Dmitrevich Dyatlenko had been killed by a fascist sniper. Dyatlenko had not been a particularly good soldier but he'd had one unequalled virtue, an ability to emit sustained farts of unparalleled volume and duration. In one competition, the artillery had produced a worthy challenger; he'd been routed by Dyatlenko, who'd managed a remarkable 47 seconds. The artillery unit had offered a double or quits on whether Dyatlenko could beat a minute. He had, with five seconds to spare. It had been agreed afterwards that nobody should light a match in the dugout for at least 30 minutes.

Only, this wasn't the sound of a soldier passing gas. The noise came from high overhead, passing from the south on its way north. The rumbling growl grew as it neared, Knyaz mentally begged it not to stop until it was past his little unit. Everybody knew that when the engine on the fascist Fi-103 flying bomb stopped, the little unmanned aircraft was about to crash to earth. To his relief, the engine kept working. The flying bomb passed on its way to wherever it had been sent. In the silence that seemed to follow after its passing, Knyaz listened hard. He was rewarded, in the distance he could hear other flying bombs on their way north. This also was something that needed to be passed back soon, but he had a feeling that headquarters would find out about the flying bombs before he could tell them.

Admiral Ernest King's Office, Washington D.C.

"Well, you were right Stuyvesant. We've had a brief message from Wild Bill. The German fleet is out, he's exchanging strikes with it now. Next time you have plans for my fleet, tell me before telling the President. Understood?"

"Yes, Sir. My apologies. The information we had came out of our economic and industrial espionage contacts and was relayed to

President Dewey as such. It sort of grew from there. I should have raised the matter with you first."

King stared at Stuyvesant and grunted. At first, the man had headed a relatively small section of the great strategic planning apparatus of the U.S. military forces. In the early days, it had seemed unimportant; a group tasked with assessing German economic strengths and weaknesses. Then, the whole war had turned out to be a matter of economics, industrial strength and production. Soon, it had become apparent that enemy moves could be predicted by a study of their industrial production and how that production was allocated. What had been a small, insignificant operation had quietly grown into a very influential part of the whole strategic planning system. That had been helped by the demonstrated ability of Stuyvesant and his team to predict German strategic decisions months before they were carried out.

"Do that. I don't appreciate being blindsided." King glared at Stuyvesant. He seemed remarkably unfazed by the attention. That was another reason why King disliked the man. It just wasn't natural the way he absorbed everything that was thrown in his direction. Stuyvesant was probably the coldest fish that King had ever met and that the Admiral did not like. King accepted that Stuyvesant was the right man for the whole United States Strategic Bombardment Commission business. He'd seen the film of the Trinity test at Alamogordo. If ever a job needed a man who was as cold as a dead fish, planning the use of those hideous things was it. That didn't change the fact that Stuyvesant made his skin crawl.

"Sir, is there any word on the progress of the battle?"

"None. There won't be until it's over. Wild Bill has better things to do that keeping us informed of tactical minutia. Filling the airwaves with that rubbish is a German specialty. Thank God. Anyway, what did you want to see me about?"

"Admiral, the President has advised you that we can expect to see the war continue until at least mid-1947?"

"He has." That was another thing Admiral King disliked. 18 months more, at least, of this futile slaughter. His carrier air groups were being battered by the losses incurred in the strikes on Western Europe. The factories were keeping pace with the attrition but there was little margin for the unexpected. If the battle in the North Atlantic butchered the Navy air groups badly, it might take months to recover.

"Well, Sir, we need to put together the naval construction plans for that period. The 1940/41 and 42/43 production programs are well advanced. The last Essex class carriers are entering the fleet now, the second group of Gettysburg class ships are proceeding well. They won't be finished by mid-47 though. The last Iowas are completing, the first of the Des Moines and Roanoke class cruisers should be entering service in '47. The question is, where do we go from there? Assuming Germany doesn't exist anymore of course."

King leaned back and thought. The prospects of post-war naval construction hadn't even occurred to him. He'd been 64 years old when the war had started but it already seemed as if it has lasted for his lifetime. Peace seemed a far-off and distant thing. Briefly, he thought of the round trip his railway pass his father, a railway mechanic, had given him when he'd been appointed to Annapolis. "In case he changed his mind" his father had said. King had never used the return portion although he still had it. Suddenly, he felt tempted to make that return trip.

"The new focus of our operations will be the Pacific, obviously. That'll require a new fleet train." King settled back in his seat and allowed his mind to run over the differences between the current war being thought in the Atlantic and a likely war against Japan in the Pacific. Slowly, he began to piece together how his Navy would have to change to meet the new environment. In the back of his mind, he still pictured the battering match going on somewhere south of Iceland.

CHAPTER FIVE
THE BLIZZARD

Admiral's Bridge, USS Gettysburg *CVB-43, Flagship Task Force 58*

"Sir, we have final loss figures from TG58.5. First wave was 64 FV-2s, 32 F4Us, 32 AD-1s. Losses including those that didn't make it home or are too badly damaged to repair and were pushed over the side, 26 FV-2s, 12 F4Us, 11 AD-1s. Second wave, 32 F4Us, 64 AD-1s, 32 AM-1s. Losses: eight F-4Us, six AD-1s, nine AM-1s. Grand total, 72 aircraft lost out of 256. The pilots are claiming five carriers, three battleships, four cruisers and twenty destroyers."

Halsey snorted. "28 percent loss rate. How many pilots picked up? And what do the radar search planes say?"

"We've got floatplanes and Mariners out of Iceland looking. They've reported a few pickups. As for the Germans? It's a wipeout Sir. Intel says three carriers, and 12 – 15 support ships were in the Scouting Group. Whatever was there, it's pretty much all gone. We've won that one Sir. As for Hunter-Killer Group Sitka, both carriers were hit. *Stalingrad* has minor damage and is operational. *Moskva* has had a serious fire, its out but she's too chewed up to operate aircraft. Air losses were heavy; most of their fighters are gone, all of their ASW birds. Sir, the Corsairs we sent down? They screwed up, badly. Very badly. They hit the Bearcats and that let the divebombers through."

"Who commanded the Corsair group?" Halsey's voice was pure ice and acid.

"Lieutenant Commander Kellen, Sir."

"Tell Mister Kellen I wish to see him the moment his aircraft has landed. Find out who is the best replacement as commander for that particular group."

A shudder ran around the bridge at those words. Halsey scowled. He'd given specific orders that the fighter pilots were to beware of the Bearcats operating around the two CVEs. Then he dismissed the task of eviscerating the Lieutenant Commander until later. There were more important things to be done.

"Any sign of the German main body?"

"Came in a few moments ago, Admiral. The scouts have them on radar. They're clear of the weather front now, about 200 miles almost due south of us. We can launch any time you give the order."

Halsey grinned. "Lights on. Break EMCON. Radio and radar as needed. All carriers to swing into the wind we'll launch as planned. 58.2, 58.3 and 58.4 to follow suit as ordered. 58.5 can miss the first wave strikes, give them time to catch their breath."

There was a gentle rumble under their feet as *Gettysburg* picked up speed and swung into the wind to launch her contribution to the waves of strikes that would soon be heading south.

Bridge, KMS Derfflinger, *Flagship, High Seas Fleet, North Atlantic*

"Any word from the Scouting Group?"

"No Admiral. Communications have been trying to raise them for the last thirty minutes. Ever since we came out of the storm. The last message we had was that they were engaging the American aircraft carriers."

"What does that fool Brinkmann think he's doing? His orders were to use his aircraft for scouting, not to go charging off after the enemy. He's left us blind. We need to know where the convoys are."

"He did find the enemy task group, Sir. It's to the west of us. And if the transmissions we're picking up are true, he's got at least two of their carriers."

"Two carriers? Out of five. And he's lost his aircraft doing it? That's no excuse. Even if he has finished them."

"Sir. Message from destroyer *Z-20*." The Comms Lieutenant's face was white.

"From *Z-20*?"

"From Admiral Brinkmann, on *Z-20*." If ghostly bells had started to toll at that point, the message couldn't have been clearer. There was only one reason why an Admiral would be reporting from a destroyer. Nothing larger was left afloat.

"What has he to say for himself."

"He regrets to report, Sir that all three carriers, three cruisers and nine destroyers have been sunk by American air attack. He says the attacks were ferocious. They were carried out by very large numbers of aircraft and were sustained until the attacking aircraft ran out of ammunition. All his aircraft are gone, either shot down or ditched in the sea when they ran out of fuel. He repeats his claim of two carriers hit in retaliation and over two hundred American aircraft shot down. That's all Sir."

Lindemann felt like hurling his cap to the deck. The Scouting Group was the heir to the famous battle cruisers of World War One. *Now it has gone without telling me where the enemy convoys were.* All it had achieved was, possibly, weakening the screening group. Still, it was possible that they'd depleted their air groups and carriers without aircraft were helpless.

Two carriers, if they were Essex class, and there isn't any reason why there should be others would make 200 aircraft. Their air groups could be so badly mauled that they couldn't fight any more. That would make it possible to hunt for the convoys with the spotter planes from the battleships. He had enough of them, more than 30. They were a trump card to hold for later. Lindemann linked his hands behind his back and stared forward. *The convoys have to be up there to the north somewhere. The troop convoy was fast, it could slide right across our nose.* That thought decided him.

"Order all ships, full speed, course due north."

He resumed his position, feeling the vibration build up under his feet as *Derfflinger* accelerated. He barely noted the disturbance on the bridge behind him. The gasp that followed it did gain his attention.

"Admiral, Sir, enemy radars. Long range air search sets." The report from the signals officer cracked slightly. "It's the radars on their carriers."

"Where are they? Make a proper report, damn you. Bearing and number"

"Due north Sir. Metox is picking them up all along the northern horizon. Sir, there are dozens of them. The Americans must have their whole fleet out there."

Lindemann stared at the officer. He was about to ask for confirmation but shook his head as he changed his mind. There was no need for confirmation, the intercepts of so many radars couldn't be ignored. Suddenly, he was seized with a desire to turn, to head south, but there was another shake of the head as that plan was negated also. *If there were that many carriers up there, their aircraft could easily outrun my battleships.*

"Are we being tracked?"

"By airborne radars. There are at least twenty, in an arc, north to west of us." That decided it. *If my ships are already being tracked there was no point in running.*

"Maintain course, the radars mark the convoys. We will head straight for them." *Nobody has ever sunk a battleship at sea with carrier aircraft before.*

140

The last piece of the puzzle fell into place. A radar contact. Long range certainly but positive. A large formation of aircraft heading straight at the battle fleet.

FV-3 Shooting Star Bolt From The Blue, *First Wave, Over The High Seas Fleet, North Atlantic*

The German flak barrage was incredible. The great battleships seemed to be outlined in fire as they hurled shells at the incoming formation. The first wave of American aircraft, from TG-58.1, hadn't known about the German formation's turn north until mid-way through their flight. The news had made them make a swift change of course. Now, they were coming in from behind the German force, hitting it in the left rear quarter. The two FV-3 squadrons dropped their tip tanks and hit full throttle, streaking ahead of the rest of the formation. They had the speed to duck the worst of the anti-aircraft fire, so it was up to them to clear the way for the piston-engined aircraft

Lieutenant Alan Bolte saw the gray shapes stretched out before him. The destroyers surrounding the back of the formation could be ignored. Their 20mm quads were lethal only at short range and the German destroyers lacked the fire control necessary to handle crossing targets. The ship at the back of the line seemed smaller than the rest. As Bolte closed on her, he could see her triple turrets. *That meant a cruiser, German cruisers had triples, German battleships had twins.* According to the briefing, the battleships were top priority. Bolte was a man who believed in obeying his orders. The next ship up the line had a single twin turret aft. It filled his gun sight as he raced towards the formation. *Bolt from the Blue* shuddered as the flak shells exploded around him. Right above the big twin guns was an anti-aircraft mount, Bolte could see the gunners loading and firing as he closed on it. *They'll do.*

He'd already closed to close range for his five inchers. Bolte thumbed the button that sent the black smoke tails streaking out before him. The anti-aircraft mount was blotted from sight as the explosions from the warheads rippled around it. There wasn't time to do much more, the German battleship, it had to be either *Scharnhorst* or *Gneisenau*, swelled up in his gun sight. He lifted the nose a little and squeezed the trigger of his six nose-mounted .50 caliber machine guns. The stream of tracer swept across the aft superstructure, bounced off the crane in a spectacular display of ricochets, then tracked across the

141

three portside 4.1 inch twin mounts. He could see the crews working their guns, then being scythed down.

The battleship was still passing him. Its gray structure flashed past to his right. Bolte left off the burst for a second, then resumed as a group of 20 millimeter mounts, some by B turret, others on the turret itself, swept into view. Another long burst, the tracers slashed at the crews at their open mounts. *Incredible! The Germans didn't give their anti-aircraft gunners shields? Had they never heard of strafing attacks? Or did they really believe they were the invulnerable supermen their propaganda claimed?*

Bolte flew past the smaller battleship. He still had no idea whether it was *Scharnhorst* or *Gneisenau*. Ahead of him were the monsters in the other column. *When dealing with a poisonous snake don't stamp on its tail, crush its head.* Bolte angled his *Bolt from the Blue* for a run on the lead battleship in the second column. To his surprise, the flak from the bigger ships was no worse than the mass he'd already flown though. Every American ship that left the building yards had more anti-aircraft guns than its predecessor. *Another odd thing about the German fleet. Perhaps they thought everything should be standard and identical. Just by ze book ja?* Bolte thought to himself as he emptied his .50 calibers into the superstructure of the German ship. His eyes took in the details quickly, the 4.1s were in turrets, not the open mounts that had got their crews slaughtered. So, his .50s wouldn't be taking them out. No matter, he'd done his best. The Corsairs and Skyraiders had better tools to handle them. He flashed in front of the German ship, almost on a level with its bridge, and ran for the clear sky beyond. As he did so, he saw an explosion lighting up the portside of the ship he'd just strafed. *A secondary explosion? Just what did I hit with my machine guns?*

Admiral's Bridge, KMS Derfflinger, *Flagship, High Seas Fleet, North Atlantic*

"Scheisse." Admiral Lindemann breathed the word in appalled fascination as the reality of the chart sank in on him. Four waves of Ami aircraft were coming at him. More seemed to be added every few minutes. Raid count, more than 200 aircraft each. *Just how many aircraft had the Amis got? More than two thousand,* the words sneaked into his mind as his eyes glazed over. He'd heard from the Army and Luftwaffe what happened when the Ami carriers came calling. They swamped the battlefield with their aircraft, they shot up

142

and destroyed anything that was in the area. If anybody tried to move reinforcements in or fly them in from other bases, they'd run into a mincing machine. A dark blue wall of death that swallowed everything thrown against it. He shook himself. *That was no way to think. The Amis were people, humans, men.* Another treacherous thought spilled into his mind. *Men who used steel and machines to fight flesh and blood.* Waves and waves of those machines were coming his way and there seemed to be no end to them.

"They're here Admiral! They're coming from behind." Lindemann looked out. Once, when he had been a youngster, he'd heard some of the neighborhood children challenging another to throw stones at a beehive. Lindemann hadn't known quite why, but he'd turned away and started to run. The challenged boy had thrown the stones causing a cloud of bees to set off in pursuit of their attacker. Lindemann had got away safely, but the boys who'd shouted the challenges had been badly stung. The boy who had so foolishly responded had been stung to death. For the second time in a day, Lindemann wanted to run. He knew that running was the only wise course of action. The American aircraft descending on the rear port quarter of his fleet looked just like that swarm of bees had done.

He'd hoped the first wave would miss him, pass aft of his formation, but they'd turned and slammed into the rear of his group. *Good tactics, come in from an unexpected angle.* He could see one group of aircraft pulling ahead of the rest. *They had to be the jets, using their speed to dodge the worst of the antiaircraft fire. It was working too, most of the bursts were behind them.* For a brief second, he thought his gunners were cutting them down. He saw black smoke and flames, but it was only their rockets. They'd seemed to have concentrated on the rearmost three ships of the line; *Scheer*, *Scharnhorst* and *Gneisenau*. The latter seemed to have been worst hit. Her superstructure almost vanished beneath the rippling mass of explosions. *The rockets the Ami jabos carry can't really hurt an armored ship. They'd have been effective enough against the destroyers but the Ami pilots had ignored them.*

"We got two Sir." The gunnery officer's voice was subdued and grim. Two out of more than thirty! The dark blue jabos had strafed three of the 'Thirty Eights' and were coming for the 'Forties'. *Anti-aircraft fire still largely ineffective,* Lindemann noted. *The jets were just too fast.* One of them was streaming black smoke; dense black smoke from its fuselage that spread even as Lindemann watched.

He won't be getting back to his carrier, he'll go down somewhere in the bitterly cold North Atlantic. Then, Lindemann hit the deck as a hail of machine gun fire showered the bridge. The armor plated screens took most of it as the jets swept over. Lindemann chanced another look. The burning jet he'd seen a split second before was huge. In that split second, Lindemann knew that the pilot realized he couldn't get his jet home and that his chances of surviving the crash were tiny. So, he'd made a different decision.

The FV-3 Shooting Star slammed into the anti-aircraft batteries that lined *Derfflinger's* side at more than 500 miles per hour. The aircraft had fired its rockets and machine gun ammunition. It didn't matter, the sheer kinetic energy and more than 50 percent fuel load in the jet made for a devastating impact. Lindemann felt his flagship reel under the impact and saw the explosion of fire amidships. That was bad, his anti-aircraft firepower had been cut badly and the column of smoke from the flames would attract more aircraft in to hammer the wounded prey. Then, he looked through his binoculars. His wasn't the only ship that had problems with fire.

F4U-4 Corsair Spider's Web *First Wave, Over the High Seas Fleet, North Atlantic.*

Lieutenant David Earnest Webb had his R-2800 engine pushed well into the red zone. War emergency power it was called and he guessed this classified as an emergency. He was wrecking his engine and he knew it. *What the heck, the Navy wasn't short of R-2800s.* He couldn't catch up with the FV-3s that had gone ahead, but that didn't matter too much. By the ripples of explosions that had covered the three ships at the rear of the formation, they'd done a good job of drawing the enemy's fangs. Or so Webb hoped. The flak coming up still looked terrifying.

He had something terrifying under his belly for the Germans. The whole point of the early strikes was to kill the German flak crews. That would leave the ships defenseless against the heavily-laden Adies and Mames that were following the fighter-bombers. They, in turn were trying to break up the German formation with their torpedoes so that the ships would be on their own against the Navy fighter-bombers. The later waves could send them to the bottom at leisure. Break the formation, that had to be the key. To do that they had to kill the flak gunners. That was why Webb's Corsair was loaded the way it was. He carried the usual eight five inch rockets under the outer wing panels.

Under the inner panels, where the cranked wing sloped sharply upwards into the fuselage, nestled two 150 gallon tanks of one weapon the Germans hated above all others. Napalm. It had never been used against ships before. There was always a first time for everything.

Three ships had been hit by rocket fire. Their anti-aircraft concentrations were spotty at best, reduced to just a few streams of fire from areas the rockets had missed. Webb held his own rockets; he had another target in mind for them. In any case, the orders for the napalm runs were very clear. Come in from the stern of the ship, along its length. Drop so the tanks bounce along the superstructure not over the side and into the sea. Those orders put his best line in the middle of the three ships that had been softened up. Streams of fire from the ships arced up at him from both sides. He was passing ahead of one, behind another. *Time to turn.* He pulled the nose around. Sure enough, he lined up just about right. The twin turret was ahead of him, the smashed wreck of a 4.1 inch twin mount above it.

Just perfect. He lifted the nose a little, then squeezed the release. The tanks under his belly wobbled clear. They arced down, tumbling end-over-end on the short trip between *Spider's Web* and the German battleship. They hit, burst and engulfed the hangar on the German ship in a rolling ball of orange and black fire. The napalm didn't spread the way it did on land. The ship was a mass of obstructions that trapped the jellied gasoline into pools. Instead they saturated their area of impact. The flames ran down the decks as the sticky gel adhered to everything and everybody in its way. Webb's first tanks had set the area around the aft mast ablaze., The tripod stuck out of the inferno that had erupted around its roots. The other Corsairs flashed past, adding their tanks to the blaze.

By the time the first squadron had completed their runs, the whole aft of the superstructure was a mass of flame. Secondary explosions marked the site of the anti-aircraft guns as their ready-use ammunition cooked off. Later pilots found their aircraft bouncing round from the turbulence of the fires so the more thoughtful Corsair pilots held their drops and placed their tanks further forward. As a result, fires spread forward to engulf the bridge and forward guns. One Corsair had the bad luck to be making its run when the torpedo tubes on the *Gneisenau* exploded. The blast flipped the aircraft out of control, so that it collided with the battleship's funnel. Its fuel and munitions exploding were barely noticeable in the holocaust swallowing the *Gneisenau*.

That didn't worry Webb. In fact he would never know what had happened to the Corsair pilot. Different squadron, different carrier. Just another loss in the list that was growing steadily as the November day ticked past. He had another thought on his mind. Up ahead of him, another battleship had been marked by an explosion, a big one. He didn't know what had caused it. Whatever it was, he was going to take advantage of it. He lined up on the battleship. It was a big one, with two funnels. The area around the fore funnel was burning from the explosion, no anti-aircraft fire was coming from there. The aft funnel was the center of a fiery mass of flak. He lined up and held his fire to the last second. Then Webb let the gunners have it with his machine guns and rockets.

At last, he was out of the deadly cones of fire and heading home. Webb eased back on the power and watched his instrument panel record the lowering temperatures and pressures. All characteristics that determined the life of his engine. He was heading home, back to *Gettysburg*. The trail of smoke behind him wasn't enough to worry about. *Spider's Web* had been hit before. She'd be hit again but it didn't matter. Today, he was going back to his carrier.

AD-1 Skyraider Bayonne Beauty, *First Wave, Over the High Seas Fleet, North Atlantic.*

In his imagination, he could feel the heat washing off the three burning ships. He knew the damage wasn't mortal. It couldn't be. It wasn't even severe. Napalm would sear the upper decks, incinerate anybody outside the armor but it would burn off. It could not penetrate the heart of the ship. That was the job of the torpedo bombers. *Bayonne Beauty* had a single torpedo nested under her belly and four Tiny Tim rockets under her wings. Lieutenant Fisher McPherson knew that the objective this early in the game wasn't to sink ships but to spread chaos and disorder. The birds later in the attack would be carrying two or three torpedoes each. They would be the ship killers.

Still, McPherson wanted to do the best he could. Even if the objective was to break the formations up, professional pride meant he wanted to score a hit. The problem was the torpedo bombers were coming in from astern of the targets, the worst possible angle for a torpedo attack. The torpedoes were consigned to a tail chase, one in which their speed margin over the targets wasn't that great. He had already decided there were other options, other targets.

146

McPherson picked his first target; a destroyer running just behind the worst-hit of the three burning enemy ships. Its anti-aircraft fire was flashing round him. That didn't matter too much, the important thing was to get as close as possible. So close his Tiny Tims would gut her. Anyway, the German destroyers didn't have dual purpose main guns. The destroyer grew closer, much closer and his rockets slashed across the gap between the Adie and its prey. Three satisfactory explosions; one of the rockets must have misfired. Now it was time for the battleship. He swerved, skimming the sea as he brought his nose around then tried to close the range as much as possible. In a stern chase like this, he had to get as close as possible if his torpedo was to stand a chance of a hit.

His torpedo launched McPherson swung away, heading out from the German ships. The fighter-bombers could indulge in wild rides across the enemy ships, strafing everything in their path. The lumbering torpedo planes were too valuable. They had strict orders. No grandstanding. Drop your fish, come back, get some more, drop those. Come back, get some more, drop them. Keep going until there weren't any targets left. The crews got the message.

Captain's Bridge, KMS Gneisenau, *High Seas Fleet, North Atlantic*

"We've lost everything aft of the tower, Captain. There's nothing left back there." The young Lieutenant gasped, not from exhaustion but from shock and sickness. He'd never seen what the Ami's dreaded jellygas had done before. He'd heard stories but he'd dismissed them as soldier's tales intended to impress the pampered sailors of the High Seas Fleet. Now he knew different. He'd seen the charred husks sitting at the remains of their guns; seen others till writhing as they died. He shook the images from his mind and carried on. "The fires are terrible but they're confined to the upper decks. The jellygas didn't penetrate into the ship. Below decks, there's no damage."

Captain Christian Lokken was only half listening. His attention was fixed on the cloud of torpedo-bombers that were closing in him from behind. "I want every turn of the screws the engineers can give me. Every one. No holding back. If there are safety margins, ignore them. Today, there is no section of the gauge marked in red. Understood?"

Engines nodded and spoke into the communication system. They'd lost contact with a lot of the ship. The fires had severed the runs in the superstructure. Thankfully, the machinery spaces were still on line. Underneath their feet the vibration picked up as *Gneisenau* accelerated. Lokken did not take his attention away from the aircraft closing in. The formation split in three. One group headed for *Scharnhorst* up ahead; another picked *Scheer* behind. The majority of the planes were coming for him.

"They're coming at us from behind, Klaus. Poor tactics on their part. A bad angle for torpedoes." Lokken tensed. There were torpedoes dropping from the Ami bombers. "Port and centerline screws hard aft; starboard screw full ahead."

Gneisenau's bow started to swing around as the ship's machinery screamed in protest at the abuse. She slid sideways through the water, combining her turn with forward motion and sideways shift, all in ways the designers had only dreamed of. Lokken watched the torpedo planes pulling away. *If he timed this right . . . . .* "All engines, full ahead."

The screaming shudder stopped. *Gneisenau* lurched forward and left the tracks from the torpedoes to pass aft, not far aft but enough. As long as they missed, it didn't matter by how much. Ahead of the battleship, the two surviving destroyers scattered out of her way. When a 32,000 ton battleship hit a 2,000 ton destroyer, it didn't take any great insight to know who would come off worst.

"*Scheer's* been hit." The First Officer spoke quietly as he saw the tower of water rise from the heavy cruiser. A bad hit; right aft where the hull dropped a deck. That was always a position of great stress. Given the questionable strength of the ship's stern, she'd be lucky to keep her rear end in place. And there was always the possibility of damage to the shafts. Captain Mullenheim-Rechberg on *Bismarck* had claimed the odds against a ship getting a crippling hit in the screws was a thousand to one against. That was nonsense of course, simple mathematics said otherwise. 15 percent of the ship's length was the screws, shafts and rudders. Assuming hits were distributed at random on the hull, one hit in six would cripple one or all of those units. One in six, not one in a thousand.

Lokken paid no attention. "Starboard, centerline screws hard aft, port screw all ahead." *Gneisenau* screamed again as her bows were

148

hauled through the sea. It was a desperate turn to try and avoid another group of torpedo planes that had caught up with her before dropping. The white streaks in the water were closing on her, getting dangerously close. Then an intercept course slowly turned to parallel and then to diverging. *Gneisenau* had turned inside the torpedoes.

"That makes at least twenty misses. The Ami's need some practice." Then the First Officer cursed his words. Two columns of water rose from *Scharnhorst*. One was way forward, between the bows and the foremost turret, the other level with the aft mast.

Lokken still ignored him. His mind was consumed with the picture of his ship surrounded by the torpedo bombers. He was fighting desperately to survive the hail of torpedoes launched in his direction. Another salvo was coming in, this time from in front. The bombers had worked around him. Now they were attacking from both sides, eight off the port bow, four off the starboard. Lokken visualized the geometry and knew it was over. That's why this attack was called the Hammerhead. To avoid one group he had to expose himself to the rest. *Well, better four than eight.* He swung his bows to starboard. "All back full."

With a little luck the sudden reduction in speed would throw the Amis off. *Gneisenau* threaded the spread of eight torpedoes. They raced past either side of him. It was close, the nearest wobbled as it entered his wake and was almost drawn into his screws. But, it wasn't, it was just a fraction too far out. The other four were racing towards her. As *Gneisenau* slowed, Lokken saw them. The first was passing well in front of his bows, the second much closer. Lokken cringed. The third slammed into his ship in almost the same place *Scharnhorst* had been hit just a few seconds earlier. Slammed home, but no explosion. Whatever had happened, the torpedo hadn't exploded. Fuze failure? Lokken didn't know. Another hit, right between Anton and Bruno turrets. That one did explode and Lokken felt his *Gneisenau* shudder from the hit.

It was over. Their bolt shot, the torpedo planes were leaving. *Scheer* was in deep trouble, listing and slowing down. *Scharnhorst* was also slowing but she seemed far less hurt. Lokken guessed it was the hit forward more than anything else. *Gneisenau* seemed unaffected by the blow she had taken. Lokken didn't need the damage control report to tell him what he already knew. The torpedo defense system had taken the hit, the damage was superficial at most. Just some minor leakage inboard. He took the opportunity to look around. *Derfflinger* hit and burning. And another blue cloud just about to descend, this time on the head of the formation.

FV-3 Shooting Star Sweet Chariot, *Second Wave, Over The High Seas Fleet, North Atlantic*

Reprisal and *Oriskany* had just rejoined the fleet after a major refit. They had the latest radars, the new 3 inch L50 anti-aircraft guns in place of the quad forties, the lengthened bow and an improved island. They also had new airgroups with the least experienced pilots in the Fifth Fleet. They hadn't even flown their first strike over France or the U.K. yet. That was why nobody had asked them to do anything clever. They had simply been steered straight at the German squadron. As a result, they were hitting it head-on.

Lieutenant Commander Bob Price knew his job. He had to assess the enemy squadron while streaking in to do the flak suppression run, then assign his aircraft to the most valuable targets. It had been a lot to do when the strike leader had ridden on an Avenger with three crew members on board. Asking a single pilot to do it while flying a Shooting Star jet fighter was placing too great a load even on an experienced man. Experienced, Bob Price was not. Well trained, talented, skilled yes, but he was asked to do a job that was way beyond him.

And yet he tried hard. It didn't help that the Germans had built their Hipper class heavy cruisers to the same general plans as their battleships. From dead ahead, telling the difference between the ships was a matter of judging size. To those who sat in armchairs and sermonized on the minute differences between classes, distinguishing between a heavy cruiser and a battleship was easy. So much so that failing to do so was a matter of derision. For a young, inexperienced pilot moving at over 500 miles per hour through an intense anti-aircraft barrage, it wasn't such a sinecure. Nor did it help that the American ship recognition instructors had hammered home the lesson. Twin turrets meant battleships, triple turrets meant cruisers. Price saw the shape, saw the twin turrets and his mind said battleship. He saw the single ship leading both columns of battleships and made a simple, honest, decision. *That ship must be the flagship. An admiral always lead his fleet didn't he?*

"All aircraft concentrate on the lead ship." The order sounded authoritative, crisp and sharp, exactly the way an order should sound. As a result, 32 FV-3 Shooting Stars and more than 60 F4U-4 Corsairs converged on the heavy cruiser *Hipper*. Behind them, the Adies swept down on the hapless cruiser.

Admiral's Bridge, KMS Derfflinger, *Flagship, High Seas Fleet, North Atlantic*

Once, when he'd been in Austria, Lindemann had seen an avalanche engulf part of a small village. The memory raised an urgent question in his mind, *just what in hell did the Amis have against the poor old Hipper?* Lindemann asked himself the question in appalled amazement as he watched the tide of Ami jabos sweep down on the heavy cruiser. *Had she done something to personally offend the Ami Admiral? Was there a special order out that the Hipper was to be sunk at all costs? Did they know something about the Hipper that I don't?* Throwing more than a hundred aircraft at a single 20 centimeter cruiser seemed very excessive somehow.

Lindemann winced as the victim of the onslaught seemed to vanish under the rippling blaze of rockets from the jets that lead the assault. Attacking from the front like that had its costs though. Five of the Ami jets went down to the fleet's concentrated anti-aircraft fire. Two of them exploded in mid air as 105mm shells scored direct hits. By coming in from the front like that they were running straight into a crossfire from the two lines of battleships.

Derfflinger's steel armor rang with the ricochets of the .50 caliber machinegun fire that hosed down her decks. The ship's center section was beginning to look like a slaughterhouse. Blood from the flak gunners ran down the deck and mixed with the soot from the fire caused by the crashed jet. It was odd, Lindemann had expected to see the burned out tail of the aircraft sticking out of the superstructure when the fires cleared but there was nothing. The sheer force of the impact had smashed the jet to fragments.

He swung his binoculars back to *Hipper*. Her flak guns were silent. She was burning from the Anton turret back to her stern where the infernal jellygas was soaking her. Lindemann had the reports from *Scharnhorst* and *Gneisenau* to confirm jellygas wasn't a ship-killer the way torpedoes and armor piercing bombs were. In fact it did very little damage at all to the ship since the fires were superficial and didn't bite deep. But the word from *Scharnhorst* and *Gneisenau* was that jellygas massacred the flak gunners and left the victim defenseless against the aircraft that did carry the ship-killers. Lindemann got the impression though that the pilots in this wave lacked the deadly precision of those in the first group. A lot of the rockets and jellygas tanks had missed completely, He watched two clumsily-dropped jellygas tanks bounce off the ship before exploding harmlessly in the sea alongside her.

By the time that had registered, the bent-wing jabos had passed over *Hipper*. They left her blazing in their wake. Their course took them through the deadly crossfire from the battleships and over *Moltke*. The same infernal ripple of rockets swathed her superstructure and her flak guns faltered. Still, four of the bent-wing bastards, Lindemann was surprised at how much venom was in his description, had crashed, their wreckage staining the sea.

It was the Ami torpedo bombers that suffered worst. Slow and lumbering, they were easy prey for German gunners who took the opportunity to exact revenge for the hellish jellygas. They got the bombers in their gunsights early as the torpedo planes closed on *Hipper*. The cheers grew as the score mounted and redoubled when it reached double figures. Twelve out of thirty plus torpedo planes had been sent into the sea by the time the survivors got to drop on *Hipper*.

Lindemann recognized the perfectly-executed hammerhead torpedo attack. Even with her decks saturated with fire, *Hipper* swung hard to port. She was trying to dodge the torpedoes closing on her but it was hopeless. Lindemann knew that and grimly counted the long columns of water shooting up from the ship's side. Six in all, four to starboard, two to port, far more than a heavy cruiser could be expected to take. One torpedo struck right forward and ripped the bows off. Another struck under Bruno turret, a third under the bridge, two on opposite sides of the ship in the engine rooms, the last right aft in the screws. The effects were almost immediate. She started to roll over, the big cruiser slipped onto her beam ends, exposing the two great holes ripped in her port side. Even if she'd stayed afloat, she wouldn't have been going anywhere. Her screws and rudders were tangled wreckage, her stern almost severed from the ship.

Lindemann swung his binoculars around, looking for survivors in the water. How men could have saved themselves through decks coated with jellygas he did not know. The he saw something he had missed when he'd been concentrating on the fate of the poor

Hipper. Z-31 and *Z-39* were going down fast, their sides ripped open by the big rockets the Ami Douglasses carried as a secondary weapon. The torpedo planes that had survived the hammerhead attack had been almost perfectly placed for a rocket attack on the destroyers and they'd done their deed well. It was then that the significance of the second attack overwhelmed him.

The American tactics were brilliant, simply brilliant. Their first wave had focused on the rear of the formation. They'd chewed up the 'thirty eights' and damaged the ships. They'd forced them to slow down and hindered their movements with damage. The second wave had been their youngest, least experienced men. They'd been given the easiest attack runs, straight at the head of the fleet, but also the most dangerous. Brilliant and ruthless, the Amis had thrown the pilots they'd miss least into that deathly dangerous run right into the crossfire. By blasting *Hipper* and her screen, they'd created a mass of sinking ships in front of the battleships. The 'thirty eights' were swinging to port and the 'forties' to starboard in order to avoid the wrecks. The Americans had sacrificed their youngest pilots but they'd pried apart the German formation. The two lines of battleships were no longer mutually supporting. Now they would have to fight on their own.

Brilliant, simply brilliant tactics. The American Carrier Admiral, was it Halsey or Spruance, was a genius. Time to be encouraging and put on a brave face. "Two waves gone, only two left. And they have only sunk the *Hipper*. Soon, we'll have them under our guns." *No need to mention Scheer, her screws smashed, her stern hanging off, limping along behind the formation. Waiting for the Amis to finish her off. Just don't mention her, hope everybody will forget that she was a dead ship.*

The Signals Officer spoke, his voice shaking. "Admiral, Sir, it's not just four waves. At least three more have joined the plot. There are five waves at least more to come."

Admiral's Bridge, USS Gettysburg *CVB-43, Flagship Task Force 58*

"Sir, Formation Able has reported in. Claiming a heavy cruiser and two battleships hit and seriously damaged. They've lost at least 11 aircraft, have 13 more with varying degree of damage." A signalman rushed up with another message flimsy. "Formation Baker, Sir. They claim a battleship sunk, another one seriously damaged and four destroyers sinking." The lieutenants voice became grim. "Baker has lost more than 21 aircraft shot down, Sir. We'll be recovering Able in 40 minutes, Baker in an hour."

Halsey nodded, absorbing information. *The days up here were short. It was already past noon and we are racing against the setting sun.* "TG-58.3 launching?"

The Flag Lieutenant nodded. "Message just in, Sir. Formation How is on its way; 58.4 will be launching Formation Ink in 15 minutes. We'll be recovering Able while 58.5 launches Formation Job."

"Very good. Take one of our Corsair groups and the remaining Adie squadron, and the CAP Corsairs from *Essex, Franklin, Hancock* and *Bon Homme Richard.* That'll give us a strike of six groups. Formation Key. All Corsairs, they're to carry Tiny Tims. If anybody's running low, 1,600 pound APs instead. The other groups are to use the groups they're holding on deck for CAP when their turn comes up. CVLs as well. We'll use the surviving Flivvers for CAP. That'll buy us another two hours to rearm and refuel. Then Able goes in again. Clear?"

"Clear, Sir."

Wild Bill Halsey looked over the sea again, south to where his prey was lurking. And to the west, the sun was beginning to sink towards the ocean. At dusk the carriers would turn north, away from the German fleet, if it still existed. And, in case it did......

"Admiral Lee is forming the Battle Line?"

"Sir, it's assembling now. The battlewagons are detaching from the Task Groups as per your orders. Uhh," the officer was about to risk the legendary wrath of Wild Bill. "The Large Cruisers Sir? Should they go too?"

Halsey shook his head. "They stay with us. They've no place in a gunnery duel." He looked out again. *Is it my imagination or has the sun sunk a little more already?* Time was the enemy, he realized that, but how little of it he had scared him. The constant stream of fighter-bombers and torpedo planes from his carriers could sink the German fleet. Of that, he was confident. As long as they had enough time.

154

AM-1 Mauler Conestoga. *Third Wave, Over The High Seas Fleet, North Atlantic*

The Germans had made a catastrophic mistake. In maneuvering to avoid the torpedo planes, their formation had started to break up. Their anti-aircraft fire had lost its cohesion, it was wild, uncoordinated, ineffective. The FV-1s streaked straight through it, unloading rockets and machine gun fire into the lead pair of battleships. Those gray monsters staggered under the blow and their defensive barrage faltered under the rippling wave of rockets. The pilots off the *Randolph* and *Bunker Hill* were some of the most experienced in the fleet and their tally of missions over France and England had paid off. None of the jets had been hit. They'd curved away at the end of their runs, leaving their targets nicely softened up for the Corsairs and their napalm.

Lieutenant-Commander Raymond Searle absorbed the position as he saw the superstructures of the two leading battleships in front of him erupt into flames. The Corsairs swung around slightly and made their runs from directly ahead of the four huge battleships. It cost them. The anti-aircraft fire from the lead ship had been degraded badly by the flak suppression runs but the following ship had not. Two Corsairs were nailed as they passed over the lead ship and tried to make their runs at the one behind. Ten Corsairs had deluged the German battleship's superstructure with 3,000 gallons of napalm, sticking to everything and everybody.

Searle watched and reflected grimly that, in this case, anti-aircraft fire dying had a very literal meaning. For a brief second he had a picture of the nightmarish inferno on the decks of the stricken battleships. Then he swept it from his mind. *They were Germans, who cared what happened to them?* Searle's younger brother had been one of the prisoners murdered at the Battle of the Kolkhoz Pass. That made hammering the German fleet personal.

The Maulers were making their runs a lot higher than the previous aircraft. There was a good reason for that. Searle had named his aircraft *Conestoga* for a reason; it could lift loads no other single-engined aircraft could equal. There was a lot of rivalry between the Adie and Mame squadrons. Mame was a bit faster than the Skyraider and it could carry more. On the other hand, Adies were easier to fly and had shown an incredible ability to survive damage. Searle had seen Adies that had no right to be in one piece, let alone still flying, bring their pilots back alive before finally giving up – after landing on the decks of the carriers. Both planes were new; both had their problems. It was the Adies that had won the pilot's trust.

The Mames had something new for the Germans to chew on. They carried a 2,000 pound rocket-boosted armor-piercing bomb under their bellies, another one on the inner hardpoint under their wings and ten 200 pound parachute-braked fragmentation bombs under the outer hardpoints. Searle flew ahead of the battleships, then swung to run down their length. Errors were usually in range, not bearing. This plan would minimize the effect of range errors. Out of the corner of his eye, he saw his squadron dropping into place. The formation had been worked out to maximize the number of bombs hitting the target. His eyes flipped down to his bombsight. Through its lens in the bottom of the fuselage he could see the sea. He changed course slightly and the bow of the lead German battleship appeared. His cross ran along it. The forward turret appeared, then, as the second turret eased into view, Searle dropped his entire load. As soon as they saw him do so, the other pilots released simultaneously.

Searle swung away and headed north. His pilots were behind him. 11 of the 12 Maulers in his squadron had survived. Beneath and behind him, he could see the Adie torpedo planes hadn't been so lucky. The two German battleships at the rear of the formation had concentrated on them. *Three planes down? That's what it looks like.*

Behind and beneath him, the 2,000 pound bombs dropped by the Maulers worked as advertized. Each was equipped with a parachute and, as they'd been dropped, a lanyard opened that chute, effectively stopping the bombs dead in mid-air. The weight of the bomb under the chute swung the assembly down to vertical. As the bomb passed 80 degrees, a simple inclinometer fired the six 5 inch rocket motors welded around the outside of the bomb. They boosted it to speeds far beyond anything a normal bomb could achieve. Pre-war analysis had been based on the assumption that, to gain any degree of penetration, a bomb had to be dropped from high enough to pick up speed on the way down. The higher the altitude, the faster the bomb descended and the greater the thickness of armor it would penetrate. That applied all the way up to terminal velocity. Beyond that, the rate of descent stabilized and wouldn't cause any further increase in penetration. Of course, the higher the bomb was dropped from, the less the chance of it hitting the target. If the thickness of armor was such that a bomb of given weight had to be dropped from a height where the chance of it hitting the target was negligible, the needs of protection were served.

The rocket-boosted American bombs didn't need altitude to accelerate. The rockets drove them. The bombs dropped from 2,000 feet up were moving far faster than terminal velocity by the time they hit the decks of the ship. They were still accelerating even after they had punched through the thin steel of those decks. That was something the *Derfflinger's* designers had never anticipated. Nor had any other battleship designer, but it wasn't their products that were under attack.

Nine of the bombs hit *Derfflinger*; ten hit *Moltke*. More hit the sea alongside the two ships, diving deep underwater before they exploded. In a way, those near misses did more damage than the direct hits. The shock waves pummeled the two ships, springing plates and bursting open welds. The armor piercing rocket bombs were something even the battered German ships had never experienced before.

Two of the direct hits were from *Connestoga*. One hit B turret. It sliced through the 130mm armored roof and scythed down the long steel barbette. The bomb's delayed action fuse was initiated by the impact and methodically counted away the milliseconds before the time came for it to destruct. The fuse designers had forgotten to allow for the fact that the bomb was still accelerating even after it had passed through the turret armor. As a result, the bomb had passed below the shell and charge magazines before it exploded.

That oversight and the small charge carried by the heavy-cased bomb saved *Derfflinger*. Fragments from the explosion ripped open the fuel tanks under the barbette and opened the ship's bottom to the sea but they didn't detonate the magazine. Earle's other hit, on the deck in front of and to port of A turret, also failed to cause a magazine explosion. The explosion there blew the ship's side out where the six bow torpedo tubes were installed. *Derfflinger* lucked out again, the water rushed through the ripped open side and extinguished the fires before the torpedoes could explode.

Compared with the wrath of the armor-piercing bombs, the two torpedoes that hit the battleship seemed almost insignificant. A few minutes earlier, the towers of water beside C and D turret would have been cause for alarm but the ship was still reeling from the bomb hits. The torpedoes defeated the torpedo protection system and ripped open the side of the ship. That was where *Derfflinger's* luck ran out.

A few seconds earlier two rocket-boosted bombs had sliced through the ship's side beside C turret, just inboard of the torpedo bulkhead. They'd exploded in the area between the bulkhead and the ship's C turret magazine, reducing the maze of relatively insignificant compartments to a tangled mass of wreckage. The water from the torpedo hit just a few feet away burst through the shambles and flooding started to spread throughout the whole area. A split second later, the second torpedo hit another area beside D turret, one that had also been mangled by a bomb hit. The two torrents of water mixed and merged as they raced through the wreckage, spreading uncontrollably as they did so. It took the water only a few seconds to find flooding paths through the ship and into C and D turret magazines.

Admiral's Bridge, KMS Derfflinger, *Flagship, High Seas Fleet, North Atlantic*

Lindemann picked himself up from the deck, stunned by the blasts. The sight had been incredible. B turret had been lifted clear off its mounting amid smoke from the explosion underneath that formed almost a perfect ring. The turret was now sitting drunkenly across its barbette. The damage reports were coming in but Lindemann didn't need them to tell how bad the situation was. He could see the bow ripped off by one of those parachute rocket bombs, He could feel the ship slow and begin to list. The word penetrated his senses somehow.

"One machinery room has gone, Sir. Direct hit. We've lost Bruno, Caesar and Dora turrets. I think Anton will flood soon. Stern's been hit. We've lost steering and the port and centerline screws. We're trying to restore power to the starboard screw but we've, the gearing has, it's all a wreck back there. Those damned bombs went straight through our armor deck. We'd probably have been better off without it. All it did was set the damned things fuses working. There are fires down below but they're under control. It's the flooding. The bombs smashed us up inside, the torpedoes opened up holes to let the water in. Admiral, Sir, the flak guns, they're gone. Those little parachute bombs exploded just above the decks, what the jellygas didn't finish off, they did. The crews in the open mounts, they were already dead, we only had the enclosed 105s. Fragmentation bombs did for them."

"Message from *Moltke, Sir.*" The Signals officer was reading from a piece of paper, his face white with shock. "Ten hits, all from bombs. Anton and Dora took direct hits, they're gone. One bomb hit beside Dora, its blown the whole side out there. She took three hits dead aft, their whole stern section had detached, she's dead in the water. Bow's gone, she took four hits forward of Anton. She's flooding freely up there and settling by the bows."

Lindemann shuddered, *Derfflinger* and *Moltke* were already slowing, *Seydlitz* and *von der Tann* overhauling them. "Signal *Z-28* to come alongside. I must transfer my flag. Order *Von Der Tann* to be ready to take command of the fleet. How long to the next wave hits us?"

"Ten minutes Sir. At most."

Incredibly their air search radar was still working. Ten minutes gave him just enough time to shift his flag to *Z-28*. Then, he could transfer to *Von Der Tann* in the next gap between waves. That raised the obvious question. "Any more waves of Ami aircraft joined the attack."

"Oh yes, sir. One more in the last few minutes. They're holding steady launch rate by the look of it. One wave every fifteen to twenty minutes. No sign of it ending."

Boiler Room, KMS Gneisenau, *North Atlantic.*

They were coming under attack again, Rheinbeck knew it. Orders came down on the telegraph, for every tiny fraction of steam that could be forced from the boilers. The violent changes in machinery orders; the canting of the deck. Rheinbeck had heard it all before. Only an hour ago. He still remembered the screaming protests of the boiler plant forced far beyond its capacity; the reversing and full ahead orders following in bewildering succession. The swerves as the battleship tried to dodge the weapons launched at her. Captain Lokken had worked wonders that time, dodging torpedo after torpedo. Then Rheinbeck had heard the crash and felt the ship shake as one of the Ami torpedoes had struck home. The torpedo defense system had held. *Gneisenau* had survived.

That had been an hour before and now it was starting all over again. Rheinbeck wondered *what is happening up there, what is happening to the rest of the fleet. Are our guns bringing down the Ami bombers as the officers had so confidently predicted. An hour since the first attack and we havn't been struck again. It has to be going well didn't it? So why are we being hit now?*

If a needle could be bending against the stop mark on the gauges, the ones on the steam pressure indicators were. *52 kg/cm² atmospheres pressure, 450 degrees centigrade in theory, the Good Lord alone knew what the temperatures and pressures in there were really like.* The piping was already groaning as it was forced beyond its capacity. Then, the deck under Rheinbeck's feet canted and he knew the attack was coming in for real. Captain Lokken was on the bridge, fighting for them all again, maneuvering his battleship as if it were a destroyer.

The vibration in the boiler room was intense, yet even through it Rheinbeck could feel the shattering effect of the hit aft. A rocket-powered 1,600 pound bomb slashed through the roof of Caesar turret. It plunged down the barbette and exploded in the ammunition hoist. It was empty. The flashtight doors to the magazine were closed and that ruled out a catastrophic explosion. The blast from the bomb's detonation went downwards, rupturing the centerline shaft tunnel and bending the middle of *Gneisenau's* three shafts. The bend wasn't that great but it caused the long, racing cylinder to rip open the tunnel and its seals. Water surged in from the sea and started to spread through the stern quarter of the ship.

The hammering of the bent shaft against the seals in its tunnel told Rheinbeck *Gneisenau's* luck had run out. The second bomb hit told him just how badly. It punched straight through the 80-millimeter thick armor deck and exploded in Rheinbeck's boiler room. The armor-piercing bomb had a low explosive charge. It didn't disintegrate into a hail of small, man-killing fragments the way a high explosive bomb would have done. Instead, it split up into a small number of large chunks that crashed into the over-strained machinery in *Gneisenau's* port boiler plant. That started a chain reaction that caused the whole installation to disintegrate. The boilers themselves were finally stressed beyond their physical limits and erupted. Pressure surged through the steam pipes, causing them to rupture also.

A few men were in the direct path of the fragments. They were the luckiest ones; the flying lumps of steel crushed the life out of them. Others were standing in front of the boilers when they flashed back.

They were less lucky. They were instantly incinerated and died where they stood. For the rest of the boiler room crew, hell was just about to start.

Rheinbeck was one of the unlucky ones. He was immersed in a scalding cloud as the ruptured boiler plant filled the compartment with superheated steam. He'd never felt anything like it; never in all the years he'd worked down here in the bowels of the ship. Searing agony as raw steam saturated the air. It filled his lungs and eyes, blinded him, ripped at his throat and nose. He ran, staggering for the hatches that lead out of the scalding hell that now surrounded him. *There was something, someone? Between him and the way out.* A figure already with his feet on the rungs that were the way to escape. Insane with pain, Rheinbeck grabbed him and threw him out of the way. His only idea was to find a way out, up to where there was no steam, where the pain would stop. He climbed up, three, then four rungs. Then he was seized around the waist and thrown to one side. He felt himself slipping, he tried to hang on but a boot crushed his fingers. He fell, back down to where the superheated steam was condensing into near-boiling water on the deck.

He could see again, slightly, as if he was peering through a dense fog. Thankfully, the pain stopped. The burns from the superheated steam had finally penetrated deep enough to sear the nerve endings in Rheinbeck's skin. He was dying but he didn't know that. All that he did know was the pain had stopped and he could see the struggling men frantically trying to escape upwards, out of the boiler room that was killing them. He crawled across the deck, leaving glove-like imprints of skin stuck to the steel. He never made it back to the way out. One of four torpedoes that slammed into *Gneisenau's* side burst open the torpedo defense system and let a flood of blessedly ice-cold water into the boiler room.

Captain's Bridge, KMS Gneisenau, *High Seas Fleet, North Atlantic*

Captain Lokken knew that *Gneisenau* was done for. He'd pulled every trick he knew but it hadn't been enough. There had been too many Ami jabos. They'd picked him out and concentrated on him. Two torpedoes dead amidships finished the work that the bombs had started, destroying his machinery plant and leaving him dead in the water. The stern was a mess. Another torpedo back there had mangled his screws and rudder. A fourth torpedo plowed into *Gneisenau* between Anton and Bruno turrets, penetrating the torpedo protection system and forcing him to flood both magazines. That meant everything had gone, machinery, heavy guns, flak batteries; everything that made *Gneisenau* a warship. It was over.

That applied to more than just *Gneisenau* alone. This wave of Ami jabos concentrated on the destroyers that had been with the tail of the 'thirty eights'. The Voughts had come in just above sea level and fired their rockets into the destroyer hulls, slowing them down for the Douglasses to finish off with their heavy rockets. Four of the screening destroyers had caught the attack. Two had already gone down, the other pair wouldn't last long. *That,* Lokken thought, *applied to Gneisenau and Scheer as well.* They were being left behind, *Scharnhorst* was struggling to keep up with *Bismarck* and *Tirpitz* despite her torpedo damage. *Gneisenau* and *Scheer* were virtually dead in the water.

The two ships weren't even close enough to support each other. They'd be picked off individually as soon as the Amis decided they were worth making the effort. What really hurt was that the last wave of Ami jabos had got away clean. Oh, a few of them had departed trailing smoke but none had been short down. The earlier wave that had taken out his flak gunners had done all too well.

Lokken looked around. The professional part of his mind told him the truth. The High Seas Fleet was finished. *It was all over for them as well.* Their formation had been cracked wide open; the two lines of battleships forced apart, then each split further. *Derfflinger* and *Moltke* had been hit badly and dropped behind the formation, leaving *Seydlitz* and *von der Tann* to try and make their run. *Strange how history repeated itself, almost 30 years earlier, those ships had taken part in another death ride against an overwhelmingly powerful enemy fleet.*

Lokken stopped himself in sheer shock at his own thoughts. The U.S. Navy hadn't committed a single battleship to this action. It had never occurred to Lokken before, but he'd never even seen an American warship. They were staying safe, over the horizon, slaughtering their enemy with airstrikes. That made him think of them as being overwhelmingly powerful. The truth dawned on him. His battleship, the battleships, were obsolete, floating targets. The Americans had known it; that's why they had built their carriers.

Lokken allowed the terrible thought to roll around his mind. *What was it the American showman had said?* 'Never give a sucker an *even break.'* It was a chilling thought. This battle was showing them applying that as a strategic principle. If it was possible to destroy an enemy without risk to themselves, that's what they'd do. The Fuhrer had cursed the Americans as businessmen but Lokken suddenly realized that was exactly correct. *They treat war as a business problem. Minimize expenditure, maximize profits. Minimize risk, maximize gains.*

The insight suddenly told Lokken the truth. The Americans would be back to finish off *Gneisenau*. They would do it with aircraft and there was nothing he could do to stop them. *Gneisenau* was sinking, slowly but inevitably. There was nothing he could do to stop that either. That left only one order to give.

"We will abandon ship. Order the men to prepare rafts. They must stay out of the water or they will freeze. They will use whatever they can find but we must get off this ship."

Lokken looked across the sea again, at the remaining 38s, disappearing off to the North. And at the dark blue cloud that was descending on them.

Admiral's Bridge, USS Gettysburg *CVB-43, Flagship Task Force 58*

"Admiral, Sir. Reports are in from Formation Easy. Formation Fox is starting its attack now."

"How long to dusk?"

The aide blinked. "Three hours, Sir. Twilight about another half on top of that. Formation Easy, Sir?"

"Yes, yes."

"They hit the left hand column of battleships, Sir. They're reporting the loss of five aircraft. Claim seven torpedo hits; four on one battleship, three on the one following it. The Mames scored big Admiral. They're claiming more than six hits on one battleship, four on another and three on a third. Strike leader reports the German formation has broken up. Sir; they're scattered, at least four big ships are dead in the water and at least two of those are foundering. Only two battleships and a cruiser are left moving. They've split away from the main formation and are heading for us still, with five destroyers as screen. Formation Fox is hitting them now, Admiral."

"Formation Fox." Wild Bill Halsey ran the figures through his mind. Four squadrons of Corsairs for flak suppression, two squadrons of Adies with two torpedoes each, two squadrons of Mames with three 2,000 pound rocket bombs per plane. This was TG58.2s heavy punch. The one that he was swinging at the last combat-effective German ships.

AD-1 Skyraider Yellow Rose *Seventh Wave, Over The High Seas Fleet, North Atlantic*

Yellow Rose was straining her engine to keep up with the rest of the formation. It wasn't that her performance was sub-standard, her R-3350 engine was behaving above and beyond specifications. It was that she was carrying three torpedoes, not two like her sisters. Lieutenant George Herbert Walker Bush had promised that he was going to get himself a battleship and that was what he planned to do. He'd started by bribing and blackmailing his crew chief into hanging the extra torpedo under his aircraft. It hadn't been hard. The crew chief came from Texas. That and a few appeals to state honor combined with a gentle reminder that the Bush family looked after its own had been enough. Overloaded, he'd been running his engine on the redline all the way to the German fleet.

The battleships were in front of them now. A pall of black smoke from the flak suppression runs hid their superstructures. Six Corsairs had gone down in those attacks but their napalm and rockets had butchered the German anti-aircraft gunners. The red beads of tracer were still coming up, but only a small fraction of the fire they'd been prepared for. Bush took the throttles back from their maximum position and felt *Yellow Rose* slow down. The other Skyraiders were going in fast, pulling ahead of him. That reduced their exposure to the flak guns but their torpedoes had a greater chance of breaking up or sinking when they hit the water. At least one of the torpedoes broached surface and sank but his eyes were fastened on the center of the lead German battleship. Right between its two funnels.

He was falling further behind by the second and Bush suddenly realized that he felt lonely, flying straight at the gray giant while the other members of his squadron had passed over it and were already heading home. He counted the columns of water erupting along the side of his target; three widely spaced and then two very close together. The first three were beautifully placed, one under each of the forward turrets and the third under the rearmost mount. All purely by chance, it was hard enough to hit a ship with a torpedo. Placing a torpedo exactly was too much to expect. The last two hits were almost beside each other, under the aft funnel. That had to hurt.

Bush was suddenly aware that there were lights flashing round his cockpit. A German quad twenty crew had either escaped the carnage or their gun had been manned by some replacements. There was no time for distraction. He slowed down a little more, nestled closer to the water and hunched down in his seat. *A little closer, just a little...* Then he punched the release, dropping his centerline torpedo first followed by the two under his wings. They were heading for the target now, in a tight group with his first fish following the others. *Now, if it went just right, that really would hurt.*

As *Yellow Rose* cleared the German ship, the 20mm gun got the range. Its shells, explosive and armor-piercing incendiaries lashed at the aircraft's wings and belly. They tore out large lumps, slashing into her systems and ripped open fuel and hydraulic lines. *Yellow Rose* staggered in the air, mortally injured by the long, raking burst. As the crippled Skyraider turned away, her torpedoes crashed into the battleship's side.

The anti-aircraft gun had shot *Yellow Rose* to shreds but the three torpedoes did damage that far outweighed the shells. The leading pair of torpedoes hit directly under the bridge, barely 30 feet apart. They blew a hole more than 150 feet long in the ship's side. The torpedo defense system had already been compromised by the earlier hits and failed completely under the stress of the twin explosions. A split second later, the third torpedo exploded in the middle of the failing structure. It turned the torpedo bulkhead into shards of razor-sharp steel that slashed inwards, raking the engine room behind with fire and fragments. The concussion from the three hits blasted open the internal bulkheads separating the diesel machinery rooms. That opened the way for the floodwaters that followed.

Limping away from the ruptured battleship, Bush had no way of telling just how much damage he had caused. He'd seen the explosion. From his viewpoint it looked like one massive blast. He was too busy keeping *Yellow Rose* airborne to worry about it any more. His engine was banging and coughing. The front of his canopy was coated with oil and the only gauges that weren't registering far into the red danger zones were the ones that didn't work at all. The rear section of his canopy was clear of oil. That let him the wings, their control surfaces ripped up and hanging loose. Objectively, Lieutenant Bush realized there was no reason why his aircraft should still be flying.

Yet, *Yellow Rose* was still flying. Even more impressively, she was heading home. Bush did the calculations in his head; he was losing altitude very slowly and could do nothing to stop it. He was losing fuel as well and couldn't do much to stop that either. He didn't think he was losing oil; by his estimates it had already gone. Why his R-3350 was still working was beyond him. But, if things didn't get any worse, he'd just about make it back to his carrier. What he'd do when he got there was another matter. Still, it was time to concentrate on flying, what happened later could wait for later.

"Hey, Shrub. What's with that German ship? How did it get you that mad at it? Blow up one of your pappy's oil wells or something?"

Bush looked around. Two Skyraiders from his squadron were forming on him, escorting his crippled bird. He waved at them and one pilot waved back.

"Damage report, Shrub. You know the panel, square one on the side, just above the tailhook? It hasn't got a bullet hole in it. All the rest have. You're streaming black and white smoke, I think the white is fuel, and there are bits falling off now and then. Guess Pappy's going to have to buy you a new bird after this."

Bush waved again. His family was rich enough to buy him a new aircraft but he suddenly found he had an intense desire to keep *Yellow Rose*. Almost as if she was responding to the thought, the engine surged a little and he was able to regain a little altitude. Then the surge died away and the temperature gauge was climbing up again. The aircraft staggered onwards as the minutes ticked by; as if she was grimly determined to get her pilot back home.

"*Yellow Rose*, this is *Kearsarge*. You're around ten miles out. You're clear for landing straight in, come to course oh-one-five."

"Negative *Kearsarge*. If I put this bird on the deck, she'll pile up. Too many other birds coming in for that. Permission to ditch her?"

166

There was a long pause and the voice on the radio came back, loaded with quiet respect. "Granted *Yellow Rose*. Be advised there is a plane guard destroyer bearing oh-three-oh, four miles out. Ditch close to her. She's getting a boat out for you."

Bush reached up and opened his canopy. Light from the afternoon sun flooded in, telling him just how blackened his canopy had been. He tightened his straps, then tightened them again. Finally, he exhaled as far as he could, the yanked the straps another notch tighter. Ahead of him he could see a Gearing class destroyer had slowed right down to pick him up. *Lose the little altitude I have left, then drop the plane onto a wave.* There was a brutal slam as the crippled Skyraider plunged into the waves. Then, another series of blows as it bounded along, spinning as one wing dipped and grabbed a wave. Then, there was a dull wump noise as the flotation bags in the wings inflated. Bush knew they wouldn't last long; they must be full of holes as well. He looked around and saw a ship's boat closing in on him.

Yellow Rose was sinking slowly. Bush felt that somehow he'd let her down. She'd fought hard to bring him back and now she was going to die out here. Well, he could do something about that, he took his kneepad and started to write out the story of what she had done to get him home. That way, his Pappy would buy him a new bird to carry on the name. He was so involved in writing it, that he didn't feel the bump as the rescue boat hit the sinking Skyraider.

"Jeez, look at that, guys." One of the seamen in the crash boat was incredulous. "Sits there, as cold as ice, writing up his reports. Damn."

Captain's's Bridge, KMS Lutzow, *High Seas Fleet, North Atlantic*

It was unbelievable, incredible. All around him, ships were writhing. They burned from bomb hits and the infernal jellygas, listed from the relentless waves of torpedoes that ripped their sides. Captain Martin Becker couldn't believe his old cruiser was still afloat. Already, according to the raid count, more than a thousand of the dark blue Jabos had raked the fleet with rockets, torpedoes and bombs. The radar showed still more enemy formations coming in, at least five. Possibly six. As soon as one wave cleared, the next had arrived; a perfect conveyor belt of death and destruction. The last wave raked the two surviving 'forties' with bombs, rockets and torpedoes. Both were now dead in the water. *von der Tann* was settling fast. She'd taken eight torpedo hits all along one side and six of those lethal rocket bombs. One had smashed the bridge, burst it open with the same casual ease as an over-ripe tomato thrown at an unsuspecting victim. Admiral Lindemann had transferred his flag to *Von Der Tann* only a few minutes before. He'd managed the dangerous task of transferring his flag under fire, only to put himself directly under an Ami 2,000 pound bomb. *All went to prove that one couldn't trick the Grim Reaper.*

The wave overhead was different. The previous groups of Ami jabos had come in low, slashing at the formation from only a few dozen feet above sea level. This group were higher; five or six thousand feet at least, probably more. *Were the Amis getting tired of the casualties from the flak? Or did they have a new trick in their book?*

It was a new trick, and it was being used on a new target. Previous waves of jabos had concentrated on the big ships. Now they were helpless and could be finished off almost at leisure. High overhead, the aircraft in this latest wave were peeling off in the traditional curve of the dive bomber, heading down in chains at the destroyers underneath. It was a familiar enough sight. The German crews had seen it often enough during newsreels of the glory days of 1940 and 1941 when nothing seemed able to stop the German steamroller. *Obviously, the Amis had decided it was their turn to suffer. Not that the destroyer men hadn't paid a grim price already.* Seven of the sixteen had been bombed and rocketed. Five had already sunk, the other two wouldn't last much longer. Those attacks though had been afterthoughts, incidental to the main weight of attack that had been hurled at the battleships. Now the Amis were targeting the destroyers for destruction.

Far away, at the head of the formation, *Z-30* vanished under a hail of bombs. The Ami Voughts had gone for her, firing their rockets in the dive; then releasing bombs. Not jellygas, the destroyer men had been spared that horror. It was a grim comment on this battle that the prospect of freezing to death in the icy seas was a mercy compared with burning in Ami jellygas. *Would Z-30 make it out of the pattern of bombs that had been hurled at her?* She did, but she was burning and losing way. *How many bombs had hit her? Three? Four? According to the books the Ami Voughts could carry two 500 kilo bombs each in addition to their rockets. They would make short work of an unarmored destroyer.*

A realization hit Becker. *Lutzow* was the only capital ship left in the formation that was even partly operational. She'd tried to make the break north with *Seydlitz* and *Von der Tann* but she'd been too old, too slow, and her diesels hadn't been up to it. She'd been floundering along, left further behind every minute. Now, there was enough separation between her and the main group that she might, just might, be overlooked.

"Helm, come to course one-six-zero. Maximum speed, hold nothing back."

"Sir?"

"You have a problem Commander?"

"Sir, the. . . . . " The First Officer was trying to find a tactful way of phrasing this. "The Admiral's last orders were to head on zero-zero-zero straight for the Ami fleet."

"Admiral Lindemann's orders died with him. Do you think he survived that?" Becker pointed at the sight of *von der Tann*, a pyre of black smoke marking a hull that already had more than a thirty degree list. The ship wasn't recognizable. Both funnels were down. The fore bridge was a mass of burning wreckage. All the turrets were at strange angles, some with their barrels up, others down. If ever a ship was a floating wreck, it was *von der Tann*. Only she wasn't the worst off from what had once been the Second High Seas Fleet.

Becker winced as, on the horizon, *Z-23* exploded. *A rocket bomb? Probably not, more likely a normal five hundred kilo that had punched through the destroyer's thin plating and touched off a magazine.* A split second later *Z-25* followed her. The eruption from her magazine formed a strange mushroom-shaped cloud. For a second, Becker shuddered with a cold horror he couldn't explain. Something much more frightening, on a much deeper level, that the death of a ship and her crew of 340 men could explain. Looking at the cloud marking the magazine explosion that had destroyed *Z-25*, Becker could only think of the expression 'somebody had walked on his grave.' *But this was Germany's fleet that was dying under the relentless air attacks. Did that mean that Z-25 had walked on Germany's grave?*

"One-six-zero, NOW. We are Germany's last capital ship. As long as we can stay afloat, the fleet still lives. The day is lost, hopelessly, irretrievably. We have a chance to turn around and save something from this disaster. Signal what other ships still can to head for home. Night is just two hours away. If we can survive until then, the Ami carriers will have to wait for dawn. Nobody can fly from carriers at night." *Lutzow* answered her helm and her bows swung south, heading for home.

"Sir, over there." The first officer spoke quietly, apologetically. Across the sea, *Scharnhorst* and *Moltke*, probably the last battleships left even partly mobile, were also turning for home. Far behind, *Scheer* was struggling with her wrecked rudder and single remaining shaft to do the same.

KMS Bismarck, *High Seas Fleet, North Atlantic*

The American tactics changed. Instead of the waves hitting a few ships in concentrated blows, now they were spreading out, finishing off the cripples. *Bismarck* was down by the bows. Her foredeck was already underwater with the sea lapping around the base of Anton turret. At least what was left of Anton. It was burned out, the barrels, blackened and drooping in the water. None of the other turrets were in any better condition. Bruno was completely off its barbette, lifted into the air and dropped back. For all the world it resembled a blackened shoe thrown carelessly into a pile. The ship was listing heavily to port. The last wave of Ami bombers had put six torpedoes into her port side, adding to the four that had already hit her. Now the port edge of her catapult deck was also level with the water. What there was left of her superstructure had been raked with more bombs. Fortunately none of the rocket bombs since she'd already taken six of those. Just a mix, 500 kilos, 750 kilos, thousand kilos, some high explosive, some armor piercing. They churned her superstructure to scrap. After a while the hail of hits had just been rearranging the wreckage.

It was a mark of how much water the ship had on board that the submerged bow and heavy list hadn't raised her stern or starboard side clear of the water. Not that the ship still had a stern to expose. An Ami Douglas had put both its torpedoes into the screws and the entire stern section had dropped clean off. A sheer, cliff-like wall now marked the point where the structure had failed. The incredible thing was, with all the holes in the hull and the thousands of tons of flood water that was surging through the battleship's insides, she was still burning down there. A huge plume of black smoke rose above the sinking ship, half-masking the blood-red sun that was slowly setting in the west.

That sun had masked the aircraft's approach. Four Corsairs came out of it, in tight formation. Their wings sparkled with the flashes of their .50 caliber machine guns. The hail of bullets swept through the men struggling to abandon ship on the sloping, burned out and wrecked decks, scything them down. The Corsairs dropped their bombs and passed over the fleet to where the settling hulk of *Seydlitz* steamed in the sea. They lashed her with their rockets and machine guns and were gone. They were probably orbiting round for another pass, that was something else that had changed, the hours when the Amis made a single pass across the fleet and left were gone. Now the ships were defenseless, their flak guns gone, their machinery useless. Their crews could only watch the Americans circled around them, placing their bombs and torpedoes just so. Coming back over and over again until their guns and bomb racks were empty.

Captain Mullenheim-Rechberg felt the battleship shudder under his feet. *More internal explosions as the fires down below eat their way towards his magazines*. He picked himself up; he'd ducked behind a wrecked anti-aircraft mount when the strafing pass had started. The men who'd been trying to abandon ship were sprawled around on the deck where the Ami jabos had cut them down.

"Why? Why? Couldn't they see we are sinking, that the crew are abandoning ship?"

One of the junior officers was almost hysterical. For a moment Mullenheim-Rechberg had sympathy for him. *He's barely more than a boy and this wasn't what anybody had expected. But panic and fear were contagious and had to be crushed quickly*. "Get a grip on yourself. You are an officer, act like one."

"Sir, *Von Der Tann* has gone! She just rolled over and went down." That wasn't surprising, she'd taken at least ten torpedo hits and twice than many of the heavy armor-piercing bombs. She was the first; but she wouldn't be the last, *Seydlitz* and *Derfflinger* were as bad. Behind *Bismarck, Tirpitz* was shattered and sinking fast. That didn't surprise him, by the time the last Ami bombers had finished with her, she'd taken a total of 13 torpedoes and a dozen heavy bombs. She would not last much longer.

171

Captain Mullenheim-Rechberg staggered as another internal explosion racked his ship, sending a fireball upwards out of the smashed ruin of her superstructure. She was rolling over more quickly, settling lower all the time. It was only a question of what would get her first, a massive explosion as her magazines went or flooding eating up what was left of her buoyancy. That decided him. There was one thing left he could do for the *Bismarck*. He cupped his hands around his mouth and put all the power in his lungs into the shout. "Scuttle the ship!"

Then, he turned to the young officer beside him, a supercilious smirk on his face. "Now the Amis can't claim they sank her."

AD-1 Skyraider Clementine *Ninth Wave, Over the High Seas Fleet, North Atlantic.*

The great German battleship rolling over had been a spectacular sight; her red belly contrasting with the black-gray sea, the tiny figures of men running down her hull trying to avoid the inevitable and fatal plunge into the ice-cold seas. Their efforts were futile, the ship's stern vanished beneath the waves and she had slipped under, leaving them floundering in the water they had dreaded. Marko Dash circled the sight for a minute, then felt his aircraft rock savagely. A second German battleship had exploded. *The fires must have reached her magazines although there were rumors that the Germans weren't too bright when it came to storing fused shells in their magazines.*

Clementine circled the sight below again. Two of the German battleships had gone. Another was at the last edge of extremity. He watched her slip under, faster and faster. He knew the mechanism, as the hull sank deeper, the pressure driving water through the holes in her hull increased and the flooding rate increased. Then, as the ship sank deeper, more holes in her hull became submerged and they too added their contribution to the mass of water that was sinking her. Finally, the shattered and riddled superstructure let the air out, leaving nothing to save the ship. That battleship, and the one behind her, were doomed.

Aren't they all? The U.S. Navy had Chance-Vought, Douglas, Martin, Lockheed. They had aircraft carriers, the Germans had battleships. What had they been thinking? Over to his left, Dash saw a single battleship, slowly, painfully, turning south. She was listing, leaving a trail of oil in the water behind her, black smoke staining the sky behind her. Marko lead his formation over to the position of the ship and looked at her more closely. She was one of the smallest German battleships, two twin turrets forward, one twin aft. Scharnhorst class. What looked like her sister ship was way behind, dead in the water. The other eight aircraft from Marko's squadron already making their attack runs on her. This one, the mobile one, was Marko's.

"All Sugar aircraft, split into two groups of four. Hit her from either side of the bows. 45 degrees off centerline; first flight hit port, my flight hit starboard." Marko's voice was confident as he rapped out the orders. TG58.5 had only enough aircraft and munitions left for a single strike and this wave was a mixture of serviceable aircraft from the squadrons on board the carriers. One good strike.

He took his plane down, skimming the waves in the now-familiar pattern of the torpedo-bomber pilot. There was some flak; a tiny amount, a few tracers here and there. Nothing like the storm that had greeted them when they'd hit the enemy carriers that morning. He knew it was a perfect hammerhead attack. The torpedoes would interlock to form a web from which even a fully-mobile ship found it hard to escape. This cripple didn't even have that chance. Marko's rockets streaked towards the target. The battleship's battered bridge vanished under the flashes of the impacts, then his torpedoes were gone. His wing cannon added to the chaos on the target. Then his formation flashed over the ship and their work was all done.

Behind him, seven columns of water rose from the ship. Two up by the bows severed the raking structure, causing it to collapse downwards. Two more hit portside, just under the funnel; three more starboard side, under what was left of the aft superstructure. *That had to hurt.* Marko watched the battleship lose the last vestige of movement. She went dead in the water, her wake faded away as she lost speed.

Marko's formation had got in and out clean. Eight aircraft had gone in, eight come out. He led the formation higher, ready for the return flight home. Below him, he saw the battleship he'd watched foundering had already gone and the one behind her was on her beam ends. That made it time to report.

"Saber control, this is Ink Five-Two Leader. Have seen two battleships sink, one explode. Fourth is on her beam ends. Attacked one battleship heading south, estimated seven hits. All torpedoes released." Marko paused. "Control, we're doing murder out here."

"Ink Five-Two leader, Washington wants a clean sweep on this one. Do a circuit of the area, see if any other hostiles are heading south."

"Roger, sweeping south now."

Marko's group swung south and started its search arc. It didn't take long. They didn't have to go very far. There was a formation beneath them; a capital ship, five escorts. For a second, Marko debated whether to call the sighting in. *Hadn't enough ships been sunk, hadn't enough men died?* That doubt lasted only a second.

"Saber Control. Ink Five-Two leader here. Sighted enemy formation. Estimated one capital ship, five destroyers, about 20 miles south-east of main formation."

"Acknowledged Five-Two Leader." There was a long pause. "Be advised that one squadron of Adies from your group is being diverted to hit them. We are contacting Excaliber and Knife to have Formations Jack and King diverted to take down that group. Come on home. The sun's going down."

Admiral's Bridge, USS Gettysburg *CVB-43, Flagship Task Force 58*

"Sir, Word from Saber." Halsey grunted. *Shangri-La* and her task group had opened the battle and her crews now had more experience at attacking ships than his other pilots. "Sir, Formation Ink reports that three enemy battleships have sunk. One more is going down now, the other four are dead in the water. The survivors, one large ship reported as a battleship but we think it's a cruiser, and five destroyers heading south. Saber requests Jack and King hit them. They're all-Corsair waves, Admiral. So are Log and Mike. We're ready to launch Nan now Sir, but we're running out of time. We'll be well into dusk by the time they recover."

Halsey thought for a minute. "Nan is Able reloaded. Get them off. They started the battle, they can finish it. Then get the Tigercats loaded up for a night torpedo attack. They'll go in if any of the Germans survive the daylight strikes." He broke off, another messenger had arrived on the bridge.

"Sir, final report from Ink just in. Two more battleships gone down, total is now five. Confirmed losses are identified as two

174

Derfflinger class, two Bismarck class, one Scharnhorst class. Smaller units wiped out. At least three cruisers and twelve destroyers sunk.

"Very well. Transmit the following message to Washington." Halsey took a message blank and scribbled a few words on it.

The messenger read the five words and grinned broadly. "Yes SIR!"

Captain's Bridge, KMS Lutzow, *High Seas Fleet, North Atlantic*

One of Captain Becker's secret vices was that he was a hopeless addict to American cowboy films. He particularly loved the endings where the good guys were holed up, either cavalry in a fort or a wagon train drawn up in a circle, hoping for rescue but determined to sell their lives dearly. That was his situation now, except he knew no rescue was coming. He'd seen the cloud of smoke on the horizon as *Seydlitz* had exploded. He'd heard the reports as *von der Tann* and *Tirpitz* had capsized. *Bismarck* and *Gneisenau* had gone as well, they'd just taken too much damage, too many hits, and had foundered. No, there was no rescue coming, that left only selling their lives dearly. At least, *Lutzow* still had her anti-aircraft guns working. She could still fight.

"Maximum power. It doesn't matter what the gauges say, get this ship moving." That was a decisive enough order. There were 16 torpedo planes coming in, already splitting into two groups of eight to catch him in a scissors attack. "Concentrate fire on the portside group. Hard to starboard." *Try and shoot down as many of the torpedo planes on one side as possible, try to take the other group head on.*

His anti-aircraft guns ranged in on the formation he'd selected. He was rewarded, first one Douglas erupted into flame and plowed into the sea, then another blew up. *Probably a direct hit form his 105s.* His 20mm guns chewed up a third, sending it spinning into the sea. The remaining five dropped at perilously close range, then passed overhead. Becker heard the roar of their rockets but his whole attention was focused on the tracks of the torpedoes. *Only eight? Two must have broken up or sunk, perhaps a Douglas hit by 20mm fire at just the wrong second?* His ship was turning hard, the tracks were slowly drifting aft of him. Seven missed, somehow, the last caught his ship under his rear turret. Becker braced himself for the explosion that never came. *A dud?*

His relief lasted only a second. *Lutzow* shuddered as two explosions up forward racked his cruiser. He cursed the bad luck that had brought them. He'd dodged the deadly beam attack that should have raked his ship with hits, only to get hit twice by torpedoes from a bow-on attack, where the book said the chances of getting hit were but slight. He could feel the ship slowing, her movement in the water changing as the buoyancy of the bows were lost. The torpedoes had hit either side of the ship, precisely between the peak of the bow and Anton turret. Now, the whole bow had gone, sheered off just forward of Anton turret.

"Report."

There was an interminable delay from up front as the damage control crews tried to get a handle on the effects of the hits. Meanwhile Becker looked around at the rest of his squadron. *Z-38* and *Z-29* were burning, *the Douglasses must have hit them with rockets as they passed.* It looked like they'd hit at least one more of the Ami bombers though.

"Damage control. The forward bulkhead is holding, we're reinforcing with timbers and sealing off now. We can't move though. If we get any way on, the bulkhead will split wide open."

Becket grimaced. *Staying here meant death.* Then inspiration struck. "You mean we can't get any forward speed on. No reason why we can't go backwards." He flipped to the engine room telegraph. "Full power astern. If we have to, we'll back all the way home!"

Admiral's Bridge, USS Gettysburg *CVB-43, Flagship Task Force 58*

"Nan is making its run now, Sir. It's the big finale. 58.2 and 58.3 got off four full squadrons of Adies and Mames each. With our group, that's four squadrons of Corsairs and ten of bombers. More than 200 strike aircraft. The officer checked a tally list, one that was a long, long column of numbers. "Sir, good place to stop, with Nan going in, we've launched exactly 1,776 sorties against the enemy fleet."

Halsey grinned. That was a number that would make headlines. "Our losses?"

"So far, 254 aircraft lost due to enemy action, 186 lost operationally, 48 are badly damaged and will need major repairs. We

176

have just over 1,672 aircraft left operational of the 2,160 we started with. Attrition is 22.6 percent of our totalled air groups." The aide thought for a second. "I've no idea whether this is good or bad. Nobody has ever done what we did today."

Halsey grunted. "What's left out there?"

"Main formation has gone Sir. One battleship and a cruiser are left dead in the water, 58.3s Adies are closing on them now. Another cruiser and five destroyers tried to make a break south. The destroyers have gone, the cruiser is crippled and heading south." The aide laughed. "She's going backwards, her bows got blown clean off. Nan and a mix of Adies and Mames from TG54.3 are hitting her now. It's over Sir, Washington got their clean sweep."

United States Strategic Bombardment Commission, Blair House, Washington D.C. USA.

"Any news?" Igrat's voice reflected the tension that had been building in Washington all day.

"Nothing official. Last I heard, the Rivets are intercepting a lot of communications from the Germans and some from our aircraft. If they're anything to go by, the Germans have lost a lot of ships and Halsey a lot of aircraft. Phillip says that means we're winning, we can replace our aircraft a lot faster than the Germans can replace their ships."

"He would. We can't replace those pilots though."

"Have you seen the output of our flying schools Iggie?" Naamah relaxed slightly. It had been a long day and she was tired. "We're actually training more pilots than we can use at the moment."

"I didn't mean it like that. The boys who get shot down, we can't be picking many of them up."

"Don't know. No word on that either. I know we've got Mariners and floatplanes out to recover as many of the splashed pilots as we can, but its winter and it's the North Atlantic. I guess you're right, we can't be getting to that many of them. Anyway, we'll know soon. Got any plans for the weekend?"

"Going up to stay with Mike on Long Island. Going to make it a long weekend. I've got a few days leave before we do the next run to Geneva."

"Be careful with Mike, he tends to be over-emotional." From Naamah, that was a serious criticism. She regarded Mike Collins as a playboy, essentially a lightweight who drank too much and didn't keep his temper under control. There was a good reason why Stuyvesant hadn't tapped him for either the Strategic Bombing Commission or the Economic Intelligence and Warfare Committee. As far as she was concerned, his only redeeming virtue was that he threw good parties. *Still Iggie had always liked dancing on a knife edge. At least she never whines when she gets cut.*

"You're not being fair, Nammie. He's tired; tired deep down inside. The troubles in Ireland wore him out, disillusioned him, and what's happening there now has finished the job. Seeing Protestants in the partisan-jaegers hunting Catholics and Catholic partisan-jaegers hunting Protestants, it really got him. He thinks nothing is worth doing, nothing is worth any effort, so he might as well have a good time. Anyway, he does throw good parties and you know what they say, a man in the bush is worth two in the hand."

Naamah shook her head and went into The Seer's office. "How's it going?"

"Nothing since you asked ten minutes ago." Stuyvesant smiled to take the edge off the remark. "And pass that to Lillith as well, It's been fifteen minutes since she asked. Got to admire her self-restraint. We're probably about an hour behind the loop though. Intel will go to Navy first, then the White House, then back down to us. All we can do is wait."

At that moment, the red telephone on The Seer's desk rang and he listened to the voice on the other end for a minute or so, no more. Then, he went out to where his assistant was sitting. "Lillith, round up the gang and spread the word. We've just had a message from Wild Bill. Message reads, and I quote. 'Sighted German Navy. Sank Same.'"

CHAPTER SIX
WHITEOUT

Headquarters, 3rd Canadian Infantry Division, Kola Peninsula, Russia

"So, Sir, we are operating in the standard two up one back formation. We have 7th and 8th Infantry Brigades on the line; the 9th is held in reserve. Most of it anyway. C Company of the Cameron Highlanders are parceled out to the various rear area elements of the division. Those Vickers guns are marvelous defensive tools, especially in this climate. The Nova Scotia Highlanders are in deep reserve; they're getting much needed R&R. That means our real, accessible reserves are the Stormont, Dundas and Glengarry Highlanders and the Highland Light Infantry of Canada.

"Two battalions in reserve for the whole Division?" General John M. Rockingham wasn't impressed. "That's very thin."

"I know, John." General George Rodgers sounded defensive even though he knew he had no reason to be. Rockingham was new to the Kola Front and had little understanding of the peculiar problems inherent in trying to fight a war up here. That's why he had come in advance of his 6th Infantry division and was doing "The Grand Tour" as it was derisively known. It was the standard practice for a newly-arriving General Officer; send him on a visit to the units in place. Save

179

him from having to re-invent the wheel. "And the front we're covering is much too long for the number of troops we have available. We need at least three full corps here, not two. Guess how much chance we have of getting that third corps. Look, the front is like a great L. The Russians are holding the bottom horizontal where most of the enemy forces are concentrated. We're holding the long vertical. Too much front, too few troops."

"Can't the Russians help? Take over a section of the front."

"They're tapped out. It's all they can do to hold the southern end. Petrograd is a hell of a force commitment and they've got every warm body they can find either holding the city or working the munitions factories down there. You know they've got women in their combat units?"

Rockingham nodded, shuddering slightly at the thought.

"There's a political angle to this as well of course. I guess you've had that explained to you? Well, from this end of the spectrum, it means we don't push too hard and the Finns don't either. It's 'All Quiet On The Western Front,' I guess. Only the Finns have the Germans pushing them as well, demanding activity. So they go in a lot for rear area raiding and attacks on service units. At first, that hurt us. Those troops weren't too well trained for combat and I guess that meant Finnish casualties were pretty light. They're hurting for manpower just like everybody else. Anyway, after we lost a few units to those raids, we concentrated them into cantonments, trained guard units for them and gave them some Vickers guns for security. Once our rear echelon people could shoot back, the Finnish raids dropped right off. Guarding against them is still draining our front-line strength though. We could use those machine guns on the front line. One Vickers gun in the right place is worth a company of infantry."

"We'll be the southernmost division of II Corps." Rockingham spoke quietly, absorbing the data he'd been given. "Our northern flank will be your southern. That'll compress your frontage a little. Any chance of some of your people briefing mine on what to expect and how to defend against it? I guess the Finns will see a new unit and guess we have the same lessons to learn as you did. Some advance training will save a few lives."

"That we can arrange." Rodgers was more than slightly relieved. Rockingham had a good reputation, but all too often 'a good reputation' meant an over-inflated ego that wouldn't listen to advice from anybody else. Obviously not the case here. "John, if I might give you some advice, take advantage of the positions of the lakes and rivers. They can cut the length of front you have to cover quite drastically.

Rockingham paused. There was something wrong there but he didn't quite know what. His train of thought was interrupted by a dull rumbling sound that reminded him of an old motorboat. The thought had only just begun to form in his mind when the air raid sirens went off.

"Doodlebugs!" The call went up from several points in the camp. Then the sirens cut off. There was an eerie silence as the troops on the ground listened to the uneven rumble as the missiles approached. Rockingham found himself willing them to keep going, to pass on to another target. Suddenly the sound cut out at the worst possible time, when the missile was almost directly overhead. "Everybody down!" The cry was universal as the entire base camp took cover. Rockingham was counting seconds until impact. *One thousand and ten, one thousand and eleven, one thousand and twelve, one thousand and thirteen, one thousand and fourteen, one thousand an . . . .*

The explosion was devastating. The early Doodlebugs had used a cheap explosive that lacked shattering power but the newer ones didn't. The missiles hit the ground in a shallow dive so that the warheads exploded above ground level. That maximized the area covered by the blast and fragments. Shattered glass from windows scythed across rooms. As always, the blast from the first explosion took strange and unpredictable paths that would leave one set untouched while the one beside it shattered into a silver rain. Even as the echoes of the first explosion faded, another took over. It rolled across the cantonment and the troops inside it. A third followed, then a fourth. Rockingham was prone on the floor of Rodger's office, waiting for the explosions to cease. A fifth went off, then a sixth and he started to relax. Then he heard gunfire from the cantonment perimeter. *Whatever was happening, the doodlebugs had been just the start.* Rockingham thought grimly that he was about to get a much closer introduction to warfare on the Kola Peninsula than he had realized.

Machine Gun Pit Baker, C Company of the Cameron Highlanders, Kola Peninsula

Sergeant Andrew Burns Currie shook his head to try and clear the cotton wool that seemed to have covered him. His Vickers gun was mounted in a solidly-constructed bunker made of pine logs set in an earthen embankment that was also reinforced with pine logs. *Thank God, wood was one item that wasn't in short supply on Kola, for it had been the stout pine logs, old timber as hard as iron, that had absorbed the blast from the six Doodlebug explosions. Most of it, anyway.* There had been enough force in the nearest one to stun him and his gun crew. Currie blinked, shook his head, and stared out of the narrow firing slot of the bunker. Sure enough, white-clad figures had already erupted out of the treeline and covered the distance towards him with terrifying speed.

The machine gun. I have to open fire. He was tempted to sit back and debate the beauties of that idea but the rational part of his mind was recovering from the shock of the Doodlebug blasts. It overcame the sluggish, unwilling part of his mind. The twin handles of the Vickers gun felt comforting. Currie squeezed the trigger, sending the first rounds of a long, long burst in the direction of the Finnish infantry. He sensed his number two man feeding the belt into the gun while number three and four were loading belts and supplying number two. Number five was making sure the water tank was full of snow, condensing the steam from the water jacket and making sure the barrel was cool.

Currie saw his first rounds go wild, overhead, scattered into the greenery of the forests. He was still seeing slightly double but the comforting, familiar hammering of the Vickers gun was curing him faster than anything else could have done. It was a sovereign remedy for blast-shock, doing something so familiar that the brain didn't have to think about it. He corrected his aim and walked the stream of machine gun fire into the group of skiers. They tumbled and fell, tangled in a heap as the steady burst chewed into them. The flat of his hand was beating lightly on the machine gun receiver, sending the barrel in a steady arc that raked the burst across the men who had been frantically trying to get to his position before the deadly tattoo could start. Then, he reached the end of his arc of fire and started back again, the same slow, steady, 450 rounds per minute beat that crucified infantry in the open.

The attack wilted in front of him. There was a special art required of a medium machine gunner, a combination of skill, patience and determination. The Vickers gunners were a breed apart, recognized by a special combat badge and by the less desirable compliment of being the hated target of the enemy. A Vickers gunner had to have the fortitude to ignore what was happening in front of him, to resist the effort to concentrate his fire on threats. Instead, he had to sweep the line of bullets backwards and forwards across his beaten zone at a steady, specified rate. If he did so, then it would be impossible for an enemy to advance through that beaten zone. They would try, and they would die, cut down by the remorseless beat of the Vickers Gun. But, if the gunner was not resolute, if he started to try and fire on the advancing threats individually, tried to use his judgment in shooting down the most pressing threats first, then the deadly web of fire would be broken and the enemy could advance into the beaten zone and survive.

Sergeant Andrew Burns Currie was a very resolute man. The stream of fire from his gun swept backwards and forwards across his assigned beaten zone. In front of him, the Finnish infantry died.

The Finns, or those that had survived, had already gone to ground, trying to escape from the remorseless machine gun. They were firing rifles at the embankment, and particularly at the machine gun bunkers, Apple and Baker. There was no problem in spotting them. Each was marked by a little cloud of steam as the Vickers guns boiled off the water that kept the barrels cool. Water, in the form of snow, was another thing that was not in short supply during a winter on the Kola Peninsula. Currie saw a concentration of impacts around the biggest group of Finnish survivors and for a moment thought that Apple had broken its swing to fire on them. He quickly realized the thought was unworthy of him, Apple was raking its beaten zone just as methodically and systematically as Baker. The impacts were coming from rifle and Bren Gun fire.

The streams of .303 bullets from the two Vickers guns and Currie could only guess how many rifles and Brens were suddenly augmented by explosions around the dip where the Finns were clustered. Currie grinned at the sight, even as his methodical sweeps ignored it. *Somebody had EY rifles up on the embankment.* A standard No.4 fitted with a grenade launcher cup. Drop a Mills Bomb in the cup, pin out of course, load a blank round in the breech, close the bolt and let fly. The Grenade would lose its hammer as it left the cup and could be thrown a good 300 yards or more. A good man with an EY rifle could drop a grenade in a man's lap at 200 yards, toss it through a window at 300. With proper timing, the grenade could be made to air-burst over a foxhole. Company Sergeant Major Clitheroe was a very good man indeed. His grenade burst over the Finnish survivors and lashed them with fragments. A second and third followed and that left them silent.

Time to switch targets. Currie elevated his barrel just a touch and now his stream of bullets was raking the treeline from which the Finnish skiers had debouched. Apple followed suit and now the two Vickers Guns were lacing the trees with their methodical patterns of fire. Neither gun stopped firing, anybody who knew the Vickers Gun also knew that they usually went wrong when starting a burst. Once they were working, they kept on working. The two steady, methodical 450 rounds per minute streams of fire never stopped. Now their interlocking patterns meant that nobody could get out of that treeline alive.

Headquarters, 3rd Canadian Infantry Division, Kola Peninsula, Russia

Rockingham lifted the wooden shoulder stock of his Capsten Gun to his shoulder and squeezed off a burst across the compound. That was an advantage the Canadian submachine gun had over the Russian and German models; its magazine loaded from the side. That made it possible for a man to fire from a fully-prone position or take cover beside a window and fire out. The Capsten had its critics, a bit of misplaced gaspipe with a magazine some called it, but it had its merits.

Unfortunately, this one was a Mark III; an older model that used the original Russian 7.62 Tokarev round. His troops had the new Mark V with longer barrel and the hot Tokarev Magnum the Yanks had developed. Rockingham squeezed off another burst in the general direction of the Finnish infiltrators that were working their way through the base.

"Watch it, John!" Rodger's voice was urgent. Rockingham had been about to sneak a look out but the warning stopped him cold. "There'll be snipers all over the shop. Those damned Finns can shoot the nuts off a mosquito."

To confirm his words, there was a crack and the wood beside Rockingham's head exploded into fragments. The sniper must have guessed where he would be and tried a shot to see if it would penetrate the wood. It hadn't, but the splinters spalling off the inside had been bad enough. Rockingham could feel his cheek wet. He tried another quick burst and changed the magazine. *Bless that side mounted feed.*

"Friend!"

The voice had come from inside. Rodgers drew his Browning Hi-Power. The double-stack magazine for 7.62 Tokarev made for a bulky pistol but it was fine when one got used to it. It gave the user a lot of firepower; much more than the older single-stack designs.

"Enter!"

Rodgers was covering the door and Rockingham swung round to add his Capsten. Even so, he nearly missed seeing the young Lieutenant who crawled in. The fear of the snipers was making everybody jumpy.

"Sir, errr, Sirs." the Lieutenant goggled slightly at the sight of two Generals in the little office. *Both putting up a gallant stand if the number of expended cartridge cases was anything to go by.* "We'll have you out of here in a few minutes. We've got an anti-sniper team clearing the area."

"Another lesson for you, John. Make sure you've got specialized anti-sniper teams trained. You'll need them. I doubt there's more than half a dozen of the swine out there and they've got the whole headquarters pinned down. What's the damage?" The last remark was directed at the Lieutenant.

"Bad, Sir. The northern, western and eastern perimeters are all holding but the Finns ran right over us in the South. Came right on the heels of the Doodlebugs. Gutsy thing to do."

Rodgers nodded in agreement, the Doodlebugs were so inaccurate that following them in like that took guts indeed. *But then, the Finns had never lacked for courage or skill. It was just they were such a miserable bunch of paranoid lunatics. On reflection, the paranoia was justified, most of the world was out to get them. But did they have to be so gloomy about it? Five minutes talking to a Finn could drive a man to drink.*

185

"Anyway Sir, sirs, we lost the Motor Pool for a while. We've got it back now; the Redcaps took it back pretty quick. Can't move the vehicles though. The Finns were in there for at least twenty minutes. Probably booby-trapped every vehicle in the place. Radio section and comms have gone, blown up. The fuel dump held but..." The Lieutenant hesitated, "....they got the RCAMC post."

"How many?" Rodger's voice was terse. "And why weren't they evacuated?"

"A dozen patients Sir. Three more who were ambulatory escaped as the Finns came in. There were two doctors and five nurses on duty. Wouldn't leave the wounded. Finns killed them all. Think so anyway; the men who escaped heard the gunfire. We won't know for sure until we recapture the place but isn't that what they always do?"

Rockingham looked shocked. Even in a war that was spiraling brutally out of control, some things just weren't done. The Germans were as hard as nails but even they never shot medical staff, not in field hospitals anyway. They'd just put the staff to work caring for their own wounded. There was a story that did the rounds that related how they'd overrun a Canadian field hospital and done just that. When German Army pay day came around, the Canadian staff found they were included, paid at full German Army rates for their work. After the Swedes had arranged an exchange, they'd come back with their pockets full of unspendable Reichmarks.

On the floor across the office, Rodgers was weighing up the situation. With half the camp disputed, comms and radio gone, transport gone and everybody pinned down by snipers, the Divisional HQ wouldn't be commanding anything for hours. That left the front line brigades of the division hanging in the breeze.

Airbase Muyezersky-5, Karelia, Kola Peninsula

"Still socked in solid."

Captain John Marosy wasn't entirely displeased to hear that. A day snowed in meant another day not having to face German Flak. There were too many quad-twenties, too many twin-thirties and even the twin-engined, armored Grizzlies suffered. The single-engined birds were even worse off; their losses were worryingly high. Lieutenant Zelinsky settled down in a convenient chair and leaned back.

"I've been having a word around. The weather's clearing but it'll be tomorrow before we can fly again. The Russians down at Three are still grounded, they're to the east of us and the storm's clearing from the west. The Canuck Williwaws at Six reckon it'll take all night to get the runways clear. Way it is out there, we couldn't even find the fight line, let alone get anybody off it."

"Winter's setting in early, that's for sure." Marosy finished off his coffee. It was cold but coffee came in by convoy and was not to be wasted. "We never had a storm this bad this early before." This was his second winter in Russia. He'd spent the first one flying A-20s.

"Heard a rumor about some of those big bases, you know, the ones up in Maine. Some say they've got tunnels underground, joining all the buildings. Why can't we have those?"

"Keep it buttoned, Lieutenant." Marosy's voice was cold. "The sign up on the wall isn't a joke. You hear a rumor and repeat it then the wrong ears pick it up. Well the rumors may be wrong, that one almost certainly is, but who knows what the Krauts will make out of it. Careless talk does cost lives."

Zelinsky looked abashed at the rebuke. Marosy decided to take mercy on him. "Look it's OK, here. We all hear these rumors. Just be careful who you're talking to. The Russians paid high for their lack of operational security back in '41. We don't want to do the same."

There had been no warning, nothing. One second Zelinsky had been about to say something. Then the whole world had just fallen apart. Marosy picked himself off the floor. The mess was a complete wreck, blasted in, tilting and about to fall. Zelinsky was dead. A fragment from the wooden wall had skewered him just as efficiently as a cavalryman's lance. The building was wrecked, a complete wreck. Marosy knew he wasn't making sense, even to himself. That didn't seem to matter at all. Then hands grabbed him and pulled him out.

It wasn't just the mess. The whole base was wrecked. The hangars were down with two of them were burning. The flight line looked sick, just as if there'd been a tornado down it. The aircraft that had been on it were thrown about like toys. "What happened?" Marosy realized with a little amazement that he'd asked the question.

"A-4 rockets. Eight of them. Krauts must have brought them in during the storm and set them up. Did well too. Good tight pattern."

"Aircraft?"

"Don't worry. Your bird's OK, Captain. She was over on the other dispersal area, that got away with it. We've lost ten, fifteen at least though. Now you stay put while we get you to the aid station."

That was when it occurred to him. *That was how the rumor about tunnels had got started. The bases back in home had air raid shelters in case of Doodlebug raids. Of course, shelters were no good against the A-4 rockets, one needed warning to get to an air raid shelter and the A-4s didn't give any. They just exploded with no warning at all.* Then, Marosy relaxed as he felt his stretcher being lifted.

Conference Room, The White House, Washington D.C.

Some meetings were pointless before they started and this was one of them. Technically, the discussion was the invasion of Europe and the various plans for it. Marine Corps General Holland M Smith was giving the overview and he knew it didn't matter. All that did matter right now was the battle going on in the North Atlantic because the outcome of that would change so much. So, the thoughts of everybody were there, not here. The clocks on the wall gave the times at various locations around the world. Moscow, of course, Madrid, Rome, New Delhi, Canberra, Tokyo, Pretoria, Bangkok. One gave the time in the North Atlantic and that was the one everybody kept glancing at. Howling Mad Smith was not pleased but in the presence of the President, he restrained himself nobly.

"Gentlemen, This time last year, we were actively planning five possible scenarios for the invasion of Western Europe. In order of preference, these were as follows. The first was Plan Red which envisioned an invasion of England being mounted directly from the USA. An outgrowth of Plan Red was Plan Emerald which envisaged a landing in Ireland. In effect, the seizure of Ireland would provide us with a bridgehead for the subsequent invasion of England. Third in preference was Plan Gold which envisaged a landing along the Aquitaine coast of France. Emerald and Gold would also be mounted directly from the United States. I need hardly tell you that an invasion mounted across the North Atlantic would be a military undertaking unprecedented in history. The fourth plan that was being actively considered was Plan Olive which envisaged a landing in Spain had that country entered the war. Finally, Plan Silver looked to an invasion of North Africa.

"Over the last year, we have continued to refine these plans. Contrary to our expectations, Spain has not only refrained from entering the war against us, Generalissimo Franco has actually moved closer to us and has provided some small, discrete, but none the less valuable services. Where the practicalities of Plan Olive are concerned, while there are suitable invasion beaches, the transport infrastructure in Spain is poor and has not recovered from the Civil War. If we were to invade, we would face heavy resistance and extensive guerilla warfare. I would remind you of what happened to Napoleon in Spain. Once we had fought our way through all that, we would still face the barrier of the Pyrenees where a much smaller force could hold us almost indefinitely. For all these reasons, it has been decided that Plan Olive is no longer a viable option and it has been discarded from future planning.

"We have also evaluated Plan Silver in depth. The problem is that a Mediterranean strategy does not get us anywhere. If we invade through Italy, we face all the problems that face us in Spain, severe resistance, guerilla warfare and a final mountain barrier that the enemy can hold almost indefinitely. The same applies to an invasion through the Balkans. If we strike at Southern France, we gain nothing that we could not achieve by way of Plan Gold. The logistics of operating out of North Africa are frightening. There are few suitable ports on the Atlantic coast and we would have to supply our forces via Egypt. This would mean an Atlantic crossing, then rounding the Cape of Good Hope and sailing up the eastern coast of Africa. Once the supply lanes have been established, their capacity is such that the port congestion we would face would make the problems we suffer at this time seem minor by comparison. Plan Silver offered us nothing but grief and trouble for no gain. It is not a viable option and has been discarded. Finally, with reference to both Olive and Silver, it is not our policy to go around invading neutral countries. We do not wish to acquire more enemies; the ones we have are quite sufficient.

"Our attention has, therefore focused on refining Plans Red, Emerald and Gold. Our studies have shown that Plans Red and Emerald are very closely intertwined. We cannot undertake Emerald and then not proceed to Red, nor can we carry out Plan Red and leave

Emerald in our rear. We have therefore merged Plan Red and Emerald as a new joint plan entitled Operation Downfall. This envisages two attacks. Operation Olympic is the invasion of Ireland to establish a forward base followed by Operation Coronet, the invasion of the English mainland.

"The alternative is the invasion of France. We have now named this Operation Overlord. Both Downfall and Overlord envisage the use of six Marine Corps divisions with a follow-up of nine U.S. Army divisions and allied forces. In the case of Downfall, the allied force would be two Free British divisions. In the case of Overlord, one Free French Division.

"It should be noted that Overlord and Downfall are inextricably linked. Great Britain is the mighty fortress that guards Europe against assault from the west. If we execute Downfall alone, we will have captured the fortress but left that which it guarded untouched. If we execute Overlord alone, we will have that great fortress in our rear and our hold on France will never be secure. Inevitably, either Overlord follows Downfall or Downfall follows Overlord. The operations are joined at the hip.

"One factor is decisive. There are few if any good invasion beaches along the western coast of Ireland. It is a rugged coast and the few real beaches there have unfavorable gradients. We would also require suitable invasion beaches along the western coast of England. Suitable beaches have been identified as the region around Blackpool and further south near Swansea. If we proceed with Operation Overlord, we can exploit the beaches in Aquitaine which are much better suited to our purposes. This gives us an interesting possibility. The beaches along the southern coast of England are more attractive from a landing point of view than those anywhere else in the country. It is thus easier to invade England from France rather than the other way around. This had lead us to the final decision, to execute Operation Overlord first and follow it with Operation Downfall. Under this scheme, Operation Coronet will take place before Operation Olympic."

"You would leave Ireland in the hands of the Nazis? Will all that is going on there?" The Senator spoke passionately.

"We have no choice. Much as it hurts every one of us that can read a newspaper, we have no choice."

"General." President Dewey also had his eyes fastened on the North Atlantic clock as it ticked away. "We are landing six divisions with a follow up of ten or eleven? Is this sufficient?"

"No, Mister President, it is not. As an initial landing it will be adequate but barely so. It is simply the best we can do. Perhaps Mister Stuyvesant can enlighten us further on the industrial and economic side?"

"That would be valuable indeed. Mister Stuyvesant, could you give us the Economic Intelligence and Warfare Committee's findings on this?"

The Seer stepped forward. Quietly, Lillith started distributing papers that provided background data. "Gentlemen, we're tapped out. So is Germany, so is Russia. We can all barely support the forces and operations we have at the moment. Germany and Russia have run out of manpower. Their reserves are barely adequate to maintain their current force structure. On paper, we have manpower enough but we are supporting a vast war production machine. We fight a rich man's war because by doing so we conserve our most precious possession, our young men. We can be the arsenal of democracy, or we can be the army of democracy. We can't be both. The force General Smith has described is literally everything we can pull together for an invasion.

"Will it be enough? On its own, the issue is finely judged. The opposition in Europe is not great. Most of the German war machine is in Russia. There are, at most, ten German divisions in France, assuming that the two French SS divisions, *Charlemagne* and *Charles Martel* can be considered equivalent to a German division. There are six German Divisions, including the two English SS Divisions, *Black Prince* and *Ironsides*, in England and two German divisions in Ireland. Plus the Partisanjaegers of course. These forces in France and England comprise the bulk of German forces not on the Russian fronts."

"English and French SS divisions! Why are these people worth fighting for?" It was the same Senator who had spoken before.

The Seer was about to speak but President Dewey held up his hand. "It is possible to find brutal, sadistic thugs in every country, in every place, in every town. It is no different here." He produced a copy of the Boston Globe from his briefcase, with the picture of the tarred and feathered woman on its front page. "Need I remind you of this? Nor do I need to remind you that she is not the only victim of such attacks. It is our great pride that the thugs who did this are reviled and hunted, not given exotic uniforms and turned into national heroes. But let us not pretend that such beasts do not exist here. Seer, do the Germans have plans for an American SS division?"

"They do, Sir. They have tried to recruit prisoners of war. Not with any great success I am pleased to say. They call it the *Robert E Lee* Division."

There was a hiss of disgust that rang around the room, none louder than from the Senators representing Southern States. The idea that the saintly Robert E Lee should have his name associated with the SS appalled them. Privately, the Seer grinned to himself. He actually had no idea what the Germans planned to call their American SS division. But the invention had had the desired effect.

"We don't know how well the British and French SS divisions will fight. The British fought well in 1942 and in 1940 the French kept fighting despite an appalling strategic situation until Halifax stabbed them in the back. But, even allowing them German-like performance, we can take what they have in Western Europe. The problem will be if they shake loose formations from the Russian Front and bring them back. They can do that, their rail network inside Europe itself is almost untouched. We simply can't get at most of it.

"There is one other thing though. I said Germany is tapped out and I meant it. They have just enough manpower, just enough industrial power to keep going at their present level. In a very real sense, they are running on capital. If they have a disaster, if they lose a big chunk of that capital, they can't replace it." The Seer's eyes strayed to the North Atlantic clock again. "We have the German fleet in a trap now. If they lose that fleet, they can't replace it. We'll own the sea, unchallenged. Unchallengeable. The German tripod will have only two legs and that will mean we can redouble our blows at one of the other legs. That way, we can bring them down."

"How long?" The talkative Senator was off again.

"18 months? About that. Perhaps two years. We can't give our invasion force air cover from the US; we have to pound German air power into the ground first. Take out the second leg of the tripod. For

192

that we need the big carriers now entering service. That'll just leave the German Army. We can whipsaw that, break it between two forces." The Seer grinned nastily. "East and West of the Mississippi?"

The allusion to the American Civil War wasn't lost. Nor was the concept of slowly strangling an enemy to death, stripping away his means to fight, one piece at a time. The Senator nodded, with reluctance. "I doubt if I'll see it in my lifetime."

The Seer smiled, nastiness replaced by confidence. "With due respect Senator, I'm sure I'll see it in mine."

Conference Room, The White House, Washington D.C.

"Stuyvesant, why do I get the feeling that this whole Overlord plan has the makings of a first-class disaster?"

"Because it does have the makings of one, Mister President. It's doomed; a catastrophe that will make Gallipoli look positively brilliant."

"I know that, Stuyvesant. It's not what I asked, I want to know why it's a recipe for disaster. And why has General Smith come up with it?"

"General Smith was assigned to come up with a plan for the invasion of Western Europe using the forces we had available. That he has done and we are looking at the result now. I would venture to say that this is the best possible plan that could be made, using the forces available. The reason why it's going to be a disaster anyway is that the forces committed to it are still grossly inadequate. What's worse, anybody who looks at the plans, and we have to assume that the Germans will, sooner or later, will know that they are grossly inadequate. They'll see it for what it is, a plan to land an occupation force *after* the war is over. And then, they'll ask, how do we plan to end the war? That's a question we don't want raised."

"So we need a bigger invasion force. You, yourself, said just a few minutes ago, that we're tapped out. So the invasion is impossible." It was a flat statement and Dewey's voice was grave. He knew well the implications of what he was saying.

"We are tapped out, in the manpower department anyway. The 95 division force we have now is all we can support. Industrially, we can do a lot more. The truth is that our economy is barely half mobilized; our production can go a lot higher than present levels if we really need to. Of course, every time we crank economic mobilization up, we make the post-war demobilization crash worse. We're heading for a pretty nasty post-war economic depression as it is. We're walking a delicate line between the level of military mobilization needed to fight this war and the level of civilian margin needed to ameliorate that post-war crunch. So, the obvious requirement is to get more manpower."

"Any ideas where from? Not the Russians surely?"

"No, Mr. President. The Russians really are tapped out on manpower. They can, just barely, support what they have. However, they're not the only ally we have. There's the Commonwealth as well. We're using Canadian troops up in Kola but there's a lot of the Commonwealth we haven't started to exploit yet. There's a lot of the British Army scattered around. We can consolidate that and make up a pretty decent force."

"The *British* have got a lot more forces? How come we never knew about this?"

"Oh, we did Mister President. In fact, the British were planning a transatlantic invasion long before we were. They started their planning back in 1940 with the idea of combining a transatlantic "relief force" with a military rebellion against Halifax's regime at home. The way they saw it, and I don't think those plans were ever even remotely plausible, was that they were looking at a re-occupation with, at most, a few skirmishes on the side. I guess they thought that getting a suitably impressive force across the Atlantic would be enough to trump Halifax. In my opinion, doing that was the easy bit. Defending the UK once recaptured, from the German response would be hard. Our sources suggest that they had the whole operation planned for late 1942, or so they hoped. Anyway, we'll never know. Their plans were forestalled by the German occupation. The forces in England, the RAF and the Army, shot their bolt holding the Germans off long enough for the Royal Navy to get out.

"In retrospect, I think The Great Escape was part of that plan. At the time, we saw it as a heroic gesture to keep the fleet out of the hands of the Germans. I think it's equally likely that it was a key move in preparing for a re-invasion. The great problem the Commonwealth faced was that their invasion fleet would be very poorly escorted. If the Germans had spotted it, there would have been a massacre. So they had to get the RN out to screen the invasion convoys. The fact the Germans got in first was an unwanted complication, but it didn't really change things. For several months after the occupation, all that was in England were the paratroopers and air landing troops who did the initial assault, some regular infantry and a few panzer and panzer-grenadier regiments who got either flown in or landed in the channel ports after they were secured. A Commonwealth-only invasion was practical even if it wasn't likely to succeed. That still left the re-invasion threat untouched. Of course, we messed everything up by getting into the war and bringing the German submarines down on our east coast. By the time they'd been cleared, the window of opportunity had gone.

"Be that as it may, the Commonwealth did a lot of planning on how to move troops around. It all proved irrelevant. Keeping the Russians in the war, holding Kola, maintaining the Arctic convoy supply line, they're taking up most of their effort now. They're still planning things of course, but it's more from force of habit than anything else. They were planning to move five corps over the Atlantic, how they'd manage it don't ask me. Apparently, it was two Canadian Corps, two British Corps and the ANZAC. Three divisions each. Then, the two Canadian Corps went to Kola. They replaced one of those corps with a mixed formation, mostly South African with other contingents thrown in. That still leaves twelve divisions and they've got plans to move them as well, without bouncing off our resources. Those twelve divisions as part of the second wave following the Marines ashore would be priceless. A 21-division follow-up looks like a serious invasion."

"How come these forces have never been mentioned before? There's something seriously wrong going on here." President Dewey was drumming his fingers with irritation.

"Partly it's us, Sir. To be honest I don't think the planners take the Commonwealth forces very seriously. Losers and all that. But it's also a reaction to how the rest of the world sees us. We're a nation of immigrant misfits. In the final analysis as a people, we're made up of everybody nobody else wanted. The very fact we exist is a reproach to their ruling elites. The fact we outperform them across the board is a deadly insult to their whole belief system. So, our unofficial foreign policy with regards to the rest of the world is, 'they see us, they insult us, we kick their ass'. As a result, we've got into the habit of not caring very much what they think of us. We just wander off and do what we want, or what we think we have to do. If they want to come along for the ride, fine, but we really don't care very much."

President Dewey was trying not to laugh. "That's not how they teach our history in school."

"Mister President, in my experience, history is very rarely how it gets written up in the history books."

"I can believe that. You know there is a problem here. Governments get so set in their ways they forget they live in a narrow, self-validating clique. We could use an outside viewpoint sometimes. How advanced are these Commonwealth plans?"

"Pretty well developed although they are intensely theoretical documents. Nobody in the Commonwealth believes that they are going to stage an invasion on their own, not now. They've got a lot of the groundwork though. Of course, if we bring in a Commonwealth force this size, it's going to throw the whole Overlord-Downfall question open again. The Commonwealth forces will insist on making the first strike at England, possibly with Ireland as a first step but definitely aimed at the U.K. Even if they go along with hitting France first, they'll want a commitment to strike at the U.K. later. I'd say no more than 60 days after hitting France. That's going to be as bad as our present plans. Another reason why we like going it alone, alliances are an entanglement."

"No foreign entanglements rings a bell. If there are Commonwealth troops out there we can get our hands on, what about the French? They had colonial interests too."

"Bit of a different case. They had troops, quite a few of them, in Indo-China but they got hammered during the 1941 war with Thailand and then when the Japanese occupied the rest of Indo-China. They have troops in North Africa but nothing like the resources the Commonwealth has. Anyway, the French are likely to be as demanding as the Commonwealth, they'll demand they hit France first and go no further. They don't like the British right now and with good reason. They were still fighting hard when Halifax folded in 1940. I'm not saying they had a chance of winning but they were still hanging on.

When Halifax signed his Armistice, they were left high and dry. If that hadn't happened they'd probably have got better surrender terms. It was just like with the police here, the first person to fold gets the good deal."

"Stuyvesant, I know you're an industrialist, not a general, but I want your honest opinion. Do you think an opposed transatlantic invasion of Europe is really possible?"

Stuyvesant leaned back in his seat, appearing to calculate the balance of forces while an ironic thought passed through his mind. *I must remember to tell Lillith and Naamah about the 'industrialist, not a general' comment.* It was a good question though, was the invasion of Europe, across the Atlantic against a properly defended Europe possible? Images of the correlation of forces surged throughout his mind.

"No, Sir. It is not. We cannot transport enough troops, support them well enough or keep them fighting once they are ashore. We'll end up with a lodgment that we are hard pushed to hold; a Russian Front in miniature. The Germans have interior lines and that's always bad news. We can't get at them without using the B-36. If we try to do so using that aircraft we trade away our trump card. The Big One has to succeed, Sir. It has to shatter the German ability to resist and it has to destroy their ability to move troops around. We have to deprive Germany of its interior lines of communication so that the Russian and European fronts are disconnected. Only then can we invade with a hope of success. That's assuming Germany keeps fighting after The Big One. All I can hope for is that the Germans see sense and surrender.

"That'll mean us just keeping order as the Europeans sort themselves out. I hope that's all we have to do."

Dewey looked at the huge map on the wall of the conference room. "It would be so much easier if the Germans do see sense after The Big One. Will they?"

"Sir, one of my staff has some suggestions along those lines. Could I impose upon you to listen to her ideas?"

The President grinned quietly to himself. The number of women high up in the Economic Intelligence and Warfare Committee had caused a lot of comment. Oh, sure, women were in the war effort, working in the shipyards and aircraft factories and doing office work for the armed forces. A few were even flying aircraft, delivering them to units, but the number of woman in senior management was infinitesimal. Except in the EIWC where they seemed to be everywhere. That had caused some snide comments around Washington. As EIWC had gained power and influence, they'd waned. "Certainly. Ask her to come in." The President knew Stuyvesant well enough to guess that the 'member of his staff' was sitting outside, waiting.

Stuyvesant picked up the phone and buzzed reception. "Nell, step inside for a few minutes will you?"

Dewey looked at the red-head with pleasure and a certain element of relief. Stuyvesant had two red-heads on his staff. This was the one that didn't terrify people.

"Mister President, may I introduce Eleanor Gwynne, she runs the section of the EIWC that is responsible for gathering economic and production data from the U.K."

"Mister President, as part of my duties, I gather information from the British Resistance concerning the forces in the U.K. and their readiness status. Over the last few months an interesting pattern has started to emerge. It appears that the a substantial number of the troops in Britain are no longer German but British. Even units that are nominally German contain a large number of conscripted British personnel, with the German elements acting as stiffening and reinforcement. For example, in a panzer-grenadier platoon with four half-tracks and infantry, the command track and two of the infantry tracks will be German, the other one will be British. The two British SS divisions are, of course, wholly made of British troops. This pattern . . . . . "

Nell spoke quietly and in detail for almost twenty minutes, running through orders of battle, morale levels, force structures and the effects of Russian front casualties on the German units. "So, Mister President, we can only see this trend continuing. If we invade, these units will fight and probably fight hard. Their German corseting will see to that. But, it is likely that, once The Big One is launched, a well-constructed, well-broadcast radio message, sent by people the British trust, Churchill and their King, will have a very good chance of causing the "German" units in the U.K. to lay down their arms. If that happens in the U.K., it is likely that the example will be seen and adopted in other countries. Ireland is a different case of course, given what has been happening there. There's no way the SS and Partizanjaegers there will surrender. Now would we want them to. There must be an accounting for what those people have done."

"How would we transmit such a message? We couldn't put it out over the BBC." President Dewey was fascinated by the concept.

"We're exploring that now. We would have to put it out over German radio frequencies. There are a number of options for doing so, all very low cost in terms of assets. Mister President, this option costs us but little and offers significant gains. Perhaps, at the appropriate time you could raise it with the King and Mister Churchill?"

"If it avoids civil war and reduces the fighting, yes, of course." Dewey noticed Nell's lips moving and though he had missed something she'd said. "I'm sorry, you hadn't finished?"

"I was just thinking Mister President, of a previous civil war in England, between King Stephen and the Empress Maud. Neither side could win so both devastated the countryside to starve the other out. Of course, it was the common people who starved, not the nobles. People said it was a time when God and his angels slept. We could apply that description to the world today."

President Dewey looked at the great map with its display of the fighting going on around the world. "Yes, Eleanor, I guess we could."

161st Rifle Division, South of Petrozavodsk, Lake Onega, Kola Front

It had been a long, long road from Alexander Ignatievich Shulgin's home, at Kineshma on the Volga, to the Kola Front. It began in August 1942 when he had been at work in his office. "They" had called him, telling him the fascists were coming and all civilians were being evacuated. He'd been given a notice telling him to pack as many of his things as he could carry in a suitcase. Everything else would be destroyed. There would be nothing left for the fascists, not food, not shelter, not clothes, nothing not even a piece of paper. While fascists remained on Russian soil, they would not even be able to ease their bowels in comfort.

The message had ordered him to be at the railway station the next morning. It had confused Shulgin. *Weren't the fascists attacking in the North, towards Moscow? There was no word of fascists attacking to the south, towards Stalingrad. Moscow was under siege and the fascists had more than they could handle there.* The newspapers had been full of stories of the heroism of Moscow's defenders, each being prepared to sell his life if doing so would add to the total of fascist dead. Comrade Stalin was there too, masterminding the resistance, cheering the people with his grim determination that Moscow would not fall.

The railway station had been a sight to behold. Crowds of people being herded onto trains heading East. It wasn't like the first evacuation, the one last year when the fascists had first struck. That had been chaos. This was well-organized, the people being pushed onto trains as they arrived and were identified.

In the background, passing the trains full of people were other lines of railway cars, loaded down with industrial machinery. It wasn't just the people who were going east; the factories were as well. The lines of people were labeled by initials. Shulgin found the row labeled S and stood there, waiting for his turn. Eventually, an NKVD man had looked at his notice, then at Shulgin. "Infantry Academy" had been his only comment. Then he'd been herded onto the train with the rest.

As the long train ride had ground on, the packed railway cars had become progressively more foul. Water had been in short supply, food even shorter. They'd been stopped, sometimes for hours, sometimes for a day or more, as higher-priority trains took up the track. Factory machinery heading east; Army units, supplies, armored vehicles on flatcars heading west. Whichever they were, the people on the trains waited until they'd gone. Then, the long journey started again. People had wept; others raged. In some of the packed cars, babies had been born. They were given special care for they were a sign that a future still existed.

Finally they had arrived at somewhere in the depths of Siberia, far to the east. Once again, NKVD men inspected the notices and this time Shulgin had been one of the younger men sent to one side. There were trucks waiting, Studebakers, and the men from the train were loaded into them. The trucks had taken them all to the Infantry Academy where the pre-war three months course had been compressed into two weeks. Then, they were made part of the 161st Rifle Division.

What had followed was a blur. A mixture of being sent to the front, assaults on fascist positions, beating back assaults on their own, fighting seemingly without end. Shulgin had felt as if he'd lived his whole life in that blur, without any past or future The 161st Rifle Division had been ground down to a shell, pulled from the line and rebuilt, then sent back. 1943 had faded into 1944. The 161st had been one of the divisions trapped in the Kola peninsula when the fascists had broken through to besiege Archangel'sk. Ground down to a shell again, rebuilt again. Somehow, without quite remembering how or when, Shulgin had advanced in rank and was now a Sergeant.

The warning came earlier in the day. One of the ski patrols, from the 78th Siberian, had spotted the fascists moving up to attack. They'd hit during the night, probably; perhaps at dawn the next day. So the 161st was going to pre-empt them. They would hit the fascists at dusk, hopefully catch them while they were moving into their jump-off positions. The company commanders had already visited their units and given their orders. The squads were to stay together in shallow trenches, covered with branches so that the fascists would not spot them. Shulgin took a tighter grip on his rifle. It was not the three-line Mosin Nagant he had trained with an age ago, but a Canadian-made Lee-Enfield supplied under Lend-Lease.

That wasn't the only thing that was different from the way he had trained in the Infantry Academy. Today, there would be no cries of "Forward!" There would be no shouts of "Urrah." Shulgin heard a quiet "Let's go, bratischka" from his company commander and saw him climb out of his foxhole. Shulgin did the same and followed him automatically. The rest of the men rose up after him. They just quietly stood up; just as quietly, they walked forward. Darkness was closing in. A mist was rising where the freshly-fallen snow steamed slightly as the temperature rose in the wake of the storm. Shulgin felt the eeriness around him, the dead silence seeming to suffocate them. Then one of the newbies in the unit started quietly rattling with his improperly carried weapons. That changed the situation instantly. The Germans picked up the sound and opened fire. First a rifle, then machine-guns. The Russian infantry hunched up and started to run forward; praying their feet wouldn't break the crust on the snow and leave them floundering. Shulgin could see only the back-pack of the man in front.

The cries of "Forward!" were already ringing through the trees. Shulgin had no idea how long he had been running forward. It could have been a second; it could have been an hour for all he knew.

He'd reached the German foxholes scraped in the snow and dropped flat into the largest of them. A firm grip on his rifle, butt tucked firmly into his shoulder. Bolt handle held between thumb and forefinger, little finger around the trigger. Not a grip taught by the Russian Army but a trick shown to them by the Canadian Sergeant-Major who'd instructed them in the workings of the Lee-Enfield. Shulgin flipped the bolt forward and back, one smooth action and squeezed the trigger with his little finger. Almost instantly he was operating the bolt again, blessing the smooth speed of the Lee action against the sticky roughness of the Mosin-Nagant. Ten aimed shots went out, then the magazine was empty. He pushed the catch that released it and inserted a loaded magazine for another ten shots.

All along the rifle line, the other infantrymen were doing the same. The rapid rifle fire cut down the fascists as they tried to counter-attack their lost positions. The squad machine guns opened up, spraying the fascists and sending them tumbling over in chaos. "Forward!" Shulgin cried out, without even realizing it. They followed up the shattered fascist counter-attack. He and his men were drove through the woods, pushing the fascists back, faster and faster. The troops that were preparing for their own attack were caught out of position and at a disadvantage. Even if they recovered from this blow, any attack they launched would be a weak and feeble thing compared with the original plan.

Smoke filled the woods. The world seemed full of explosions, shooting, the crash of grenades going off. In Shulgin's eyes, the whole battlefield was littered with people. Some were motionless, others convulsing from pain. Then, something hit him from the side, sending him flying through the air. He tried to get up but his foot turned under him. The agonizing wrench seemed to turn his whole leg to jelly. He couldn't even move to get back to where the medical unit was. He started to crawl back but stopped. *Why go back when I can go forward?* He changed direction and found a wooden stump that offered some cover. He couldn't remember what happened next; only a blaze of pain from his ankle when somebody tugged it. Shulgin rolled over, bayonet at the ready but held the thrust. One of the aid women was staring at him, contempt in her eyes.

"What the hell are you doing here? Advance, coward. Good men are dying because you skulk behind a tree."

"My foot; it's wounded. I can't walk."

202

"What wound?" Her voice was scornful. Nevertheless, her fingers felt his ankle, none too gently. "Oh, I see. A dislocation. Well, I can fix that."

The aid woman grabbed his ankle. Shulgin expecting her to bandage or splint it. Instead, she just wrenched hard and the joint snapped back into place. Shulgin screamed, then let fly with a stream of curses. He'd never guessed he knew such language, let alone use it. The aid woman shook her head and crawled away to try and find other wounded to treat.

He'd scurried forward. His ankle still felt like fire but at least the shooting pain and weakness had gone. The Russian troops were getting artillery support now that surprise had gone. The shells howling over their heads to the German positions beyond. By the time Shulgin had rejoined his company, they had been joined by several 57mm anti-tank guns Somehow the crews had manhandled the heavy weapons through the trees and into position. His company commander waved him over. Their company had lost so many men they had been assigned to protect the guns rather than hold a section of the line. The good news was that the gunners had brought some extra Degtyarev light machine-guns with them. That would make up for the casualties they had taken.

"Bratya! The fascists will be counter-attacking soon so we can all make sure my watch is set right!" There was a burst of laughter from the troops. Every veteran knew that the fascists took exactly 30 minutes to come to their senses and organize a counter-attack; not a second more or less. "Don't forget what we are here for! We cannot hold without these guns. We must stop the fascist beasts from getting close to the guns. If we protect the artillerists, they will protect us from the tanks and half-tracks. Machine-gunners, cut the infantry off the tanks. The tanks will try and destroy our machine guns first. If we can get rid of the infantry, the artillerists will see to the tanks. If every man does his duty, we will hold!"

A good speech, thought Shulgin, *short and to the point, stirring and just long enough to keep the men's minds off the fact that fascist tanks were coming.* Fascist propaganda always showed them pouring masses of tanks in every assault but most of the time they would have a couple of tanks if that. They would sit at a safe distance and shell the Russian infantry positions. They would try to spot the Russian guns and suppress them but they would not close, not unless they were desperate to break through. Of course the answer to that was to position the guns on a reverse slope so that the tanks had to close to short range. Then, there would be a lethal, bloody duel. The tanks would fire. The half-tracks with them would close with their panzer-grenadiers. The 57s would make short work of them. Then the machine gunners could cut down the fascists as they abandoned their vehicles.

Shulgin took his place in the trench, his rifle ready and waiting. Another change from the old days. Back in '42 he'd been taught to dig one- or two-man foxholes, laid out in platoon formations. The problem was that they collapsed under fire. Worse, the men in them were on their own. They were completely isolated unable to hear or see the orders. That had made leadership and command almost impossible. Every man believed the others were already dead or retreating, that he was the only person left alive. Then it seemed that enemies were all shooting just at him. So now the rule was to dig trenches, full depth if there was time, half depth if there was not. But every man could see his comrades and they could see him. A man's spirit might fail if he was on his own, but to show cowardice when one's comrades were watching? Impossible!

"Here they come!" Tovarish Major called out. Sure enough, it had been 30 minutes to the second. It was obvious from the strong rumble of explosions that the attack on the frontline had started. The sounds of explosions drew closer, and was joined by a massive roar of engines. That meant the enemy tanks were coming. Shulgin saw the forward security pickets appearing at the ridge and running towards the anti-tank guns. They ran to the company commander, explained something to him and the order went out. "Prepare for the tank attack!" There were no drugs in the 161st. The troops were in their half-trenches. The artillerists tried to camouflage their guns with branches, mud anything they could find.

At that moment some people in Russian khaki appeared on the ridge. They ran towards the guns as fast as their legs would carry them. To Shulgin that meant just one thing. The front line was completely broken and an avalanche of tanks and Panzergrenadiers was about to descend on them. The artillerists were waiting by their guns, the barrels were trained along the ridge, ready for the first vehicles to cross. They didn't have to wait long. Fascist tanks, at least ten of them, crossed the ridgeline and rolled forward at high speed. They fired their machine-guns at the fleeing infantry. Shulgin identified them. *4th series tanks; they looked archaic compared with sleek Panthers and hulking Tigers but they were deadly enough.* They were running down the hillside, firing their main guns non-stop. Shulgin sneered at that, *it was a trick that worked against inexperienced drugs but veterans know it was almost impossible to fire accurately on the move.*

Shulgin had to remind himself of that. He wanted to flee, his legs kept trying to run but he forced himself to remain still. Then two loud explosions as the fascist tanks hit some mines. An engineer platoon had hastily laid them while the infantry were digging in. *Two tanks, out of ten!* Shulgin cheered, the more so because one of the tanks was burning while the other had spun on its wrecked roadwheels. The rest lumbered on, bearing down on the infantry. One came up on a trench. It spun around on its tracks, driving along the length of the ditch. When it came out the other end, Shulgin could see its wheels and tracks were bright red. A 57mm cracked and the shot hit the tank square in the side. It started to burn, its crew struggled to get out but they were shot down before they had a chance.

More shots from the 57s; return fire from the 75s in the tanks. Shulgin and the infantry stayed down. They had to let the tanks pass through their positions and stop the Panzergrenadiers before they could get to the artillerists. There was one small problem with that plan. It was such a minor problem he was sure it had escaped those of higher rank who were paid to think on such things. The problem was that the tank was made of steel, and infantrymen were not. It wasn't impossible to knock out the tanks with grenades and satchel charges, but it was even harder escape afterwards. Even if they disabled a tank, that didn't end the matter. The crew might not abandon the immobilized tank, they might stay and continue to fight. That was why the order had come down. "You should always burn the tank."

The remaining tanks were almost on them. The 57s fired to the end, Shulgin could see one gun, its crew slumped around it. The artillerists had fought their gun to the muzzle, until they'd been cut down by a shell from a tank. One of the fascist tanks was very close. For a moment, Shulgin thought he was dreaming because he saw two members of the dead crew come to life. Their gun had been loaded and they'd been waiting their chance. It wasn't only fascist tankers who could stay at their post and continue to fight. The armor-piercing shot from the 57mm smacked into the side of the tank, just under the turret. There was a split second of silence then the tank erupted in an explosion. Smoke and flame poured out of every hatch, every port in the armor.   Panzer grenadiers were all over one gun crew, the artillerists were fighting back with pistols, clubs, anything that came to hand. They fought their gun to the muzzle and beyond so that the fascists could not claim they'd captured a Russian gun while a member of its crew still lived.

Shulgin had been firing his rifle on remote control. His thumb and forefinger worked the bolt, his little finger squeezed the trigger. He'd run out of pre-loaded magazines and was loading from stripper clips, the same way his old three-line rifle had been loaded.   Another tank was burning in front of him. The Company Commander was beside him, clapping him on the back.

"Well done Bratischka. A well thrown grenade indeed!"

Shulgin shook his head, he couldn't remember throwing grenade at that tank. All he could remember was firing his rifle at the panzer-grenadiers surrounding the 57mm. *Perhaps the man who had thrown the grenade was dead and command wanted living heroes, not dead ones.*

"Men, fall back. Our work here is done. Help the artillerists with their guns."

The words made no sense. Shulgin looked around.   The fascists had fallen back. They'd nearly made it through but not quite. Six tanks knocked out, and three half tracks burned. Many figures in gray spread around the Russian position; many figures in Russian khaki as well.   Shulgin went over to the gun whose crew had fought the fascists hand-to-hand around the barrel. Only three were left.

"Tovarish artillerist, let me help you with your gun."

They nodded, dumbly, still in shock at the ferocity of the fight. In the gloom of the near-night, the survivors of the Russian force started manhandling the anti-tank guns back to their start line. Falling back before the fascist artillery could pound them in their positions.

"Tovarish Shulgin, I must inform you that Sasha has been killed. I wish you to take his place." The Company Commander looked tired and gray. Shulgin looked around. As far as he could see, the company was reduced to 10 to12 soldiers and only one of the lieutenants still lived. *Why?   What had this attack achieved, they'd seized the ridge, then just given it up?* It didn't make sense. His company had been chewed up again, for nothing. He shook his head sadly, they'd advanced this evening, he'd thought he was a few steps closer to his home in Kineshma on the Volga but now they were back where they'd started.

The Company Commander looked at his new Sergeant Major and knew just what was running through the man's mind. *It was so easy to explain in a classroom. A spoiling attack, one that pinned down an enemy unit, bloodied it so it wouldn't be able to fight somewhere else. A fascist plan ruined, their units wrong-footed. So easy to say in a classroom. How to tell it to a man who was helping push an anti-tank gun because not enough of its crew were left alive to do it for themselves?* The Company Commander lead the way back through the darkening woods in silence because he lacked the words to explain what they'd achieved this evening. He didn't think the words existed, not in any book a man might want to read.

Curly *Battery B, US Navy 5th Artillery Battalion, Kola Peninsula.*

"Early for dusk?" Commander James Perdue spoke cautiously. The darkening sky seemed threatening somehow. It shouldn't have; the snow had finally stopped and there was but a light sprinkling still coming down. It was the clouds that did it. The setting sun was between them and the ground so the light reflected off the overcast, drenching everything in a sinister yellow glow.

"It's those clouds." Captain Walker McKay confirmed it. "They're bringing down the dusk a whole hour early. At least they'll keep the warmth in."

That was one of the lessons of the Kola Peninsula. A clear night was incredibly beautiful, the stars shone brilliantly, the moon seemed larger than it should – but the same clear, dry air sent the temperature plummeting downwards to depths that were killing cold. A clouded night was better, even if one couldn't admire the stars.

Perdue looked around again. The Russian ASTAC work crews were already clearing the tracks of the last splattering of snow. The Allied Strategic Transport Administration Committee had been one of the first organizations founded when the Americans had started to arrive in Russia. Supplies that were desperately needed on the front had been piling up in Vladivostok instead. The Americans wanted to move them and were prepared to do whatever it took to get the supplies shifted. So were the Russians. The problem had been coordinating the two. ASTAC had grown as a result; an organization flung together out of American, Russian and Indian transport experts to make sure the railways, ports and Air Bridge worked to maximum efficiency. The Americans had been shipping in track, rolling stock and traffic management expertise. The Indians had built the Afghan and Persian railways. The Russians had put in the backbreaking labor to keep everything running.

It was something that left the Americans quietly in awe, the grim, silent determination of the Russians that they would not be beaten. Not by the weather. Not by the Germans. Not by anybody or anything. Quietly, at night, the American officers asked themselves one question about their allies. *How could the Germans have thought that these people would ever give up?* Even after the frightful battering they had taken in 1941 and 1942, the Russians had fought on; on the front lines, deep in their own rear areas to produce the tools their army needed, deep in the enemy rear as partisans. The work crews here had labored with that same grim determination. They were supposed to keep the tracks clear for the great guns to use, and they were going to do just that.

Captain McKay had already left *Curly* and was well on his way towards *Moe* 400 yards away when the air raid sirens went off. At first Perdue thought it was the siren warning of an outbound shoot or inbound artillery fire so rare was the air raid warning. It took a second or two for the wailing's real identity to sink in. By then, muscle memory had taken over and he was running for the shelter of *Curly's* locomotive. He'd just made it when four Focke-Wulf 190s swept over the hill, their wingtips almost touching, their noses and wings sparkled with the flashes of their cannon and machine guns.

Almost as soon as they had appeared, the twin 40mm guns that surrounded the railway artillery battalion opened up. Twelve mounts, two one each train, six on the ground surrounding the site, all with on-mount radar fire control. German fighter-bomber tactics were different from American. American pilots would have gone for the anti-aircraft guns first and come back for the trains. The Germans made a straight line for their primary targets, the three railway gun trains.

Perdue heard the concussion of the aircraft bombs going off. *Eleven hundred pounders? Sounded like it.* Then the crash was drowned out by a rippling, tearing noise. He knew what that was. German aircraft carried a container was filled with hundreds of two-pound fragmentation bombs. They'd be released at low level and would shred anything not under cover. Perdue flinched and tried to squeeze himself deeper under the protective bulk of the locomotive. Then, the crackle of bombs and the roar of the engines was gone and there was a strange, eerie silence. At last it was broken by the wail of the "all clear."

He got up, looking around at the sight of the artillery unit. It didn't seem too bad. A lot of smoke and obviously some fires somewhere, but not so bad.

"Sir, Commander, Sir." One of the young Lieutenants was gasping for breath. "Captain McKay is dead. They got him in the open. Your orders, Sir?"

Perdue looked at him. "Get me a status report now. I want to know the exact condition of each of our guns. And their trains."

Perdue didn't actually know whether he was in command or not. With Captain McKay dead the command devolved upon the senior gun commander. That would be Commander Dale with *Larry*. Somebody had to do something though, somebody had to be in charge and Dale could always take over later.

"Sir, *Larry's* locomotive took a direct hit, it's gone. Commander Dale is missing." *Well, that solved that.* "The railway lines have been torn up. It looks like the 190s carried two 1,100 pounders each and one of those cluster bomb things. We can't move any of the trains, even if the locomotives were working."

"What's wrong with *Curly* and *Moe*?" Perdue turned around, *Curly's* locomotive was swathed in steam."

"Both damaged sir, strafing hits."

"Very well. Get the commander of the ASTAC unit over here."

The Lieutenant doubled away, then came back a few minutes later with an engineer.

"Tovarish Major." An idle thought ran through Perdue's mind. *If his father had heard me using the Russian "comrade" so familiarly when growing up, he'd probably have taken a strap to my backside.* "How soon can we repair the tracks?"

The Russian pursed his lips, thinking. "By mid-day tomorrow certainly. If these were normal trains, we could do it much faster than that but these heavy guns? They are more tolerant of bad tracks than normal railway wagons but still we must take very good care to make sure the tracks are bedded down properly."

Perdue nodded. It was too long. "How badly is the bombed locomotive wrecked? Can we use some parts from it to repair the other two?"

It was the Russian's turn to nod. "We can. Or my men can repair the parts that are damaged. But only two locomotives. The bombed one will never move again."

"Then we need only repair two lines then yes? How soon can we manage that?"

"By dawn. Certainly by then, if your men can help as well."

"Very good." Perdue looked around. The ridge to the west of them was stained by a column of black smoke where one of the Focke-Wulfs hadn't escaped the anti-aircraft guns. "I will give orders that every available man not needed for the guns will join you."

Perdue walked over to the command carriage and sat down with the communications lines. Ten minutes later, he had a better picture of what was going on. There were three German thrusts. One from Finland that was biting deep into the Canadians holding that front. A second between Lakes Ladoga and Onega. The Russians had pulled a fast one, a pre-emptive attack with their 161st Rifle Division. The division had been chewed up, badly, but they'd knocked the Germans off balance. That thrust was stymied. The third thrust was due south. That was reported to be moving up relatively fast. It would be at his position shortly after dawn, assuming the Germans fought through the night. They probably would. Some of their units had the new-fangled night fighting equipment.

Three thrusts, obviously aimed at encircling and destroying the troops holding the southern part of the Kola Front. Perdue had his orders. If he couldn't get his guns out, he was to blow them up. The Germans must not be allowed to capture them.

Perdue looked at the three great railway guns. In his heart, he knew that blowing them up and exfiltrating his troops was the right way to go. The Germans would move fast, even at night. His unit couldn't stand off the forces that were reportedly moving up on him. If he wasn't careful, his guns could be captured in the chaos of a night action. But, although it was the sensible decision, he wrote it off. *Larry* was beyond saving. With its locomotive gone, it couldn't be moved. He'd shoot with it all night if he could then blow it up. But *Curly* and *Moe* could be saved. Perdue decided that he would be damned before he'd blow them both up as well.

Front Held By The 3rd Canadian Infantry Division, Kola Peninsula, Russia

The lakes had been the way through. Ever since the Continuation War had started, the lakes had been barriers to an attack. In summer, they were impassible, they were large enough to need a full-scale amphibious operation to cross and that would alert the defenses the other side. In winter, they were thickly iced enough to cross but the hard sheet gave no cover and any infantry that tried would be exposed as the machine guns cut them down. That was just a way to commit suicide. Normally; not this time.

The storm had been the worst in living memory. It had blanked the moon out for days, leaving the nights pitch-black. Its sub-zero cold froze the ice unusually thick for the time of year and it had dumped almost three meters of snow on top of that ice. That had provided cover and turned what had been a barrier into a highway through the Canadian defenses. A highway that Lieutenant Martti Ihrasaari and his platoon had exploited. Now, they were deep behind the Canadian positions, blocking the road that the Canadian unit behind them would have to use for its retreat.

The Canadian unit had been hit in front by artillery fire and a determined infantry assault. The Canadians weren't Germans whose orders from the top had always been to hold their ground at any cost. Nor were they Russians who held grimly on out of sheer bloody-mindedness. The Canadians believed in a flexible defense. When hit by prepared artillery barrages, they fell back, out of the line of fire. Then they regrouped and regained ground by counter-attack. A sensible tactic; one that the Finns themselves used. This time they intended to turn it against the Canadian troops.

Ihrasaari's platoon was dug into position, covering the road when the Canadian unit appeared. Mostly infantry moving back, some Universal Carriers. Ihrasaari had already pushed the bolt on his rifle home and was taking careful aim, selecting his target with scrupulous attention. One of the Canadians was showing initiative, watching the men retreating back along the hastily plowed road. *An officer, possibly, an NCO probably. One who was looking after his men and that professionalism would cost him his life.* Ihrasaari took a deep breath, held it and then fired. The man spun around and fell down. First blood.

The bolt on the Moisin Nagant was sticky. They always were. Ihrasaari wrestled with it, bringing the cocking handle up to vertical with repeated blows of his hand then forcing it back. Once the adhesion in the chamber was broken, it worked smoothly enough but that initial bout of struggling took too much time. By the time he'd leveled the long rifle back to aim at the Canadians, they'd gone to ground and were firing back. Their Lee-Enfields didn't have bolts that glued up with lacquer deposits in the chamber. Ihrasaari didn't know what size force he was up against. *Probably a point platoon for an infantry battalion, but they had more firepower than I do.*

His own machine guns were hammering, spraying their bullets at the Canadian riflemen. There was a streak across the battlefield. One of the Finnish Panzerfausts had scored a direct hit on a Universal Carrier, dissolving it in a fireball. Almost instantly, the Panzerfaust gunner died. A grenade, launched from one of the many launcher rifles the Canadians had, exploded over his head. The crackle of fire from the sub-machine guns that dominated the battle. The Finnish Suomis and the Canadian Capstens exchanged bursts as the gunners tried to pin each other down. The two guns were evenly matched. There wasn't that much difference between the 7.62 Tokarev and the 9mm Parabellum although the real nitpickers reckoned the extra penetration of the 7.62 gave it an edge. The Suomi was more controllable though.

It was the racket of the grenades going off that would decide the battle though. As always, the Canadians were throwing them around in profusion. These days every Canadian soldier seemed to have a shoulder bag full of the evil little Mills bombs. They'd been shocked by the firepower of the German assault rifles and this had been part of their answer, hand grenades used in extra-large quantities. Every time Canadian troops moved, they did so behind a shower of Mills grenades.

Ihrasaari fired again, cursing the sticky bolt on his rifle and the long length that made it difficult to aim. Long rifles had almost gone from the Russian Army. They used either the M44 Mosin Nagant carbine, the PPS-45 or the SKS; all short, handy weapons. The Finnish riflemen still had the full length 3-line Mosin Nagant, many of which had been captured back in the glory days of the Winter War. Then it had been 'gallant little Finland' fighting the hulking Russian bully. Now, Finland was just another German ally, to be treated with contempt and hammered whenever the Allies had nothing better to do. He squeezed his shot off at the muzzle-flash of a Capsten. The snow bank exploded upwards as his bullet plowed into it. Then his own cover erupted as a Canadian Bren Gun zeroed in on him.

He felt the sting across his face, probably just ice thrown around by the bullet impacts. *Time to leave.* He slid down the bank and squirmed along to find himself a new position. He froze several times as grenades exploded near him. *Those damned grenade launchers.* They worked in conditions where a mortar would not, where a mortar round would bury unexploded in the snowbanks. The Finns had rifle grenade launchers as well, but not as many nor were they as effective as the Canadian weapons. By the time he got back to a firing position, the firefight was dying down. The Canadians had driven the Finns back, away from their positions on the road, and had dug in. Ihrasaari guessed they were quite pleased by that.

The Finns were pleased as well. They'd forced the Canadian units to dig in along the road. That meant they were fixed in place. Ihrasaari's platoon was one of many that had infiltrated through the snow-covered, frozen lakes and dispersed through the rear areas of the Canadian Third Infantry Division. If the plans had worked, that division had been chopped up into a series of small packets, isolated along the communications line leading to their rear areas. That meant the real work could start, eliminating those small pockets one at a time. Just the way Soviet infantry divisions had been wiped out during the Winter War. Only one uneasy thought disturbed Ihrasaari's mind. *These weren't Soviet infantry divisions. In fact Russian infantry divisions weren't the same as the ones that had been wiped out in 1939. And this was the Continuation War, not the Winter War.*

Headquarters, 71st Infantry Division, Kola Front

"Captain Still would like to see you, Sir." Major-General Marcks stared at his aide coldly. There was a time and place for such remarks. This was neither. The aide whitened slightly and spoke again. "Captain Lang would like to see you Sir."

"Send him in." *This,* Marcks thought, *might be interesting.*

"Sir, thank you for seeing me, Sir."

"Are your orders assigning you to Colonel Asbach's command clear?"

"Very much, Sir, I thank you for giving me this chance. I know I have much to learn and my start here was not good."

"Others have been worse. Is there anything else?"

Lang didn't reply but rubbed his ear reflectively. It was a well-understood silent question. *Was this room secure?* Marcks nodded briefly.

"Sir, the attack we are to launch tomorrow, it's part of a much bigger operation." Marcks remained silent letting the Captain talk on. "It's not just Army forces along the Kola front involved, or the Finns. We are one major part yes, but there is another. The fleet is out, trying to cut the supply convoys to Murmansk."

Marcks nodded. He'd heard that as well. Lang wasn't the only one with well-placed sources.

"Sir, I have friends in OKW. The whisper there is that the naval part has gone very badly. The American fleet was waiting in ambush and our casualties have been very heavy. Worse, the supply lines have not been cut. I thought you should know this."

"Have you told anybody else this news?"

"No Sir. Other than you, my lips are sealed on this. But I thought you should know. You know what happens when operations turn out to be disasters."

Marcks did. The politicians would blame the military high command. High command would deny that its marvelous operations could possibly fail and that they could only be so if they were deliberately sabotaged by the field officers. So scapegoats would be hunted down and given a quick show trial before being hanged. It hadn't always been this way. Once it had been understood that every so often things went wrong. But those days were long gone. Now failure was treason. Those high up would hang those lower down, or be hanged themselves.

"You will continue to say nothing of this Captain. This conversation never happened. And I wish you success in your first field operation tomorrow."

Curly *Battery B, US Navy 5th Artillery Battalion, Kola Peninsula.*

There was another roar as *Larry* hurled a shell south, towards the German lines. There was no specific target. The great gun was firing at random, it was enough that the shells landed inside German-held territory. Technically, it was harassment fire. In reality it was just to wear the barrel out before the gun was blown up at dawn.

The trains were being reorganized. The empty shell and charge wagons were being detached from the trains and moved to one side. They'd be left behind and blown up as well. The remaining ammunition was being concentrated into the magazine cars that were left. The surplus fire control car was being attached to one of the two remaining trains. The anti-aircraft wagons from *Larry* split between *Curly* and *Moe*. One of the two locomotives had already been repaired and was moving backwards and forwards, getting the consists sorted out. Come dawn, this whole area would be abandoned. The ASTAC engineers were already planting demolition charges on the lines. That was something the Russians had down to a fine art. When they pulled out, there was nothing left but scorched earth.

"What's the word?" *Moe's* gun captain spoke quietly in the silence between *Larry's* roars.

"Huns are advancing all right. They've pushed the Russian infantry down south back and bust a hole wide open in the front. There's tanks and armored infantry probing north, they'll be here by mid-morning. Just to make life interesting, the Finns have caved the

Canadian Third Infantry in and they're edging east. Looks like the plan is to bag the whole of the Kola Front. Anyway, that's the bad news.

"Good news is that the weather has cleared. There's F-61 intruders up already. They're hunting the German supply columns. The poor innocent lambs think they can move at night without the Black Widows finding them. Or the ones that haven't tried it do. The rest of the Kola Air Force will be covering us come dawn. We'll have Grizzlies trying to blast a way through if we need them. Which I rather suspect we might."

"What are our orders? Any changes."

"Nope. Still get the guns out if we can, blow them up if we can't. Err on the side of caution. These guns and their fire control must not fall into German hands. *Larry's* a write-off but we'll try and get the other two out. Take a look at this."

Perdue spread a map out on the deck of the battalion command car. "The bridge will be fixed well enough for us to cross by dawn. Then we'll head north along this line here. It's a straight run, no real problems except for fuel and the Mikado locomotives can burn wood if they have to. Lucky they're not oil-fuelled. The Russians are setting up a stop line here, using the White Sea Canal as a base. Once we're over that, we can set up again and get back to work."

"Suppose the lines are gone? If they've been hit here, they may have been taken down elsewhere."

"I thought of that, that's why we're taking some extra cars along. We'll persuade the ASTAC engineers to ride with us, that's why I wanted to speak with you now. They'll want to stay and try and hold back the Germans but we need them to help get the guns out. Anyway, it's a waste of good railway engineers to throw them away as second-line infantry fighting panzers. So, I'll order the commander to bring his men with us. He'll argue, then you join in and we all stress how much we're going to need them around to get the guns out."

Larry crashed again, sending another of its dwindling pile of shells south.

CHAPTER SEVEN
A KILLING COLD

HMCS Ontario *Flagship, Troop Convoy WS-18 en route from Churchill to Murmansk*

"Message from the Yanks, Admiral."

"I do hope it's a bit more informative than the first one.

Captain Charles Povey took a deep breath. The first message had been "Sighted German Fleet, sank same" which hadn't been terribly informative. Melodramatic certainly, even by Yank standards. It had at least slowed down the process of planning a battle in which a couple of light cruisers would take on a whole battle fleet. They'd got to the point of getting in to the middle of the German fleet, firing at everybody and hoping the Germans would hit each other in the crossfire. It had worked with MTBs in the Baltic, sometimes.

"Well, let's hear it then?" Admiral Vian was impatient. He hadn't been looking forward to that battle and needed to know that he wouldn't have to fight it.

"Americans have finished recovering their carrier planes. They've lost more than four hundred aircraft." A set of low whistles and the sounds of teeth being sucked filled the bridge. "They're claiming they've got the lot. There are some smaller ships, a cruiser and a couple of destroyers last seen heading south east, probably towards Norway, but they've been hammered badly and Halsey isn't going after them. Not with his planes anyway. By the sound of it his air groups are pretty shot up. But all eight battleships and three carriers are confirmed sunk."

Cheers echoed around the bridge, spreading throughout the ship as the word passed from man to man. As always, shipboard rumor spread the word faster than even the most sophisticated communications system could manage. Vian shook his head sadly. "We're at the end of an era gentlemen. After today, nobody will take battleships seriously any more. The Old Queen has handed her throne to her successor. What's Halsey going to do now? Any offers?"

"He's got to pull back, meet up with his support groups and get some replacement aircraft. Then, I guess, he'll take a swing at the north of Ireland, just to remind the Huns it's still business as usual, before going home to bomb up again. God knows how much ammunition he's thrown at those battleships."

"Sounds about right. Anyway, our way's clear to Murmansk. Order the convoy to make full speed, we've got a Canadian division to deliver. And, by the sound of things, they're going to be needed."

Bridge Wing, USS Charles H. Roan, *DDE-815, North Atlantic*

Captain Hubert Wilkens knew that what he was seeing would haunt his sleep for the rest of his life. The sea was covered with wreckage, some shattered, some burned, some just strewn around. As *Charles H Roan's* searchlight flickered across the scene it saw many other things as well. Bodies floating in the sea; hundreds, no thousands, of them. Some were just floating in the sea. Others were sprawled across wreckage.

"Air temperature is 15 degrees Fahrenheit Sir. With wind chill, its about ten below. Water temperature, 26.45 degrees. That's a killing cold, Captain."

Wilkens nodded. His eyes scanned across the dreadful scene. He could feel the bitter cold biting through him, even here in the shelter of the bridge wing, wrapped up in the warmest clothing the United States Navy could provide. *Perhaps it was a mercy that the water was so cold, the sheer shock of going into it could kill a man and even if he survived that, his survival time was measured in a very small number of minutes. It was a quick death.*

"Sir, movement out there!"

"Where away?"

"Directly on the port beam Captain." The searchlight scanned across and illuminated a crude raft, made from timber strapped to what appeared to be oil drums. It had sides, giving whoever was on it some protection from the wind. Behind him, Wilkens heard the whine as the power-operated 40mm quad mount swung to bear on the raft.

"*Taney* Justice Sir?"

"No. These are surface sailors, not U-boats. Anyway, there's a lot they can tell us. If anybody is alive on that raft, we'll pick them up. Get scrambling nets over the side. Detail a rescue team to check the bodies there for survivors."

The *Roan* pulled alongside the makeshift raft and four figures climbed down the nets. There was a pause for a couple of minutes then a voice came over the radio link. "Sir, twelve men here, three alive, just. An officer, two ratings. We'll need some help to get them up. They're literally frozen stiff."

Wilkens gave the orders and looked at the scene. The sea seemed jelly-like somehow, as if it were on the point of freezing and only kept from doing so by its constant, restless motion. Already *Roan* was accumulating ice where the spray was hitting her rails and plating, freezing solid in an ever-increasing white coat that was adding to her topweight by the minute. The northern North Atlantic wasn't a friendly place for destroyers. Across the TBS radio, he could hear other destroyers from the Battle Line screen searching the field of floating wreckage; hunting for any other sailors who had beaten fearful odds and survived long enough for the destroyers to pick up. There were a few triumphant calls as more isolated patches of survivors were found and brought on board. They were pitifully few. In his heart, Wilkens guessed that the death toll here had to be the worst in naval history. *How many? Twenty, thirty thousand men? The Germans had overly large crews on their ships.*

"Any idea how many?" His voice echoed around the frozen bridge.

The OOD knew what Wilkens meant. "We're running a count Sir, so far, less than a couple of hundred. Message from Admiral Lee, Captain. The Battle Line is casting to the south east and east but they report no contacts. Looks like the fly-boys got the last of them. He's ordering us to finish sweeping this area for survivors before rejoining the Battle Line."

"Make it so." Wilkens thought for a second. "Close up anti-submarine crews, maintain full sonar watch. If there's a Type XXI around here, I'm not giving him a free shot. If the sonar crew as much as sniff a submarine, we go for it."

"Very good, sir."

Wilkens stood on his wing, looking out across the debris field to the dim shapes of the other destroyers methodically searching. After a while he felt his engines pick up slightly. They'd reached the end of the wreckage field. If there were other survivors out there, they'd lost out.

"Any sign of any of our pilots?"

"No sir."

That figured. Most of the lost Corsairs and Skyraiders had either blown up in mid-air or plowed into the sea so fast their pilots had little chance of escape. The chances of survival when pressing home attacks from wavetop height were very poor. In this battle, ships, planes and men had survived together or died together. There had been very few who had found a middle way.

"Sir, Doc Tulley wants to see you, the German officer we picked up has recovered consciousness."

Wilkens left the bridge and found his way down to the sickbay. Doc Tulley was waiting outside. "Captain, one man has come around, the officer. He's in a bad way. Exposure, frostbite, you name it. His temperature is 81 degrees, it's a miracle he's alive. We're trying to do core warming and we're using a new trick, inhalation warming, getting him to breathe heated air. If it's enough, I don't

220

know. I don't think anybody has ever picked up men this frozen who were still alive."

"Core warming?"

"Preferentially warming his body, with hot water bottles and bricks the boiler rooms have been heating, but not his arms and legs. The army has found if you warm those, cold, acid blood from the extremities flows back to the body and stops the heart."

"Will he make it?"

"He might. If gangrene doesn't set in. If he doesn't develop a pneumonia we can't control. We have some penicillin on board, so he has a chance."

The sickbay was oven-hot; the heating turned up to maximum in an effort to get some warmth into the frozen men who had been brought on board. Wilkens sat down by the bunk. The man in it was breathing hoarsely, his face a mass of red chaps and cold-blisters.

"I am Captain Hubert Wilkens, Commanding Officer, the United States destroyer *Charles H. Roan*. Is there anything I can get for you?"

The voice was so distorted it was hardly recognizable, as if the cold had frozen and broken his vocal chords. "Captain Christian Lokken, battleship *Gneisenau*. My men, any saved?"

"A few, not many." Wilkens decided to keep the news of just how few to himself.

"You picked us up." The hoarse, faint, cracked voice sounded surprised.

"Admiral Lee, commander of the Battle Line detached some of his destroyers to search for survivors." Again Wilkens decided to be economical with the truth, the orders had been to search for shot-down pilots. Nobody had expected any German survivors.

"The Battle Line." Lokken seemed shocked. "Battleships also, how many?"

"Ten."

The number seemed to stun Lokken although he should have know it. His voice faded even more. "It was all for nothing. If we had survived the jabos, we would still have lost. This was surely our death ride."

Captain's Bridge, KMS Lutzow, *South west of the Battle Line, North Atlantic*

There was no reason why they should still be afloat. *Lutzow* had taken three more torpedo hits and her superstructure was a mass of tangled, unrecognizable wreckage. She was still moving backwards. Her engines thudded with the grim determination to get her crew to safety. Her pumps strained beyond their maximum capacity to keep the flood waters at bay. Captain Becker had organized bucket chains to try and keep the flooding from overcoming them. They were helping a little, not much but a little. They were keeping the survivors of the crew busy and their minds away from the water that was, despite all their efforts, slowly gaining on them.

Off to port, their last destroyer, *Z-27*, was painfully keeping up with them. She was crowded. She'd picked up survivors from *Z-28* after that destroyer had been battered into a wreck during the last, furious, American assault. Becker had been listening as *Scheer* went down, too crippled to evade the horde of aircraft that had studded her with their torpedoes then drenched her with bombs and rockets. It had been a miracle that *Lutzow* had survived; a miracle Becker didn't understand, he could just accept that it had been so.

Then, they'd had another miracle. He'd got the reports from his shattered ship and realized there was no way he could make Norway. It was more than 350 miles away. At his painful 6 knots, backwards, that meant almost three days transit. His ship simply could not stay afloat that long. But, southwest, that was different. He was only just over 130 miles away from Torshaven in the Faroe Islands. Less than a day's transit and he could make that. Just. So he'd swung his stern southwest and started the long, painful journey. Six hours later, he'd detected a large formation of ships. They were obviously enemy but had crossed his path, some 30 miles behind him, heading east. At a guess, the Amis had detached surface ships to mop up any survivors. He'd read somewhere that was their doctrine; carriers batter the enemy, then surface ships move in for the kill. Only, his change of course for the Faeroes had meant they'd missed him.

"Damage report?"

"We're holding our own, Captain. The bucket brigades are helping a little and the pumps, well, they're far above their rated capacity. The old girl is fighting hard, Sir."

Becker nodded. "And we can save her yet. We can't get into Thorshavn, but we can beach her outside. Then we can get the crew ashore. If *Z-27* makes it, she can probably get into the harbor." Becker laughed grimly. "It looks like the Faeroe Islands have just acquired a Navy."

Admiral's Bridge, USS Gettysburg *CVB-43, Flagship Task Force 58*

"Sir, aircraft secured, pilots are sleeping it off. We've got an initial debrief, we'll do some more details tomorrow. Our F7Fs are spotted on the deck, ready to go if there's a need."

"Any word from Admiral Lee?"

"No, Sir. They've done a sweep south and east of the kill zone, they found nothing. Formation Nan must have got the cripples. He's complaining bitterly Admiral. He says you might at least have left him something for his guns. Oh, and the destroyers have picked up some survivors from the German ships. They're in a pitiful state Admiral; the cans are doing what they can." The Exec thought for a second. "Sorry Sir, that was a horrible pun."

"I'll forgive it. Any word on our pilots?"

"Mariners picked up a dozen; floatplanes from the cruisers about the same. A few ditched close enough to the screen to be picked up, total of about 30. As for the rest, we'll have to assume they're gone Admiral. On board the carriers, we've about seventy or eighty with wounds and burns from deck crashes. We've got around 400 dead in all. Group Sitka says it's lost about 200 with the same number wounded. They're heading west for Churchill and a repair yard."

"Pass word out to the groups. We'll pull back; west then south west. All groups to make up a strike wave to hit whatever targets we have listed in the Londonderry area. Since we're passing, we might as well make use of what munitions we have left."

The Exec consulted his flipboard. "We're OK for land attack munitions. Lots of HE stuff, we didn't use much of that. We're out of Tiny Tims and rocket bombs, pretty much out of torpedoes and badly down on armor piercing 2,000 pounders, 1,600s and 1,000s. We've hardly any 500s. We're low on chemicals for napalm as well. We can give one set of land targets a good seeing to. Wouldn't be wise to hang around too long though."

"Agreed. The courier plane is ready?" Halsey had spent hours writing up a detailed account of the battle. What had gone right, what had gone wrong, the lessons to be learned. It was only a preliminary document. The day's action would be as closely and avidly studied as any in naval history. There was a naval historian on board, a man called Morison. He would be writing the popular history of the battle, one that would be a rare example of a history written by an expert who had actually seen the events in question. That raised an interesting point. "I guess we have to give a name to this battle."

He walked over to the chart and looked down. It was smeared and smudged with the notations that had been put on it in the frantic planning that had taken place over the last 24 hours. Halsey wished he could put on his reading glasses but they wouldn't fit the image, not here on his command bridge. The nearest patch of land was a small group of islands about 250 plus miles south west of them. The problem was that he couldn't make out the name.

"These islands here. What are they?"

Across the chart table Ensign Zipster glanced at the map. He couldn't make out the name either, but he was aware of the need for a young Ensign to impress his Admiral at every chance. Anyway, there was only one group of Islands north of the UK wasn't there? The British had a naval base in them or something. "They're the Orkneys Sir." Zipster spoke with authority, tinged with a slight level of condescension that nobody else had known.

Halsey looked at him sharply. He hadn't missed the inflection in the voice. Still, it was the information he needed. "Very well then, We'll call it the Battle of the Orkneys."

Airbase Muyezersky-5, Karelia, Kola Peninsula

Despite the Russian work teams who had been out all night, there was still slush on the runway. Just enough to drag on the wheels and lengthen the A-38Ds take-off run. Captain John Marosy mentally calculated how much the effect was likely to be as he ran his R-3350 engines up. His hands moved, dropping the flaps to the 20 degree setting, while his eyes watched his instruments as the engine temperature climbed. The R-3350 was a temperamental beast with a habit of eating cylinders when it overheated. A valve's temperature would climb beyond the limits and burn. Then the head would disintegrate and chew up one of the eighteen cylinders. Next, the cylinder would go airborne and chew up the whole engine. At that point the hydraulic fluid would be lost and he wouldn't be able to feather the prop. It would over-speed and come off, slashing at the fuselage on its way. Usually at that point, the whole engine would seize and twist right off the wing. On the whole, it was better not to let the engines overheat.

He was pressing hard on the brakes but *Hammer Blow* was still shifting forward. Ready or not, it was time to go. Up ahead of him, the runway clearance crews saw the A-38 start to pick up speed and scattered to clear the way. Most of them anyway, a few took the chance of stopping to clear one last spadeful of slush before jumping clear. Then, the white and gray A-38 raced past them, its twin tail lifted as the aircraft picked up speed. A few waved as he passed but Marosy didn't respond, not now. His hands were full dealing with the Grizzlies take-off run. Like most over-powered aircraft, its flying characteristics were unforgiving. The torque on its take-off run was as much as he could control. Ground-looping would be a sad way to start a mission. Embarrassing.

Marosy blinked as *Hammer Blow* rotated and lifted over the snowfield. The storm had past and the air was crystal clear, the early morning sun reflections off the snowfields blinded him. Blinded wasn't an understatement, snow-blindness was a real problem. That was why the Americans had brought along one of the war's less obvious secret weapons. Sunglasses; available in huge quantities. They were bringing them in by the millions and distributing them as needed. The wire-framed dark glasses had even become something of a fashion statement back home. Those who could get them flaunted them. Beside him *Lightning Bolt* had moved into position on his wing. There were supposed to be four aircraft in this formation but *Angelina* had been one of the aircraft destroyed in the A-4 bombardment while *Worst Nightmare* had developed engine trouble and been pulled from the flight line. That left just two.

"Where are we going?"

In the back, Sergeant Bressler had his map spread out on the table. Originally, the second crewman on the A-38 had controlled the two twin .50 machine guns in remote controlled turrets. The D-model had those stripped out and replaced them with four fixed guns in the outer wing panels. The reduction in weight had reduced the strain on the engines and added a little to maximum speed. Now, the second crewman served only as a navigator and radio operator. He was vital in that role. He could speak with the forward air controllers on the ground and leave the pilot to worry about avoiding German flak.

"Hitting an armored column moving up from the south. Its threatening one of the Navy's railway gun batteries so we're to slow it down a bit. Steer course 178, hold altitude, 2000 feet. We're about 15 minutes out."

"Armored. Panzers?"

"Panzer-grenadiers. According to the recon patrols, it's a mixed column. Mostly mechanized infantry with an armored car unit and a self-propelled artillery battery."

Marosy sucked his teeth. Panzer-grenadiers meant flak, a lot of it. Each half track had a 20mm gun and there would certainly be at least one quad twenty or twin thirty. And that wasn't the worst of it. If there were infantry, there would be spirals. They'd only appeared in the last few months and weren't that effective but they were yet another thing to worry about. He scanned downwards, trying to pick out the vehicles on the ground against the glaring snowfields. There were theoretical armchair "experts" who decried camouflage, who would point at the vehicles on display or in pictures and sneer that the elaborate paint schemes didn't fool him. Well, it was interesting that people like that were very keen to fire off their opinions but very reluctant to get involved in any other form of firing.

Up here, trying to spot white vehicles against a white background, camouflage was very effective. It cost aircraft. It meant that the Grizzlies had to stay higher so they could search more

226

effectively, then dive down for their attacks. That gave the Germans a few seconds of warning, time for them to start to disperse and get their guns lined up. *No,* Marosy thought, *camouflage was effective all right.*

His eyes continued scanning downwards, looking for the tell-tale signs of a vehicle convoy moving. It could be anything; tracks on the snow although thickness and freshness made that unlikely. The vehicles would be moving on the roads. He wouldn't see the roads themselves, they were white as well, but he might see the shadows. The sharp, clear sun was a friend as well as an enemy. It cast shadows of banks and vehicles where the object itself wasn't so easily seen.

In fact, it was the sun that helped him, although it worked in a different way that he had expected. His eyes caught a flash on the ground, a reflection off a windshield perhaps, or a pair of binoculars. Whatever it was, it caught his attention and focused him on a section of road underneath. That's when he saw the vehicles and knew that they had seen him. Given the snarl of four R-3350s and the altitude he was flying at, they would have had to be blind, deaf and stupid to have missed the pair of Grizzlies. They were dispersing as much as the ground and the snow let them. He knew for certain that they were getting their flak ready.

"*Lightning Bolt,* I've got them. 11 o'clock, about two miles out. There's a ridgeline over at 3 o'clock. We'll run from behind that."

"Got you, *Hammer Blow.*"

Marosy put *Hammer Blow* into a long curving dive, heading for the terrain masking provided by the ridgeline. The two Grizzlies would make their first run from there, trying to see the anti-aircraft vehicles and pick them off with their 75mm guns. The ground swept up. The ridge masked the position of the German unit as the Grizzlies leveled out behind it. Then, the two aircraft swung around, skimmed the top of the rise and went straight at the German half tracks. They'd already spread out, trying to reduce the casualties when the inevitable napalm drops started. The first flicker of tracers were already starting to lick out. These days, every German half-track had a 20mm cannon, the days of the vehicles having rifle-caliber machine guns were long gone. That was why the A-38 had replaced most of the other twin-engined ground attack aircraft; its 75mm gun could knock out the flak guns from outside the range of the 20mm.

Marosy saw one of the half-tracks giving a dense stream of tracers. It had to be a quad-twenty vehicle; probably the biggest threat. He lined up and squeezed the firing trigger. The aircraft lurched as the 75mm in its nose fired. Through the muzzle flash he saw his first round had landed short. His second was a little to the left but the third turn the half-track into a red and orange fireball. Then, he saw something else, streaks of gray smoke leaving the ground and heading for him. Spirals.

Mechanized Column, 71st Infantry Division, Kola Peninsula

"Disperse! Get those vehicles separated. Gunners open fire when you have the target." Colonel Asbach yelled the orders out. They had little time to prepare for the attack that had suddenly developed. They'd seen the Grizzlies of course, and heard their engines. For a while it seemed that the Ami jabos had missed them and would head off south. Then, the aircraft had turned slightly towards them, before diving away to the west. Everybody in the column knew that they had been spotted. That meant the column would soon be fighting for its life.

At the rear of the column the six self-propelled 150mm howitzers were frantically backing up, trying to get clear of the rest of the column. Their trucks were doing likewise and doing a better job of it. The English-built AECs were renowned for their ability to cope with bad conditions. When they worked at all. The British truck workers had a habit of building subtle defects into their vehicles; an axle over-tempered perhaps so it fractured under stress, or a towing bar whose mounting welds would fail when an extra load was put on it. More importantly, they weren't overloaded. The self-propelled guns were. Like most German self-propelled artillery, the guns used captured enemy tank chassis. In this case, some British cruiser tank captured back in 1942. The Covenanter or something similar. It didn't matter, what did was that the chassis was overloaded and clumsy. Still, the battery was better than towed guns.

The two anti-aircraft half tracks attached to the artillery battery had already swerved to a halt. The crews on the quadruple 20mm guns elevated their weapons and scanned for the approaching jabos. Ahead of them, the half-track belonging to the anti tank squad of one of the mechanized infantry platoons had also stopped. Strange figures were emerging from it, looking like running tents with a stove pipe sticking out. The stove pipes were the Panzerschreck rocket launchers, the running tents were the men who were going to be firing them. To his astonishment, Sergeant Heim saw Captain Lang jump from his kubelwagen and run over to that half-track. *What, he wondered, was Captain Still up to now? And would any of the unit survive it?*

"Sergeant! A cape, a Panzerschreck launcher and a Fliegerschreck rocket. Now!" Lang's voice was urgent, there was little time. In the back of the vehicle, the anti-tank unit Sergeant looked doubtful. Captain Still's reputation had spread beyond the artillery unit. Lang's hand dropped to his pistol. "Now, Sergeant."

That did it. The Sergeant passed out the equipment demanded. Lang hurriedly checked the cape. The white side was out. It was shaped like a cone, with two tubes for his arms. He slipped into it, then took the Fliegerschreck rocket and checked the fuse. It was the standard Panzerschreck rocket but fitted with a powerful booster and had a time fuse on the end. Lang dialed it down to minimum, then slipped it into the rocket launcher. The Grizzlies had already come over the ridge and were heading for the unit when Lang got into position. He knelt exactly the way the user manual for the Fliegerschreck said, and aimed the clumsy launcher at the lead of the two aircraft.

Two aircraft, that was odd, the Ami jabos usually flew in fours. Perhaps the A-4 bombardment of their bases had hurt them worse than anybody had expected. Lang hoped so, his contacts on the General Staff had whispered that the navy part of this operation was truly a disaster. *The Amis had to lose somewhere didn't they? And they had no equivalent to the A-4 rocket, the weapon that gave the German artillery the ability to strike deep into the heart of an enemy rear area.* Whatever the reason, there were only two jabos and that gave the mechanized column a fighting chance.

Lang was already starting to sweat inside the clumsy protective cape. The first Panzerschreck launchers years before had required the users to wear protective capes but their back-blast was nothing compared with that of the Fliegerschreck rocket. The booster needed to give the rocket the speed and range necessary to engage an aircraft would immerse the operator in a ball of fire when the rocket ignited. Without the tent-like cape, survival was not an option.

Through the glass panel in the front of the cape, Lang saw the first Fliegerschreck rockets go out. First, the long streak of the booster, then the wild spiral as the Panzerschreck rocket detached for the final spurt. There was something odd about firing things in stages; it didn't work very well at all. Lang had heard that the Peenemunde group's efforts to build two-stage versions of the A-4 had been failures for that reason. They were still trying, still working towards a rocket that could cross the Atlantic and strike at American cities, but the problems were proving intractable. Quietly, one of Lang's General Staff friends had told him it wasn't likely that the multi-stage rockets would be anywhere near usable this decade. Looking at the wild gyrations of the Fliegerschrecks, Lang could see why.

The lead Grizzly, Lang's target, was already firing. Its first two shells had missed, but the third had hit a half-track down the road. Tracers from the 20mm guns were already surrounding it but they seemed to be brushed off by white monster that was coming for him. Lang took a brief breath and settled down, still tracking the target in his sights. It was so tempting to fire, but Lang resisted it. He waited for the optimum moment. Then, he squeezed the trigger and felt the furnace-like heat seep through the protective cape as the rocket soared away.

He watched it fly, needle straight, for the Grizzly. Then the second stage separated. It didn't even have a chance to start spiraling before the time fuse ignited. The rocket exploded almost directly under the starboard engine of the Grizzly. Lang watched the whole nacelle erupt into flames; a brown and red streak stained the sky behind the stricken aircraft as it reared up. Lang saw the propeller detach. It spiralled away and broke up, lashing the fuselage with its fragments. Then, the pilot got the aircraft under control and curved away, still surrounded by the firefly tracers from the 20mm guns. The second Grizzly broke off the attack instantly, moving to cover it's stricken team-mate. That's what the Ami jabos did; they covered each other. Normally, there would have been two more aircraft to carry on with the attack on the unit but not this time. The two Grizzlies disappeared; the one trailing smoke quickly losing altitude.

Land peeled off the cape. The residual heat from the rocket blast stung his hands but he ignored it. There were cheers coming up from the vehicle crews, cheers that lifted Lang's heart. He saw Sergeant Heim running over to help him with the cape and the clumsy launcher.

"Well done Sir! Superb shot! May I ask, sir, where did you learn to use a Fliegerschreck?"

Lang grinned, in relief more than anything else. It was the first time his men had referred to him with anything other than carefully-concealed derision. "I was the adjutant to the head of the team who developed this. It was my responsibility to write the operating manual and to do that I had to know how to use it. I must have fired fifty of these things." Lang good-humoredly wagged his finger at the sergeant. "Never say that doing one's paperwork doesn't have its uses, Sergeant."

A-38D Grizzly Hammer Blow *Over the Kola Peninsula*

Marosy saw the gray streaks coming straight at his aircraft but that didn't mean much. If the spirals flew in a straight line, they could be evaded. The Germans had been more cunning than that. There was a flash as the main rocket separated from the booster, then the Spiral started cart-wheeling through the air, There was no way of predicting where it would go so it couldn't be evaded. A turn could just as easily put the aircraft into the wild gyrations of the spiral as avoid one. It was purely a matter of luck whether the damned thing went into the aircraft or off into the sky. That's what made the spirals so dangerous.

This time, the first salvo of spirals exploded well clear of the pair of Grizzlies. Marosy was lining up his aircraft on one of the self-propelled guns at the rear of the column when there was another streak of gray. This one had no time to start spiraling. It was still going straight when it exploded underneath his starboard engine. He felt the lurch as the R-3350 started to fly apart from the damage; heard the crash as the propeller ripped off the shaft and its fragments tore into the fuselage. Much more importantly, he saw the sea of warning lights as the aircraft's systems started to fail from the damage inflicted by the warhead fragments. There was only one way to interpret those lights; *Hammer Blow* was finished. The best Marosy could hope for was to put her down somewhere reasonably safe. The worst was that the ruptured fuel lines would feed a mid-air explosion.

"Don't look good, boss. We got fire out here." Bressler's voice was deadpan.

"Hitting the extinguishers now." Marosy thumbed the buttons and glanced sideways. The fire subsided a bit, but not much. At this rate, the main wing spar would fail soon. That would mean *Hammer Blow* would lose a wing and spin in. A part of his mind recorded that he had broken off his attack and was trying to separate from the column he had just been attacking. Only a remarkably stupid pilot bailed out over the troops he had just strafed. There had been all too many cases of such pilots being killed on the end of their parachutes or being thrown into the burning wreckage of their aircraft. Another part of his mind recorded the streaks of 20mm tracer around him. Once they had been a matter of concern; now they were almost inconsequential compared with the danger he faced from his crippled aircraft.

"*Hammer Blow*, this is *Lightning Bolt*. You better get down fast, the under surface of your wing is falling apart. Fire is spreading in there."

"Roger that, *Lightning Bolt*. We're losing fuel, oil, structure, ideas and hope. We're going in as soon as I can see somewhere to do it. Well away from the Krauts."

"I hear you, *Hammer Blow*. We're ready to do a pick up."

Marosy looked out in front. There was some flat ground up ahead. The question was whether he could make it. *Hammer Blow* was giving up fast; the port R-3350 was overheating with the stress of keeping the aircraft flying. It was a question of whether he would run out of altitude before he could make somewhere a crash landing was possible. The A-38 cleared one ridgeline but doing the next was almost impossible. *Abort that*, Marosy thought grimly, *clearing the next ridgeline was impossible*. He swung the nose around, feeling the controls stiffen in his hands. Time was running out.

The pine trees were the next problem. *Hammer Blow* couldn't quite clear the trees as she started to belly in. The tree tops lashed at the windscreen, thundered against the structure of the aircraft, and ripped the port propeller apart. Then, the A-38 flopped on her belly into a long, flat patch of snow. It was soft enough to absorb the impact but the crew were still thrown against their straps by the impact. Something caught the port wing, spinning the aircraft around. The tail broke off, sliding away from the main fuselage while the rest of the aircraft skidded to a stop.

"Out, out, out!" Marosy yelled. In the back, Bressler knew if he said 'what?' he would be talking to himself. He flipped up the aft canopy, heaved himself out and started to run. At some point he had grabbed the walkie-talkie kept in the rear compartment; he had no memory of doing so. By the time he and Marosy got to the treeline, *Hammer Blow* was already burning furiously. The explosion that destroyed the aircraft was almost an anticlimax by comparison.

"We're coming in for a pick-up; be ready to get out fast." *Lightning Bolt's* voice was urgent.

"Negative on that *Lightning Bolt*. The snow's feet thick. If you land, you'll ground loop. We're going to have to walk out. We'll try and link with the partisans."

"Roger *Hammer Blow*. We'll spread the word. Good luck and God's Speed."

Marosy knew that was the minimum he'd need. If they didn't meet up with a partisan group, their chance of getting home was slight. "Bressler, time to start walking. North I think."

"Sounds good to me. Damned Spirals."

Curly *Battery B, US Navy 5th Artillery Battalion, Kola Peninsula.*

"Is it safe?"

The ASTAC Major commanding the bridge repair detail stared at the jury rigged repairs, his lips silently moving as he computed the risks. The bridge had been hard-hit by the German railway guns and the earthquake effects of the big shells meant that its structure had been undermined. Had it been fatally undermined? He didn't know. His men – and women - had been working all night to get repairs done but were they adequate to take the weight of the great railway guns? He didn't know that either. Yet the answer to both questions was critical.

"Is it safe, Tovarish Major?"   Commander James Perdue repeated the question. *Larry* was rigged with explosives. C4 demolition charges were wrapped around the vital parts; the breech was stuffed with split propellant bags. The gunners had managed to squeeze fifteen of the bags in, more than 50 percent more powder than the breech was designed to take. Then they'd taken a sledgehammer to drive the tompion solidly into the end of the barrel. The gun crew had made a lot of rude jokes about that. Meanwhile other demolition teams had been at work on the battery fire control center, rigging it with both C4 and the contents of more propellant bags. The battalion fire control center had been detached and added to *Curly's* train, giving the gun both battalion and battery command cars. A number of the magazine cars were empty and they'd been detached to save weight. *Curly* had been reduced from 14 cars to nine; *Moe* to eight. The surplus cars were parked on the sidings, also rigged for utter destruction.

"I think so, yes. But it will be a very near thing. You will send the diesels over first?"

Perdue shook his head. "*Curly* goes first, then *Moe*. Once they're over we'll hook passenger cars to the diesels and send as many over as the bridge will take. Each train is going to damage that bridge a bit more and we have to get the heaviest stuff over first. If the bridge goes, whatever is left this side will get blown up as well." That would include the diesels if they got trapped. They were only shunting engines, intended to move cars around, but they would still be useful to an enemy that was short of rail transport. The partisans had seen to that, they had a talent for devising innovative ways to sabotage steam engines.

"Very well. I wish you luck Tovarish Commander. My men and I will buy you what time we can."

"Tovarish Major, I beg you, please, we need you too much to leave you here. None of my men understand how to repair railway track or work on the lines. We have no knowledge of what the capacities of the tracks are or anything like that. The Hitlerites are all over the place, they may have cut lines, bombed them, shot them up, who knows? If there is damage, we do not know how to repair it. We need you and your men Tovarish; if we are to get these guns out, your experts are vital. And beyond that, skilled railway engineers are worth their weight in gold. Once the bridge has been blown, the fascists will be stuck here for hours anyway. There is little you can achieve by staying here, but there is service of incomparable value you can perform if you come with us. We have room set aside for all your men in the trains. After the miracles they performed last night, we cannot afford to leave you."

The ASTAC Major looked bewildered at the impassioned appeal. Before he had time to commit himself to a refusal, Lieutenant

234

Commander Enright from *Moe* cut in. "Tovarish Major, my Commander speaks nothing but the truth. There is a major fascist offensive going on. The damage in the rear areas will be heavy and we all know the railway lines are the first targets. We will need you and your men if we are to get these guns out."

Major Boldin looked at the two American Navy officers and sighed. Their appeal made sense and he was under no illusions about how little a group of railway engineers armed only with bolt-action rifles could achieve when fighting a panzer-grenadier unit. It was just that he had his own chain of command to worry about.

"Very well. I will order my men to cross the river and wait for your trains there. After that, we will ride with you. For my files, please will you give me a written explanation of why we must ride with you?"

Perdue hid his smile carefully; he had anticipated that. There was still enough of the old days left in Russia to make written orders a valuable commodity. He had already written a paper that explained the problems of getting his guns to safety and how essential the help of the ASTAC unit was. "That can be arranged, Tovarish Major. If you will excuse me for a few minutes I will prepare it for you now."

As Perdue went to get the letter, he saw the ASTAC Major telling his work teams they would be riding with the guns, not staying here to fight. The air of general relief was quite unmistakable. Then, *Curly's* Mikado engine sounding its whistle drove everything else out of his mind. The trains were about to start moving.

The bridge looked as shaky as he had suspected. It had been repaired all right, but the work had been done fast and had used whatever materials were available. As the first train had moved up, the ASTAC work team had flooded over the bridge, combining an urge to run for the safety of the other side with a last check on the hasty repairs. Perdue swung up into the Mikado's cab where the engine crew were getting ready to move off.

"How do we do this? Get over as fast as we can?"

The engine driver spat over the side of the cab reflectively. "No Sir. No way, We take this slow and steady. We try to run over and we'll shake this contraption apart. We take it careful-like and Mike here will get us over."

The engine started to move. The strain of towing the 16-inch gun and the rest of its consist showed in the faces of the cab crew. They were moved steadily forward and watched their speed pick up slowly. The engineer kept the pressure just right to hold at the correct speed. Perdue could tell when the wheels hit the bridge. The sound changed dramatically and he could feel the structure groaning beneath him. He tore his eyes away from the gauges in the cab and looked out at the river below. Then, he wished he hadn't. He could see the train swaying on the bridge and, out of the corner of his eye, what looked suspiciously like bits of the bridge structure falling away to splash in the river below. Ahead, the far side of the river seemed to be receding rather than getting nearer. *That had to be an illusion didn't it?* They couldn't be going backwards.

They weren't. The sound changed again as the Mikado's wheels left the bridge and were once more on solid ground. Perdue jumped down as the train started to slow and went over to the ASTAC officer who was watching with anguished anxiety.

"Well done, Tovarish Major. Your crews did a fine job. We have saved our first gun."

Major Boldin smiled weakly. The American Navy officer hadn't seen the bridge sagging under the train or the supports that had been hammered into place, breaking loose and falling into the river. "Tovarish Commander, can you order your gun to go down the line so we have room for the next. We must hurry, we have little time."

Perdue nodded and spoke into the walkie-talkie radio. The other side of the river, *Moe's* train started to move. He could see why the Russian was so worried. The bridge seemed to be stretching under the weight, only there was no 'seemed' about it. The track was stretching. It had to, the way the railbed on the trestles was arching downwards. He heard the Mikado starting to strain as it pulled *Moe* up the slope to the side of the river. The underside of the bridge now dropped a steady rain of fragments into the river. Finally, the train made it, the Americans and Russians joined in a prolonged barrage of cheers. The guns were over, anything else that made it was a bonus.

The next to try was a diesel shunting engine towing two carriages. The demolition teams were on board those and they had one last job to do before they took the perilous ride over the river. That was to start the fuses on *Larry* and the rest of the gun site working. Once they'd finished, their diesel started to pull them over. By then, the bridge was clearly on its last legs. It swayed from side to side as well as up and down. The fragments that detached from it were larger, obviously from more than just the track bed. The diesel and its carriages made it, just; it was clear nothing else would. The remaining two diesels and the carriages that were left were going to have to go.

As if to emphasize the point, there was a despairing groan from the bridge. Then the whole structure started to collapse into the river. The tracks and rails detached as it fell. The roar of the bridge's descent was drowned out by a massive explosion from the site that the battery had used for so long. Perdue could see the huge cloud boiling over the hill that separated them from *Larry's* explosive demise. It roiled upwards, towering over them, dropping yet more debris into the river that was already three quarters blocked by the remains of the bridge. Unidentifiable objects rained down. Perdue had a nasty feeling they were parts of *Larry's* barrel. Then the original explosion was joined by more than a dozen more as the rest of the rolling stock was destroyed.

"Well, that's it." Perdue was as sad as he sounded. It was a hard thing to blow that gun up.

"Not quite." The demolition engineer had a nasty grin on his face. When Perdue thought about it, he realized that all demolition men had nasty grins, most of the time. "We left a few surprises for the Nazis."

Perdue nodded. *Anything to buy time.* Then he turned to the ASTAC major. "We head east, for Murmansk?"

"I would recommend not Tovarish Commander. The fascists are coming through that way, a right flanking move. They will cut the line soon. We should go west. We can go that way, then pick up a spur line that will take us to the northern trunk line."

"There isn't a spur line on this map."

Major Boldin grinned. This day was his. The bridge had held for the two vital trains, he'd got his people out with all the paperwork to justify it and now he knew something the American did not. "Of course not, Tovarish Commander. To put all our railway lines on a map the fascists may capture? I think not. There are some lines that are not shown on these maps and some that are shown do not exist. That is why we always have guides on trains that are heading off the main routes."

"Very well. West it is." Perdue turned around; he just couldn't resist the chance. He waved his arm like an old-fashioned wagon train guide and gave the time-honored order, "Wagons West!"

Mechanized Column, 71st Infantry Division, Kola Peninsula

The huge pyre of smoke rolled over the trees a few seconds before the rumbling crash of the explosion rocked the column. Colonel Asbach cursed; fluently and with great imagination. The devastating blast had come from the site of the railway guns he was supposed to be seizing. A coup de main wasn't much use if there was no coup to put in the main. His monologue, to which his men listened with great, if discrete, glee, was brought to a halt by another rippling crash of explosions. *That would be the rest of the rolling stock at the site being blown up,* he thought bitterly.

"Right, follow me, We'll see if the Amis have left anything for us to salvage." Not that there was likely to be. The Russians were the skilled ones at destroying things with minimum use of explosives, the Americans just stuffed everything with every type of explosive they could find and blew the whole lot up. *The Amis were like little boys sometimes, obsessed with creating bigger and better explosions.*

"Sir, where are the Ivans?" Captain Lang spoke tentatively. Since shooting down the Grizzly he had gained a little respect and he didn't want to risk it by asking foolish questions.

"First thing Lang. Out here, no salutes and we don't use the word Sir. The Russian snipers are too damned good and there's no point in marking their targets out for them. Secondly, the Ivans?" Asbach waved his hand around and the snow-covered fields and the trees. "They're out there, probably all around us. Regular troops, ski units, partisans; one or all of those is watching us right now."

238

Lang looked dubious. While serving as an adjutant to OKH, he'd heard of defeatism and poor morale being prevalent and a deep concern. This seemed bordering on paranoia though. He couldn't see anybody out there. Then he reflected on his first disastrous days here on the front. Those days made him cringe every time he thought of them. He reflected grimly that, since that time, he had learned just enough to realize that he knew less than nothing about the realities of soldiering on the Russian Front. On the other hand, Asbach was a veteran of the siege of Moscow and had taken part in the almost legendary Operation Barbarossa.

"It's that bad?" Lang hoped that would be an acceptable phrasing of the question.

"Worse. We live and fight in a goldfish bowl. Everybody knows what we do before we do it. I said there's partisans out there; well, you can take that for granted. They're always there. Once winter comes down, ski troops as well." Asbach glanced at the Captain beside him. The man seemed incredulous and suspicious, but was also listening intensely. "Lang, if we go off the roads, how fast can we move."

Lang was about to say 52.5 kilometers per hour, the book maximum speed of the 251 when the incredible stupidity of the comment surged through his mind. He nearly bit his tongue stopping himself. *It was the sort of thing Captain Still would say.* He looked at the deep snow either side of the cleared road and pictured a 251 trying to force its way through. *The wheels would break the crust at the top and the tracks would dig their way in.* He pictured the vehicles floundering, digging themselves in deeper every minute.

"We can't move at all, S...... Asbach."

"Very good, Lang. We're roadbound. Trapped on this road. The partisans live here; they know where to go and what to do. They can go where they want. The ski troops are even worse. You know what division we face here?"

"The 78th Infantry Division?"

"No, Lang, the 78th *Siberian* Infantry Division. The Siberians are born on skis. They grew up in weather than makes Kola seem like a summer resort. They can move cross-country on their skis faster than we can move in our vehicles." Asbach's face went blank for a minute, remembering. When he started speaking again, his voice was small. "We met them outside Moscow for the first time. They came through the forests like ghosts, they'd hit us and vanish into the snows again. We couldn't hold. We had to retreat from Tula but they never stopped slashing at us. We called them the white wolves but no wolf was ever as deadly or as merciless as those Siberians. Any man who was on his own for more than a minute or two would be their prey. They'd slide out of the forest, cut him down and be gone before anybody could do anything about it. We'd find a defensive position, set up our forces and try to hold. Then we would find they were already behind us, hacking up our rear area troops. For two months they drove us back and nothing we could do could stop them. That's the people we are fighting here, Lang. That's why I know they are watching us."

"So why don't they attack?"

"Could be any number of reasons. They may be calling in artillery, or Ami jabos. They could be under orders to watch and report. They may be moving themselves. Just don't ever delude yourself that they're not watching us. They were bad enough before the Amis started giving radios to everybody. Now, they're ten times worse. So, what do you think we should do?" Asbach looked at Lang sharply.

"If they could be calling in artillery, we should keep moving. The Amis will have things like crossroads and bridges pre-registered, we need to avoid them as much as possible." Lang stopped with the realization he was being Captain Still again. "I'm sorry, that's stupid. We're trapped on the roads, we can't avoid crossroads and bridges. We just have to move as fast as we can and hope to keep ahead of any artillery."

"Good man. So, let's get moving. And our first objective?"

"The railway gun site. See what's left, what can be salvaged. Then, once we've fulfilled our primary order of seizing the site, we have a relatively free hand."

"Very good. So we move out." Asbach turned away, a small glow of hope burning inside him. He'd been right; there was a soldier inside Lang, trying to get out. It had been crushed, stifled, by too much work in the rear area, too much contact with the top brass who gave the orders without understanding what it was they were asking, but the spark was there. It just needed to be patiently coaxed into life.

The site that had once been the railway gun battalion was devastated. There was a great pile of steel scrap in to one side. A burst barrel forlornly pointed at the sky; a disemboweled breech had been hurled across the tracks. That had once been one of the guns he had been ordered to try and capture. The tracks had been torn up by other explosions. At the neck of the network of lines were the remains of two lines of carriages headed by diesel shunters. The carriages were burned-out skeletons; the diesel shunters hardly recognizable. The stench of burned wood and the bitter, acrid smell of explosives saturated the area. It was enough to make eyes water. Asbach surveyed the destruction and shook his head. When the Americans had first arrived in Russia, the material they discarded or abandoned when it wasn't convenient to withdraw the stuff would keep a German unit in comfort for weeks. A bit of an exaggeration, perhaps, but the Germans had been stunned by the wealth the Americans couldn't be bothered to save. Only, they'd learned the lessons taught by the Russians well. Now they blew up or burned even their garbage.

That thought perturbed Asbach and he turned around towards where a group of his men were starting towards the wreckage, looking for salvage. "Halt, right there. Nobody move until the area has been checked. Engineers, start looking for booby traps."

It didn't take long to find the first one. A pipe bomb buried beside a pathway that lead to what appeared to be a bunker. The bunker was just a shallow hole dug deep enough to give the impression of a tunnel in the snow. An explosive ordnance disposal man from the engineers quickly defused the pipe bomb and made it safe. Then the engineers started to check the site in detail. Asbach stopped them. There was nothing here worth keeping; all that was necessary was to clear a path through the site. That meant clearing out the main track, that was all.

It was there that they found the real surprise. A thin wire, buried under the snow, leading to a standard push-pull detonator. Only there wasn't just one charge; there were half a dozen, spaced down each side of the main road through the site. If they had been tripped off, the whole column would have been immersed in explosions. It took the bomb disposal expert nearly an hour to defuse the intricate web of charges and detonators. Eventually he did so and stood up, stretching his back.

Fire one shot, they know you are there. Fire two and they know where you are. The sniper, be he a partisan or a member of a ski patrol knew his – or her – job well. Lang heard only a single shot and saw the explosives disposal expert crumple with a terrible finality. He looked at the trees surrounding them and saw nothing. He finally understood what Asbach had been trying to tell him. They were being watched. All the time.

CHAPTER EIGHT
THE ENDLESS SNOW

Somewhere on the Kola Peninsula, Heading North.

"Well, now we have a problem."

The sight before them would, under other circumstances, have been rather beautiful. A landscape covered with a pristine snowfall, unmarred by tracks or stains. Out of it poked small collections of pine trees, spotting the landscape as it dipped down into a shallow valley As the ground rose the other side, the patches of trees grew larger once more. Under these circumstances, the same vista was a depressing sight.

Captain John Marosy and Sergeant William Bressler had been moving through the trees for hours after *Hammer Blow* had been shot down. That made good sense. The snowfall had been too heavy to allow easy going anywhere except where the pine forests provided protection from the worst of the blizzard. Not that staying under the trees was actually easy; it was just less back-breakingly exhausting. Their current problem was a simple one; there were no more trees. It wasn't even a question of backtracking and finding a new way around. The forest in this area was in the shape of a giant hand. They'd been moving down a steadily-narrowing finger of forest for some hours. Going back would virtually take them all the way to the wreck of *Hammer Blow*. Even then, they'd only be able to select a new finger and hope that it ended in a more favorable position.

"We could try and make our way down and across." Bressler didn't sound too happy about that. Marosy didn't blame him.

"No way Bill. We'll be floundering for hours down there. Stuck out in the open like a pair of plaster geese. The snow will have drifted in the valley. It's not too bad up here, but it'll be feet deep down there. And even if we do manage to make any distance, we'll be leaving tracks a blind man could follow."

"So what do we do, Boss? Wait here until somebody finds us, and hope it's the partisans, not the Krauts?"

Marosy thought carefully. "In the short term, yes. We made good time under the trees. We're well clear of the wreck. We'll hole up here until dusk. Try and keep warm and rest. We've got two things running for us. One is that the boys know we're down and they'll be looking. If they find us, they'll send a ski-equipped Dragon Rapide out to get us. The other is that we're in the snap-back after the storm. Temperature is higher than normal for a few hours but it'll drop like a stone tonight. By midnight, the snow will be freezing and crusting and we should be able to make better time if we do have to cross that valley."

"Wouldn't put too much faith in the boys looking for us Boss. We've lost what, twenty, thirty aircraft in the A-4 bombardment? And there's a big Kraut push on. The rest of our boys will be working round the clock. They won't have time to look for us. At best, they'll keep their eyes open going out and coming back."

He was right, of course and Marosy knew it. It was obvious that the German offensive had obviously been carefully planned. They had to have had this stashed away for months, waiting for the conditions to be right.

"There's always the partisans. They'll know a bird went down and they'll be looking for us as well. When they find us, they'll get a message out."

"Provided the Krauts don't get us first. What do we do then?"

Marosy was beginning to find Bressler's pessimism a touch irritating. "We pick a nice strong tree to get hanged from; what do you think?"

Bressler nodded and started looking at the pine trees around them. "That one looks about right. Got a nice view across the valley as well. Especially of the German troops gathering to watch down there."

"Not a funny joke, Sergeant."

"Not a joke at all, Boss. Take a look."

Marosy scanned the tracks at the foot of the valley. Sure enough, in the last few minutes, a group of trucks had pulled up and were disgorging white-clad infantry. He took out his binoculars and had a closer look. They were Germans all right; the banana-shaped magazines on their rifles were all too apparent. Even as he watched them milling round by their trucks, he saw some pointing up at the hills around them.

"Sorry Bill, you're right. Krauts. We'd better get out of here. Back the way we came, we don't have very much choice."

They started edging back through the trees. Marosy paused for one last look. It seemed like most of the Germans were coming his way. *Had they seen a flash of light from his binoculars?* Perhaps they were making a shrewd guess based on the crash site and time elapsed. One good thing, the men were floundering in the snow, it would take them some time to get up to the easier going under the trees. That gave him and Bressler a chance to get clear.

Headquarters, 3rd Canadian Infantry Division, Kola Peninsula

"What's happening out there?" General John M Rockingham wanted information and wanted it now. He was in de-facto command of the 3rd Infantry since General George Rodgers had caught a blast of grenade fragments and gone down. Which raised another point. "And what's happened to the RCAMC post? Have we got it back yet? What are we doing about our wounded?"

The Lieutenant spoke very carefully, his voice clipped to avoid it shaking. "We've recaptured the field hospital Sir. They're all dead in there. They shot the patients in their beds, made the doctors and the nurses lie on the floor and then one of them walked down the line, putting a bullet in each of their heads. Boys are hopping mad about it, Sir. They're in a killing mood now; there's no disguising it. We won't be seeing prisoners any time soon. We've set up an

245

emergency facility using some first aid post people who happened to be here and some of the not-so-badly wounded who learned first aid in the Boy Scouts."

There was a quick pause while the Lieutenant composed himself. He'd seen the scene inside the RCAMC post himself and wouldn't forget it in a hurry. "As for the rest, we're just mopping up now. We've cleared out the snipers. The EYs did a grand job as usual. We've restored the Southern perimeter as well and driven the Finns out. We guess they're retreating. Should we pursue them?"

Rockingham thought for a second. "No. Secure the perimeter, then we'll get set up and get the headquarters back into operation. Lord knows what's happening out there while we've been pinned down. Any prisoners?"

There was a bitter laugh from the Lieutenant. He hadn't exaggerated. After the RCAMC post, there hadn't been any interest in taking prisoners. A couple of the Finns had tried to surrender but they'd been shot or bayoneted, or both. "No, Sir. The Finns are fighting to the last man and the last bullet. No prisoners."

"And nobody prepared to take any I'd guess. Very well. Lieutenant. Pass word around that if we can get some, it would help us find out what the hell is going on here."

"I'll pass the word, Sir." 'And a fat lot of good it will do' was the Lieutenant's unspoken addition.

Rockingham slipped out the Division Office and made his way to the communications office. The Royal Canadian Corps of Signals had their radio sites set up but it was a gamble whether they had any operational capability back yet. He made his way from building to building, keeping well under cover all the time. There were wise words he'd heard from a fellow officer once. 'All situations are tactical until you have proved otherwise for yourself. Never take somebody else's word for it, if you do you could earn the unfortunate distinction of being the last casualty of the battle.'

The firing had stopped and the battle here at the headquarters unit did seem to be over. He reached the RCCS bunker and announced himself. Entering a defended building unannounced was another good way of becoming the last casualty of the battle.

"Have we contact with our forces yet?"

"No, Sir. Re-establishing now. We are receiving but we're not able to transmit yet. We're re-rigging the aerials; we should have that solved soon. We're picking up a lot of transmission from our units, Sir. It seems like the Finns infiltrated between them during the storm and set up road blocks and so on. All our front line units are cut off. They're in a series of hedgehogs, spiny side out, where our front line used to be. They're holding firm but calling out for air and artillery support. It's a mess, Sir. The whole divisional front is a gaping hole, if those hedgehogs collapse, there'll be nothing to stop the Finns going through and rolling up the whole of Second Corps. Or heading north and hitting First Corps in the rear."

"Well, they'd damned well better not collapse then, hadn't they?" Rockingham looked at the map, envisaging what his front like had to look like. "And there's no damned reason why they should. This infiltration and hedgehog trick is all very well. The Finns made good use of it during the Winter War and the early stage of the Continuation War, but those days are gone. We've got more tactical air than we know what to do with and our units are a lot more self-contained. When we get through to the units that have been cut off, tell them they are to hold their ground and not try to break out. We'll come to get them. Tell them that if they run short of supplies, we'll drop them by air. Get that out as soon as we have transmission."

"Sir, we heard about the RCAMC post. Is it true?'

"So I'm told, I haven't seen it for myself." The Signals sergeant swore under his breath, quietly vowing to get word of what had happened out to the front line units. They would take a due and dispassionate revenge for the crime.

Rockingham left the bunker as carefully as he'd entered it. Next thing was to get to the aid post that the survivors of the medical unit had set up and exchange a few rude jokes with the wounded. All part of keeping unit morale up. While he was doing it, he could find out how long General Rodgers was going to be out of action for. Then back to the radio bunker to start coordinating with the units that were cut off. Telling them to hang on, stand fast and wait to be relieved in place was one thing. He had to make sure they could see they were getting the support they needed to do it.

247

"Major Gillespie? A word please." Lieutenant Colonel Haversham had got the orders a minute or so earlier.

"Sir?"

"Divisional headquarters are back on the net. Their general orders to all units are to hold in place; we're not to try and break out. Instead, we will fight our ground where we are. The rest of the division will come and fight their way through to relieve us."

"Makes sense Sir. I've been reading up on what happened to Russian units that got cut off like this. It wasn't being cut off that chewed them up, it was their own efforts to break out. They weakened themselves so much that when the Finns finally moved to liquidate the pockets, there wasn't much the Russians could do to stop them. So we're to stay put?"

"That's right. Rocky's arranging for air and artillery support and says we'll get supply drops if we need them."

"Rockingham's arranging it? I thought he was 6th Division when it finally arrives?"

"He is. I guess General Rodgers is out of it and Rocky has taken over in his place. There's bad rumors coming out of Division. Apparently the headquarters units got chewed up. Including the RCAMC detachment."

"Damn."

"Anyway go spread the word, everybody to dig in deep. Make sure the front line is continuous. The Finns are masters at slipping through any holes that we leave and we don't want them in our back areas. Above all, nobody and I mean nobody leaves the perimeter until we get relieved. And if we've got artillery and air coming in, we'll be calling it in almost on our own heads. The deeper we dig in the better. Last thing we want is casualties from our own supporting fire."

"Especially if the Yanks are delivering it. You know what their pilots are like. Over-enthusiastic."

That, Haversham thought, *was putting it politely.* The Canadian troops had a saying about the Yank fighter-bomber pilots, they were unerringly accurate. Every bomb they dropped hit the ground. Somewhere. Then, he had a strange sensation, as if his own thoughts had been turned into reality. A whistling noise.

"INBOUND!" The shouting was all over the perimeter, Haversham glanced around to see figures diving for cover. That was probably a good idea and he copied it. The explosions followed a split second after he made it to the ground. *They were mortars, 82s? Perhaps 50s? They were light cracks, not the heavy thuds of the medium mortars.* The ripple of explosions lasted for barely minute and then the scene was silent again.

"Fire back, Sir?" Gillespie picked himself out of the snow. All over the hedgehog, the troops were doing the same. Miraculously despite the number of explosions, nobody seemed to have been hurt. The tiny charge on the German 50mm mortar had combined with the thick snow to produce a lot of barks and no bites. Haversham knew they wouldn't be that lucky again.

"No. Waste of ammunition. Those were 50mm mortars, the crews will have moved long before we can put fire down on them. That's what they're trying to goad us into doing. Plus get a measure of what we've got in here. See if we can get support from the outside. We need to hoard what we have in here with us. Goes for food as well as ammunition. Gillespie, get an inventory made of what supplies we have here and what we need urgently." Haversham sprinted over to the radio section. It was time to fight a war the Yank way. Hole up, form a defensive perimeter around their radio operator and let him fight them with the divisional artillery. It wasn't soldiering the way his father or grandfather would have understood, making sure a kid could eat his can of beans undisturbed while he blasted the enemy with somebody else's artillery but it was the low-cost way of fighting a war. Low cost in terms of Canadian lives anyway. That was what was important.

"Get in touch with headquarters. Tell them we're coming under fire. If there's support available, we could use it on the perimeter." *It was time,* Haversham thought, *to start educating the Finnish Army on the facts of life. One of the earliest lessons would be that there were consequences for actions.* That lesson could be applied on a lot of levels.

249

Finnish 12ᵗʰ Infantry Division, Kola Front

Lieutenant Martti Ihrasaari wasn't particularly happy at this point. Having been detached and sent on this infiltration mission had allowed him to get out from under the crushing dead weight of the divisional and regimental commands for a while. When the Canadian division had collapsed, the rest of the division had moved up as well. Now he was back under their command. He'd got a cursory 'well done' for his roadblock that had this battalion bottled up along the road but now he was just back to being a small cog in a big machine. One that didn't necessarily have his interests at heart.

What had just happened was a good example. That quick flurry of mortar fire had been supposed to wake the Canadians up and make them fire off their counter-battery salvoes, wasting their ammunition and revealing their position. The crews of the little Model 36 mortars had gone as soon as they'd finished their fire mission of course. That was the one good thing about those mortars. It was a good tactic in theory, but it had no regard for the people who were left and who couldn't move away. The really annoying point was that it hadn't worked. The Canadian position was still silent.

Then Ihrasaari heard a threatening roar, one that came from overhead and grew closer all the time. He knew instantly what it was. Artillery and not the pipsqueak little 50mm mortars either. This was the big stuff, Canadian 5.5 inch guns or Ami 155s. He felt his stomach clench and his body try to drive itself deeper into the snow. There was one good thing about this. Artillery came down at an angle and the shells would bury themselves in the snow before exploding so much of their force was directed down into the ground. The little mortar shells came straight down and their explosions were much more effective – for their size. That didn't change the fact that their size was tiny compared with the big inbounds.

Ihrasaari was wrong. The shells didn't explode deep in the ground. They burst in the air above the Finnish positions around the Canadian hedgehog. Their fragments lashed down at the troops in their dug-outs and foxholes. The first two patterns of shells were bad enough, but the third was sheer hell. Those shells didn't explode in the air; they hit the ground and went off with a curious muffled explosion. The burst pattern was strange as well. The cloud of smoke was greater than he'd expected and had curious white tendrils that leapt out of it.

250

Perhaps tentacles was a better word, Ihrasaari thought, *they reminded him of the octopus he had seen once at an aquarium.*

Ihrasaari saw the white smoke cloud rolling towards him. *A smoke-screen? Were the Canadians trying to break out of their fortifications already?* He knew that's what the divisional commanders wanted; the besieged troops to exhaust themselves in break-out attempts but this was very early for that. When the smoke engulfed him, Ihrasaari felt the heat creasing his skin. It caught him in the throat and caused him to erupt in an explosive fit of coughing. He saw his men were surrounded by a snowstorm of small, white particles that floated down upon them. Then, he realized what the rounds were and the idea filled him with instant terror. *These were white phosphorus rounds, incendiaries, anti-personnel.* The men who had been hit by the little snowstorm were screaming in pain and terror. Their clothes sizzled and burned as the flakes landed. They tried brushing them off but the effort only made things worse. When their hands touched the stuff the little flakes caused a horrible burn, increasing in intensity as it burrowed into their flesh.

He tried to run over to his men. Some were rolling in the snow, trying to put out the fires that were eating into them. He knew it was no good, that the white phosphorus was dissolving into the fatty tissues of their bodies where it would prevent the wounds healing. As he thought that, he heard another roar overhead. Another series of the airbursts flailed the ground with fragments. His suspicions had been right. This wasn't going to be like fighting the Russians.

Hedgehog, The Regina Rifle Regiment, Kola Front

"That's all we're getting Sir. Battery shoot. Two rounds per gun of proximity-fused airbursts, one of Willie Pete and a last proximity salvo as an envoi. I hope that for what the Finns received they were truly grateful." The forward artillery observer switched his radio link off and went back to eating his lunch. A can of beans, Haversham noted.

Bridge, KMS Lutzow, *North East of the Faroe Islands, North Atlantic*

"More problems?"

Captain Becker rubbed his eyes. He was deathly tired and the bitter cold had long seeped into his bones. There was no shelter from

251

it, *Lutzow* was too torn up for that. Just a shattered pile of steel slowly, painfully, heading her way towards an inevitable end on the rocks outside Thorshaven. "Diesels are overheating. It's not surprising, we were never built to go backwards this long. The intakes are designed to scoop up water while we are going forward, not backwards. The flow isn't enough and the engines aren't being cooled properly. Can we turn around and go forward for a while?

The Damage Control Officer thought, or tried to. His mind wasn't working properly; hunger, cold, exhaustion and fear had shrouded him in a blanket that seemed to strangle every thought before he could even get it out. He breathed deeply, trying to compose himself. "How far are we out, Sir?"

"Thirty kilometers, perhaps fifty? No more than that. If we can just keep running for four more hours, we can make it to the rocks."

"We've got more timbers up on the false bow, we've stiffened it a bit. Provided we don't go too fast, it should hold. For an hour or two, to cool the diesels at worst, get us in at best."

"Captain." The Navigator's voice was slurred also. "Why don't we send *Z-27* ahead? If we go down, there's nothing they can do for us. If we don't, they can spread the word, get us some help. Get the men ashore across the rocks or get fishing boats out to take off the wounded. Anything."

"Good idea. Do it. By signal lamp." Becker rubbed his eyes again and saw *Z-27* pulling away from the sinking cruiser. "Turn us around, we'll go forward."

The orders were carried aft by word of mouth since the ship's internal communications had long since failed. Under his feet, Becker felt *Lutzow* shudder and start to swing. Behind him, the long line of men passing buckets of oil-stained water from below stopped work and looked around. Was the ship going down at last? Then they saw her make her slow, anguished turn and realized what was happening. Wearily, they started the bucket chain again, painfully passing the flood water from one hand to the other.

One of the men looked down suddenly at the contents of his bucket. "Hey, I recognize this lot. We threw it over the side three hours ago."

There was a tired surge of laughter from around him; then back to throwing the buckets of water over the side. Becker found himself looking over the brutally-amputated bows of his ship. She was going forward again.

"Engineers? How are our engines?"

"Cooling slightly Sir." He nodded. *That had solved one problem but had it created another?*

"Damage Control, what is the situation up forward?"

The reply came quickly. "Leakage is down a bit, Sir. Water still coming through but it hasn't increased the way I thought it would."

"Suction." Another officer spoke quietly. "When we were heading backwards, the cut-off area acted like a transom stern. There was suction there, pulling the timbers outwards. Now there is pressure pushing them back together. It will mean that when the leaks start again, they will be worse, but until then, not so much."

Becker nodded and suddenly looked through his binoculars. "There, in front of us. You see it? On the horizon? Land. Just another couple of hours, that's all."

Another officer looked. "Might just be cloud, Sir?"

"Perhaps, but for the men's ears it is land ahead."

It was. For the next hour, Becker saw the shadow on the horizon solidify and enlarge. It was land. It had to be the Faeroes. He saw something else as well; a small boat coming out to meet him. It took time to pull alongside, He saw it was a fishing boat, a sailing craft. He didn't find that surprising since the Faeroes probably hadn't seen diesel fuel for years.

"German battleship. Are you heading for Thorshaven?"

"We are, God willing."

"Your destroyer told us where to find you but you cannot bring your ship into our harbor. You will block it when she sinks."

"We do not wish to. We would beach her outside."

"That is good. There will be other boats and men on shore to help your crew. Can you steer a course?"

"Not with accuracy. We are setting the rudder by hand. But we can try."

"Set ten degrees to port. This will put you on to a sand beach. Your men will stand more chance there than on the rocks."

"Very well." Becker gave the helm order and felt *Lutzow* shift again. The island grew in front of him, quickly swelling in size. He had to make several more small changes of course to try and hold the line the Faeroese fishermen wanted but they managed it. Soon, he could see the beach, a small cove, sheltered, welcoming. Much better than he expected.

"Get everybody out from down below. Minimum crew for running the ship only. Everybody else on deck."

"German battleship?" The voice came from the fishing boat again, still distorted by the loud-hailer. "We can take your most wounded if you wish. There are other trawlers coming out. If you lower your wounded down to us we will take them to Thorshaven."

"Thank you." Becker wanted to say more but he couldn't think of the words. He was just too tired.

Slowly, *Lutzow* was surrounded by fishing craft. Her crew lowered the worst of the wounded down to the larger trawlers. More small craft were joining them by the minute, ready to take the survivors off when the sinking cruiser hit the beach. That wouldn't be very long now. Becker could feel her getting more sluggish as the water filled her hull.

"Time to go. Engineers, full power from the diesels, the harder we hit that beach the better. Means we'll be closer to dry land. What's the tide?"

"High tide, Sir."

"Good."

There was a blast on *Lutzow's* sirens and the ship started to pick up speed. The wooden false bow started to disintegrate as the water lapped at it but it really didn't matter anymore. Becker felt the vibrations as the hull started to touch the bottom followed by the vicious slam as his ship grounded fully. The engines pushed her ashore, through the bottom sand and onto the rocks beneath. Eventually, she stopped, hard aground, barely fifty meters from the high tide mark. When the tide went out, she would be almost wholly exposed. Becker felt something else. As his ship had grounded, she'd changed. Something had gone from her. In his heart Becker knew the truth, *Lutzow* was dead. She'd got her crew to safety and she'd died doing it.

Alongside, the small craft were pulling men aboard, catching them as they climbed down from the decks and pulling them to safety. The little boats ran them ashore before coming back for more. Then Becker saw something he couldn't credit. Groups of Faeroese Islanders were running into the sea, long chains of them secured by lifelines. They grabbed at the German sailors and manhandled them back to the beach, just as the same sailors had manhandled the buckets all through the night. Others waited on shore with blankets. They wrapped the survivors in them as they reached safety and rushed them off to be warmed and sheltered. Quietly Becker marveled. After the ruthless bombing the day before, it was almost too great a contrast to bear.

As custom demanded, he was the last man off. He even made a tour of the ship to make sure she was deserted down below. Then he came to the demolition switches. There he hesitated. The standing orders were to blow the ship up but he held his hand. It wasn't the ship, the cold, empty stillness told him more clearly than anything else that *Lutzow* was dead. Whatever it was that made her a ship rather than a steel coffin, was gone. But her tanks were half full of oil. If he blew her up, that oil would wreck the fishing ground on which these people depended. They'd risked their lives in the freezing water to save his men; he couldn't repay them by coating their island with a scum of fuel oil. He reached carefully down, disconnected the detonator and disarmed the scuttling system.

Back on deck, he dropped down into a fishing vessel, the one who had come out to meet them. Its Captain was staring at him.

"It is all right, Captain." Becker spoke slowly. "The ship will not explode. Her tanks are half full of fuel oil; if your people can get it out, it is yours."

The fisherman nodded and took his boat in, Becker marvelled at the skill with which the sailing ship was handled so close in. When its bow touched sand, he jumped off, involuntarily yelping at the coldness of the water that came up to his knees. Then, another fisherman grabbed him and pulled him out of the water on to the beach.

"There is somebody you must meet."

The fishermen lead him to another figure. He wore a khaki uniform with an odd, boat-shaped cap without a peak, made of wool with a button on top and ribbons hanging down behind. The man turned around and Becker saw the Union Jack flash on his shoulder. "Colonel Ian Stewart 2nd Battalion, Argyll and Sutherland Highlanders, Free British Army."

"Captain Martin Becker, German Navy Ship *Lutzow*."

"Captain Becker, I must advise you that you and your men are prisoners of war. However, due to the peculiar circumstances that prevail here, I will offer your men parole. There are no facilities to keep prisoners on this island and I would not wish to keep you all locked up in your destroyer."

"You have our parole. I will order my men to cooperate. Colonel, my ship's fuel tanks contain oil these Islanders will find valuable, I promised to them. You will honor my promise? They deserve much more than a few gallons of oil but we have little else to give."

"Of course." Stewart waved and men on the hills stood up. They had Bren guns and Becker realized just how easily this beach could have been turned into a bloodbath. "We will send you out when our supply ships arrive. There are too many of you to go out in one trip but we will get you all to Canada in time."

"Supply ship?"

"Of course. We've been occupying these Islands for more than two years now. We have a supply run set up. Fast minelayer out of Churchill.

Becker nodded. He had no idea the Faeroe Islands had any garrison, let alone a British one. The he started to laugh; more a result of released stress than anything else. Stewart looked puzzled. "Colonel, when we were trying to get here, we thought that a wrecked cruiser and a shot-up destroyer would at least be a start for a Faeroe Islands Navy. Now we find they have an Army as well. And at the rate the world is killing itself, soon they will be a world power of great importance.

Stewart joined the laughter. "Aye, that they could. And they're good people here. The world could do worse than them." Then he looked at Becker. "It was bad out there?"

Becker shuddered at the memory. "The Amis, they never stopped coming. One wave of jabos after another. They just battered our ships to death. Even when they were dead in the water, they kept on until they sank. How we survived I shall never know."

Supreme Command Headquarters, Berlin, Germany

The guards outside the door could hear the screaming even through the thick wooden paneling. Screams of rage and fury that went on and on without break or interruption. Eventually, the doors opened. A white-faced figure in an Admiral's uniform left, shaking with rage. His aide rushed up to him, only to be pushed away.

"Don't touch me I have leprosy. So has the whole Navy. You would be well advised to find another uniform to wear."

"Sir?"

Admiral Karl Doenitz looked across at the young officer. "The Navy is a waste of time and resources. We have never done what the Fuhrer wants. We have never fulfilled even his lowest expectations. Every promise we have made has been broken. Our U-boats failed in 1942 and even our Type XXIs have failed to cut the Atlantic convoys. The S-boats failed to command the Baltic. We cannot even destroy a single convoy when using the entire battlefleet. How many tanks could we have built with the steel squandered on those ships? How many aircraft could fly with their engines? Where could we have gone with the fuel they burned. So asks our Fuhrer.

"If the Navy had failed him once or twice, those might be the fortunes of war. But the Navy has failed him every time and that means it is staffed by traitors. So says our Fuhrer. It is not worth keeping, it is a failure. So concludes our Fuhrer. The remaining ships are to be scrapped, all of them. So orders our Fuhrer."

"All of the ships Admiral, even the sub...."

"All of our ships, so commands our Fuhrer. We are to scrap them all." Doenitz looked quickly around. "The Fuhrer certainly means to include the submarines in that list but we know that submarines are not ships. In a few days, a week of two, somebody will ask that question and the Fuhrer will have calmed down enough to give an answer that will save the submarines. A few of them anyway. The missile launchers certainly, perhaps some of the rest. But the Navy is gone. Not that there are many ships left to scrap."

The aide ran through the list of ships left after the disastrous sortie. A single old cruiser, three or four destroyers, a dozen or more torpedo boats, a lot of smaller ships. What about the minesweepers? The way the Amis were laying mines off France and around the UK, decommissioning the minesweepers would bring coastal shipping to a complete halt.

"What about the minesweepers, Admiral? If they are laid up?"

"Then we will soon be unable to move supplies by sea. I know. But the Fuhrer has given his orders and they are not to be questioned. Young man, if you can find another place for yourself, I would do so. The Navy is not a place for a young man with ambition anymore."

"Admiral, you must come with us." Two men, SS officers had appeared. Doenitz squared his shoulders and turned to go with them. His death wasn't inevitable not yet. He still had a few cards to play. The missile attack submarines, the only weapon Germany had that could strike at the mainland USA, was one. The minesweepers that the Army needed desperately was another. He could play those to save his life. Others too. But he was too much of a realist to believe that his hand was strong. As a desperation play, he had a chance. No more than that. But his precious Navy had none. What the Amis hadn't sunk with their carriers was doomed by the orders of the man who ran the country. A man who was completely insane. If Doenitz had ever doubted that matter, the display in the conference room a few minutes ago had shattered those doubts.

"Wait outside." The voice was not one Doenitz had expected. Hermann Goering was sitting in the office. He'd been weaned off morphine over the last year and looked a world better as a result. After crashing to the bottom and losing most of his influence in the middle of the war, he was now, slowly and painfully, rebuilding his position. The two SS men left.

"Well Karl, your Navy really screwed up, didn't it?"

Doenitz looked at him "If we'd had more planes, proper carriers...."

"You'd still have lost. My people think the Amis had almost three thousand aircraft on those carriers. They'd have swamped anything we could have put up. Anyway, that's what we're going to be discussing you and I. All about carrier warfare and how our aircraft performed at sea. We'll keep on discussing it until the Fuhrer has calmed down and your neck is not due to be stretched by a piano-wire noose any more. Then we'll edge you back into, well, not favor but tolerance.."

Goering settled back in his seat. He had acquired another ally. That meant one additional piece in his plan to re-establish his authority was back in play.

C-99B Arctic Express *Seattle Airport, Washington*

The main wheels touched the runway with the usual heavy thud. The C-99 wasn't like a normal aircraft. It was much more like a ship in the way it wallowed through the air. It was also unresponsive. The aircraft made little attempt to follow its pilot's instructions and fine adjustments were hard to achieve. That was why the landing run started a long way out; the aircraft had to be lined up perfectly before it got too close to the ground. More than one C-99 had been lost because the pilot had made an abrupt change in angle too late and a wingtip had dug into the ground. Flying a C-99 was an art form, one that took practice to perfect. That was why a growing trend in the C-99 groups puzzled Captain Dedmon. It seemed as if just as a crew got experienced enough to handle their big birds in the Arctic conditions of the Air Bridge, they would vanish, posted away to some other group. The official explanation was that they were assigned to crew training; giving new pilots some insight into the handling characteristics of the C-99 before they came up here to fly the Bridge.

It seemed as if more than enough experienced crews were being reassigned to train the number of C-99 crews needed up here though. There were rumors that more C-99 units were being formed and sent to the Pacific; used to move supplies and troops around. Dedmon knew for a fact that every so often a C-99 would turn up with a load of supplies made in Australia. Equipment that had been produced in Australian factories but paid for by the U.S. and charged against Russia's Lend-Lease account. So perhaps that was where the crews were going. It would make sense, another Air Bridge lifting supplies up from Australia. With the C-99's range and payload, almost anything could make sense.

Alongside the transport, a flock of ambulances were already following *Arctic Express* ready to pick up part of its cargo. That was another reason why Dedmon had brought his aircraft in carefully. The lower deck was full of casualties, almost 150 of them with doctors and nurses moving as best they could between the litters. Normally the faster C-54s were used for casualty flights but there had been a rush of evacuation cases. *Arctic Express* had been available so she'd been loaded up with the wounded soldiers. Another 150 passengers were on the upper deck. They were men coming home on leave. In a week's time, they'd be on their way back to the Russian Front.

Dedmon swung off the runway, onto the taxiway, following the orange and black jeep that was showing him the way. As he cleared the long tarmac strip, he could see a C-99A at the other end starting to move, the first step in its long flight to Russia. He guessed that the troops on the upper deck would be watching, knowing that all too soon, they'd be on a flight just like it. The U.S. had been supporting its armies in Russia for three years and had got it down to a fine art. The heavy equipment went by sea; the men were flown in.

The jeep broke right, onto the hardstand and Dedmon followed it. *Arctic Express's* tires squealed as he made the turn. Then, the rumble of the nose doors opening started as soon as the engines behind the wings spooled down. The casualties on the lower deck would already be the centers of a rush to get them off the aircraft and on their way to hospital. The very fact they were on this flight meant that their wounds were serious enough to be flown back to the Zone of the Interior, not treated in Russia. Dedmon's thoughts were interrupted by the curious throbbing snarl that was the C-99's trademark. The C-99A he'd spotted a moment earlier was already lifting off; its flaps pulling up and its undercarriage retracting as it set off to Russia. Behind it, a C-54 was already taking its place at the end of the runway. Its crew did their final checks before they left, probably for Anchorage, then Anadyr and down to Khabarovsk or one of the dozens of smaller strips that were spreading across Siberia.

The flight deck crew finished their shut-down checks and Dedmon signed the chit that handed his aircraft over to its ground crew. They'd take responsibility for her; get her prepped and ready for the next flight out.

"Anything special, Sir?" The crew chief tapped the clipboard reflectively. There had been a time when each crew had its own chief and own ground crew but that had all been changed. Now, maintaining the aircraft flying the Air Bridge was done on a production line basis. If a specialist's services weren't needed on one aircraft, then he'd be shifted to one where he was. That simple change had quadrupled the availability of the transports.

"No, Chief. She's behaving real well. Like a true Lady." Dedmon signed the remaining dockets and stretched himself out of his seat. His back and legs were stiff; it took a long time to get from Khabarovsk to Seattle at under 250 miles per hour. The navigators did a fantastic job on these flights. Before the Air Bridge had been set up, nobody had even guessed at the problems involved in making flights this long.

Inside the terminal, Dedmon's crew started to disperse. That was another slightly odd thing about the Air Bridge. A lot of the pilots were the older, more experienced types, about half were already married with families. His co-pilot, Jimmy York, broke away to where his wife was waiting. Dedmon did a slight double-take at that. When they'd left, Susan York had been a blonde; now her hair was jet black. He'd heard there'd been some problems on the East Coast but that didn't reach out here did it?

"Bob? Can I have a word with you for a minute?" Colonel Sutherland was almost running across the base building. Another slightly older man, a holdover from the pre-war Army Air Corps. "You're going out in two days?"

"Guess so, Sir. Haven't seen the orders yet." It was a fair bet though. It took two days to turn the big, complex C-99 around and get her ready for another long haul to Russia.

"Take my word for it, you will be. A cargo of aircraft tires, I think. Look, I'm appointing you my new Operations Officer for the group."

Dedmon mentally paused. "Tommy Kincaid's all right?" Enough aircraft were lost on the Air Bridge; that was why the wings and tail were painted bright orange-red. Made it easier to spot a wreck in the snow.

"Oh, he's all right, sure enough. Got his orders out yesterday, going to another group so they say. Why can't they just let us settle down? I can't be expected to run a transport group when my best crews keep getting transferred out. You'll be gone soon; mark my words. Anyway, I want you to take over as Operations."

Dedmon smiled his thanks and watched Sutherland scurry off. *Why hadn't Sutherland had his transfer orders yet?* The slightly insubordinate thought made Dedmon smile as it crossed his mind.

Somewhere on the Kola Peninsula, Heading South.

"They're catching up fast." Bressler was right. Marosy knew it although he would rather not admit the fact. The Germans had started closing in once they'd got out of the deep snow in the valley. Now here, in the trees, they were moving a lot more quickly than the two American airmen.

"Might be time to pick our ground, Bill." Marosy looked at the trees. There wasn't much cover; the pine trees tended to kill off undergrowth. "There's some rougher ground over there. It'll give us some cover."

Bressler winced. The day had been quite a come-down, from a semi-automatic 75mm cannon to a pair of .38 revolvers. There was a grim joke about those .38s. According to the aircrew, their only use was to make sure the Germans came in shooting. Getting shot was a lot less painful than slowly strangling on the end of a rope. "Won't it be better to get a little further south, John? We can try and give these buggers the slip at least. Once we make a stand, it's all over."

Marosy tried to make his mind up but the cold was seeping into him. In the end, it wasn't the possibility of getting away that decided him but a flat crack and an eruption of snow around them. The lead Germans had caught up, almost.

"Too late, can't even get to the rocks. Down there, now." The two airmen dived into a slight dip, one that offered only a bare margin of shelter. Even as they hit the bottom, bruising limbs on the rocks that were under the snow, more shots echoed around them. It was indeed a very bare margin of shelter.

There were more than a dozen Germans, moving quickly through the trees towards them. Marosy drew his pistol and cursed the Air Force that bought these weak and useless .38 revolvers when they could have had the Colt M1911s. It was as if the Air Force had to consciously reject everything that its once-parent Army had selected. There was a short lull in the German fire as their troops moved forward. Marosy knew what was in their mind. They had a chance to get their hands on two of the hated fighter-bomber pilots that had first made their lives a misery and then tried to end it by dousing them in napalm. They were concentrating on that objective and he intended to make sure they didn't achieve it by capturing this A-38 crew alive.

His .38 shot sounded feeble in the pine forest but Marosy was astonished by the result. At least three Germans had gone down. Even less explicable was that two quickly joined them, great blotches of red erupting over their white coveralls. At that point, Marosy was suddenly aware that the gunfire had changed, there was a staccato clatter of rifle fire but with it, a ripping noise that was far faster than any machine gun Marosy had ever heard. The Germans were cut down by the ambush. A few trying to retreat backwards through the trees but the gunfire followed them. They never made more than a few feet.

After the deafening sound of the gunfire, the woods seemed silent. Marosy and Bressler felt they couldn't move as they watched figures get to their feet from a ragged L-shape that surrounded the obliterated German unit. Marosy raised his hands and called out "American pilots."

One of the ski troops emerging from their positions called back. "We know."

The man walked across while the rest of the troops started to check the dead bodies of the Germans. Out of the corner of his eye, Marosy saw one man dip his fingers in the blood of a German and smear it on the face of a young soldier. Then he called out, "Comrades, we have a new Brat today."

"I am Lieutenant Stanislav Knyaginichev." The Russian spoke slowly; obviously thinking in Russian, then translating slowly and carefully. "We have been tracking you for more than an hour."

"Captain John Marosy, Sergeant William Bressler. Thank you for the rescue, Lieutenant."

"Call me Knyaz. We were told of your crash by a partisan group. They also told us where to look. You were leading the Germans very well, so we left you to get on with it. Then it was easy to set up a good ambush for them." The lieutenant's voice was slightly strained. He was trying to conceal his amusement at the way the two Americans had been stumbling around in the snow. "Did your survival people never teach you how to make snow shoes from branches?"

Marosy shook his head. He watched with awe at the way the Russians were moving with casual ease in the snow. He'd thought the Germans had been skilled. Now he saw them as inept blunderers compared with the ski troops around them. *And if they'd been inept blunderers, what did that made me and Bressler?*

"Another thing you Americans must lean about the Russian winter." Knyaz was trying to stop himself laughing as he reached out and tapped the American's flight suits. "Snow is not green. Come, we must move away from here. Can you ski?"

"A little, not as well as your men."

"No matter. Our vehicles are only a few kilometers away. My men are finding you some skis and some camouflage suits that are not too badly bloodstained. We are heading home now to rejoin our

264

division and we will take you with us. Also you can carry a banana rifle, we have captured quite a few this time out."

That was, Marosy thought, *an improvement over a .38.* As he and Bressler struggled into the German snow camouflage suits, they saw the young soldier with the bloodstained face getting slapped on the back by the others. Knyaz saw the look and explained. "When a recruit joins us, he is a drug, a worker. He is fit only to do the dirty jobs in the unit. But when he has killed his first Hitlerite, he becomes a comrade, a brat. A brother. Then, he can make other drugs do the dirty jobs for him."

"Ah, I see. You speak English very well Knyaz."

"Thank you. I learned some in an American hospital. My division always tries to have one who can speak English with each ski patrol, for just such times as this. Now hurry; we must move on before the fascists can follow up."

Arado-234B "Green Seven, Reconnaissance Flight, II/KG-40, over the Kola Peninsula.

It was a good thing to be in the reconnaissance units; they had been first to receive the new jets. The Arado Lieutenant Wijnand was flying was a good example, a neat, twin-engined recon aircraft that could outfly pretty nearly all the fighters up in this benighted part of the world. Well, not the Ami Shooting Stars, but there weren't that many of those around, not yet, not here on Kola. Mostly they were on the central part of the Eastern Front, where the Amis fought. Wijnand and 11/KG-40 had been stationed there for a while and it had been a nightmare. The Amis never seemed to run short of fighters; their Thunderbolts and Kingcobras were everywhere. The bomber squadrons were still flying Ju-188s and they'd been caught badly. That was why the group had been moved here, so they could recover on a quieter front.

Wijnand looked down. The snow-covered landscape really was quite beautiful. Then he looked more closely. Way off to the left, heading off in a quite different direction from that the experts had predicted, were two long clouds of smoke. Wijnand banked around and set off to have a closer look. Sure enough, it was what he was looking for. Two trains pulled by steam locomotives.

A closer inspection with his binoculars showed that they weren't just what he was looking for. They were the ones he was looking for. The front two trains had each had one huge gun with a line of carriages. Following them, in a desperate effort to keep up, was a diesel locomotive pulling two more carriages.

"Base, this is the Flying Dutchman here. I have found the prey, heading west." Wijnand looked at his maps and carefully calculated the position, then read it out over the radio.

"Well done my little Dutchman. The map shows a bridge up ahead. We already have bombers ready to go, we will take that out. Headquarters wants those guns captured and already the Amis have blown one of them up. So we will make sure the muddy-feet get a chance at the two remaining. Stay with them; we will tell you when the bridge has gone.

Ju-188A-2 W+KQ, II/KG-40, over the Kola Peninsula.

This was the sort of raid the Ju-188 was good at. A quick take-off, a sneak over the lines at a specific target and back before the Amis or Ivans could react. The 188 was fast low down. It could make almost 450 kilometers per hour and it could slide under the radar surveillance that the damned Amis had set up almost everywhere. Mind you, low down was all that mattered on the Russian Front. The Ivans flew low and the Amis not much higher. A fight 5,000 meters up was a rare thing.

Captain Schellberg spread his map out on his knees. He was getting routing instructions from his navigator but he wanted to see the terrain for himself. The raid was a very specific one; a railway bridge that should be other the next ridgeline. His eight bombers would be making their runs along the length of the bridge. The bombing errors were likely to be in range, not deflection; so a run along a bridge gave a higher chance of a hit than one across.

There it was. Schellberg grabbed his radio. "Second section, make your runs now." Second Section were the novices; the newbies with only one or two missions under their belts. There were all too many of those these days. Give them the biggest targets. If they brought the center spans down, Schellberg's veterans could drop the end spans. But if the newbies missed, then Schellberg's section could still rectify matters.

The first of the Ju-188s crested the hill and started it's run. The two thousand-kilo bombs wobbled free and lurched downwards sending up fountains of water beside the middle spans. *Shaken it up a bit,* Schellberg thought, *but still standing.* The second pair of bombs were way short. Good for line, they chewed up the railway tracks short of the bridge, but the bridge itself was still standing. The third pair were very close. The water spouts actually soaked the bridge girders but still no collapse. The fourth pair hit home. It was as if the crew had watched what the others had done and averaged out their errors. The explosions blackened the sky around the bridge. When it cleared, the center span was down, one end in the river and the pier it had rested on broken.

"Well done Number Four! First section follow me."

Schellberg put his Ju-188A into a dive, aiming the nose at the abutment where the bridge met the bank. He held his breath slightly, squeezed the release just so, and saw the boiling black cloud erupt as his thousand kilo bombs slammed into the target. The bankside span crumpled and collapsed.

As Schellberg pulled away, he saw the damaged center span collapse into the river as two more bombs took down the remaining pier holding up its other end. Three of the four spans were down now. It was down to the two remaining aircraft to deal with the last. Schellberg saw the cloud of smoke rising from the bank and cursed. Thick as it was, he could see the last remaining span of the bridge was still standing. Still, the bridge was down, decisively down. That meant the mission was achieved.

The eight Ju-188As headed back for home. Just for once, it had been an easy mission. The Ami and Ivan fighters had been tied up hitting the German units advancing in the southern section of the Kola Front. The Canadian aircraft were supporting their troops fighting the Finns. There had been no flak around the bridge. It would be a long, long time before there was another mission like this one.

Curly, *Battery B, US Navy 5th Artillery Battalion, Kola Peninsula.*

It was still called the TBS even though it wasn't used to talk between ships. In fact, this particular set wasn't even installed on a ship. It was used to communicate between the carriages that made up the gun train of Battery B. Yet, this was a United States Navy train, traditions still held good and it was called the TBS. The signals Lieutenant answered it. The message wasn't good news.

"Sir, we've just received word. The bridge we were intending to use has just been blown. German bombers took it down about an hour and twenty minutes ago."

"Damn." Commander Perdue wanted to put it rather more strongly than that. "Ask Major Boldin to join us. And order all the trains to halt."

Perdue stared at the map. Unless there were spur lines that weren't shown, they were trapped. The spur they had intended to use was on the other side of the now-destroyed bridge. The only alternative was to go back east and hope that the German advance hadn't blocked that particular route out. A faint hope and one that exposed his guns to risk of capture, the one thing he was under strict orders not to allow. It was a situation that deserved something better than a single damn.

The ASTAC Major entered the command car and Perdue explained the situation briefly. "So, Tovarish Major, is there any chance of repairing that bridge? If not, can we get out by retracing our steps and heading out east then North? Failing those two options, what can we do?"

"The bridge? It is destroyed. We cannot repair it. According to the partisans, the central pillars and the far side piers have gone. We would need to build an entirely new bridge; it will take weeks. As for going back, that also is impossible. There is nowhere to turn the trains around and to go backwards so far, with such a load as we have, we cannot do this." Boldin stared at the map. "But there is one alternative, very risky, very dangerous; but open to us."

"Better than giving up and blowing up our guns here."

"Indeed so, Tovarish Commander. But when I said very dangerous, I am not joking. You see this ridge that runs along here, parallel to us, you can see it to our right. That ridge has deposits of low-grade coal in it. Not good coal, but useful. So, before the War it was decided to dig new mines in that ridge to recover the coal. Two such mines were dug here and here. " Boldin's finger tapped the map at two points a few miles in front of the trains. Points on almost opposite sides of the ridge.

"And to get the coal out, they needed a railway siding. One for each mine. Don't tell me there's a tunnel through the ridge at that point. Where the mines join?"

"Sidings yes, both sides of the ridge. There is no tunnel through the ridge. If there are points where the two mines join, there almost certainly are, a simple safety precaution, they would be man-sized only. Not big enough for great trains like these. But, the two sidings are joined by a line that goes over the ridge. We can take the trains along one set of sidings, over the connector and out by way of the other set. That will take us out onto this line here. We can head east along it, then north along here to rejoin our original route at this point here." Boldin's finger tapped out the route.

"That seems to be ideal." Perdue paused. "There's a problem isn't there? We can't be this lucky."

"There is indeed a problem. The mines never produced good quality coal and when the war started, all the available equipment was concentrated on the mines that could. These particular mines were closed, their equipment taken away for use elsewhere. We would have taken up the railway lines as well but there was not time. The Hitlerites advanced so fast we never got the chance. So the lines are still there, but they have not been maintained since 1941. Four years of winters and summers, of snow and ice forming then melting. They will not be in good condition, those tracks.

"There is another problem. The tracks were built in the years of the great purges. The engineer was told to get the cross-ridge line completed by a specific date. A party congress perhaps or somebody's birthday, who knows? Now the original design was to run the rails up the side of the ridge, keeping the slope to a minimum, about three percent, then turn the tracks through 180 degrees on the level ground at the top of the ridge them bring it down the other side. Only there was not enough time and not enough track. So rather than complete the job late and run risk of liquidation, he took some short cuts. The slopes up and down are much steeper than they should be. So much so that the coal trains had difficulty managing them and there were some accidents. To take these great guns along those tracks..." Boldin shrugged. "It may be possible. It is our only way out."

Perdue thought the problem over. "There are sidings both sides of the ridge?"

"Yes Tovarish Commander."

"So we can try this. We will take the guns to the foot of the ridge and the mines there. We will park the guns in the siding and use both locomotives to pull the carriages over to the other side. The diesel shunter should be able to manage without help. Then we use both locomotives to bring each gun over in turn. The problem will be coming down the other side. Will it be possible to turn the train around so that we can have the gun in front of the engines, that way they can act as a brake? Then we can assemble all the trains in the sidings the other side of the ridge, sort ourselves out and be on our way."

Bolding thought carefully. "I think this may work yes. Your Mikados are powerful engines, this I know." Then he smiled brightly. "Tovarish Commander, you are very determined to save your guns, yes?"

"Very much, Tovarish Major. If I lose another one, the Navy will take the cost out of my salary."

United States Strategic Bombardment Commission, Blair House, Washington D.C. USA.

"General LeMay to see you, Sir." Naamah made the introduction without giggling over the 'sir.' In the anarchistic environment preferred by those who worked on Project Dropshot, the word was rare indeed.

"Curt, it's good to see you. How goes SAC?"

"My B-29 bomber crews are getting shot to hell in Russia. The new groups are short of planes, pilots, equipment, everything we need. Apart from that its going well."

"That bad? I thought the D-models were rolling off the lines now."

"They are. And most of them go straight into modification centers to have faults fixed or be modified. I've got groups out there with three serviceable aircraft. The 100th has been operational since

270

October, on paper. In reality, it's got twelve bombers out of the 75 it's supposed to have. We're flying the birds around the clock; one crew brings them in, another takes them out. I have to tell you, that's putting a lot of hours on the airframes that aren't too strong to start with. Don't sweat it though. We'll get the crews ready, it's the planes that worry me."

"We can treat the D-models as a training cadre. The first really operational ones will be the E-ships. When they start arriving we'll be converting the Ds to tankers."

"Glad to hear it." LeMay paused for a moment. "Look, Phillip, it isn't really that bad. The B-17 program was worse and the 29 production problems were even more chaotic. You remember what happened with my first B-17 group?"

Stuyvesant shook his head. "Not from the inside, no."

"December 1941, we were supposed to be based in Iceland. We'd packed up to go, our ground echelon, all our spares, baggage, tools, everything was on its way to Iceland. Then they start to talk about sending us to Hawaii as an emergency deployment instead. Can you imagine, 35 B-17s suddenly arriving at Hickam without any of the thing needed to keep them flying? Disaster. Only thing worse would be arriving in the middle of an air raid. What the hell caused that flap anyway?"

"Never got to the bottom of it Curt. The Japanese were up to something. For a while, it looked like they were going to hit all ways at once. Phillippines, Dutch East Indies, Malaya and Singapore, you name it. Some of the radio intercept guys even suggested the Japs might pound on Pearl. Then suddenly, it all went away. The Japs stood down and poured their military power into China instead. They're still there, making headway, and we're turning a blind eye because the supply line to Russia runs right under their nose.

"Well, nobody told us that; just that orders for the Pacific were coming down. I had to get the whole group out of the zee-oh-eye before the orders to they arrived. At least we haven't had that with our big birds. If Consolidated can get the production sorted out, we'll be ready. We're ready now if we really have to be. We can put about a 150 birds up for a strike. Some of them are older and slower than the rest but they'll still give the krauts hell. You give us the packages,

271

Phillip, and Consolidated the birds, we'll take their whole damn country off the map." LeMay shifted his pipe from one side of his mouth to the other. "So, how's your side of the planning going?"

"Pretty good; we're refining the target list now. Looks like around 200 targets for optimum. Fewer than that, we leave bits of the war machine working. More and we just start rearranging the rubble. I want to hit some targets, Berlin, Munich, Nuremberg, with more than one device. They're political targets. We wipe them off the map to make a point. Other targets are going to need at least two devices. They're hardened targets like shipyards and certain factories. So, I'd say somewhere between 220 and 260 devices. You're still planning three-plane sections?"

"Right. We've been trying all sorts but that seems to be the best for the big bird. We can position them so all the approaches are covered by gunfire from the turrets." LeMay shifted his pipe again. "Spent a couple of trips up there myself, talking the birds into position. It works, if we need it to. Might not. You hear about Paul Tibbets' experiment?"

Stuyvesant shook his head.

"Boeing stripped a B-29B right down; took out all the guns except the tail mounts, all the armor, everything not strictly needed for flight. Even took the arms off the seats. Tibbets took the lightweight bird up to 30,000 feet and some P-47s tried to intercept him. He outmaneuvered them all, chased them all over the sky. Nobody could believe it but he did it, right in front of them. Nobody expected the result to be so dramatic. Even the people who designed the birds are saying there's something about these big birds high up we're not allowing for. But, you're right, three plane sections. Those sections are called Hometowns by the way."

"Right, so with 75 planes per group, we should be able to use between eight and ten groups to drop the devices. That gives us a heck of a margin for safety. We'll be OK for the big birds Curt."

LeMay laughed. "Stuyvesant, you're a great planner and a great industrialist but you don't know squat about running a bomb group. Look, each group has three wings right? 24 birds per wing. That's eight three-plane sections. Each Bomb Wing will be doing well if it gets five of those sections up; three if we're unlucky. The rest of the big birds will be down for repair or in the shop for modification. Then, there's the crew. We have to keep some of them back in reserve for additional strikes, the first crews in won't be flying again for days after a two-day mission. So call it four sections per Bomb Wing. That's 12 sections per group, not 25. You do your maths again."

Stuyvesant did it in his head. "21 groups, possibly 22. Remember what I said about a safety margin? Forget it. AWPD-1 back in '41 planned for 44 Bomb Groups of big birds by 1947. You're saying we'll need half of them for the package deliveries and the rest for the conventional strikes."

"Looks like it."

"We can manage the package delivery but you've just shot the follow-up full of holes. And we're going to have to make sure Fort Worth, Wichita and Segundo hit their production standards. The E-ships will be entering the production cycle in April. They've got the uprated engines. You know, if Tibbets is right about the guns being counterproductive, that's going to ease the production situation a bit. That remote controlled gun system is complex and takes a lot of time to build. Getting rid of it would be a good thing."

"Agreed. That's why I'm here, Phillip. I need to have some big birds built without guns and armor, just to see what they can do. Can you authorize it?"

"I can't but I can make sure the people who can do. But are you sure that's the way you want to go on this? Flying those bombers virtually unarmed is going to be a hell of a risk."

"The kids in the B-29Bs and RB-29Cs are taking that risk right now. Few nights ago, one of the RBs outflew a kraut night-fighter. Pilot did a damned fine job, evaded the fighter, got his radar pictures and brought them back. Then flayed the debriefer alive for telling him the Krauts didn't send night-fighters out after single bombers. But the point is, his RB-29C did outfly the fighter and they aren't stripped down the way Tibbets stripped his. They're taking losses but not prohibitive ones. Of course they're flying in at night, not in broad daylight. Any reason why we can't go in at night?"

"Accuracy. The packages are destructive but they still need to be placed right. We've got radar pictures for some of the targets but not all of them. Some, we're going to have to hit the hard way. That's why we need the recon birds to go in first. The recon big bird is going to be as important as the package carriers. They have to do weather recon, plot the defenses and draw their fire and do the target navigation on the way in. And, just to make it fun, the recon groups are still flying a mix of RB-29s and RB-23s. Not a recon big bird in sight yet."

"And that's even more big birds we need. Hell of a problem isn't it." There was not a trace of sympathy in LeMay's voice. He had enough problems developing the tactics to use the big birds. Getting them to him was somebody else's heartache.

CHAPTER NINE
SNOW DRIFTS IN THE WIND

Mechanized Column, 71st Infantry Division, Kola Peninsula

"They got the bridge." There was a triumphant note in the report. It wasn't often that air-ground cooperation went smoothly but this time it had. A recon aircraft had spotted the trains heading west. That had been a disaster for the mechanized column. The destruction of the bridge had left them stranded on the wrong side of river and the nearest crossing point was about an hour's drive east. There just weren't any to the west. That had put them so far behind the escaping trains that there had been no chance of catching them. Only the recon aircraft had got through to its base, the group commander had worked miracles getting a flight of eight bombers armed and off and the pilots had been phenomenal. The bridge had gone down. Now, the only way for the trains to escape was east. Right back into the arms of the mechanized column.

Asbach got his maps out. "We can drive along the rails. They're pretty much clear and give us a good footing. We should be able to get, what, 25 kph?"

"I think so. And the train cannot go much faster, it will have to back all the way. Can a train back that far?"

"I do not know. Do we have a railway man in the column?"

"No, not this column. I read the personnel files the night before we left."

Asbach raised his eyebrows slightly. That was taking devotion to paperwork a bit far. "A bit of advice, Lang. Just read two or three files and remember a key fact from each, a commendable one. Then repeat it in front of the men. They'll think you know everything. The rate this front eats men, we will never keep up with doing things the right way.' He watched Lang nod slightly, absorbing the message. Then Asbach frowned. "What are these here?"

Lang peered closely at the point Asbach was indicating. "These are old Finnish maps of the area?"

"What else? They are the best we can get. These date from 1936."

"Well then, those look like markings for mines. Coal probably, might be iron ore."

"Lang, have you ever seen a coal mine without a railway spur and marshalling yard? And look, see how those mines are between the two lines? Do you want to make a bet there is a railway line there?"

"And if those mines are coal, the engines can stock up on fuel. Perhaps water as well. If there is a railway line there."

"There must be. If there are mines there are railways. That will be a way out for them. If the lines are still there."

Asbach stared at the map, chewing distance, speed and time over in his mind. "How about we try this, Lang. We go west, along the railway lines to this point here. If the trains are coming this way we'll meet them by then. If we have not, we assume there is a line across this gap, through the mines. Then we turn north and head though the gap here up north to this junction. We can wait for the trains there and they will walk right into our arms. See, it's like a triangle, the trains must go along two sides while we can cut up along the third."

"But if the trains are coming east, just slowly?"

"They still have no way out. The rest of the Corps is heading north off to our right. There's no way out there. We will not get the honor of capturing the guns but the guns will be captured. But the more I think on this, the more sure I am that there is a railway spur not shown on this map. The Russian maps are useless. They are never right; that's why we use Finnish ones. We head west then north Lang, and intercept the guns at the junction of the east-west and northern lines." Asbach grinned in a friendly manner. "And we can get you your first piece of over-decorated tin, yes?"

Torshavn, the Faroe Islands, North Atlantic

A second destroyer had joined *Z-27* in the harbor. Becker read her bow number with some difficulty; the ship was blackened by fire and badly burned. Still, he made it out in the end. *Z-20*. She had been one of the destroyers with the carrier group. By the sound of it, she was now the only survivor of the Scouting Group. Becker was staring at her when he heard a sound behind him.

"*Z-20*. She's got a lot of survivors on her, all of them in a pretty bad way. Admiral Brinkmann as well." Colonel Ian Stewart was standing behind him.

"Thank God, I'm not senior officer here anymore." Becker was genuinely relieved. He was tired, sick, he just wanted to rest.

"I'm afraid that's not so Captain. Admiral Brinkmann is," Stewart hesitated, "not himself. Not at all himself. He had to be carried from *Z-20*, and he's . . . .uhhh . . . . . unresponsive. In the previous lot I think the medics called it shell-shock. I must ask you to carry on as Senior German Officer. Otherwise, I'll have to ask one of the destroyer captains and, well, you'll do a better job I think."

Becker nodded. "Very well Colonel. What do you want me to do?"

"Two Free Royal Navy minelayers, *Ariadne* and *Manxman*, are on their way down. They'll be in after midnight. *Ariadne* was due to go back to the States for a refit but she's doing this last run extra. She's empty; she can be loading your men while *Manxman* unloads supplies. I want you to go through all the survivors collecting here in person and pick out the sickest. They go back to Iceland first. The fitter men can wait for the next runs."

"Enlisted men take priority of course." Becker was simply stating a fact. No officer worthy of his rank would take an early ship out and leave enlisted men behind.

Stewart nodded. "Aye, goes without saying. Each minelayer can take about two hundred, so we can get four hundred out tonight. We have nearly two thousand of your men here, from *Lutzow* and the destroyers. And few are in good health. It's a fourteen hour run from here to Iceland. You'll have to get the men ready for a fast boarding. The ships have to be well out by dawn."

Becker nodded. The last thing these men needed was to be trapped on another sinking ship. As if to reinforce his thoughts, the vicious growl of a radial engine split the afternoon open. Becker almost whimpered as he recognized the sound of a Corsair and dived for the ground. The dark blue fighter skimmed overhead, pulled up at the end of its run then came back. For a moment, Becker thought it was a strafing run or even worse he'd see the ugly, wobbling tanks of jellygas split away from the aircraft. He was wrong. The Corsair charged overhead then vanished off into the afternoon sun.

"Photo-reconnaissance run. That was an F4U-7P. Probably getting pictures of the ships here." Stewart saw Becker staring at him from the ground. "We get to be very familiar with American aircraft here."

Becker climbed to his feet, a little sheepishly. "Colonel, I'll get the sickest men selected and ready. One other thing."

"The name's Ian. We'll be working closely together for the next few weeks I think."

"I am Martin. Ian, I disabled the scuttling system on *Lutzow* and *Z-27*, but on *Z-20*? It may need to be attended to."

"Aye, it will. You need help in seeing to this?"

"No, I think not. I can take some of my men to do it. But if you could have some of your men to aid us if it gets ugly?"

278

"I'll see to it, Martin."

"The General will see you now Sir." The airman in the outer office put an accent of almost supernatural terror on the first two words. Stuyvesant followed him in.

"The Seer's here."

"Right, you are dismissed."

Stuyvesant waited until the door was closed. Like all the USSBC offices, this one didn't have an intercom system. Too great a chance of it being left on and the wrong words getting broadcast. "I had a word with a few people, Curt. We can't get any big birds built to stripped down configuration. Consolidated are getting ready to shift to the E series and it would disrupt that. What is happening is that Wichita have six C-ships in house and they'll strip those down for you. Take out all the guns but the nose and tail mounts, all the armor. Be ready in six weeks. That'll give us an idea of what we can achieve by stripping them down. I've got a couple of my people working out what else we can strip out from them and what the likely gains will be."

LeMay thought for a moment. "I can find no cause for complaint with that."

"Another thing, Curt. I was thinking about your crew problems. Would it help if we brought the B-29 groups back from Russia? They'd act as cadres for more units; might accelerate the build-up."

"Not a good idea, Phillip. Two reasons, one is that crews aren't the problem; we're getting as many as we need by using the Air Bridge as a training ground. We just take them off the C-99s as we need them. The other is that those B-29 outfits are hard-luck groups. Take a notional group right, we'll call it the 49th Bombardment Group. There isn't a 49th Bombardment in the USAF. It arrives in Russia, its inexperienced, a bit sloppy. Don't fly the boxes as tight as they should perhaps, a bit careless on making their turns. The Luftwaffe give it a pasting, shoot down a lot of birds. So our 49th gets a load of replacements who are even less experienced, a bit sloppier. So the 49th

279

gets hit again. Soon, its efficiency is shot to hell. It's a hard luck group, nobody expects anything good of it. They don't expect any good of themselves. Pretty much all our B-29 groups in Russia are like that now. Once we're done, I don't plan to keep any of them. I have neither the time nor the inclination to distinguish the incompetent from the merely unfortunate."

"Which reminds me, Curt, you said that if we had to, we could put 150 bombers at Germany?"

"Mixture of Bs, Cs and Ds. Be a hell of a mess but we can do it. I've put all the best groups, the ones that have the most experience and a reasonable strength on hand in the First Air Division. We're just starting to form the Third Air Division now. Four groups per Division, 300 birds total."

"Right, well, if Germany does a special test, we go straight away. With whatever we've got. At the moment we have three Model 1561s and 24 Mark 3s either in the dumps or final assembly. Production is leveling off at around 10 Mark 3s per month. What I suggest is my people do a short target plan, updated on a monthly basis, using whatever we have. Give that to you. You can work out how to do it with what bombers you have. If it does drop in the pot and Germany does do a test, then we can go with the latest plan."

"We can do that. We'll keep that between ourselves though. If people know there is a small-scale emergency plan they'll want to use it right away. We do not want that issue re-opened."

Stuyvesant laughed. "That we can be sure of. It was damned hard work convincing General Groves that we shouldn't be trickling the packages onto their targets as they came off the production lines. I can imagine circumstances where that might work, if the enemy was on the verge of defeat for example, but we don't face that situation."

"Trouble with the Army, they never understood the strategy of air power. Always thought of doing things in small packets. Same when I took the '17s south on friendly visits. Army never understood what was involved. Stuyvesant, we've got a chance here to crush an enemy from the air, totally. We can't waste it."

"No, we can't. And we won't."

Disused Mining Complex, Kola Peninsula

"How are the tracks, Tovarish Major?"

Major Boldin pushed his lower lip out and thought the matter over carefully. "The diesel has taken its two carriages over the ridge safely, that is for certain. But the Mikados and the guns? They are a very different matter. It is as we feared. There have been more than five years, five winters, since this mine was closed and the track beds have been damaged. The sleepers are breaking up. There is much risk that the rails will spread apart when the full weight of the guns bears on them. If that happens then it will be all over."

"What can we do?" Perdue was frustrated. He didn't like being dependent on other people for the safety of his guns but he had no choice. Anyway, the ASTAC Major and his crew were proving their skills were real enough. The way they had cleared these old tracks and started their inspection proved that.

"Perhaps your men can get the first gun coupled to the two engines. Mine are walking the tracks now. We have some spare ties and other pieces to repair the worst damage. And we can fill in the bedding where the freezing has moved it. Then we can move your first gun to the top of the ridge."

Perdue nodded and turned to the crew of the lead Mikado. "Jones, Allen, couple both Mikados to *Curly* and get ready to tow it up to the top of the ridge. There's a siding up there, so leave *Curly* up top, come down and get *Moe*, take it up as well."

"Sir?" Jones's voice was curious, wary.

"We'll have to turn the trains around at the top. Major Boldin says we can do that using the siding at the top of the ridge. We'll put the gun in front and the engines behind it for the descent the other side. That way the locomotives will act as a brake and stop the guns running out of control."

"With respect, Sir. No, Sir." Jones was deferential but firm. Perdue stared at him; he hadn't expected that. The other side of the rail, Boldin's eyebrows met his hairline. This was something new to him. He'd never seen an American officer shoot one of his own men before. Well, there was always a first time for everything and this looked like it would be one of them.

"The other side of the ridge is as steep as this one, steeper perhaps. With the weight of the gun, it's going to pick up momentum very quickly. If we put the locomotives behind the gun, they can act as a brake, they can prevent the gun from picking up speed and running out of control."

"With respect, Sir, that won't work." Jones bit his lip. Before being drafted for the Navy he had handled heavy freight trains all over the United States and twenty years of that experience told him the right way to do this was not the way this officer thought it was. But how to explain it? "Look, Sir, meaning no disrespect Sir, but think on this. If we have the gun in front and the engines behind as you suggest, the weight of the gun will be pulling one way and the pull of the engines in the other. If we have the engines in front pushing back against the gun, the gun will be trying to push down, the trains pushing the other way. The first load is tension, the second is compression. We don't want a doubled tension load on the drawbar. It'll distort it at best; at worst it will rip the bar clean off. We could end up with the couplings so damaged we won't be able to pull the guns at all."

It made sense. Perdue had to admit it. His thoughts were interrupted by the sound of the diesel shunter arriving. It was about to make the next trip over, towing the battalion command car and a battery fire control car over the ridge. Up on the long cut that lead up the side of the ridge, he could see the Russian railway engineers walking the tracks, carefully inspecting the rails to make sure they would be secure for the guns.

"Very well Jones. Do it the way you recommend." *And may the Good Lord help you if you're wrong* was the unspoken addition.

"Very good Sir. We'll take *Curly* straight over, up one side and down the other. Then we'll leave the gun there and come back for *Moe*. Save a bit of time as well that will. Major Boldin, Sir, your men, have they got grit they can throw on the rails if we start to slip?"

Boldin started, slightly shocked that the aging railwayman was still alive to speak with him. *He wouldn't have been if this was a Russian Army unit. Speaking to an officer like that, it could get a man shot. Or worse.* "Yes, we have that. The men will walk beside you with it ready."

"Right then. Mr. Perdue, Sir, we'll get rolling with *Curly* as soon as the shunter reaches the top."

"Make it so. And, Jones, I'll be riding in the cab with you. I want to see how this goes. Lieutenant Tavernor. Are the guns and other cars fully rigged?"

"Yes, Sir. Cars and guns can be blown any time we have to."

"Good. If the Krauts turn up, don't hesitate to blow what's left this side of the ridge." Perdue paused for a second, a thought occurred to him. "Jones, why don't we put the diesel behind the guns with the two steam engines in front? The diesel won't push or pull, it'll just act as a sort of safety stop, prevent the guns putting too much stress on the couplings."

"That'll work, Sir. We're to wait until it rejoins us this side?"

"Correct. We can use the delay to make sure everything's secure this end."

The sun was starting to set by the time the first train started its run up and over the bridge. Jones had started the strange consist moving, taking the slope slowly and steadily. Alongside the two locomotives, Russian ASTAC engineers were walking. Every so often they would sprinkle handfuls of grit under the wheels. Jones could see Perdue watching curiously. "Improves traction Sir. We've got wet steel on wet steel here. That's why we're taking everything so slowly. If Mike here starts to slip or the gun does, we're in a world of hurt. Just like driving on ice; take it slow and steady, don't do anything sharp. Guess our tankers learned that, Sir."

Perdue chuckled. The tribulations of American tank crews trying to move their Shermans and Grants during their first winter in Russia had been notorious. There had been a joke that one could follow an American unit in those first months by the line of Shermans upside down in a ditch. Still, they'd learned, just as Perdue was learning now. "Is that why the slope is so shallow? When they said it was steep, I was expecting something much worse."

"Three percent is bad, Sir. For a train like this, and these tracks are six and a half or even seven percent. We'd think long and hard before building track like this in the States. If there was another way around, we'd take it. Situation like this, we'd have drilled a tunnel before taking track over the top like this." Jones was interrupted as the locomotive lurched suddenly. Perdue saw him go pale and check the load behind.

"It's OK, Sir. The bedding must have been loosened by the . ice. It shifted a bit." He looked behind again. "Thought so. The ASTAC guys are already there, packing it back in."

"This is dangerous isn't it?"

"That it is, Sir. Going down will be worse just the way you said. Still, it's something to tell my grandchildren about. We won't be stopping on the crest if that's all right with you, Sir. Going straight down, it'll put less strain on the drawbar."

Perdue nodded. The train eased up onto the ridge and he took the opportunity to look out. The view was beautiful; the reddening sun reflecting off the snow fields below. Ahead, he could see the wide sweep as the track made its 180 degree curve before heading down the other side of the ridge. All too soon he was looking down at the track dropping away in front of him.

The train crew were working hard, stopping the great gun they were pulling from starting to build up momentum. Perdue had no idea what they were doing and he was beginning to realize just how presumptuous his 'planning' had been. He really had no idea what was going on. Trying to keep out of the way, he looked out of the cab again. This time he watched the Russian engineers try to get the right amount of grit under the wheels of the locomotives. Without any warning, one of them took some steps alongside the tracks and slipped. It might have been a patch of ice, it might have been a sleeper that was broken and jagged. Whatever it was, he lost his footing and fell against the locomotive. In a second, he had fallen under the wheels. Perdue heard the scream ending abruptly as the train ran him down.

The sound was still making him shake when the two Mikados got *Curly* down to the sidings at the other end of the ridge. Perdue jumped off the train. He'd already decided to stay here with *Curly* while the engines went back and got *Moe*. After that, it was just a matter of resorting the trains again and getting back under way. There was a cloud of steam around him. He heard the train's whistle sounding before the two Mikes set off on the long haul up the slope. As their sound died away, Perdue suddenly felt very lonely.

It seemed like an age had passed before the two engines reappeared with *Moe* behind them and the little shunter making up the rear. It was far into dusk; in the fading light, Perdue could see the constant stream of gravel and ice being dislodged by the weight. *Moe* was visibly swaying as the gun's weight compacted the railbed and crushed the gravel weakened by years of ice-bound neglect. Once, Perdue thought they'd lost her. The gun started swaying and then appeared to lurch downwards. The dusk dimness highlighted a shower of sparks that shot out from the lead Mikado's wheels, then Jones, or the other engineer on the locomotives caught her, or perhaps the little diesel had added just a bit of stability and they brought it back under control. *Or had it just been a trick of the light?* Eventually, *Moe* joined *Curly* on the sidings that had once served the northern mine. Perdue looked thankfully at the two guns and reboarded the first Mikado.

"Jones, we'll keep the diesel here to move the carriages around. The two Mikes can get the rest of the trains. Take as many trips as you feel easy with, the hard part's done now. There's coal here as well. We'd better stock up before we pull out."

They were all suggestions, not orders. Jones nodded in agreement. "Good plan Sir. Although the coal here is pretty foul stuff." He paused for a second. "That last trip was rough, Sir. We nearly lost *Moe* when the bed gave way. Still, it all worked out at the end."

Williwaw H-AC, over Third Infantry Division Hedgehogs, Kola Peninsula

It was called a Cab Rank. Six Williwaws circled the area, high enough to be safe from flak and Spirals. Their engines were throttled right back and the mixture leaned out so they could stay for as long as possible. They were waiting for a call from one of the hedgehogs down below; Canadian infantry units cut off by the Finns. Only, the Canadians weren't trying to get out. They had dug in and were staying put. They were fighting the Finns with artillery and airstrikes. That was why the Cab Rank was here. A forward observer on the ground would call them directly and put them on the target. Or he'd coach in one of the little Australian Boomerangs. They would mark the targets with white phosphorus smoke rockets for the bigger, faster, Williwaws.

We're a strange team, Flight Lieutenant Digby Dale reflected. The Boomerang was something the Australians had cobbled together from a trainer and a few spare parts they happened to have available. Intended as a fighter, it had been too slow for the job, but its small size and agility made it perfect for the Forward Air Controller job. Boomerangs had been supplied to the Canadians and Russians for that job. The Russians used them as night harassment raiders as well. There was a whole regiment of Russian Boomerangs flown by women. Or so Dale had heard.

The Williwaw, or the Williwarmer as it was disrespectfully called, was pretty much cobbled together as well. The starting point had been a Canadian attempt to fit an R-1830 radial engine to a Hurricane. That had been an attempt to make use of the airframes that were piling up in Canada after the Coup in Britain had shut down supplies of Merlin engines. The obvious candidate for the Canadian-built Hurricanes had been the Allison V-1710, but American aircraft needed all available supplies of that engine. So the complex job of converting the Hurricane airframe to a radial engine had started. Halfway through the effort, Hawker engineers had arrived with blueprints for a better aircraft called the Tornado. The only problem with the Tornado was that it needed one of two British engines, the Sabre or the Vulture, neither of which was available. So Canadians and refugee Brits sat down together and redesigned the Tornado to use the American-built R-2600 engine. It went into production in 1943 as the Chinook. It still equipped quite a few Canadian squadrons. More had gone to the Russians as Lend-Lease.

In the fullness of time, the Chinook's performance was found wanting and more power was needed. That had led the engineers to shoe-horn an R-2800 into a developed version of the airframe to produce the Williwaw. 71 Fighter Squadron had only received its Williwaws a few weeks before and were still getting used to them. It was fast and agile, no doubt about that; but what Dale really wanted was a jet. Just like the Yanks and Krauts had.

"King Flight, this is Duffle. Come on down, target is green smoke, say again green smoke." There were a string of numbers that gave him his coordinates. Dale did a wingover and dived down, followed by the other two members of King Flight. Hard to see in the fading daylight was a cloud of green smoke. *Spotting rounds probably fired from mortars.* He lined up and squeezed the button on the control column. It unleashed the twelve rockets under his wings. There were bright red streaks coming the other way, as always they seemed to be coming straight for him only to flash past on either side. *Lucky these were Finns down below. The Germans had a lot more Flak guns and a lot more skill in using them.*

The green smoke was being lacerated by rocket fire. Dale shifted his finger and released his two 500 pound bombs. The snow-laden trees were approaching fast. He had just enough time to fire a quick burst from his cannon and that was that. Dusk was coming, time to go home. Behind him, the ground erupted as six 500 pound bombs speared the center of the green smoke cloud.

"King Flight, this is Duffle. Well done lads. Target had been done to a turn. Off you go; mummy's waiting."

Dale led his flight away, on the long haul back to their base. 71 Squadron had been lucky. Their base hadn't been targeted by the Huns with their damned rockets. He'd heard that the American bases had taken a right pounding the day after the storm. That was the trouble with the Hun rockets. Their doodle-bugs were easy targets for a fighter or anti-aircraft units, but nobody had come up with a way of stopping the German rockets yet. There were even rumors that the Russians had captured some intact and were trying to copy them. Still, useful as they were, they still couldn't replace a manned fighter-bomber.

"Break left, break left!"

The alert broke through Dale's reverie. He hauled the stick over and rammed the throttles forward to full emergency setting. The Williwaw stood on its wingtip and spun left. Dale's eyes grayed out as the G-force drove blood from his head. He still caught a glimpse of the attacking aircraft as they flashed by. Twin tail, single jet engine mounted above the fuselage. He-162s.

Dale reversed his turn, swinging in to attack the pair of German jets. It was too late, they were already far away and streaking back towards German-occupied territory. They were a hundred miles per hour faster than the Williwaws and were using every scrap of that speed to get clear. Dale had read the intelligence reports on the He-162. They rated it well as a fighter but it had only 30 minutes of fuel on board. That meant its pilots were restricted to a single pass at a target. Unless they were over their own bases, they simply couldn't hang around to dogfight.

The two retreating aircraft were the only ones. Dale had been half expecting another pair of He-162s to come out of the clouds, but the attack was over, barely a second after it had begun. There was a black stain across the sky. One of the three Williwaws in the formation hadn't got the message in time or had been a bit slow in making his turn. The aircraft was now a funeral pyre on the snow below.

"Control, this is King-1 here. We just got bounced by two He-162s. We lost H-AB. The 162s got away clean."

"162s? You sure of that?"

"No doubt. Single jet above the fuselage, twin tails. And they went through us like a bat out of hell. 162s for sure."

"Confirm King-1. Control out."

A hundred miles to the north, the fighter controller slipped her earphones back. There weren't supposed to be He-162s on this front. That didn't excuse King-1, though. It was the old case of endofmissionitis. They'd been on their way home so they'd dropped their guard. And paid for doing so.

Automobile Club, Andrews Air Force Base, Washington D.C.

"Curt?" The Seer looked around the dimly-lit room. A half-built car was in one corner, a pair of greasy, coverall-clad legs stuck out from underneath. Another half-person in even dirtier coveralls was bent over the side of the car, apparently working on where the engine should be.

"Socket wrench, quarter inch." The voice came from under the hood. The Seer picked up the required tool and passed it to the outstretched hand. "Thanks." The hand vanished inside the car again.

288

"Phillip?" LeMay's voice came from under the car. There was a faint rumble and a wheeled platform with Curtis LeMay on it rolled out.

"Curt, the cover story's out; we released an official statement an hour or so ago. It tells the world that a C-99, on a routine training flight prior to assignment to the Air Bridge, crashed on take-off. No survivors. Nobody's questioning it; no reason they should. That's one good thing about the big birds going in. They've so much fuel on board, by the time its finished burning up the magnesium and aluminum, all that's left are the engines. Nobody can tell what the thing was."

"Hell of a thing to say about 15 men isn't it? They burn up so thoroughly nobody can tell what they died in. Phillip, have you met General Francis Griswold? Commander, Third Air Division. Frank, this is Phillip Stuyvesant. More commonly known as The Seer these days."

"Pleasure to meet you General. I see our current situation is much like our professional relationship." Griswold looked puzzled. "I get the tools and you guys use them."

"Very good, Stuyvesant. I used to follow the races where the yachts your yard built ran through their paces. Didn't know it then of course. I was surprised to find you were the man who owned Herreshof behind the scenes. Always thought you were an aircraft man."

"Got interests all over, Sir. The yachts were more a matter of love than anything else. Long time ago, I met a Navy Senior Chief who taught me how to handle a sailing boat. Sort of caught the bug. What on earth are you two up to here?"

"Frank needs a car for his family. Can't buy a new one of course. So we got an old chassis, an engine and the rest of the parts and started to build one. No cause for complaint so far; project's going well. Even with gas rationed the way it is, people still want a car if they can get one."

"And we just burned up a couple of hundred thousand pounds of the stuff. Any idea why the big bird crashed, Curt?"

"Wing Commander is coming down tomorrow to tell me all about it. On the carpet in front of my desk." Griswold gave a grim chuckle. There was a piece of moth-eaten carpet in front of LeMay's desk where those who had explaining to do stood until their explanation met LeMay's exacting standards. "You know what he'll tell me? 'I can't understand it, Sir. They were my best crew.' They always are, have you noticed that?"

"Can't speak ill of the dead syndrome?"

LeMay shook his hear irritatedly. "Hell no; I could understand that. It really is the experienced crews who go in for idiotic reasons. Pure negligence on their part. The stupid, inexperienced crews don't crash. You know why? Because we have manuals for every single job on the big birds. Doesn't matter what. Pilot, navigator, radio operator, each has his manual. It's got all the procedures laid down. The inexperienced follow them exactly, by the book. It says 'read the check list out. Don't do it from memory.' So they read the check list exactly the way they're supposed to. But you get some smart-assed crew who think all that stuff is for the new recruits, not for them. They've got 'experience.' So they take short cuts, ignore procedure and one day it kills them."

"Any idea what cased this crash?" Griswold was interested. His formations were only just starting to run through the training process.

"First assessment? They tried to take off with a propeller in reverse pitch. There's no mention in the tower report of them doing a Vandenburg Shuffle before heading off. That's one thing the Wing Commander will be clearing up for me tomorrow; just how many of his crews miss the Shuffle. Before he takes over his new command at Wendover."

Griswold winced, Wendover was a hellish posting, right on the Utah/Nevada border. One could lose all one's money gambling in Nevada and then have the Mormons in Utah make one feel really bad about it. Nobody liked Wendover. Some people even preferred the Aleutians. LeMay caught the gesture and continued. "People get killed in war. Can't be helped. But if I ever meet the men who died under my command I want to be able to tell them 'we did everything we could to prepare you. We made the best plans possible under the circumstances. We maximized enemy casualties and minimized our own. That having been done, I consider your life to have been properly expended.' Won't make them feel any better of course."

"One thing's been bothering me a little, Curt. You told me that there were going to be four groups to an Air Division? My people ran some numbers today and that seems too few. If we go by base location and capacity, we should be able to have eight groups in each Division. I know the normal span of command is three to five but it might be a more efficient use of resources to go for eight."

"I'll take that under advisement Phillip." LeMay was interrupted by the bang of the outer door opening. Blackout regulations meant all the buildings on Andrews had double doors. A second later, the inner doors opened. An airman entered, blinking owlishly at the lights and squinting around.

"Hey guys, need a hand here. My battery has gone dead."

"We might have a spare around here somewhere." Griswold was very carefully keeping his voice neutral. "We'll help you put it in."

"No need for that. I got a spare at home; saw it for sale a few months back and grabbed it for when the old one died. Didn't think it would go this soon, though. If you can give me a push to get started, I'll swap them over at home."

A few minutes later, LeMay, Griswold and The Seer watched the masked tail lights of the car vanish into the darkness. LeMay broke the silence that had followed the bang of the car being push-started. "That's a smart kid. Thought ahead to the time when he would need a new battery. Anybody see what his name was?"

"Badge said 'Martin'."

"I'll keep him in mind." LeMay grunted suddenly. "I hope that kid never finds out who we were."

"Why, Curt?"

"If he ever discovers who he asked to push his car, he'll drop dead of heart failure.

291

"On the whole though, it is better not to get shot down."

Lieutenant Stanislav Knyaginichev translated the American's remark and listened to the guffaws of laughter from his men. They'd built the zemlyanka quickly and efficiently as usual. In the process, they'd 'shown' the Americans how to do it as a way to stop them from trying to help and thus disrupting the well-oiled routine. Then they'd shared their vodka and food with the two pilots. The Americans had rewarded their generosity with ground attack mission stories that usually featured vivid descriptions of German units being doused with copious quantities of napalm. Russian units never seemed to tire of those accounts. The last story had ended with their Grizzly being hit by a 'Spiral.' That had taken a little translation work but eventually they had made it. Then one of the Russians had asked a question about fighters.

"Rifleman Kabanov asks if you have fighter escort when you fly against the Hitlerites?"

"Our Grizzlies, usually no. We fly low down and there we are faster than the fighters, except the jets of course. But if we fly higher up, as bombers rather than ground attack aircraft, then we have an escort, yes. When I flew A-20s, we always had escorts. Usually Thunderbolts. If we were lucky we had Yaks to protect us."

There was a stir of pride when Knyaz translated that. "So the Russian pilots are better then." It was more a statement of satisfaction than a question.

"For us in the bombers yes, very much so. The Yak pilots remember their duty. They chase off the fascists but then stay with us in case more arrive. Our fighter pilots leave us to attack the enemy aircraft, but then go chasing off after them so we are unprotected when more Hitlerites appear. We were always pleased when we heard a Yak regiment was to be our escort."

"And now we shall escort you as well." Knyaz shifted to Russian. "Bratischka, the fascists have advanced north of us but they have not broken through. Our men have formed a defense line further north and the Hitlerites have failed to penetrate it. The Finnish attack

292

has also failed. They have broken up the Canadian division they attacked and isolated it in small pockets but those pockets are holding out. Not just holding on but their artillery and aircraft are bleeding the treacherous fascists white. We are winning this one, Bratischka. Now, our orders are to head north as well, to rejoin our parent unit. And, of course, to bring our American friends back with us. Let us do that task well, Bratischka. You have all heard how they have made the fascists suffer for invading our soil."

Torshavn, the Faroe Islands, North Atlantic

The two ships were blacked out; just shadows that were very slightly darker than the land against which they were silhouetted. Becker ran his eyes quickly over them. Three large funnels amidships; two twin four inch guns forward, one twin mount aft. They sat high out of the water. Their freeboard was increased by the mine deck that was the whole purpose of their design. Today, that mine deck was an extemporized field hospital, crowded with German seamen; most were badly burned, all suffered from exposure. Becker had picked the worst casualties for the first run to Iceland. The Faroese Islanders took their fishing boats out in the pitch black night to help speed the loading process. Once again, Becker had been awed by their skill at handling the small craft and their dedication to helping the wounded.

"Aye, they're good people in these Islands. They can hold their heads high in any company I can think of." Colonel Stewart was watching the two minelayers getting ready for sea. "The thing is, if our positions were reversed, they would still be doing the same. They don't care who's right or wrong in this. They're sailormen and when they see fellow sailormen in trouble, they drop everything to help."

"We could learn a lesson or two from them." Becker lapsed into silence. His mind was occupied by the images of the battle. The screams of the men burning as his ship had been hammered, the way she had shaken as the hits reduced her to scrap. And, always, the vicious snarl of the Ami jabos as they had pitilessly pounded her. They'd won in the end. His *Lutzow* was dead, a hopeless wreck on the rocks.

"I got the reports from Task Force 58. The destroyers attached to the battle line have picked up some more survivors. They combed the battle area but the numbers aren't good. A couple of hundred. Stewart kept the rest of the message to himself. By the time

293

the Americans had finished pushing aircraft too badly damaged to be worth repairing over the side, they had lost almost 500 planes. And yet, Halsey was going to take another swing at the British Isles before he left to repair his air groups.

"There's one last group of survivors to be loaded before the minelayers pull out. They're on the way out now."

Becker looked curiously at the Scottish Colonel. "I thought we had the worst of the wounded on board already."

"We have. These are something different. Some of my boyos speak German and they've been listening to what was being said. Quite a few of your lads are pretty devout Nazis so we've separated the worst ones out and are getting them out first. Better for us that way, they'd be the ringleaders in any trouble. Better for you, they'd be the ones to dispute any orders you give." Becker nodded. It made sense. "One thing, Captain. We separated out the ones we could recognize. We can't have got them all. The ones that are left aren't going to appreciate the difficulty of your position and they won't like the way the ships have had their scuttling systems disarmed. If I were you, I would watch my back very carefully."

27th Canadian Armoured Regiment, Kola Peninsula

The M27 Sheridan tanks of the 27th Canadian Armoured Regiment (The Sherbrooke Fusiliers) had stopped all along the road leading to the besieged Third Canadian Infantry Division. Night had fallen. Too many German tanks had night fighting equipment to make chancing a nocturnal firefight acceptable. Better to wait until daybreak when the Allied fighter-bombers would be swarming over the battlefield again. That was the theory, anyway.

Captain Michael Brody didn't have much time for theory. He had even less when he could see the brigade chief of staff approaching. Although his military career hadn't been that long, it seemed otherwise. Any length of time on the Kola Front felt like eternity and had taught him a senior officer never brought good news.

"Michael, do your boys feel like a little night-time drive under the stars?"

"Sir?"

"That's my man. The infantry have got a wee problem and they've asked us for some help. Take a look at this map. There's a dominant hill up ahead, with a house on it. Old farmhouse, probably, but it's got thick walls and the infantry couldn't take it without tank support. Anyway, infantry battalion commander came to me and said 'Give us a couple of tanks old man, they're just parked alongside the road with the crews getting cold and bored.' I gave him a good cursing of course, told him my boys needed some sleep. Anyway, all said and done, I promised him a pair of tanks to shoot up that house for him so his men could capture it. You were my first choice for the job, good of you to volunteer. Here's the orders, off you go."

The Chief of Staff took off down the road again, back to the Regimental headquarters. Brody toyed briefly with the idea of shooting him with the coaxial machine gun but dismissed it. There were probably written copies of his orders back at HQ so it wouldn't do any good.

"Sergeant, we got a job to do. There's this little house on the hill over there, it's on the reverse slope, I guess we could hardly see it. The krauts have an artillery observation position there. Defenses are ringed around it; trenches and a mortar battery. The infantry want us to blow it apart. We got a good HE load?" It wasn't really a question. The sixty-odd rounds of 90mm they had on board were split evenly between HE and HVAP.

The house was indeed on the reverse slope. There were times when Brody would have preferred the old M4 Sherman with its low-velocity 75mm. The arching trajectory meant they could have dropped shots over the ridgeline. The 90mm gun was flat trajectory; the first two shots only succeeded in blowing the roof off. Then Brody and his companion tank went up the hill along with the infantry riding behind the turret. Something the Canadians had learned from the Russians; in operations like this, tank-riders were decisive. As the house rose into view, the two tanks methodically pumped more shells into it.

Behind the hill the Germans had trenches and a mortar battery. The Sheridan was almost blind when closed up. Brody, like most of the other tank commanders in the Sherbrooke Fusiliers, drove his tank with the turret hatch open. This time it paid off. The Germans hadn't been expecting tanks at night and they were caught completely flat-footed by their appearance. While the Sheridan's main guns blasted the little house, the bow and turret top machine guns laced tracers into the defensive positions around it. The German mortars were firing over the ridge at the infantry they assumed were making their way up the slope. It was the first time Brody had ever seen mortars close up. By the look of it, it was the first time the Germans seemed to encounter a Canadian tank at close quarters. Brody snapped out short bursts from his .50 machine gun. The big slugs tumbled the German infantry as they tried to organize a resistance to the tanks.

Behind him, Brody heard the infantry commander yelling "Go forward! Get 'em boys!" The Canadian infantrymen jumped off the back of his tank. His driver was spun his tank left and right, trying to give the infantrymen cover as they rushed forward into the German pits and trenches. His machine gun was useless. It was too high up, and couldn't be brought to bear close in. The powers that be had thought of that and given Brody a Capsten Mark V SMG. He sprayed it at a group of Germans who were trying to run towards the smoldering ruins of the house. Another German suddenly appeared with a Panzerfaust aimed directly at him. The infantry were too fast for him. Three of them were all over him, their bayonets and rifle butts rising and falling.

Brody had reached the mortar pits. The Germans were still trying to fight but it was hopeless. He drove over the pits to crush the mortars. His driver shifted the tank right-left-right as he crushed their crews under his tracks. Brody heard the screams from beneath him but had more important things to think about. The tank accelerated out of the pit, Brody still firing his Capsten at the Germans fleeing in front of him.

Ahead of him he saw a red light in the treeline. "Gunner, engage left! Infrared Searchlight." The turret spun and the 90mm crashed. Almost simultaneously there was an explosion on the frontal armor. The flash blinded him and Brody felt his face burn. Ahead of him, the red light went out as both Sheridans pumped shells into the position of the half-track. That was the weakness with the German night-fighting system. They had to have infra-red searchlights to illuminate the targets. There was another brilliant flash off to the left. He heard the shell scream just in front of him. His driver didn't need orders, he spun the tank around to face the German tank. That was another advantage of fighting opened up; when the hatch was open, everything could be seen. His crew noticed anti-tank guns as soon as they started firing, and started maneuvering at once. If they waited just one little bit they'd get hit in the side. It was bad news to be hit in the side; a frontal hit wasn't so dangerous.

The 90mm guns crashed again. This time there was a fireball from the treeline. The German crew hadn't been fast enough. They'd given away their position with the muzzle flash from their gun and they hadn't cleared position fast enough. The American 90mm would make very short work of a Panzer IVK. And had.

If there were more tanks, they'd pulled back. They couldn't save the house. If they stayed, the Canadian infantry would be all over them. The two Sheridans started backing up, moving to a position just behind the crest of the ridge where they could sit in overwatch. The infantry commander was jogging up and shouting. "Hey tracks. We've got a medic; you look like you could use him"

Brody felt his face. It was covered with blood and he could feel a steel fragment stuck in his cheek. He waved acknowledgement at the infantrymen. Once his tanks were in position, he decided it was time to take advantage of the offer. The first aid post pulled out the fragment and bandaged his cheek. Then they gave him a half full bottle of vodka to take away the pain.

F-61D Evil Dreams, *over the Southern Part of the Kola Peninsula*

"Anything moving down there?"

The radar screen was masked under a curious cone-like arrangement that was supposed to shut out all non-essential light and make the dim display more readable. It worked, after a fashion, but it meant that the radar operators on the F-61D Black Widows could be picked out by the circular bruise around their faces. The constant jolting of an aircraft being flown at low altitude meant that resting one's face on anything would result in steady, minor injury.

"Can't see anything, Boss." Sergeant James Morton squinted hard. There had to be something down there. The Germans had staged a major offensive, both sides of Lake Oneda, and had run into heavy opposition. There had to be supply columns moving up behind the lead German elements, there just had to be. Nothing was moving in daylight, the Grizzlies and Thunderstorms were seeing to that. So, the supplies had to be moving up at night. Which lead back to Lieutenant

Quayle's question. *Was anything moving down there, and if not, why not?*

"They could be man-packing stuff, Boss. We wouldn't see that on the radar."

"No way Jimmie. The krauts have thrown the best part of their Army Group Vistula into the attack. Lot of tanks, even if they are moving slowly. There's got to be gas trains and ammunition moving north. Don, anything you can see out the back?"

Donald Phelan looked out through the glazed portion of the F-61s central fuselage nacelle. The whole rear section of the nacelle had been made transparent; why Phelan couldn't quite work out. Probably it stemmed from the Black Widow's ancestry as a night fighter somehow but it did seem excessive. Technically, Phelan was the aircraft's gunner, controlling the quadruple .50 caliber machine guns in the turret on top of the fuselage. His real job was to look out for targets on the ground below. The F-61s had been replaced as night fighters by the faster, more agile Grumman F-65 Tigercat, but they'd found their role as night intruders. They could lift a fearsome array of bombs and rockets, while their SCR-720 radar had proved very useful at finding targets in the darkness. It was a pity that radar wasn't showing anything now.

"I'm going to try a bit further south. The Germans may be moving north more slowly that intelligence is suggesting. That would mean their supply convoys will be further back."

Evil Dreams turned south. Her R-2800s droned steadily, her radar swept the ground ahead of her. This was the hard part, actually finding something to shoot at. Once she had a target, *Evil Dreams* had the bombs and rockets, not to mention her four 23mm cannon, to do something fairly disastrous to it. But first she had to find it. The minutes ticked by, slowly draining the fuel from her tanks.

"Hey Boss, got something."

"Worthwhile?" There had been all too many times when a F-61 had expended its bombs and rockets on a target of little value only to have a rich group turn up when she was on her way back home, her racks and magazines empty.

298

"Collection of vehicles; definition isn't good enough to count how many." There was a rustling of maps in the bulky radar compartment. "OK, there's a railway junction ahead. East-west line meets a north-south line. I think the contacts are clustered around the buildings at the junction." The resolution of the SCR-720 wasn't that good, it was barely adequate to show that the targets were there.

"OK, we'll take them down." Quayle swung *Evil Dreams* around in a wide curve, getting her lined up on the radar contacts below. There was nothing to be seen down there. Every unit on Kola knew that keeping itself blacked out was essential if they were to survive. The Americans had their sophisticated Black Widows with their array of weapons and radar. The Russians had their partisans on the ground, all too ready to spot a target and steer in one of the little night-intruder Boomerangs. The Germans had their night fliers as well; everything from the old Hs-123 biplanes to Ju-88Gs and He-219 night-fighters. An array of nocturnal pests whose activities condemned the troops on the ground to a night of sleepless darkness.

"Target's in front of us now Boss." Quayle reached down and selected the inner bomb racks. They had something new, a device that allowed three 500 pound bombs to be carried on a single pylon originally intended for a single 1,600 pound weapon. The price paid was that the triple rack was draggy and pulled their speed down. That's why a wise pilot dumped those bombs first. Next step was to put the nose down, taking *Evil Dreams* into a long, quiet dive that allowed him to throttle the engines back. *No point on giving the targets more warning than I have to.*

Morton quietly read the range to the cluster of targets on the ground ahead. Then, he stopped; they were too close in for the radar to be effective. It didn't matter. Quayle had seen the shadows of the buildings in front of him and had lined up perfectly. Then, he punched the bomb release and slammed the throttles forward. The big Black Widow leapt forward with the added power from its R-2800s. Staring out of the back transparencies, Phelan saw the ground erupt with the six explosions from the bombs. Then two more, bigger, fireballing blasts.

"Secondary explosions, probably fuel or ammunition going up. Whatever had been down there, we've hit something." He paused a second. "Problems Boss. We've got a bandit out here. I'm picking up Lichtenstein emissions and we just gave him the flaming datum to end all flaming datums." Morton scanned his radar warning equipment.

There was no indication where the enemy night-fighter was, but it was out there and it had a good idea where the intruder it was hunting could be. Phelan slid away from his observation post and climbed into his gunner's seat. If they couldn't find the enemy night-fighter, defending against it would be his job.

In the cockpit, Quayle was weighing odds. *The fighter couldn't be to the south or west of us, otherwise we'd have picked it up. It had to be north and east, probably on its way back to base. And it had to be above us.* In daylight that would be a bad disadvantage for *Evil Dreams* but at night, things were different. The lower aircraft would be hidden against the shadows of the ground; the higher aircraft would be silhouetted against the brighter sky. Provided the differential wasn't too great, the plane below had the edge. Quayle remembered something else; an urgent intelligence warning that German night-fighters carried upwards-firing cannon. *No. Here, now, being below was good.*

As *Evil Dreams* turned, her radar scanning arc cut across the sky, searching for the hostile night-fighter. The Germans had a radar warning system too; one that could detect the SCR-720. That was probably how they knew *Evil Dreams* had been in the area.

"Got him, Boss. He's turning our way but we're behind, below and outside his curve. About 5,000 yards ahead. Closing steadily, his speed's around 200, perhaps 250." Quayle glanced down, *Evil Dreams* was doing just over 330 mph. Within two minutes, they should be able to see the target. Theoretically, it was possible to do an entire intercept using radar sightings but nobody ever did. They waited to see their target first.

"He's straightening out Boss. Probably going to reverse his turn." That would make sense, the German pilot would be snaking, trying to expand the search arc of his radar. This time though, the turn would take him right across the Black Widow's nose.

"Got him! There he is." Quayle ran the identification through his mind. *Twin radial engines, twin tailplanes, glass cockpit extending to the nose. A Heinkel 219. That was good, they were the best night fighters Germany had and downing one is a real prize.* The German fighter was dark against the sky. To cut down shadows, the Germans painted theirs dappled gray. The Americans used a darker slate gray.

"Turret locked forward, Boss; transferring gun control to you." Phelan settled back. His turret was now part of *Evil Dreams'* forward-firing gun battery.

The He-219 was already starting her reverse turn. Quayle corrected slightly and started to turn with her. The red pipper on his gunsight moved up the aircraft's fuselage to a point just forward of its nose. A quick glance to check that he had selected all eight guns. A gentle squeeze on the trigger was all it took.

There was no stream of tracer. No sensible night fighter crew used the stuff. He could see the shells strike, the brilliant flash of the 23mm shells ripping into the German's cockpit; the smaller flashes as the 0.5 machine gun bullets danced across the disintegrating mass of metal and plastic. The He-219 was armored, but *Evil Dreams'* 23mm guns had been designed to bust tanks. An aircraft was easy meat for them. The American and Australian crews had fallen in love with the V-Ya cannon and they were taking most of the production these days. The Russians preferred the heavier 37mm guns for their ground attack aircraft, so everything had worked out.

Up ahead of them, the He-219 was a mass of flame. It spun out of control. Quayle ceased fire and throttled back, diving away to get clear of the blazing wreck. The night's work wasn't over yet.

Mechanized Column, 71st Infantry Division, Kola Peninsula

There had been no warning. They'd heard the engines of course and knew there was an aircraft up there. They hadn't known who or what it was. The younger men, those with the sharpest ears, said it was twin-engined. That had seemed right. It wasn't one of the Russian women in their damned sewing machines. That meant it was either American or German. Everybody knew which way the odds favored in that bet. So they had listened carefully and heard the engines fade away as the unidentified aircraft departed. Lang had almost started to relax when Asbach had suddenly leapt up. "He's coming back; get down!"

Lang had obeyed even though he couldn't work out how Asbach had known. He'd thrown himself flat just as the quiet purr of engines turned into a roar that almost drowned out the whistle of the bombs coming down. Then the sound of both was lost in the explosions. Lang counted them; four, five, six. By the glow that suddenly lit up the night he knew that some of them had bitten. He looked up, cautiously, carefully. One of the buildings around the station was ablaze where a bomb had flattened it. A trio of half-track trucks were a mass of orange-red flame. One of the sub-units had just lost its reserve fuel. Not a great cost. If the unit had been concentrated, it might have been far worse. Asbach insisted they disperse though, and his experience had, once again, paid off.

"There are two aircraft up there." The young sergeant was speaking almost to himself. "I think one of them is ours."

That would mean a night fighter come to rescue them, probably drawn by the explosions. Lang listened carefully. The young man had been right; there were two aircraft up there. It was a fair bet they were stalking each other. He watched, the time seeming to drag by. A crash and rattle was clearly heard over the sound of the engines. It was to the north of them. Lang swore he could see the muzzle flash of the plane's guns. There was no doubt about where the other plane was. It exploded into flame, a brilliant red crucifix against the dark night that twisted and fell, distorting as it tumbled from the sky.

"I wonder who it was?" Lang couldn't help ask.

"We'll never know. Nobody got out of that alive." There was a crash. The flames seemed to spread out as the destroyed aircraft hit the ground, ten, fifteen kilometers north of them.

"Everybody get to cover, disperse away from the buildings." Asbach rapped out the orders. If the American aircraft had survived, it would be coming back.

F-61D Evil Dreams *Over the Southern Part of the Kola Peninsula*

"Going back for them, Boss?"

Quayle shook his head, then keyed the microphone. "Don't think so. They'll be dispersing down there. Anyway, I've had a thought. I was wondering why they were grouped around a rail junction."

Phelan thought for a second. "They were waiting for something. Supplies."

"That's my guess. They must have moved pretty fast to get here and I bet they're down on gas. Ammo too, probably. So, they're waiting for a resupply. Now, since they're waiting for a resupply by a railway line, doesn't that mean the supplies are coming. . . . ."

". . . . . by train." Morton finished the sentence off.

"Right. If we work back along the rail lines, we should find that train. A whole trainload of supplies. Jimmie, plot me a course to follow the railway line west. Don, back to your turret. The guns are yours. That kraut may have had a friend."

Evil Dreams fell back into its usual routine. The Black Widow cruised west. When the contact came, there was no mistaking it, a brilliant return whose glow lasted the entire sweep of the scanner. "Boss, we've got it. Big train by the radar echo. There's a lot of metal down there.

"Any friendlies down there?"

"We're far behind enemy lines, Boss. Must be as supply train. Krauts must be desperate to run a train this big. Either that or they're really short of engines." That was part of the briefing the night intruder pilots got. The Germans were desperately short of locomotives. They'd started the war short. They'd looted the countries they'd conquered to make up the numbers. That had left them with a mixed fleet it was impossible to maintain. They'd never built, or captured, the heavy cranes and wreckers that were needed to salvage damaged or derailed locomotives. The path of the German armies was marked by a trail of rusting locomotives abandoned by the tracks they had left. Then the partisans had displayed incredible imagination in sabotaging what was left and the Americans made busting trains a specialty. All in all, the German railways were in a sad state

"Check the book anyway, Jimmie."

Morton got his briefing notes out. It only took a second to check. "Nothing friendly round here boss. There's a Navy train getting out but its far to the west of us; other side of the river and heading north by now. This one's a kraut, no doubt about it."

Quayle banked the Black Widow around and headed north before turning down to hit the train side on. Recommended method of hitting trains was to strafe along their length; there was a good bet this train was loaded with ammunition and flying along it was a sure way to get hit by debris. He thought for a second, then selected the twelve five-inch rockets hanging under the outer wing panels. Selector set to two. They would fire of in pairs; each pair a split second after the one before.

Once again it was the shadows that were his first indication of the target. To his surprise there were three separate trains and he'd blundered; he'd lined up on the last of the train convoy. It was too late to do anything about it. He gunned his R-2800s and made his pass, pouring the rockets at the engine and cars behind it.

"Gee, look at that secondary!" In the back, Phelan was watching the eruption and fire as the rockets tore into the target. It had been a beautiful pass.

Curly *Battery B, US Navy 5th Artillery Battalion, Kola Peninsula.*

"There's a plane up there." Perdue was searching the sky but he could see nothing. *The aircraft seemed to have turned away, whatever it was probably didn't matter too much.* Then he heard the faint growl of the engines picking up and he knew it would matter very much.

It was sheer luck that he saw the twin-boom Black Widow. It streaked across his trains, pouring rockets at the poor little shunter at the end of the line. The orange streaks of rocket fire gave him just enough light to make a tentative guess. The roaring fire as the rockets exploded in the supply of diesel fuel and propellent bags stored in one of the shunter cars confirmed it. A Black Widow night intruder had spotted the trains and decided they just had to be German. Perdue swore to himself, *damned Black Widow squadrons hadn't been informed we have been forced to change their route.*

"What's the colors? For God's sake hurry!"

"Green to white." The voice was unidentified, unidentifiable in the roaring noise of the inferno that had engulfed the shunter and its consist.

Perdue grabbed the flare gun and rammed the correct flare into it. Time was short. The Black Widow would already be turning for another pass at the trains underneath. The flare went skywards; burning green, then turning to white. Even before it had completed its burn, Perdue fired a second, then a third. It must have been enough because the Black Widow thundered a few feet overhead without firing.

F-61D Evil Dreams *Over the Southern Part of the Kola Peninsula*

Quayle was lining up on the remaining parts of the train group when the flare exploded almost in front of him. At first he'd thought it was a spiral but it had burned green, turning to white. Two more had followed it.

"Don't shoot Boss! It's one of ours."

Morton's scream of warning stopped Quayle just in time. As *Evil Dreams* flashed over the trains, he saw the two great guns in their carriages. "Jimmie, that Navy train; was it railway guns?"

"Sure was, Boss."

"Well, it isn't far to the west of here. We just shot the holy living shit out of it. We'd better warn control, we'll radio it in."

Curly, *Battery B, US Navy 5th Artillery Battalion, Kola Peninsula*

The shunter and its consist were a write-off. Eighteen Americans and six Russians had died with it. Perdue was already having their graves dug beside the tracks. It was hard to tell which corpse was which, the combination of diesel fuel and propellent had charred them beyond recognition. Perdue knew he was probably burying Americans in a Russian grave and vice versa, but he guessed it didn't matter too much. They'd fought together, died together, did it really matter which was which?

Sickbay, USS Gettysburg *CVB-43, Flagship Task Force 58*

The bang and roar shook Captain Christian Lokken out of his uneasy sleep. For one hideous moment, he thought he was back on his shattered *Gneisenau*, experiencing again the merciless pounding from the Ami jabos. Then he saw lights above him and the instructions on the cabinets. The gray paint; the stenciled note 'Property of the U.S. Navy.' Almost as soon as it registered there was another bang and roar directly overhead.

"Noisy aren't they Captain?" The voice was professional-cheerful, the one doctors used to critically ill patients whose chance of survival was still in doubt. "Aircraft taking off. We're launching strikes, hitting targets around Londonderry. Especially the SS barracks and training center there."

"A carrier? How?"

"You were transferred over from the *Charles H. Roan* last night. The destroyers are doing what they can, but they're just not equipped to handle casualties like this. You're a very sick man, Captain."

Lokken slumped back into his cot. "My crew, how many survivors? Do you know?"

"We think a total of fifty three. There may be more in the Faroe Islands; three of your ships made it there. Two destroyers and a cruiser. We think there may be between 2,000 and 2,500 survivors on board them."

"And you will be bombing them again." It was a flat statement. After the nightmare of the day-long assault, Lokken couldn't believe the Americans would leave those ships afloat. A thought that was emphasized by another bang and roar over his head.

"I don't think so. We sent a photo-Corsair to have a look. The cruiser's on the rocks, finished. The destroyers are Free British prizes. Anyway, Captain, you've got pneumonia, frostbite and Lord knows what else. Rest for a while; later I'll give you some exercises to get the fluid out of your lungs. If you want to survive, its critical you follow the instructions I give you. Another thing, don't even try to leave the sickbay. The change in temperature will kill you. Going for a walk is literally more than your life is worth."

The doctor left the sickbay, nodding to the two Marines on guard outside. His words to Captain Lokken had been the absolute truth but not for the reasons he'd given. A lot of *Gettysburg's* crew were Irish. The majority of them reckoned they had scores from 'the old country' to settle with a convenient German. There was another bang and roar from overhead. More Corsairs on their way to pound the SS units headquartered around Londonderry.

CHAPTER TEN
ALL THINGS MUST PASS

1st Platoon, Ski Group, 78th Siberian Infantry Division, First Kola Front

"A Hitlerite battle group."

Knyaz surveyed the railway junction with his binoculars. A few feet away, Noble Sniper Irina Trufanova was doing the same using the PMU telescopic sight on her rifle. At the moment she was under orders not to fire. This was a covert scouting mission after all. If the patrol was spotted, her first job would be to drop anybody giving orders. Still, no sign of that yet.

There were half tracks scattered around the buildings. Instinctively Knyaz counted them. *Almost enough for a full battalion of Panzergrenadiers.* There probably had been enough once but there were six bomb craters in the middle of the building cluster and at least two burned-out vehicles. That had to be the work of the Night Witch whose report had caused his patrol to be diverted here.

"What do you think they're doing here?" Captain John Marosy was watching as well; rather hoping the force gathered around the junction was too strong for the ski unit to take on.

"There is one of your naval gun trains west of here." Knyaz spoke slowly. He hadn't told the Americans of the radio messages he'd received that morning. A Russian officer told nobody any more than he had to, a hangover from the bad old days. Ski units were more closely knit than most. Even so, operational security was paramount. Not because Knyaz didn't trust his men; because lifting a man from a unit and getting him to tell everything he knew was a past-time both armies practiced. A few carefully-chosen barbarities and that man would tell whatever he knew. What he didn't know, he couldn't tell. Which could be very tough on the captured man, of course. "It is trying to escape to the North. The original line was cut by bombing, now it must come through here."

"So the unit is trying to block it. Can they stop the train?"

"They do not have to. This junction splits the line two ways. A line to the north that takes the trains, eventually, to Murmansk. The other line goes east but eventually curves back south. Would you like to guess which way those points will have been set?"

Marosy didn't like the way this was going. "They'll be set so the train goes south."

"That is so. The combat group is set up so it will stop anybody changing the points. If the train stops, it will be captured. If it does not, it will curve south, go deeper into enemy territory and still be captured."

"So we will have to capture the points and change them. Put the train on the right track." Neither comment was a question, much as Marosy would have liked them to have been. He was very unhappy about this. He'd heard of the horrors of infantry fighting on the Russian Front and that was quite enough.

"An easy thing to say, Tovarish Captain. Look at what we have down there. At least three mechanized infantry companies, an artillery battery, a platoon of armored cars with 50mm guns in turrets and another with 75mm anti-tank guns. That is much more than a battalion; far too much for a full-strength infantry platoon. And we will be under strength for I must send men to warn the train of what awaits it."

Marosy thought carefully, An old proverb ran though his mind. *'If you're going to a fight, bring all your friends. And get them to bring their friends.'* He knew few people in the American Army, let alone the Russians. He did have friends in the Air Force. To make matters better, he was trained as a forward air controller. "Knyaz, the switches for the junction, they are by that small shack, yes?"

"If this is the same as all the other lines, yes. And things are very standardized."

"Well, suppose we had some air support. In fact, a lot of air support. Could we take that hut, it's close to us, and hold it long enough to reset the junction and let the trains past? Then the trains pick us all up and take us North?"

Knyaz thought carefully also. His unit was small but very skilled and were veterans. If the Americans threw their aircraft in to the battle and kept the fascists under fire and if the trains were lucky, they might get past. And they might be able to pick up the remains of the ski unit. That was so many ifs but if they all came to pass, it would be good to ride a train on the way back home. There was the problem of the vehicles of course, but if their crews could take them further north, they could be picked up later.

"Can you get us air support?"

"Have you a radio I can use?"

Curly, *Battery B, US Navy 5th Artillery Battalion, Kola Peninsula.*

"Sir, up ahead. Men in white."

That could mean anything, Perdue thought. *Everybody wore snow camouflage up here.* It was very, very hard to tell who was who. The banana-shaped magazines of the German rifles were a pointer, certainly, but enough captured weapons were floating round to make them an unreliable guide at best. *So who were these people?*

"Sound General Quarters. Get the men with rifles ready. If this is an ambush, we'll have to shoot our way out of it."

Ahead, one of the white figures was standing on the railway line, waving his arms in the traditional "stop " sign. Perdue had no intention of doing that, no intention at all. Not until the situation was a lot clearer than it was now. "Slow down a bit, but keep going." *Let the situation mature as the mud-puppies say. Trouble was if one let the situation mature long enough, it all turned into manure.*

"What's he doing?"

"Still waving, Sir. Now he's making a 'cut' gesture. Looks like a guy on the carriers doesn't it?"

"It does indeed." Perdue's binoculars were shaking too much from the vibration of the engine to allow clear vision but the guns carried by some of the men had the drum magazines of the PPS-45. That and the American-type 'cut power' gesture decided him. That and the fact he had a lot of riflemen on board.

The gamble paid off. The lone figure on the track ran forward when the engine came to a halt and saluted at the foot of the engine cab.

"Sergeant William Bressler, Sir. Navigator of the A-38 *Hammer Blow,* shot down a few days ago. We've been with a Russian ski unit since then."

"Commander Perdue, United States Navy. We?"

"My pilot is Captain John Marosy, Sir. He's with the rest of the ski unit. Sir, I've got bad news for you. The krauts have a reinforced battalion battle group around the junction up ahead. Mechanized infantry, artillery, those big armored cars with tank guns, you name it. They're blocking the junction and the points are set to send you back south."

That was it, Perdue thought, *game over. Blow up the guns and hope we can infiltrate ourselves back North.*

"Damn, we got this far too."

"Sir, the ski unit commander has a plan. Captain Marosy is calling for air support. Given the situation, he thinks he'll get it. The ski unit will attack under the cover of that air attack. They will seize the points and reset them. Then, while the aircraft are still bombing, you crank these engines up, open the throttle as wide as it'll go and just crash through the krauts. The line north is fairly straight; it's the southern branch that curves north. As you get clear, slow down and pick up the ski troops and then make a run north."

"Not a man for subtlety is your Captain." Perdue thought it over. There was a certain simplicity about the plan that made it hypnotically attractive. *Just go flat out and crash through.* "Suppose the krauts block the line?"

"They haven't, Sir. I guess they expect you to either stop or take the southern branch. Their unit is pretty spread out as well; a Black Widow hit them last night and cut them up."

"Know how that feels." Perdue grunted. His mind played with the images of what he had been told.

"Well, it means that if the bombing pins them down, they won't be able to concentrate on the ski unit."

"How are we going to coordinate this?" Perdue decided that just running his guns past an entire kraut battalion was too much of an opportunity to pass up. *Just like Farragut in the days of old.*

"Captain says just watch, Sir. And listen out on this frequency. No need to coordinate in advance. You just stay put here and wait for the bombing to start. Then just come through as fast as you can."

Top Floor, Bank de Commerce et Industrie, Geneva, Switzerland.

"Interesting document from Lucy, Loki." Branwen put the file on Loki's desk. "And a . . . . messenger . . . . from Sweden is waiting to talk to you."

It was a bit hard to decide what to call the visitors from Sweden. Messenger was a good approximation but messengers didn't have the powers to negotiate things or give opinions. Ambassadors would have been a good option, only sovereign countries didn't send ambassadors to banks. Even to banks that were a lot older than most countries. *Supplicant might be a good term,* thought Loki, *or delegate perhaps?*

"What's the document?"

311

"Very interesting. It's a description of German plans to deal with damage from bombing attacks. Everybody was expecting to get bombed right at the start of the war, you know that, but it never really happened. There was Rotterdam of course, and a few raids on England, but mostly no bombing until the B-29 raids. And they've more or less stopped now. I guess H.G. Wells must be really upset. He was so proud of *The Shape of Things To Come*."

"So, what's the gist of it?"

"Basically, if heavy bombing of their infrastructure starts, the Germans plan to disperse and decentralize their facilities. They will split the existing large factories into many small ones; perhaps as many as forty or fifty. No manufacturing process other than final assembly of aircraft is to be permitted within one and one-fifth miles of airfields. They'll organize their plants so that the primary plants are dispersed to at least two different places. That way a firm with four plants today will have eight or more different sources of supply. The idea is that if one or two of these places was destroyed, it should still be possible to maintain approximately the same level of production by using salvaged parts from bombed plants.

"The problem is that Speer and his teams believe that dispersal, in their experience, is costly and inefficient. A plant which is subdivided into many sub-units, feeder plants and small shops cannot possibly manufacture as economically as can one large integrated unit. They believe that dispersing the production facilities will reduce production by about 20 to 30 percent. This is due to the need for large control system with many non-productive workers, the duplication of non-productive departments, such as fire prevention, first aid, social and recreational activities, increases in supervisory personnel and the impossibility of duplicating highly specialized single-purpose machinery and equipment."

"Germany is just about hanging on now. Production equals losses, more or less. Except for their fleet of course; no way that's being rebuilt."

Branwen nodded. "Their damage control provisions are interesting as well. Their plan is to form flying squads, in convoys of cars who will go to the site of a bombed installation and organize the work of bringing it back up. The plan demands 'energetic men' be recruited, ones with a wide spread of expertise and who will be prepared to work as long as it takes. Their job is to immediately round up military personnel, available civilian labor and volunteer forces to help clean up, aid in casualty rescue, etc, and analyzed the damage.

"The intention is to produce a plan that lists the required machine tool replacements necessary building repair materials and man-power, emergency tarpaulins. Speer's ministry has completed an inventory of all machine tools in the country with the plants they are located in and the priority assigned to those sites. Using that index, the damage control team can pick up suitable machine tools available in the immediate area and in plants of lower priority than the assigned one. This allows the higher-priority plant to be put back into production quickly. The stated target for the damage control teams is to have the plant up and running in 48 hours or less."

"So it doesn't matter what the importance of the target plant is then. It doesn't even matter of we do manage to identify the key industrial plants. The damage will be repaired by stripping out less important ones. The Americans would have to bomb the same plants over and over again until there are no reserves of machine tools left. Well, Douhet came up with a nice theory but Speer and his cronies have just buried it. The Seer needs to see this; put it in with the next package out to Washington. When are Henry, Achillea and Iggy due over here next?"

"About five or six days."

"They need to be here sooner than that. Ask them to come right over now. Next, send in our Swedish friend please."

The door closed quietly behind Branwen. A moment later she opened it for a middle-aged man in a dark suit. "Mister Loki. I am afraid these are not happy times."

"No Mister Erlander, these are not indeed. Why did those damned fool Finns have to go and do it?"

"You know the Finns Loki, obstinate, self-centered, conceited to a fault. Convinced they have the wisdom of all the world and unable to recognize they are a small part in a very large machine. It appears that the Germans convinced them that this offensive couldn't fail and it was the way to Finnish greatness. They still believe that. I have been in quiet contact with Risto Heikki Ryti. He is not prepared to listen to reason. He told my representatives that Germany would win the war in the end. Even if it could not win, it would hold on long enough for America and Russia to give up from exhaustion. So Finland had nothing to fear from the allies but much to fear from the Germans. And I tell you this, he may well be right. How much longer will Russia lose its young men in a war that never ends? And how many more of its young men will America lose to keep this war running?"

Loki leaned back in his seat, luxuriating in the soft leather. Once, so long ago, such a chair would have been a throne for a king. "You have heard what has happened to the Germany Navy of course?"

"Of course. But the Navy is hardly the most important part of the German forces."

"No, but it was a part of them. Now it is gone and what is left is to be scrapped, broken up. The allies own the seas of the world now."

"The survivors are to be scrapped. I did not know this?"

"They are. Hitler was apparently not pleased. I feel that this whole mad scheme may well have been his. Perhaps, perhaps not. But the fleet is gone. Doenitz has disappeared; probably dead by now."

"That does not change the fact that this war is being fought on land. America may rule the seas now, but how does a shark fight a wolf?"

"Carefully, I would think. The Finns need to understand this and you must tell them it. They have harmed themselves greatly by taking part in this offensive. They will be punished severely for breaking the peace on their front line. I have heard from my contacts in Russia that they will lose the Aland Islands at least and some of their southern territories. Much of their southern territories. And not a small amount in the north"

"If the allies win."

"Yes, if the allies win, Tage. If they win. If they do not, then we will all have much more important things than Finland to worry about."

314

B-27C Terrible Trixie *424th Medium Bombardment Group, Approaching Railway Junction 18 West*

The Super-Marauders were spread out. Their formation was designed to give the best possible bomb pattern on the ground 27,000 feet beneath them. Normally, they were closed up to give a tight pattern that would devastate the target beneath them. Not this time. That was only one strange thing about this mission, the way the aircraft had spread out to disperse the bombs over a wide area. It was almost as if the brass didn't really want this target destroyed. If that was so, why had they sent the 424th to bomb it? At short notice too; today's mission had been to hit another railway junction in the German rear areas. It was a much more normal target for the mediums than one almost on the front line like this. Normally, a target this close in would be assigned to the fighter-bombers.

Around them, the fighter escort of F-80As weaved a defensive fence around the bombers. Originally the B-27 had been designed as a high-altitude version of the older B-26 Marauder that would be harder to intercept. Experience had quickly put an end to that idea. It wasn't that the fighters could easily reach them; they couldn't. The FW-190s were running out of steam way below them and the Me-109s were operating at their margins. At first, most of the German fighters had been loaded with additional guns to deal with the B-29 raids. Taking off the extra weight had meant they could get up to where the B-27s operated. Then, the Ta-152 and the new jets had arrived. They had fewer problems getting up to the 27,000 feet where the B-27s flew. Without escorts, the bombers couldn't get to their targets without crippling losses. For all that, the main problem was accuracy. It was just too damned hard to hit targets from up here. Since high altitude hadn't given the bombers the expected level of immunity, the B-27s usually flew at around 18,000 feet and had a heavy escort. That meant their concentrated bomb pattern could devastate a target.

Now, for once, they had gone back to the high altitude game. Odd. Once again, Colonel Joseph Patroulis thought that it was as if the brass didn't really want this target destroyed. *As if they were going through the motions somehow.* Anyway, whatever the brass was up to, the bombers would be starting their bomb runs shortly. "All gunners, keep a sharp watch out. This is where the kraut fighters are likely to hit us." That went without saying. Once the bombers had settled down into their bomb run and were trapped flying straight and level, the fighters and flak would turn on the heat.

315

"Flak bursts, Sir. Way below us." That was the one good thing about being up here; only the heavy German flak could reach them and there was little of that in the front lines. Heavy anti-aircraft guns also made good anti-tank guns and it didn't take much effort to guess which was the preferred use.

Down in the nose, Major Leo Andrassis settled down and applied his eye to the Norden bombsight. His orders were strict; bias the aim to the right of the target complex and beyond it. The 'beyond it' bit made sense. He was the lead bombardier and when he dropped, so would everybody else. That meant the bombs would walk back, along the line of sight. If the point of aim was beyond the target, the pattern of bombs would be in the right place. But a right-hand bias was unusual. "Bombardier to pilot, bomb doors open. I have the aircraft."

Patroulis took his hands and feet off the controls. "Pilot to Bombardier, confirm, you have the aircraft."

Andrassis started to make his fine adjustments as he saw the magnified picture of the railway junction approaching. A slight touch on the controls, and the picture shifted slightly. The buildings passed underneath and he started counting to himself. *One Mississippi, two Mississippi, three Mississippi and go.* He pressed the release. Eighteen 250 pound bombs dropped free from the belly. Behind him, the other 27 aircraft in the formation saw the release and dropped their own loads. "That's it boys; we're done. Bombardier to pilot, you have the aircraft. Now let's go home."

Mechanized Column, 71st Infantry Division, Kola Peninsula

It wasn't like the night attack. That blast that had come from the darkness without warning. This time, the air raid sirens sounded well in advance and given plenty of warning. The troops had dispersed into their foxholes. The flak guns had been prepared to open fire although the alert had said medium bombers and those would drop from far above the range of the 20mm and 37mm guns equipping the column. Some units had the new 55mm gun, but not this one. The Heer came a long way behind the SS when it came to the new equipment.

"There they are." Asbach pointed out the flashes in the sky as the sun reflected off the silver bombers. *Typical of the Amis. They*

316

never bothered to camouflage their aircraft. The he frowned. "That's odd, they're much higher up than usual."

Beside him, Lang raised an eyebrow. Asbach grinned in reply. "The Amis tried bombing from high altitude. They couldn't hit anything. Nobody can from up there. So they gave up and came back down to below 5,000 meters like everybody else. I was expecting a strike after that Night Witch hit us, but this is odd."

"Perhaps it is a new group, just arrived? And like all newbies, they think they know it all." Lang had an innocent expression on his face. Asbach saw it and smacked the officer on the back.

"Indeed so. Terrible people, newbies." *And you've come a long way my friend. Old Lenin was right, there is a soldier inside you trying to get out. We just had to give it the chance.* "Look out! Here they come. . . . . . ."

The first set of explosions shook the ground. A rain of earth and mud descended on the troops around the junction. The bombs were way over, so far beyond the buildings that their fury was wasted on trees and snow. Asbach knew that wouldn't last. The bombs would walk back over his command and devastate it. *Or perhaps not.* He risked a peep over the edge of the foxhole. The bombs were scattered all over the place, a loose pattern, not the tight group that the American mediums normally produced. That was the altitude of course, nobody could hit a target from 9,000 meters, but something was nagging him. *This was wrong, the Amis didn't fight like this.* They were unimaginative, repetitive, they found something that worked and stuck with it.

"Sir, air raid warning."

"I would never have guessed." Asbach fixed a mock-serious glare on the radioman who had risked his life running through the bombs to carry the message.

"Sir, not this. Jabos coming in right behind. Single- and twin-motors."

Damn. Grizzlies and Thunderstorms. That is all I need. The sense that something was wrong got worse, with the Amis it was either mediums or jabos, not both. It was almost as if..... Then the penny dropped and Asbach risked another quick look over the rim of his foxhole. What he saw threw him back to 1941 and the horrors of the retreat from Moscow that first winter of the war. White-clad Siberian ski-troops skimming through the snow, slashing at the Germans freezing in their first taste of a Russian winter. They were here again. They had broken out of the tree line even as the bombs had fallen and were racing across the snow towards the small cluster of buildings around the set of points that were the whole reason for this little way-station existing. This bombing raid wasn't aimed at destroying the junction. It was a covering barrage for the attack by the ski-troops. It was aimed at seizing the controls that operated the junction itself. An attack that was already well on the way to succeeding.

"Out! Ski Troops! Siberians!" Asbach yelled the warning but it was lost in the last roar of bombs. He was not the only one who had seen the attack though. Others had done also. Already a defense was being mounted. An MG-45 put out one of its vicious bursts that bowled over at least three of the skiers. For a moment Asbach had thought they had more, but some of those who went down opened fire on the German positions in return. *Either wounded or just covering the attack,* Asbach didn't know which. The rest of the Siberians made it to the huts around the junction itself and Asbach guessed what would be happening. They would be resetting the points so that the gun train would head north, back to the allied lines. Still, to do that, they would have to capture this junction first and a single ski-platoon wasn't going to manage that, even if they did have the Ami Jabos in support.

1st Platoon, Ski Group, 78th Siberian Infantry Division, First Kola Front

"Damn. We made it!" Marosy looked in amazement at the group of shabby little huts that surrounded them. Old, weathered and half-rotten wood, they offered but little cover. Most of that little was of the morale variety. Over on his right, three of the strongest Russians were already wrestling with the level that manually changed the points over. As they had guessed, the points had already been set to send the gun trains south again. Now the challenge was to make the frozen lever move far enough to send the trains along the north bound line. They had to do it; they had to do it fast and they had to do it under fire.

There was a crackle of fire mounting from the main cluster of buildings used by the Germans. The shock of the medium bomber attack had allowed the ski troops to get across the open ground towards the railway lines but now the Germans were grimly determined they shouldn't stay there. The problem was, the Siberians had to. They had to hold the lines until the trains had got through. What happened after that didn't matter. Amidst the sound of the rifles and machine guns, Marosy heard the roar of engines starting. The Germans were getting their armor ready. They didn't have heavy armor here but even their half tracks and armored cars were deadly enough against unsupported infantry. It was Marosy's job to change the unsupported bit. The Russians were betting their lives on him being able to do it.

"Eagles this is Ground Crown. Do you read me?"

"Ground Crown, this is Little Eagle Leader. Keep your heads down. We're coming in with rockets and .50 caliber. And be advised, the Big Snakes are on the move."

Curly, *Battery B, US Navy 5th Artillery Battalion, Kola Peninsula.*

"The mediums are making their run now, Sir." Perdue had already seen the formation of B-27s high up in the morning sky. Everything was timed to run off the first sighting of the mediums. If they screwed up, the whole plan would fall apart. It wasn't a good way to run things but it was the only way that stood a chance of working. The rain of bombs from the B-27s was the signal flare that started the race. For the two remaining guns of the 5th Artillery, it was exactly that. A race.

"Roll. Maximum speed, give her everything we've got." This whole attack depended on speed to get past the German unit while they were still recovering from the shock of the bombing. Every man on both trains had a rifle or grenades, A few had anti-tank rockets. The windows in the carriages had been knocked out. In front of the frames, extra pieces of wood had been nailed to give an illusion of extra protection. Now the trains looked like an old-fashioned ship of the line with the guns sticking out of their sides in rows. That was one thing running for them, the hail of fire the men on board could put out. Another was that the long straight run to the junction was downhill. That would allow the trains to build up speed nicely ready for the charge through the railway junction. Under his feet, Perdue felt the Mikado pulling as it got *Curly* and the rest of the train moving. Behind her, *Moe* had started to follow.

The buildings were ahead, just as the model had shown. A large group in the middle, a smaller group surrounding the points. The Germans were scattered around the former; the Russians dug in around the latter. The fountains of smoke and debris from the B-27's bombs were already subsiding, clearing the way for the raking bursts from the Thunderstorm's six .50 caliber machine guns. Some of the armored vehicles were already covered by the blue clouds that showed their crews were trying to get them started. *Copperhead* changed her heading slightly. Eight five-inch rockets streamed out from under her wings to bracket one of the half tracks that was starting to move forward. The vehicle stopped and a thick black cloud rolled out. A kill.

Mechanized Column, 71st Infantry Division, Kola Peninsula

"Get those vehicles moving!" Asbach knew he had only minutes if that to get some sort of attack mounted. "Block that line!"

He'd guessed what the Amis had in mind. *They've come up with nothing so subtle as seizing the junction and driving his unit out. They were just going to crash the trains straight through.* He glanced over his shoulder and saw what he had expected. Five kilometers away, the gun trains he had been chasing had crested the ridge and were heading straight for him. The ground was already beginning to shake with their weight. *Did that make sense?* Asbach realized it didn't. What was making the ground shake was the salvoes of rockets and hail of machine gun fire from the Jabos making their final run towards him.

Off to his left was a strange sight. A white cone running across the ground with a stick in its hand. Asbach recognized Lang in his white Fliegerschrenk cape with a loaded launcher in his hands. He dropped to one knee in the precisely-approved position, and held his fire despite the fountains of bullets whipping the snow around him. Then he fired. The rocket sped straight and true, scoring direct hit under the lead Jabo's belly.

Copperhead reared in the air, lurched over on one wing then plowed straight into the ground. The wreckage bounced through one of the flimsy buildings before exploding. Lang lowered his launcher and started to reload, taking a new rocket from the three round pack he had brought with him.

1st Platoon, Ski Group, 78th Siberian Infantry Division, First Kola Front

Noble Sniper Trufanova saw the man in the cape shoot the American sturmovik out of the sky and guessed who he was. The American pilot had spoken of this unit. They'd said it had one rocket man who was better, braver and more skilled than the others. The one who had shot down his *Hammer Blow*. It was her duty to kill any Hitlerites who were better, braver and more skillful than the rest. The less skilled and less brave could be dealt with after victory was won. She aimed at the man and squeezed her trigger, then watched him crumple as the bullet struck home. Through her sight, she saw the body moving. That was when she broke the sniper's code, operating the bolt of her rifle and putting another shot into the crumpled rocket man. That extra shot cost her life.

Mechanized Column, 71st Infantry Division, Kola Peninsula

Asbach saw Lang fall as the sniper shot him. Then he saw the body lurch as another shot struck home. Only, this time he was watching. He saw the muzzle flash from the rifle. So did three of his machine gunners. They saturated the whole area with bullets. *There would be no more shots in the head from that one.*

Over by the tracks, a driver moved a half track onto the rails so that the way for the trains was blocked. Asbach's Puma armored cars were already on the move. Their 50mm guns cracked shots at the Russians holding the buildings around the points. Then one of them exploded. The second wave of jabos, Grizzlies with their big 75mm guns sticking out the nose raced overhead. Asbach knew what was coming next. Jellygas.

Then he heard the thunder of the approaching trains. He spun around. They were very close; their sides lit up with a rippling wave of flashes as those inside poured rifle fire at the German troops milling around. He guessed very few of the shots were hitting anything, but the sheer volume was making his men put their heads down. He was expecting the trains to slow down as the drivers saw the track was blocked but there was no sign of them doing so. It suddenly occurred to him; they weren't going to.

Curly, Battery B, US Navy 5th Artillery Battalion, Kola Peninsula

"You know, I've always wanted to do this." The engine driver spoke contemplatively, but there was a glimmer of sheer joy in his statement. Ahead of them a German half-track blocked the railway line. Its gunner was intent on firing his machine gun at the Mikado bearing down upon him. Suddenly the German realized the awful truth and leaped out of his vehicle to run clear. He just made it. The locomotive smashed into the half track and spun it around before the disintegrating wreckage was hurled through the air to land in a blazing heap at one side of the track.

Perdue heard and felt the crash, but it didn't really register. He was leaning out of the engine cab, firing his pistol at the Germans to one side of the train. The roar of gunfire from the carriages hadn't stopped. The ripping noise of the PPS-45s and captured banana guns mated with the slower cracks of the SKS, Garand and Mozzie-Nag rifles to make a thunderous role of musketry that seemed to dominate the air around the train.

One of the armored cars had turned to fire on them. It could hurt, this one had a 75mm gun in a semi-fixed mounting. Its first shot screamed straight through the wooden carriage it had been aimed at, probably the crew had loaded armor piercing shot by force of habit. They didn't make the same mistake twice. Its next shot was explosive and it devastated the carriage, leaving its thin wooden box in ruins. The carnage inside had to be awful. Then the armored car stopped firing and broke away, trying to escape from the shots of a Grizzly that was closing in on it.

The Mikado was slowing, Perdue turned to the engine driver. "We hit?"

"No sir, points coming up, we have to take them a bit careful like. Or we'll go over." Perdue nodded. It was fortunate the northern branch was the part of the points that went straight, not curved off but the slowdown was going to be dangerous. The rifle and machine gun fire from the Germans was hitting the carriages. That had to be hurting but the points were coming up. As the train slowed, the men on the first flat car reached down, hauling the Russian ski troops on board. Then *Curly* accelerated away. The remaining ski troops would have to be rescued by *Moe*.

Knyaz had the remaining part of his force forming a rear guard, holding back the German troops while the rest got clear. The Ami-fighter-bombers were strafing the German positions. *Perhaps they would hold the Germans back long enough for my rear guard to board the second train out.* That second train was in trouble. Two armored cars, Pumas, were shooting at it with their 50mm guns. The damage was easy to see. The great gun had been hit several times and many of the carriages were little more than splintered wood. A few meters away, the American pilot was talking to the sturmoviks, steering them to the targets. A couple of Grizzlies were already lining up for a pass on the Pumas. Knyaz saw their noses disappear in the flash of the 75mm guns firing. One of the Pumas blew up. The other stopped firing and backed away fast. Its crew knew what was to come. Sure enough, the napalm tanks wobbled free. Rolling orange and black clouds from the inferno shrouded the second American gun train from the Germans.

"Bratischka, quickly, while we are screened by the fire!" The Russians left their positions and ran to the track where *Moe* slowed down to take the points and make the pick-up. They ran alongside the train, grabbing the arms held down to them and being hauled on board the flatcar behind the engine. Knyaz was last on board, and he looked quickly around. "How many?"

"We have lost eight dead, and have four wounded." The voice of the Sergeant was heavy. Twelve was a heavy toll for a small unit. Then Knyaz looked at the train he was on, saw the damage and the bodies scattered in the wreckage. The men on this train had paid a much heavier price than his little unit.

Mechanized Column, 71st Infantry Division, Kola Peninsula

Asbach looked at the trains pulling away. *That was impossible. That shouldn't have happened. One just can't do that with trains.* He stopped an orderly who was collecting casualties. Once the trains had escaped, the jabos had left. "How is Captain Lang?"

The orderly chuckled. "The Captain is still with us, Sir. A bullet in the shoulder and one through his ear but still alive. He refuses to be put on sick call Sir. That's why the men call him Captain Still Sir. No matter what the enemy do to him, he still turns up for duty."

"Very good. Give the Captain my commendations and ask him to come to me immediately. We must reassemble the unit and get after those guns."

Asbach stared at the cloud of smoke that marked the position of the escaping guns. If he could get moving and kept up the chase, he would have one more chance to intercept them.

27th Canadian Armoured Regiment, Kola Peninsula

"Right boys, this is the last stretch. We're hitting the outer edge of the Finnish forces that have got our infantry bottled up. We break through here and we've punched through to the hedgehog. They're Finns ahead of us; not Germans. So we can expect a lower standard of equipment. They're hard bastards though; they'll fight. And remember what they did to the RCAMC detachment back at Division. There's payback due for that." A stir of agreement ran around the tank crews and infantry gathered for the briefing.

Captain Michael Brody looked at the assembled team. His squadron of Sheridan tanks had been reinforced with a troop of armored infantry carried in Kangaroos, old Ram tanks that had been converted to armored infantry carriers. There were rumors that the Yanks were producing a new armored carrier, one that was completely enclosed and bullet proof. If it was, that would make a change from their existing half-tracks. Until that rumor became reality, if it ever did of course, the Kangaroo was the best infantry carrier on the battlefield. Well, the least vulnerable anyway.

"The word is, take it easy. There's no hurry over this. Our hedgehogs are in no danger. The Finns have been trying to break into them for days now and had no luck. Time isn't long enough for supply to be a problem so we don't have to crash through. When we contact the enemy, open fire; pin them down and call for artillery. We've got lots of it and even more airpower. The Yanks are over on the other front so we don't have them to worry about. It's just us and the Russians overhead." An exaggerated sigh of relief went around the meeting; the American fighter-bomber pilots were notorious for hitting friendly targets. "Right, so everybody mount up. The ground's hard, we're not stuck on the roads. First troop, left flank, second troop on the road, third troop out to the right flank. Line abreast. Infantry, you follow on behind. Enemy infantry we'll take care of, if we run into

Pak guns, you take over and handle them while we cover you with HE."

"Any word on the Paks, Sir?"

"Word is, since its Finns, 50mms." A murmur of discontent at that. Although the 50mm was technically obsolete, at the ranges the Finns fired them it didn't make much difference. The 50 was much smaller and easier to hide than the 75s and 88s the Germans used. Usually the first time somebody saw them was when a tank was knocked out. It was a 50 that had brewed up the tank used by the previous commander of A squadron and put Brody in command today.

The relative warmth of the day before had softened the mass of snow that had fallen during the storm and caused it to compact. The cold of the night that had followed froze that compacted mass hard and turned a soft field that would bog tanks down into what amounted to near-perfect tank ground. Brody's command had three troops of tanks. Technically, he should have had a total of fourteen M27s; but his squadron, like everybody else's was under strength. Including his own vehicle, he had eleven operational tanks, spread out into a rough line abreast. There were patches of forest ahead, ones that would grow larger and closer together as the site of the besieged Canadian hedgehog got closer. The plan was to plow through the defenses before the Finns could react, force them out of their positions and back on to that hedgehog. It was a classic hammer and anvil approach; Brody's tanks the hammer and the Canadian infantry in the hedgehog the anvil.

"Tank destroyer, in the woods, one o'clock." Brody swung his binoculars and stared hard. Lost in the trees, almost, was the sleek shape of a Hetzer. *Not one of the more modern German tank destroyers, some of them were real swine with long 88s and thick armor.* The Hetzer had the same 75mm as the Panzer IV and was built on the old Panzer 38t chassis. The Germans had passed most of them along to their allies. The Hetzer was cheap, easy to build and maintain. It was also a lot less capable than the German tank destroyers. Allegedly one of the reasons why the Germans had given it to their allies was to make sure that, if said allies decided to change sides, they would be outgunned enough to make sure they did not survive the attempt. Brody reflected that trust was not a dominant feature of the German make-up.

"Load AP."

325

"Up."

"Shoot!"

Five M27s fired almost simultaneously. Their 90mm shots raising fountains of dirt around the concealed Hetzer. A black, oily cloud rose from its position. The sight appeared to have woken the Finns up, *or perhaps they had been waiting for the M27s to get into closer range?* Three more Hetzers broke cover. They maneuvered to try and get lined up for shots at the fast-moving M27s. That was a problem with the little tank destroyers. They were cramped inside and their guns had very limited traverse. Tracking the Sheridans meant they had to spin the whole vehicle on the suspension in order to get out their shots.

The Finns had obviously been expecting the Canadians to stick to the road. They'd set their tank destroyers up to cover that arc. The wide, spread out Canadian line had thrown that plan to the winds. To make matters worse, most of the Canadian tanks were to the right of the position occupied by the Hetzers and the Hetzer had virtually *no* right traverse. The time taken for them to spin their vehicles around and aim was just that decisive few seconds too long. Four more of Brody's tanks concentrated their fire on to the nearest tank destroyer, sending more fountains of frozen snow up around it. They were rewarded by another boiling cloud of orange-shot black smoke. Brody saw one of his tanks lurch to a halt. One of the two surviving tank destroyers had scored and put at least one of the M27s out of the battle. Two of Brodys tanks took a Hetzer each and demolished it with 90mm rounds. That was another problem with the Hetzer, it's cramped interior made loading painfully slow. In this case, fatally slow.

"Watch out for Paks. Those Hetzers won't be on their own." Brody sent the word out while scanning the tree line for the flashes that would reveal the position of the Finnish Pak guns. They were there. He knew it, he could sense them; he could feel the gunner's eyes on him. "Driver, hard left, now!" His tank swerved and there was the ripping noise of an anti-tank shot missing his vehicle by a few feet. "Load HE"

"Up."

"Two'clock, by those three big pines, shoot."

The 90mm guns of his third troop crashed, flinging their shells in the general direction of the Finnish position. More fountains of dirt, the anti-tank gun apparently silenced. Brody knew better than to believe that. "Diamond, this is Coronet. We've found the enemy defense line, map reference," he fumbled with his map and read out the numbers. "Anti-tank guns and tank destroyers."

"Coronet, on its way." That was his forward artillery observer. He would take over the shoot now, walking the shells from whatever guns he had been allocated on to the Finnish position. Brody heard the express-train roar overhead and instinctively ducked into his turret. By the time he looked up again, the second salvo had struck home. *25 pounders* he guessed. *The Yanks preferred their bigger 105s but the 25 pounder could fire eight rounds to the 105s six and in this sort of work it was the number of bangs that mattered, not their size.*

"Coronet, hold position, there's some Sturmoviks coming in as well." *Now that was an interesting surprise. I didn't think I was that important.* He looked overhead, searching for the aircraft while the shells from the artillery battery supporting him continued to pulverize the tree line. Keyed by a flash as the sun reflected off a canopy, he saw them, a dozen aircraft already forming into a circle over the target area. Like buzzards waiting for something to die.

The lead aircraft peeled out of the circle and dived on to the forest. At the end of the dive, the rockets under its wings flashed out with long black-gray trails that ended inside the wood. As the Il-10 pulled out of its dive, it released a shower of small 10-kilo fragmentation bombs that exploded with flat, vicious cracks inside the cluster of pine trees. The second Il-10 was already diving on the position below.

"Infantry move up to within 100 yards of the woods, then debus. Diamond, have we still got the artillery?"

"That we have Coronet. As soon as the Il-10s have finished, they'll do a rolling barrage right through the woods."

Brody nodded. Overhead, the Russian sturmoviks had finished their first cycle of attacks and were now diving on the Finns. This time, they used the 37mm guns in their wings at whatever they could see. As soon as the last aircraft was clear, the express train roar of inbounds resumed. "Infantry, rolling barrage. Follow it in. Keep it nice and tight." That was another advantage of the 25 pounder; its smaller shells meant the infantry could follow the rolling barrage that much more closely. There was a belief, never said but real, that the best way of judging whether the infantry were following the barrage tightly enough was whether they took casualties from their own fire. It was one of the grim equations of war. A few dead from one's own artillery fire meant a lot more saved by the suppressive effects of the barrage.

Brody sat back in his turret as the infantry platoon followed the barrage into the heart of the Finnish defense. It would be time for the tanks to move in soon enough. At the moment they were better placed here on overwatch.

Finnish 12th Infantry Division. Kola Front

It had all gone wrong. Lieutenant Martti Ihrasaari knew it and he suspected the top brass knew it although they wouldn't admit to the fact. They'd be telling everybody how chopping up this Canadian division had been a great victory that showed the great fighting spirit and skills of the Finns. The problem was that Ihrasaari knew the truth, the 'great victory' had achieved nothing. Oh, they'd split the division up into a series of motti all right but that was as far as it had gone. The Canadians had just dug themselves in and proceeded to shoot at everybody around them with artillery and air power. It had been days since Ihrasaari had slept and his eyes felt as if they were full of sand. He was sick as well, his arms and hands had been burned by white phosphorus. The medic had dug the wicked fragments out of his flesh but the ill-effects hadn't ended. His skin was yellowing and it hurt to urinate. The phosphorus was still there, still working.

No, the Canadians hadn't exhausted themselves trying to break out. They'd just waited for the outside relief forces to break through to them. Ihrasaari had a disturbing mental picture, of drops of water on a glass plate. At first the drops of water would be well separated, just as the Canadians had been in their motti. But, as more water was added, the droplets spread out and joined together. Soon, they had the dry bits of glass surrounded and were squeezing them out of existence. Ihrasaari had a bad feeling that he was in the shrinking dry bits. The besieger who had become the besieged.

The very fact he was here proved that. This morning, he and what was left of his platoon had been pulled out of the line facing the

328

Canadian motti and sent to reinforce a sector of the front that was crumbling under a Canadian armored attack. What his dozen or so riflemen could do against tanks was an interesting question. They had a Molotov cocktail each. They would have to do, if they could get close enough. Otherwise, they had their rifles, an average of 15 rounds and a single hand grenade each.

Up ahead, there was the sound of an approaching battle; the constant staccato cracks of rifle fire, the ripping noise of submachine guns and the longer, deeper rasp of machine guns. And, the trademark of the Canadian infantry; the crash of grenades as the Canadians threw them at everything that moved. By the rate the noise was approaching, the infantry up front, the ones Ihrasaari was supposed to be supporting, were falling back fast. Behind the noise of the gunfire, he could hear another noise, the roaring of engines. That would be heavy vehicles pushed their way through the open pine forest. In the movies, they'd be shown pushing the trees down but that was just the film maker's idea of what might happen.

The Canadian appearance was unexpected. One moment the woods up ahead were empty, the next figures had appeared. The first group ran towards him, then went to ground to lay down covering fire for the next. They were white-and-gray camouflaged. Not that that meant much, nearly everybody's uniform was either light gray, white or a mixture of both on Kola. What betrayed them as Canadians was their machine gun, the slower thumping noise of a Bren Gun. Spray erupted around a group of branches and rocks. An obvious strongpoint, one far too obvious to be used by the battle-hardened Finns. Ihrasaari's men held their fire. With ammunition in as short supply as it was, there was little point in wasting it until there were better targets.

Those targets came quickly, more Canadians, moving through the snow. Swiftly, probably on snow shoes, but not as swiftly as Ihrasaari's ski-troops could manage. He took aim at one of the figures and fired a shot. His target crumpled into the ground. All the others went down. The covering group switching their fire to where the shots had come from. Spurts of snow jumped up a few feet short of his position. Off to his left there was a crash and a scream. It might have been a mortar but was more likely to be an EY rifle, that odd contraption that used a blank round fired from a worn-out rifle fitted with a cup discharger to throw a grenade much further than a man could manage. The Canadians had experts with that thing that could make a grenade explode a meter above a man's head. Even as he thought the words, Ihrasaari heard another crash and felt the sting in his back as a fragment found its home.

He reached into a pouch for another clip. His fingers told him this was his last, just five rounds left. The Canadians were moving up fast. Each group covered the others, keeping a constant stream of bullets and grenades on the Finnish position. Ihrasaari pulled the pin out of his grenade and threw it. He ducked down so that he wouldn't see the results. The problem with grenades was that their blast could throw fragments further than a man could throw the grenade. Still here, the snow tended to tamp their exuberance a little. He looked up as the blast faded. The Canadians were still approaching. Then he remembered his Molotov cocktail. He pulled the bottle out of its pouch, turned it upside down quickly to soak the fuse, lit it and threw. He heard the whoomph as it shattered and heard a scream. Another quick look showed him the Canadians were very close now. More shots from his rifle and a final despairing click as it ran dry. They were almost on top of him. That only left one thing to do. He stood up and raised his hands in surrender.

The Canadian soldier looked at him with loathing. "Too late, chum." They were his only words and his submachine gun crackled. Ihrasaari felt the impacts and fell back against the snow. His last sight was of the Canadian taking careful aim and his finger closing for a short, vicious burst that Ihrasaari neither heard nor saw.

Hedgehog, The Regina Rifle Regiment, Kola Front

"Sir. Message from Brigade. Coronet has broken through the Finnish lines. They're on their way to us now. We're to exercise full caution, Sir. The first troops will be infantry and they've had a hard fight. They've got M27s from the Sherbrookes backing them up."

Lieutenant Colonel Haversham read the message flimsy. People getting killed by their own side was a serious danger. The infantry and tanks coming in would be ready to shoot at anything that moved. The troops out on the defenses could easily make a mistake and assume this was another Finnish attack. "Major Gillespie, spread the word fast, to everybody and I mean everybody. Even the cooks and bakers. Friendly forces coming in, the colors of the day are….. blue to green with response green to white. Nobody to shoot unless fired upon and then only if they are absolutely sure the shooters are Finns or Huns. Better to take a few shots than start an blue-on-blue here."

Gillespie nodded and started his rapid circuit of the perimeter, passing the urgent orders along the line. Especially to the Vickers gun crews. One mistake with those murderous water-cooled guns could turn the relief into a massacre. Then, he took up his position and watched. He could see the trees moving slightly as the vehicles passed between them. He guessed that the incoming infantry already had seized positions along the treeline. Now was the time. He took his flare gun and a flare from the recognition pouch, religiously checking that it was indeed blue turning to green. Then he fired it upwards and followed it with his eyes. A blue train of smoke that arched upwards and turned to green as it descended. A second or so later, another flare arched upwards from the treeline. A flare that started green and turned to white.

Cautiously, some white-and-gray figures detached from the treeline and started to move down towards the hedgehog. Gillespie focused his binoculars on them and checked details. The top-mounted curved magazine of the Bren gun, the sideways mounted magazine of the Capsten. They were Canadians. He stood up and raised a Bren gun over his head. The figures broke into a run and closed on the defensive hedgehog. About 30 yards out they stopped and a voice echoed across the trees.

"Reginas?"

"Aye, that's us. Welcome home."

"We'll be more sure of that when you tell us where the mines are."

"You're clear. We didn't have enough for a circuit, so we put what we had on the roads in case the Huns brought up armor. Come on in"

The relief force broke out of the trees. *The best part of an infantry platoon* so Gillespie guessed, *and eight tanks. Plus three of the Kangaroo armored carriers.* "Lieutenant Marcelle, Sir. We've got wounded with us, mostly grenade fragments, none too bad. One man badly burned. Finnish bastard threw a Molotov at him. Could I ask the loan of your field medics?"

"Certainly, Lieutenant. Seeing you here today, you can have anything we have, including the services of my wife and daughters. If

331

they were here of course, which, of course, they aren't. Otherwise I would not be making the offer."

There was a roar of laughter from the Canadian troops surrounding him. "Your medics will be more than gratefully received. In response, I must tell you I am reliably informed the tanks have bottles on board. I believe that Captain Brody may even have a bottle of Canadian Club."

Gillespie looked heartbroken for a split second. "Lieutenant, you're a hard man. Get your wounded over to our first aid tent. Be careful to identify yourself. After we heard what happened at Division, it's unmarked and heavily guarded." Gillespie dropped his voice slightly. "We heard, unofficially. Are the stories true."

Marcelle looked grim. "Sir, it's true. Heard it from a Sergeant who was in the fighting at Division. The Finns killed them all; even the nurses. Don't think we'll ever know why. All the Finns that attacked the camp got killed. The bastards fought to the last man on the way in here as well. We've taken no prisoners we can ask and I very much doubt that any of the other columns have either."

His words were silenced by the roar of tank engines as the M27s nosed into the hedgehog. "Sir, Captain Brody, Squadron commander. Where do you want us?"

"Captain Brody, a little bird tells me you have some Club on board. Is there any truth to that scurrilous rumor?"

"Well, Sir, we have now, but if you'd like to confiscate it……"

"A generous offer, Captain. Could you accompany me to meet Lieutenant Colonel Haversham? Perhaps we can have a little chat over a glass and find out what comes next."

CHAPTER ELEVEN
CLEARING THE DEBRIS

United States Strategic Bombardment Commission, Blair House, Washington D.C. USA.

"Igrat, we've had another message from Loki. He says he has some information of critical importance that we need to see right away. Won't say what, says it's too critical even to talk about. I'd like you, Achillea and Henry to make another Geneva trip to pick it up. I know it isn't scheduled but if it is as important as Loki says, then we need to get it here."

"Assuming this isn't one of Loki's practical jokes." Igrat flicked her heavy black hair, smoothing it into a cascade that ran down her back to her waist. One of the troubles with Loki was that he was an inveterate practical joker.

"Loki's never staged a practical joke with the intelligence data he sends back to us. If he ever does, I'll add Geneva to the target list." Igrat knew that Stuyvesant wasn't joking. Nobody knew what had started it but the feud between the two men had started a long time ago. They despised each other. Their present fragile relationship was the product of the war; nothing else. She doubted if Stuyvesant would actually have Geneva bombed just to deal with Loki but he would do something drastic.

The telephone rang. Phillip Stuyvesant picked it up. He listened and made a few affirmative grunts before putting it down. "OK, we've got your tickets on tomorrow's flight to the Azores and Casablanca fixed up. Henry and Achillea will pick you up at six. Enjoy."

Igrat gave him a brittle grin and left. Getting up at 4am was a real hardship. Still, there was a war on.

Top Floor, Bank de Commerce et Industrie, Geneva, Switzerland.

"Iggie, Achillea and Henry are coming over early to pick up the latest package. They'll be here mid-day tomorrow and be going straight back." Branwen glanced at her pad. "And the representatives from Sweden and Russia are here. I've got them in separate waiting rooms of course."

Loki nodded. The last thing he needed was Alexandra Kollontai and Tage Erlander at each other's throats before he could get in and separate them. It wasn't that Sweden and Russia had major issues in this war. They didn't; quite the reverse if anything. It was just that the old-time radical Bolshevik and the studious, formal Swede were an explosive mix. Quietly, Loki wondered how many wars could have been avoided if the nations involved made sure their respective ambassadors actually liked each other. All too many was his calculated guess.

"Good afternoon, Madam Kollontai." Loki rose to his feet as the Russian woman entered his office; an act that caused her mouth to purse in disapproval. "Welcome to Geneva. Mr Erlander will be joining us any moment. Did you have a good trip here?"

"Comfortable, thank you." Kollontai took her seat in front of Loki's desk. "The Constellation is a good way to travel."

"So I am told, although I haven't had the opportunity to fly on one yet. Ahh, here we are. Welcome to Geneva, Tage. Please take a seat. Madam Kollontai, I understand you have a message from the Russian Government?"

"Indeed I have. I have been asked to tell you that the Russian Government has been gravely disappointed by the Finnish decision to resume active hostilities against us. Nevertheless, despite their

334

treachery, we are prepared to offer peace terms even now. We will grant an armistice to Finland and cease operations against the country provided the following conditions are met. In order to avoid further threats from Finland, the following adjustments to the Finno-Russian frontier will be made. In the North, the border between Russia and Norway will be defined as the Tana River. This will transfer significant portions of the Finnmark presently in Norway to Russian hands. To compensate Norway for this loss, the area of the Finnmark, centered around Lake Inari and presently in Finnish hands will be divided between Russia and Norway. The dividing line will, again, be the Tana River.

"The long westward pointing finger of land separating Sweden from Norway, centered on Enontekio will be handed over to Sweden. These adjustments will simplify the borders in the area and remove any threat to Murmansk. The Finnish Government will be permitted to remove any of its citizens who do not wish to transfer their allegiance to the new rulers of the area in which they formerly lived.

"In the South, the province of Ita-Suomi and the eastern half of Etela Suomi, the dividing line being drawn from Kotka by way of Kuovola to Lake Vuohijarvi, will be surrendered to Russia. The Russian Government will no longer tolerate the threat to Petrograd that has twice this decade resulted in war. Finland will also disarm all German troops and military forces in its remaining territory and surrender them to Russian control. Finland will pay war reparations to Russia in the amount of 600 million U.S. dollars. The whole amount is to be delivered within five years."

There was a profound silence in Loki's office. The terms Russia was offering were savage; Finland would be losing almost a third of its territory. Madame Alexandra Kollontai looked apologetic. She was actually sympathetic to the plight of Finland but her position as an emissary in these 'talks-that-were-not-happening' did not allow her to say so. Loki and Erlander knew that, to some extent, the very fact that these unofficial meetings were taking place at all was due to a moderate influence on Russian government policy. If Zhukov and Vatutin had their way, they would deliver their terms with a tank army driving through Helsinki.

"Is there anything else?" Erlander's voice was mild, devoid of any hint of sarcasm.

"Yes. The Aland Islands are presently held jointly by Sweden and Finland. Russia will take over Finland's position there. However, all we are interested in is maintaining a naval base on those islands. If that is provided, as far as we are concerned Sweden may administer the Islands as if they were wholly Swedish and issue the inhabitants Swedish passports. Also, Finland will not be permitted to maintain armed forces. The country may have an armed police force, without armored vehicles or aircraft, and may have a coastguard but that is all."

Erlander shook his head. "I will carry these terms to the Finnish Parliament and ask Risto Heikki Ryti to present them but he will not do so. He is convinced that Germany will be victorious. I am sorry Madam, but this bird will not fly." The Americanism did not go unnoticed.

"I can sound out the Americans. Perhaps they may intervene on Finland's behalf. Perhaps they can secure a moderation of these terms." Loki did not sound hopeful and in truth he thought that any attempt to do so would be doomed to failure.

"There is no cause for leniency. Finland has brought this disaster on itself. You know the price they were offered for their participation in this attack? The whole of the Kola Peninsula, including Petrograd. I ask you, Herr Erlander, with such an addition to Finnish strength, how long will it be before Sweden falls victim to Finnish aggression? Months? A year or two at most? Yet we restrain our demands to the territory needed to secure our borders and guarantee the safety of our cities. And we are treating generously with Sweden, out of respect for your role as intermediaries, despite the fact that many Swedes serve with the SS against our troops."

Erlander looked saddened. "I cannot deny that. I can say that the Swedish Government recognizes both the generous nature of the Russian approaches and its forbearance of the asinine stupidity of some of our citizens. Citizens who will be punished, that I can assure you."

"And I can also assure you of that." Kollontai's expression was deadly serious.

"So we are agreed then. Mr. Erlander will take these proposals to Finland and ask for them to be submitted to the Finnish Parliament while I will approach my contacts with the American Government to see if some grounds for flexibility can be located." Loki looked at his two guests and a series of nods were attained. Then he reached out for the intercom on his desk. "Branwen, some refreshments please?"

A second later, Branwen pushed the doors open with her hip and wheeled in a trolly loaded with bread, beer, vodka and cold meat. "I am sorry, but the meats are Italian. No smoked fish, I tried but, without access to the Baltic....."

"Never mind Branwen, this looks delicious." Erlander cast his eyes over the tray. "Madame, I hope the vodka is to your taste?"

Branwen left. The three loaded their plates with the food she had brought. Once they had regained their seats, they looked at each other. The bristling near-hostility of the official exchanges had gone. Erlander leaned back and spoke slowly. "Honestly Loki, will the Americans use any influence here?"

Loki thought carefully and shook his head. "Not a chance. Not after this attack, no. The Finns had a good deal going for them. They stay put, keep quiet and don't cause any trouble. In exchange, the allies don't start hammering on them and, when the war is over, they get 1940 boundaries and no reparations. Now, they've reneged on that, the Americans will wash their hands of them. The generosity to Sweden is well-thought out as well. There are many more Swedish voters in America than Finns. No, the Americans will not intervene. Aleksa, how open are the Russian Government to negotiations on this?"

Kollontai knocked back a glass of vodka and stared at Loki. She was remarkably young-looking for a woman of 75 and had been fortunate – and skillful – enough to survive being a vocal critic of Stalin's policies in the late 1930s. How she had managed that, Loki didn't quite know. It was rumored that she had been summoned back to Moscow from a diplomatic posting but had somehow escaped the usual fate for those so recalled. When she spoke, her voice was saddened.

"They are not open at all. Even getting this much for Finland now is hard. They have cooked their own goose with a vengeance and the deal on offer now is the best they will ever be offered. If they keep fighting, then the terms will become progressively worse. One day, the Russian Army will be in a position to attack with all its force. Then there will be no terms. Finland and its people will vanish from the history books for all time. If they do not forestall that somehow, then their fate is inevitable."

"If the Allies win." Erlander's voice was gloomy.

"Oh we will win. We have scored two great victories in the last few days. The German Navy has been destroyed and a German land offensive has been stopped in its tracks. It may take a long time but the fascists will be crushed and our armies will overrun their lair. They will take a just and proper revenge for the atrocities the fascists have inflicted on our people." Kollontai's voice softened further as the women's rights activist took over from the politician. "And when they do, that will not be a good time to be a woman."

There was a profound silence as the truth of her words sank in. Eventually Loki broke it. "And there we have it. That leaves it down to you, Tage. Somehow, you've got to convince the Finns that they'll have to accept these terms. And Aleksa, somehow, you've got to convince the Russian Government to trust the Finns when they make another 'live and left live' offer. Because the alternative is too terrible to think about."

HMCS Ontario *Flagship, Troop Convoy WS-18 en route from Churchill to Murmansk*

"Final run in now Number One." Captain Charles Povey looked around the bridge with an air of satisfaction. They had land-based air cover for the troop convoy. Catalinas flying out of Murmansk circled overhead, watching for any signs of enemy submarines. The convoy itself had angled south and was on the last leg of its long run. The ships had picked up speed. Nobody wanted to get sunk when the safety of Murmansk, dubious though it was, could be within sight any hour.

Lieutenant Commander Murray checked the charts. "Three hours. Possibly four, Sir. No signs of any enemy action. It looks like Halsey's knocked the stuffing out of them."

"Same word from PQ-17." Admiral Vian's voice beat the 'Admiral on the Bridge' warning by a split second. "It's as if the Huns have been so thoroughly spanked, they've all gone home. No word of subs anywhere. I was expecting a major effort by the submarine fleet to try and salvage something from the disaster they've suffered but they've gone. PQ-17 reported some scattered attacks from aircraft based in Norway, mostly Ju-188 torpedo bombers, but even they seemed to lack determination. Mostly they just scattered when the fighters got to them."

"Any word from Halsey Sir?" Povey wanted to know the details of the destruction of the German fleet. He fancied himself as a naval historian and had in mind making his great opus the Second World War history of the German Navy.

"Not a word. We know from German intercepts that his aircraft hit Londonderry this morning. Destroyed schools, convents and orphanages according to the Huns. I'd guess they took out the airfields and partisan hunter barracks myself. But, no word from them. Won't be until they get back from Churchill. One thing we do know. Three German ships turned up in the Faroe Islands, a cruiser and two destroyers. Cruiser's on the rocks, finished. The destroyers have surrendered to the British garrison there. As far as we can tell, they're the only survivors."

There was silence on *Ontario's* bridge. The officer's minds filled with the reality of what the last minutes of the German ships and their crews must have been like. A dreadful choice between drowning and freezing. Eventually, Povey shook himself and banished the images from his mind. "Sir, any special orders for sailing into Murmansk?"

Vian thought for a second. "No, just make sure the Canadian troops are ready to go ashore as fast as possible. If the Huns really are stunned into immobility, we want to get back before they recover.

Curly, *Battery B, US Navy 5th Artillery Battalion, Kola Peninsula.*

"*Moe* is coming up Commander." Perdue turned around to look down the line. The locomotive towing *Moe* was indeed approaching but he could see that something as seriously wrong. There was far too much steam around it and its speed was way down. Another problem to be faced.

"Thank you. Get the rest of the Russian vehicles loaded on to the flat cars. Finish cleaning up the carriage." There was no need to specify which carriage. It had been hit by short-range gunfire from machine guns and the heavier weapons on the armored cars leaving it a

339

splintered ruin. The forty men in it were mostly dead, their bodies laid out by the side of the track.

"Lieutenant Knyaginichev, your men will stay with us until we reach our lines? We are just Navy men and railway engineers here. We desperately need your expertise as skilled infantry."

"My orders are to regain our own lines and rejoin my division. So yes, we will ride with you. I think there are still problems to come though."

"Grazhdanin Knyaz is right Commander. There is indeed a problem yet to come." Boldin had his maps out. "The railway does a bend where it swings north. It forms a loop, a big one certainly but a loop nevertheless. If the German is clever and gets moving, he can cut across the neck of the loop and be ahead of us again. Here I think. This time he will not take time to try and capture the guns. He will tear up the lines so we have to stop or be destroyed. We must move soon to have any chance of beating him."

The three officers stared at the map. Eventually Perdue said what they were all thinking. "Even if we do, he will still be ahead of us right." There was a murmur of agreement. "Very well, so there is no point in hurrying. We must think this over and do it right." His words were interrupted by them being enveloped in a cloud of steam. *Moe's* engine had come to a halt behind them.

Perdue turned around and looked at the Mikado. One side looked like a scrapyard. "How bad is it?"

"We're done, Commander. This Mike is finished. We've been losing steam pressure ever since the junction and there's no stopping it. We're shot up too badly to go any further."

Perdue turned to the driver of *Curly's* engine. "Can a Mike tow both guns? If we leave the carriages behind?"

The railwayman started to shake his head but was interrupted by a Navy Lieutenant. "Sir, you better see this before making any decisions."

Perdue followed him back. When he reached *Moe* he could see what was coming but the Lieutenant pointed it out anyway. "Sir, see the barrel there? A 75 armor piercing round hit it. Deflected away of course, but it took a big chunk out of the metal, right down to the rifling inside. There's three or four more just like that all down the barrel. And the breech, Sir. It got hit bad. 75s and 50s, three or four of each. *Moe* is really torn up, Sir."

It was that, Perdue could see it. If anything the Lieutenant was being over-optimistic. The German gunners had made good practice on *Moe* and they'd done for the great gun. It was a write-off, irreparable. Behind it the carriages were in a terrible state. Riddled with bullet and shell holes, frozen streams of blood staining the sides. Moans were still coming from inside the carriages while rescuers sorted through the shattered timbers to find the last survivors. *Curly* had got through relatively unharmed. *Moe* had taken the worst the Germans could throw at her. How the train had got this far was a miracle.

"We lost over a hundred men, Sir. Many more wounded. Hardly anybody not wounded."

"Ours or Russians?"

"Just who the hell cares?" The Lieutenant caught himself. "Sorry Sir. No disrespect meant. Some ours; some Russian, most too badly chewed up or burned to tell which. All for nothing. The gun's gone."

"Not for nothing Lieutenant. We got the rest of the men through and we can blow the gun up here. Get the teams together. Rig *Moe* for complete destruction, so there won't even be splinters left. Use propellant bags for explosives in addition to the demolition charges. Rig the Mike and the carriages as well. Make sure they're blown up and burned. Rest of the men, get the bodies out. Put them with the casualties from *Curly*. There's a junction here; that's why we stopped. We can resort the consists so we can get the most valuable coaches out. We need another flatcar for the ski troop's vehicles."

Perdue looked at the doomed gun and shook his head. He'd hoped to get them both out but the German gunners had been that bit too good. Meanwhile, there was *Curly's* train to get ready and the dead to bury. At least here, by the railway, they'd be easy to find in the Spring when they could be buried properly.

"Right, men, to work. We've got a train to blow up." Then Perdue went back to Boldin and Knyaz so see what they could work out by way of breaking through the next ambush. Ahead of him, *Curly* started moving down the line so it would be well clear when *Moe* was blown up.

Rue Henri Fazy, Geneva, Switzerland.

"We're being followed." Henry McCarty made the observation casually but it wasn't a casual matter. Normally these pick-up runs were a matter of routine, things that just went ahead without any great fuss. To actually be followed was quite unusual. It had happened before, but it had always turned out to be a matter of routine. The Abwehr or Gestapo just following three visiting Americans to see if they were up to something or were just daring tourists. It was not as if they were obviously military party; not an old man and two young women. If Henry had to make a guess, he would say the Gestapo file on them would say that he was some sort of businessmen depositing illegal business earnings in his Swiss bank account while the two women were his mistresses he had brought along for the ride. *Most Europeans assumed that American businessmen were also gangsters,* Henry reflected, *Hollywood films had a lot to answer for.*

"The black Mercedes?" Their driver had also noticed the tail. "He has been with us since the airport. What do you wish me to do with him?"

McCarty quickly thought over the options. A gun or knife battle in the middle of Geneva's old town would attract unnecessary attention. "Lose him. But don't do it obviously. Throwing a tail will prove we have something to hide. At the moment we could just be normal visitors."

"Very well Sir." The driver thought for a second and then made a hard right into the Rue des Granges. "Up ahead of us is the Hotel les Amures. It is a hotel well known for those who wish discrete lodgings for a short period. You take your two ladies in there and book a room, being careful to mention a Herr Klagenfeld when you do so. I will wait down in the street outside for you. That will excite no attention. Eventually, the persons in that car will go inside to check. A man booking in with two ladies will be remembered and the hotel staff will, with some encouragement, confirm you are upstairs. But you, Sir,

342

and the ladies will go up to the third floor, across the fire escape to the Restaurant La Favola on the Rue Jean Calvin and down through the kitchens and out. Another car from Loki will be waiting for you there and you will be gone. As soon as I see the men going in to the Hotel, I also will be gone. There will be nobody for them to follow. Anyway, one cannot get from the Rue des Granges to the Rue Jean Calvin by car. There are many steep steps in the way."

"That sounds good. Do it."

Henry settled back in the seat. Beside him Igrat was frowning. "Henry, I don't like this. Why are we being followed? It smells like somebody was expecting us to arrive. Have we got a leak?"

"*We* don't." Henry was quite certain about that. "And for the same reason we can be sure that Loki and his Orchestra don't. But you're right, this doesn't smell quite right. We'll have to play along and see what develops."

The car stopped outside a large, square building that was as undistinguished as the rest of Geneva's architecture. McCarty got out and opened the door for the two women, then reached inside to get a case. There were two reasons for that. Nobody went into a hotel with one woman, let alone two, without her case. Anyway, the case held his guns.

"Good afternoon ladies, gentlemen." The hotel clerk betrayed just a slight hint of surprise and a little admiration at the plural. "May I help you?"

"We would like a room please. One on an upper floor for preference. We will be leaving in a few hours, we have a four-thirty appointment with Herr Klagenfeld. But we will be back after dinner."

"Third floor be suitable? I thought so. Sign here please, Sir." The clerk looked down at the register. "Ah, Mister John Smith. So many of our guests come from the family Smith. Room 335." The clerk was not concerned with the women's signatures, they were likely to change with every visit this American made. Anyway, the slender one looked like a demimondaine if ever the clerk had seen one.

The three took the escalator up to the third floor and walked down the long corridor. Room 335 was at the end, right next to a metal fire escape ladder. The ladder itself was shared with the building next door, accessed by a common metal platform. Henry led the way across it, then in through the door to the next building. This one had only two floors due to the slope on the hillside, so the party went down the steps into the restaurant kitchen. The staff very pointedly did not notice them as they passed the preparation tables until Igrat stopped and sniffed a pot-au-feux that was simmering gently.

"Guys, we have got to eat here tonight." The she turned her attention to the chef who was already beginning to preen himself. "Let me guess. That was left to you by your grandmother and you have willed it to your grandchildren."

The chef's smile turned into a beam. "Madame, you understand perfectly. May I have your autograph?"

Igrat sniffed again, enjoying the heady aroma. "If it's as good as it smells, you can have a lot more than my autograph." She made for the exit, swaying her hips suggestively.

There was an appreciative laugh around the kitchens. The sous-chef discretely shook the chef's hand and promised that his wife would never find out. McCarty shook his way out and went into the main room of the restaurant. The maitre d'hotel indicated a car that had just pulled up outside. "Herr Klagenfeld has sent a car for you. I trust we will see you again at La Favola?"

"Oh yes. You can be sure of that." Igrat tossed the remark over her shoulder as she left. The three of them piled into the back of the new car. One that appeared identical with the old one.

"Any danger of them tracing us through to Loki?" McCarty never took things for granted.

The drover turned around. It was Branwen and she smiled at them. "The hotel and restaurant think they are working for the Abwehr and, probably that you were ducking either the NKVD or the Gestapo. Loki had me wait here just in case. He does for all your visits but it's never been needed before. Anyway, welcome back to Geneva. Did you remember to bring stockings for the girls?"

McCarty laughed. A mass of American nylon stockings completed the inventory of contents in the suitcase he was holding.

Not only was it a kindness to the Swiss girls who worked in the bank, it also fitted his cover as a black-marketeering industrialist.

HMS Manxman, *Free Royal Navy, Between the Faroe Islands and Iceland.*

Captain Becker looked around, trying to spot the men who were watching him. No sign of them, but he was being watched. He was sure of it. He had felt their eyes burning into his back for hours now but he couldn't see who they were.

There were enough men to choose from. What had once been the mine deck on the British fast minelayer had been converted to cargo space for the runs to the Faroe Islands. Now it was serving as a floating prisoner of war camp. The British had decided to rush the removal of the surviving German seamen from the Islands and the deck was packed almost solid. Still, it was only for a few hours. Then the men would be disembarked in Iceland and transferred to prisoner of war camps in Canada. What would happen to them then was unknown. There were few enough German prisoners of war in Canada. Prisoners taken in Russia stayed there, in Russian-run camps. There were only a tiny handful of German Navy prisoners. U-boats rarely sank in ways that gave their crews a chance of survival and "Taney Justice" reduced that chance to near-zero.

Quietly Becker cursed the unknown German U-boat captain who had machine-gunned the survivors of the Coast Guard Cutter *Roger B Taney* in the water after he had torpedoed their ship. Despite an investigation that had run deep, nobody had ever identified who he was or why he had committed the atrocity. Most of the German Navy had been as appalled as the Americans. There had been talk of a court martial and firing squad for the guilty officer. It had made matters worse that the Americans had looked on their Coast Guard sailors as life-savers and protectors, not warship crews. The bullet-riddled bodies that washed ashore had brought American demands for vengeance to an irresistible pitch.

The next time a U-boat had been sunk and there were German survivors in the water, the American destroyer had machine-gunned them. And so it had started, a descending spiral of brutality and atrocity that did nobody any credit. Becker had heard that the Americans had sent destroyers to pick up the survivors of the German fleet, that they had declared "Taney Justice" applied only to submariners. If so, it was a sign of hope, albeit a small one. *Perhaps the world hadn't gone completely mad. Not yet anyway.*

Becker sighed and turned away from the mine deck to the small group of 'cabins' set aside for German officers. They were partitioned off from the mine deck by hastily-thrown up wooden bulkheads but offered little that the enlisted men didn't have. A little privacy, that was all. Becker pulled the curtain that served as a door aside and went though, closing it behind him. Then he stopped. The curtain that normally shielded his 'cabin' had gone. He half-turned to see what was going on when something struck him.

The half turn saved his skull from being crushed. Becker knew that, but he was still stunned from the impact, barely conscious, when the curtain was thrown over him. He felt boots thudding into his ribs. The wooden thing that had been used to bring him down hit him again, this time across the back. He had tried to rise, but the extra blow felled him and he couldn't.

"Get the traitor up on deck." The words were hoarse. Becker felt their meaning wrap around him, even as he was smothered by the curtain over his head. He was picked up, half-dragged, half-carried, half-pushed, upwards through a hatch out of the mine deck towards the main deck of the minelayer. He could feel the chill on the air as they emerged into the night and the exposed deck. Becker could hear the throb of the engines, the sound of the water, the gentle breath of the wind in the superstructure. He was painfully aware of the fact those could be the last sound he would hear. At least they beat the snarling radials of Corsairs and the crash of their bombs.

"You have been found guilty by court martial of fleeing from the enemy, of abandoning your command, of disobedience of orders and of handing your ship over to the enemy. You have also been found guilty of dereliction of duty by not demolishing your ship to prevent her capture." That struck Becker as a little odd. *Not the way a Navy man would phrase it.* "You are sentenced to death. Throw him over the side."

The unseen men rushed Becker to the rail, ready to tip him into the freezing water beneath. Then something happened. A series of sounds, violent motion, and the ripping noise of a sub-machine gun. The curtain was pulled from Becker's head. He saw two of his attackers on the deck, the dark pool of blood around them had already begun to freeze. Four more knelt on the deck, their hands on their heads.

"You all right Captain, Sir?" A Royal Marine carrying a Capsten sub-machine gun was grinning at him. "You're in good hands, Sir. Colonel Stewart of the Argylls asked us to keep an eye on you. When we saw these six beauties hustling you up here, we kind of thought this might be what he had in mind. Do you recognize any of them?"

Becker looked at the two dead men on the deck and then at the four kneeling prisoners. "This one, he was my first officer." He switched to German. "Why, why this?"

"You betrayed us. Our orders were to head north but you ran when the Amis came after us. You left the rest of the fleet to die and ran to save your own skin."

"That made no sense at all." One of the Royal Marines, a sergeant, spoke quietly. "Oh yes, I speak fluent German, Captain. You did the right thing, trying to save your men when the rest of the fleet was being slaughtered. I am sorry you could not also save these."

He turned to the four prisoners. "Get those two bodies over the side."

"They are entitled to military burial." The *Lutzow*'s first officer was blustering.

"They are murderers. By intent at least. Get them over the side." The sergeant's voice was uncompromising. The four men rose, picked up the bodies and dumped them over the side of the ship. As they dropped, the Sergeant's Capsten hammered out another burst and the four prisoners followed them down. Six splashes in the water were hardly noticeable.

"Captain, you're going to the sickbay for the rest of the trip. Under guard, of course. You'll be safe there. We'll spread the word that those little rays of sunshine succeeded in dropping you over the side before we killed them. After that, we'll get you to a safe PoW camp."

Becker looked aft to where the bodies in the sea had already vanished. *Perhaps the world didn't have any sanity left after all.* The thought left him profoundly depressed.

Mechanized Column, 71st Infantry Division, Kola Peninsula

"Welcome back, Lang. How is the ear?"

"Sorry Asbach?" Lang made a great play of being deaf, leaning forward with his ruined ear cupped in one hand.

"Good man!" Asbach smacked the junior officer on the back. "You are privileged. Not many survive the attentions of a Russian sniper. To survive two shots, not one, is a very rare distinction. We got the sniper by the way. A woman, of course. Most of the best Russian snipers are. We dumped her body in a ditch with the rest of their dead. Counting her, we got eight of the Siberians and six more Russians. They probably fell from the trains as they went through. And two American sailors; they probably fell off too. No matter. We threw them all in the ditch and the wolves can have them when we leave."

"What now Asbach? Go home?"

"I think not. We have another chance. That air strike hurt us badly. We're down to the equivalent of an infantry company in half tracks, we've got three out of five Pumas left and two out of five tank-hunter-armored cars. Plus two flak guns and four of your self-propelled 150s. We've still got a force, Lang; still got a chance. Look, the railway line goes around here, more or less following the curves of the ridge. But if we cut across the neck of the curve, we can come out here, in front of them. This time, no nonsense about capturing the guns. We'll tear up three hundred meters of the track, more if they give us time, that way they'll have to stop. Then we kill them all. If the guns are still intact when we've finished, fine. But if not, well, fortunes of war."

Lang nodded and tapped the map. "We can set up here, behind this ridge. They'll come around here, straight into us. We can have them under fire before they are aware we are there."

Asbach sighed quietly. Lang was coming along but he still had a lot to learn. "Lang, the Amis and the Ivans can read maps just as well as we can. They'll work this out too. Not sure what they'll do about it but they'll see just what you have seen and think the same things. So don't expect miracles about surprising them. Just stopping them will be entirely good enough."

Lang nodded, absorbing the lesson. Back at staff, it was a running joke that the Ivans were idiots who only stayed in the war because of the way they threw away human lives and the Amis would be lost without their massive piles of equipment. Out here, he was learning differently. Out here they were all Winter Warriors and what one could see, another could also.

His reverie was interrupted by a blast. It was distant, but still loud enough to be startling and to shake the earth under his feet. On the horizon, he could see the bright ball of a great blast rolling skywards. For some reason the sight filled him with nameless dread. Asbach was already looking at his map. "15 kilometers away at least; probably nearer twenty. And that puts it on the railway line. I'd say the Amis have just lost another one of their trains."

Headquarters, 3rd Canadian Infantry Division, Kola Peninsula, Russia

"How are you doing with my division, John?" General George Rodgers was wrapped in bandages to the point where he would have done honor to a Hollywood horror film. The blast of grenade fragments that had brought him down had left him covered with wounds, none of which were mortal. Why that was, nobody would quite explain.

General John M Rockingham had the combat reports of the 3rd Infantry under his arm. His first problem was to break the news to his old friend. "The Third's mine now, George. You're being evacuated out, to Murmansk, I'm keeping Third; you'll get Sixth when its ashore and formed up. I guess your first job will be to send the Huns tumbling back to their start line.

Rodgers nodded sadly. He doubted he would be getting Sixth, not after the way Third had been cut up. "The Huns have lost then?

"They made about thirty to forty five miles but we stopped them. The jaws of the encirclement never closed, so we're fine. We held the Finns almost on their start line. Oh they split the division up into hedgehogs and surrounded us but that was it. The hedgehogs held, all of them, until relief forces shot their way through. Now, with the supplies the convoy brought, we can roll the Huns out of here.

"John, how did the Finns do it? How did they get through the lines to cut us up like that?"

"The lakes, George. The ones we used to shorten our lines and conserve forces? In the storm, they froze and the driving snow stopped us seeing them use them. I guess they had this plan for months, waiting for the right conditions. We never saw it, but it doesn't matter. The division's linked up again now and we're starting to drive forward. We've got new orders as well. Push into Finland proper. No more of this phony war on the frontier. The Finns want a real war, they're going to get it." Rockingham dropped his voice "I've even heard the B-29s may hit Helsinki. That's really hush-hush. Anyway George, you'll be getting a better briefing than this later. Until then, wrap yourself around this."

Rockingham produced a bottle of Canadian Club whisky. Rodgers looked at it with delight. "John, how did you get that?"

"Oh, a tank officer smuggled it over in his tank. Hid it in the barrel, I guess. That's where they usually hide them. Anyway, he gave it to the officer commanding a hedgehog he relieved and Colonel Haversham sent it up to you with his best wishes. A great sacrifice on his part I'd say, George."

"Aye, that it is. John, be a good fellow. Help me drink it before the nurses confiscate it."

B-29A Carolina Sings, *11th Bombardment Group, Second Air Division, Just Outside Murmansk.*

Dusk was falling and the B-29s would soon be on their way. The 127 B-29s of the 5th, 9th and the 11th Bombardment groups had arrived, flying a roundabout route over the Arctic to get from their bases behind the Volga. Nobody was under any illusions about the Germans not being aware of their arrival, but it was still worth going through the motions. It was an odd reversal of normal thought processes; try and evade detection even though it was pointless because the attempt was normal. Acknowledge that it was pointless and that made the flight abnormal and worth noticing.

The whole mission would have been impossible a few days earlier. Then, aviation fuel on the Kola Peninsula had been in short supply and was reserved for the fighters and tactical support aircraft. Even the medium bombers had been on short rations and their use restricted. Feeding the fuel-hungry B-29s was entirely impossible. Now, things were different. PQ-17 had arrived safely and it contained a disproportionate number of tankers. That fuel was being pumped ashore and it made the operation of heavy bombers from Murmansk possible. A timely thing because this raid was a very important one. Briefly at least, it was a one-off. A demonstration and a punishment for the Finnish decision to break the unofficial ceasefire along their border and go on the offensive. The bombing tonight would drive home the stupidity of that decision. Germany's cities might be out of reach but Finland's weren't. It had other purposes as well, but Colonel Thomas Power wasn't aware of those.

"Four are down Sir. We can go with 123 aircraft." The sergeant spoke apologetically and apprehensively. Power was known for a ferocious temper and strict ideas on discipline. It was whispered that the two going together was not a good thing. Faults tended to be unreported rather than risk his wrath.

"Four down? Why?"

"Engines, sir. The 3350s again. They're just not as reliable as the Wasp Majors."

Power shook his head. For some reason, the R-3350 had remained under-developed while most effort had been placed on the R-4360. That showed in the reliability ratings. Once notorious for catching fire in mid-air, the R-4360 was maturing into a fine engine. The problem was limited production. All the R-4360s were needed for F2Gs and F-72s so the fighters could take on the German jets. That left the B-29 with the R-3350. An engine that ate cylinders with dismal enthusiasm. "Very good, Sergeant."

The mission had called for 120 aircraft. Technically, the two bombardment groups totaled 225 aircraft, but they were all under-strength from losses and had managed to make only 135 aircraft ready. Eight had aborted and turned back for base. Now four more had gone from the strike mission. Only three more to lose before the mission would be under-strength. Still, the last hurdle had been crossed. The bombers were loaded with their incendiaries and explosive bombs; they were ready to go. On a nearby field, a group of F-65 night fighters were already warming up, ready to escort the stream of heavies. A group of F-61s would be strafing the flak batteries defending the target. The mission plan was simple. Fly due south, all the way inside Russian-held territory and under heavy escort. The Germans would assume this B-29 strike was aimed at their rear areas, depots, defense areas and so on. But, at the appropriate time, the bombers would swing west, cross the Finnish border and head for Helsinki.

The city was the target and the bombers were loaded to do the maximum possible damage. Officially, the targets were the great Ilmala railway marshalling yards and the factories around them, Skatudden Island, its port and factories and the Lansisatama port and factory area along with its marshalling yard. Knocking all three out would, according to the briefing, seriously damage Helsinki's capacity as a transport and production center. Of course, everybody knew that with bombers hitting at night, using radar and under fire from ground defenses, the bombing wouldn't be that accurate. The three spaced out targets probably meant that most of the city would be hit. That was regrettable but a new phrase had already been coined to cover it. Collateral damage. The collateral damage in this raid was likely to be high, all the more so since the 605 miles to the target made this, by B-29 standards, a very short-range mission and the aircraft were carrying bomb load instead of fuel. So much so, they were even using the rarely-touched underwing hard points for additional bombs. Most had their explosive loads under their wings, leaving their great bellies full of incendiaries.

Power climbed up the ladder into his lead B-29A and settled into the aircraft commander's seat. "Tower. This is Black Chalk Leader. We are ready to go."

Geneva Station

Geneva Station was quite luxurious as railway stations went. Apart from its ticket office, it also had a reasonably good restaurant and the waiting room was clean and comfortable. That didn't mean that Henry McCarty liked using it. The train ran too close to the border with occupied France before it swung south, through the Simplon Tunnel and out to Italy. The airport was even worse. It was literally on the Swiss-French border which was why the courier party never used it. Even driving past it, as they had coming in, made McCarty nervous. That was the problem with Geneva, it was a finger of land that stuck

352

into German-occupied Europe. One day, the Germans would hack it off. The Swiss made a big thing about their armed population and fortifications but they hadn't helped against Napoleon and wouldn't against Hitler. McCarty had a nasty feeling that Switzerland was running on borrowed time. He didn't want to be around when that time ran out.

Meanwhile, there were other interesting things to amuse them until their train set off on its run to Rome. Like the couple who were having an increasingly-heated altercation in the booth opposite the bar. McCarty didn't know what had started it, but it looked like the woman was telling the man with her that he was being dumped. He didn't like it. Then, as she got up to leave, he grabbed her arm and dragged her back, none too gently. She yelled something at him. McCarty imagined it was along the lines of 'get your hands off me' and jabbed at his hand with something silver. *A nail file?* The man yelped and pulled his arm back. Then the woman made another effort to break away, this time succeeding and stalked away across the floor.

That's when it got serious. The man grabbed a beer bottle from the table, smashed off the end and went after the woman. She saw, screamed and tried to run. Achillea and McCarty both moved forward to stop him but the Railway police were faster. One tripped the man up; the other stared beating him across the kidneys with his baton. Once the man was subdued, they dragged him away. McCarty and the senior officer exchanged nods, the situation was under control. Or he thought it was because that's when he heard Achillea's quiet "Henry, where's Igrat?"

He looked around, Igrat had vanished. He realized that the fight had been a diversion and that he and Achillea had fallen for it. With a brief "Achillea, follow me." He headed for the exit and the area outside. It was deserted except for a police officer standing in the car park

"Officer, has a car left this car park in the last few minutes? One with a black-haired woman and at least two men?"

The policeman looked at Achillea and decided a straight answer was the best policy. "Certainly, madam. A black taxi. With the woman and two men as you describe."

McCarty cursed. "The young lady is a member of my business staff. I have reason to believe she may have been abducted by those men. They could be in France by now."

"No Sir. The border is closed, from both sides. If your friend is in the taxi, she is still in Geneva." The police officer hesitated. Then he realized there was more going on here than met the eye. "I have the taxi number if that will help."

"Thank you officer." Achillea was at her most charming which tended to be slightly frightening. "Henry, we better get in touch with Loki and trace this. Otherwise, one of us is going to have to get in touch with Washington and tell the Seer that Igrat's in the hands of the Gestapo and we haven't done anything about it."

McCarty thought about that and winced. Stuyvesant very rarely lost his temper. When he did, the results tended to be spectacular. "Too right. Get on the phone to Branwen, now." He turned back to the policeman. "Officer, I need to speak with my bank, the Bank de Commerce et Industrie, right away. There may be a ransom demand and I must make the necessary arrangements."

The police officer had a discrete but immediate reaction to the name of the bank. All banks had a very close relationship with the Swiss Government, to the point where it hard to say where one ended and the other began. The Bank de Commerce et Industrie was something quite special. They had influence even the other banks lacked. If this American banked with them, he was a man of much importance.

B-29A Carolina Sings *11th Bombardment Group, Second Air Division, Approaching Helsinki.*

Power eased *Carolina Sings* down to the prescribed attack altitude, 2,000 feet. Power thought this was insane. The whole purpose of the B-29 was that it could bomb from high altitude, 25,000 – 30,000 feet where flak was almost ineffective and fighters were struggling. Only, the high-altitude raids had failed. They couldn't hit the targets accurately enough. So, tonight, the B-29s were coming in low, fast and in darkness. It would either work or be a catastrophe and Powers was betting on the latter. That's why he was in the lead bomber. If he was sending the men under his command to a massacre, he would lead them in himself.

354

Around him, the formation of B-29s was splitting into three sections; one aimed at each primary target area. Powers had taken Lansisatama himself. It was the most hazardous of the three. The others were on the outside of the city; the bombers could hit them and turn away. To get to Lansisatama, they would have to fly over the whole city and take flak all the way. Then do the same getting out. Night fighters didn't worry Power too much, the Finns had few of them and there were more than sixty F-65 Tigercats guarding the bomber formations. It was the flak batteries that were the problem. The Huns had too much low-level flak for this to work. That had been considered; hence the sixty F-61 Black Widows, assigned to shooting up the flak batteries when they opened fire. Of course that meant they would have to unmask themselves by opening fire first – and those opening shots could be the end of a B-29.

"Pilot, come around four degrees to port. We're starting the run now." The bombardier almost cuddled himself with joy. Power had a well-deserved reputation as a martinet. Some described him as a sadistic fascist; his enemies were far less forgiving. But on a bomb run, the bombardier commanded the aircraft, not the pilot. That made it a heaven-sent opportunity for a junior officer to give Power orders. The Eagle radar showed the city ahead very clearly. That was another reason why Helsinki was being bombed tonight. Its weird geography and coastal location gave vivid contrasts between land and sea on the bombing radar. It made picking out the targets easy. Two of them anyway. The Ilmala targets were inland and the bombers would have a harder job picking them up on radar.

The bombers had cruised out at around 15,000 feet. An easy, steady cruise that allowed the escorting fighters to formate around them. The normal pattern would have been for the formation to climb to around 25,000 feet for its bomb run. There had been a time when the B-29s had tried to bomb from above 30,000 feet, but the effort had been a failure. Unexpected winds and atmospheric effects tossed the bombs miles from their target. That problem was not easy to overcome although Power was aware that great efforts were being made to solve it. So the raids had been steadily dropping in altitude. This one was merely the last stage in the process. The formation had stayed at 15,000 feet when it crossed the Finnish border, then dived to its present level.

Major James Kaelin, the lead bombardier for the 11th Bombardment Group checked the radar display again and then looked through the Norden bombsight. He could see the long wharves of the Lansisatama clearly on radar but the optical bombsight was made useless by the overcast. Still, a radar release was better than nothing. He watched as the cross hairs on the radar picture approached the end of the port wharves. Kaelin punched the bomb release. The four 2,000 pound bombs under the wings released first; the shower of the incendiaries from the bomb bay afterwards. If they dropped right, they would saturate an area 1,500 feet long by 300 feet wide. With the bomb load gone, his attention focus evaporated. He suddenly was aware of the B-29 bouncing in the flak thrown up by the city.

"Bombardier to commander. The bombs are away. How goes things up there?"

"We've lost *Fifi Trixibelle*. Flak got her. She just blew up in mid-air. Others are swell. On our way home. Navigator, gunners, do your jobs and stop worrying about the rest of the formation."

Up in the cockpit, Power turned *Carolina Sings* back for home. Straight home; no need for a deceptive routing. The Germans had been fooled. Their light flak had been silent, they'd been expecting a high-altitude raid and the gunners had been assigned to the 88s and 127s. They weren't so effective against targets this low. The heavy guns had had problems tracking the low-flying targets and most of the fire had hit the tail end of the formations. *Fifi Trixibelle* had been unlucky. Power thought she had probably caught a 127mm in the belly just as she started to release her bombs. He didn't know how many bombers had gone down, at least six was his guess, perhaps eight. However many it was, he seriously hoped the brass wouldn't believe they could try this trick again. The Germans could be fooled once, never twice. Behind him, the city of Helsinki was starting to burn.

Residence of the Kantokari Family, Kaartinkaupunki, Helsinki, Finland

The air raid sirens woke Kristianna Kantokari before her mother pounded on the door. The wailing sound wasn't quite unheard-of. There had been air raids on Helsinki in the Winter War and in the early days of the Continuation War, but the Russians had only used a few aircraft and the damage they had done was little indeed. So, there was no great sense of urgency as the family gathered itself and started to make their way down to the bomb shelter they had prepared in their basement. As they trooped downstairs, solemnly carrying water and food for the stay, their house began to shake. A curious rhythmic buzzing roar drowned out the sirens. Ignoring her mother's warnings, Kristianna ran to a window and peered out.

There was a great silver beast in the sky. It seemed to be skimming over the rooftops and filled the whole window with its glow. Kristianna recognized it immediately from the German newsreels that were shown in the cinema when she went there with her boyfriend. It was a B-29, a 'Grosse Viermotoren' as the Germans called it. Only they were supposed to operate high up. This one was so low it seemed like it would crash into the street at any moment. There was a red ripple under its nose that sent red flashes streaking into the darkness. There were others as well; dozens of them. The great B-29 was trapped in searchlights; perhaps six or more coning in on it. The light made its silver fuselage and wings glow. Then, one of the searchlights abruptly went out. She realized the orange flashes were the gunners on the bomber trying to shoot out the lights. Then, another aircraft swept out of the darkness, a dark gray one with twin tails. Its nose and fuselage lighting up with gun-flashes and fire swept from under its wings. She heard the thunder of rockets as they devastated the searchlight battery.

Kristianna would have looked longer but her father dragged her away, swearing at her for her foolhardiness. His words were partially drowned out by four great crashes that made their whole house shudder. Suddenly, getting to the bomb shelter was very urgent. They barely settled in to their shelter. At first they were cowed by the explosions that seemed to never end. Then they were terrified by the smell of burning, faint at first but growing steadily stronger. Then their stay was ended by a hammering on the front door of their house.

"Air Raid Police. Open up and evacuate. The city is burning."

"Where, where is the fire?" Kristianna's father had opened the door and was asked questions of the harassed-looking men

"Shut up. Get your family out of here and don't argue." The answer was curt and reinforced by a hand dropping to a pistol holster.

Antti Kantokari gathered his wife and three children and led them into the street. Out here the burning smell was so strong it was choking and the night was bright enough to read by. Kantokari glanced to the east, where the bomber had come from. There he could see the glow of the fires already spreading across the roof-line.

"Go west Antti; go west." It was a local policeman, one who was trying to be more helpful and comforting to the people who he worked with every day. "The Americans dropped incendiaries and the Skatudden is burning. The fires are spreading this way. If you don't get away from them soon, you never will. Stay in the wide roads, in the middle. The snow and slush will stop the fires from getting to you. Now go, quickly. And be careful. The American aircraft are still overhead."

All around them, people were scurrying from their homes, some empty-handed; some carrying pots and pans or their household treasures. Some had bags of food. One was even carrying a flowering plant in an ornamental pot. All around them, bright little flakes were beginning to drop, strange fireflies in the cold of the night. Kristianna reached out for one. She yelped as it burned her hand.

"Embers from the fire." Her father sounded genuinely frightened. "The fires are spreading fast. The police are right; we must run for our lives."

"But our things." His wife wailed, thinking of the home she had carefully built over the years.

"Are already gone. We have only our lives. If we stay we will lose those as well."

Already, the crowd was beginning to run for the west. Now, the reason why those who abandoned everything would live while those who paused to try and recover their treasured possessions or encumbered themselves with their goods would die, became obvious. As the crowd moved, a strange filtering mechanism started to work. Those who could move fastest and had least to carry moved to the front. Those who hesitated or had their arms full, fell to the rear. And the fires were closing in all the time.

Overhead, a late-arriving B-29 swept past, heading for its target. Normally such a straggler would be easy prey for the anti-aircraft guns but the Black Widows were watching and waiting. Streams of tracer arched up from the ground. Before they could contact the bomber, two Black Widows dived in on the source. They hosed it with gunfire, then released four objects that wobbled as they fell on the gun battery. Kristianna saw great orange balls rising into the sky and the anti-aircraft fire ceased as suddenly as it had started.

"Jellygas." Kristianna's father muttered, "They are dropping jellygas on the city." His stomach squirmed with fear at the ugly orange balls and what he knew they represented. And all the time the embers descending on them were getting thicker and hotter.

There was another thunder from behind them. At first Kristianna thought it was another bomber releasing its load, but it was a house collapsing. Helsinki was made of stone and stone doesn't burn but the wood and the paint and the fabric inside stone buildings do. The bombs had blown windows in. That let the fire inside to gut the houses. Deprived of support, the stone shells were collapsing. She risked a glance behind and realized that the house that had just collapsed was in the street she had lived in. Her own home would follow, as surely as if it were already ablaze. If that was not already the case.

Nobody said anything. She and her family broke into a run, pushing anybody who got in their way to one side. They had to head west, as fast as they could. Ahead of them was the Mannerheiminte, a wide street that would act as a firebreak. Helsinki was lucky. The snow of the great storm turned the streets into rivers. They would stop the fires wouldn't they? Only when the family saw the Mannerheiminte, it was already crowded with people, running south.

"Go back, go back! The Ilmala is burning. The fires are coming."

Above the yelling of the crowds, Kristianna could see the glow of fires to the north as well as the east. There was no choice and Antti Kantokari knew it. He grabbed his daughter's hand and the five of them plunged into the stream of people fleeing the fires started by the air raid. Already, the street was littered with discarded possessions as people threw away everything in the desperate urge to flee faster, to run further. Already, the old and the young started to collapse as the run for safety exhausted them. Over the sound of the fires, the cries of the crowd, yelling, weeping and sobbing, hammered at the ears. Over on the left, the great San Nicolas cathedral was already a mass of flames. That told Kantokari the truth. The Mannerheiminte lead east. It was taking the crowds on it back into the mouths of the fires. In running down it, people were simply heading back to their deaths. He grabbed his wife and daughter's arms and angled his family across the road. They took the first westward-leading street he could find.

"They told us to stay on the wide streets." His wife was sobbing with exhaustion.

"Not the ones that lead east. The fires are north and east. We must go south and west." He looked around, this street was quieter. Perhaps all the people had already run to the west. "Come, we must go."

Head of them was a small park with people already crowded into it for shelter. Kantokari lead his family into it in the hope it would give at least a temporary respite. The snowy slush made sitting down impossible but at least they weren't running. Overhead, the Black Widows were prowling; goading the anti-aircraft funs into opening fire. One passed directly over the little park. For a moment Kantokari thought it was going to drop its jellygas onto the crowded spot of green but it ignored them and vanished again into the darkness.

"Father, look." Kristianna's voice was quiet. She pointed at the buildings to the west. They were highlighted by an evil glow of red. There were fires to the west as well. They were spreading towards the park that had seemed such a refuge.

Kantokari cursed to himself but thought quickly. *There were only two ways out of this park that did not lead north or east, and one of them led back to the Mannerheiminte. The other was diagonally across the square. They did not have time to waste.* "Come, we must move."

"I cannot." His wife was crying. "We must wait."

"If we do we die. The fires are coming from the west as well. As soon as people realize it, they will try and escape and there is only one narrow street out of here. If we wait, we will not get to it in time."

They set off. They moved as fast as they could towards the one street that promised a hope of safety. By the time they got there, the danger had become obvious. People were converging on it, driven by the reflections of fire in the windows and the steadily-increasing rain of embers. There was a crowd of people, fighting to get on to the one road out. Antti Kantokari waded into them, kicking and punching. He threw others out of his way, dragging his wife and daughter with him. His two young sons tried to help him through. It was primeval survival. Everybody was fighting to escape from the death-trap that had so recently been a place of refuge. Antti Kantokari broke through, dragging his daughter with him. He turned to reach for his wife and sons but they were swept away and beaten down by others, equally desperate to escape the fires. He tried to get back to them. The sheer force of the torrent of people forcing through the narrow gap gave the crowd irresistible momentum. It drove him and his daughter down the street.

Kristianna realized how desperately late their escape had been. Already, the buildings down one side of the street were burning. Flames tried to reach over to the fresh fuel on the other side. She saw people who got in the way of the hungry reach of the fires just burst into flames themselves. They fell to the ground in miniature copies of the great fireballs made by the jellygas. She knew nothing, except the need to run, to get away from the fires, to escape. *What if the fires were in the south as well?* Her mind held a map of the city, the Americans had started these terrible blazes to the north, east and west of the city. They blocked off every way out, trapping everybody in the great fires. The road she was on led south, towards the great church of Saint John. Beyond that was the Kaivopuisto park. *Surely that would be safe?*

The road split. One part led west back towards the dockyard. Kristianna avoided it. She looked for her father as she did so. He had gone; swept away in the crowds or caught by the fire. Saint John's Church was already burning. The sight dissuaded many from taking that road but Kristianna ignored the fire and took the southern path. She skirted the inferno and headed away from the great fire to the north. She was exhausted. Her legs felt dead but they continued driving her south, past the fires that closed in from the Helsinkihafen on the east and the Aker Shipyard to the west. They carried her south, through the narrowing bottleneck between the three great fires that were gutting Helsinki and into the Kaivopuisto Park. Her legs only stopped when they took her all the way to the sea. There she collapsed. She lay on the beach as the waves washed over her. The long run had left her unable to move as she watched the fires converge on the city center.

Later, much later, she managed to half-drag, half-walk, half-crawl her way over to Harrakka Island, just a few hundred feet offshore. There with the rest of the refugees who had made it, she was safe. In her heart, she knew the truth. She was the only one of her family who had survived.

1st Platoon, Ski Group, 78th Siberian Infantry Division, near Letnerechenskiy, Kola Peninsula, Russia.

"Bratischka, the army calls for the assistance of our gallant comrades in the partisans!" Lieutenant Stanislav Knyaginichev looked around at the men and women who had answered his call. His words had been carried on the winds, to the units hidden in the villages and in the forests. The men and women had recovered their carefully-hidden weapons and come to aid the Army in its moment of need. Knyaz looked at them with pride. To do so took more courage than could easily be measured. The Army would fight its battle and be gone. The partisans would still be here when the fighting was over and the Hitlerites came to take their revenge. When the people had bravery such as this, the Rodina was safe. Embattled, hungry, besieged but safe. In his look at the Partisans around him, he had noted something else. They were better-armed than his men were. Every Partisan carried a German banana-rifle and were supplied with large numbers of grenades. Even those who had rocket launchers, either the German Panzerfaust or the Russian RPG-1 copy, still had a rifle and grenades as well. That was the measure of these men and women. Every banana rifle they carried meant a Germans soldier lying dead in the night.

"And how may the Partisans assist the Army, Tovarish Lieutenant?" The speaker was the leader of the largest of the partisan bands. It was rumored he had a brigade of no less than fifty men and women answering to him.

"There is a great gun on the railway; a gun that belongs to the American Navy. The fascists want to capture that gun very badly but it has escaped them. Every trap the Hitlerites have laid, the gun has escaped. American sailors, Russian engineers, my own Ski-troops; all of us are fighting together to get the gun to safety so that it can once again fire on the fascist beasts."

"Why do they not give the gun to us? We could use some artillery!" There was a murmur of agreement that swept around the meeting.

Knyaz grinned. "Bratischka, this is a forty centimeter gun!"

362

The partisan leader lifted his hands up, about 20 centimeters apart at first and then spread them apart so they were about the diameter of the railway gun. There was a few muffled cheers and some gasps of admiration. This was certainly a great gun. *A Tsar of guns* thought some of the older men. They were careful to keep the description to themselves.

"It needs much preparation and special railway tracks to fire. When it does, it hurls a shell fifty kilometers and the shell makes the very ground turn to jelly under it. Truly, bratischka, this is a great gun and of much value. The Americans have fought hard and sent many aircraft to help it escape. Now it is we who must make a great effort. The Hitlerites have set an ambush just short of the river bridge. The survivors of a mechanized battalion, about a reinforced company in strength. With artillery and anti-tank guns. They have torn up the railway tracks so the train must stop. The engineers cannot repair the tracks until the fascists are killed.

"Bratischka, I will be honest with you. The men on the train have done well but they are sailors and railway engineers. Even so, they have beaten the fascists like a drum, inflicting great loss on them. But they are sailors and railway engineers, not real soldiers. This task is beyond them. My men are the only real infantry on the train and there are but twenty of us left. Can I count on you to join us, to kill the fascists and show the American sailors what the partisans can do?"

There was a moment's silence. Then the leader of the largest of the groups stepped forward and hugged Knyaz in a bear-like embrace. "Tovarish Lieutenant, we will be there at your side. Now, how are we to go about this task?"

Knyaz got out his map. "The train is coming along the line here. It will stop behind the ridge where it is safe and as many men as can be spared will come forward to a position on that ridge, facing the fascists. We will move in on the fascist's flanks and rear while they are watching the ridge and attack them. Then we can drive . . . . . ."

"My apologies Tovarish Lieutenant. I have news we all should hear. The Americans have just bombed the lair of the Finnish Hitlerites. They have set the whole city on fire. The radio in Petrograd says they can see the glow of the fires from streets of Petrograd itself. The fascists are calling fire brigades from all over southern Finland to try and stop the fires spreading further but they struggle in vain. The fires have created a great wind storm and nothing can stop the spread of the flames."

The meeting erupted in cheers. Knyaz felt his back being pounded by the Partisans. The Americans weren't around to get the praise, but he was with them and that was near enough.

"Yes, Tovarish Lieutenant, we must indeed help the Americans save their gun. The whole city on fire? Good, that is very good."

A Room, Somewhere in Geneva

"You might at least have given me a cushion to sit on." Igrat's voice was indignant. Half her mind was in a screaming panic but she had locked that part away. Instead she concentrated on the task in hand. That was buying time so Henry and Achillea could catch up with her.

She was sitting in an old-fashioned wooden chair. Her wrists had been tied to the rails at the back, her ankles to the chair legs. It was a good, old-fashioned interrogation set-up that had her facing a desk with several lamps on it. The brilliant bulbs had been angled so they shone right in her eyes. She could see very little of the rest of the room; just the vague shadows of two men. One of them had a very heavy German accent. The other never spoke at all. He had opened her blouse and was pawing her, like a schoolboy, roughly and crudely. Igrat had noticed his hands had been shaking when he had unfastened the buttons. She looked at his shadow and put as much sympathy into her voice as she could. "You don't have much experience with women do you?"

Silent-One whinnied with outrage. His fist came out of the darkness, hitting her in the face. She ran her tongue around her mouth noting the salty taste of blood.

"Where did you get the papers from? Talk to us." It was German-Voice speaking.

"You want me to talk to you? Fine." Igrat looked at the shadow of Silent-One. "You hit like a girl. OK? And by the look of your pants, you have to pee like one as well."

The fist that hit her that time meant business. Igrat's vision exploded into brilliant flashes and pinwheels. When they cleared, her sight was distorted and she could feel the eye on that side swelling shut. German-Voice was speaking again. "Tell us what we ask or by the time we finish with your face, your own mother will not recognize you."

"She wouldn't recognize me anyway, she dumped me in the trash outside a brothel as soon as I was born." *That,* Igrat reflected, *was quite true enough but I doubt it is what these two idiots wanted to hear.* The panic started to rise again. She squashed it down ruthlessly

She was right. Her reward was another flurry of blows, some full-force punches, other slaps. She could sense the bleeding in her mouth was much worse and she let the stained saliva trickle from the corner of her lips. She was tempted to spit it at the men but resisted. The time for defiance like that would come later, when her chances of survival had gone.

German-voice was screaming at her. "What is in the briefcase?"

"My sandwiches. The food on the train is terrible so I got a packed lunch."

"You want more beating?" There was urgency and lust in the voice. He looking for excuses to hurt her. That scared Igrat more than the beating.

"Well, look if you don't believe me." Igrat was genuinely irritated in addition to putting on an act for the men's benefit. She was telling the truth and the idiots wouldn't believe her.

"And the case is booby trapped and we all get blown up, right?"

That was when Igrat's mind snapped at the way the phrase was constructed. The same way fish snap at bait. She'd thought that German accent was too heavy to be real. *Well, hello, fellow American.*

"With me in the room as well? Don't be a bigger fool than you can help." German-voice hesitated for a second and opened up the case. Inside were three packages, wrapped up in paper. The faint odor of salami and cheese was more than noticeable.

"So where are the papers and where did you get them from?"

"I don't know and the sandwiches came from the deli on the Rue Henri Fazy. My boss likes Limburger but no way am I carrying that. He'll have to make do with Helvetia."

The reply got her another serious of blows. She felt the crunch of her nose breaking and fill with blood. She snorted, trying to breathe through the sudden rush that threatened to suffocate her. "Now look what you've done. That blouse is silk, I'll never get the bloodstains out of it. You know how many coupons a new one will cost me?" *None at all.* thought Igrat. *If I can't wheedle some parachute silk out of somebody, I'm losing my touch.*

There was another enraged whinny; this time from both men. There was a rattle from the desk that forced Igrat to fight the blind panic back into its corner again. "Last chance." German-Voice was really beginning to lose it. "Where do you get the information from?"

"What information?" Igrat gasped as the doubled-up length of tow-chain hit her across the chest. Suddenly her breathing was painful. *Rib fractured at least.* She coughed and some blood splattered out. The chain hit her again; the pain was on both sides of her chest. She was expecting another blow from the chain but instead something hard and heavy hit her over the kidneys. The pain was excruciating. Her efforts to scream through the broken ribs doubled and redoubled her agony. Her vision started to gray out. Igrat began to believe she was dying.

That was when the door exploded. Igrat had seen Achillea kick doors down before but never from this side. The door just fragmented, only wooden splinters were left to hang in the lock and hinges. Normally Achillea would have landed on her left leg and dropped straight into her fighting crouch but this time she hit the floor rolling. The reason was simple, Henry McCarty was following her, moving terrifyingly fast for an old man. His right hand was blurring. Three shots, a tiny, almost undetectable pause, and three more.

By the time Igrat could register what was happening, both German-Voice and Silent-One were down. Behind Henry, a figure switched on the lights. Achillea was already up and moving over to the desk, flipping off the lamps as she passed. The semi-darkness was a blessed relief. Igrat still found the effort to keep breathing unbearably painful.

"Henry, call for an ambulance. Emergency ward, right away. This isn't good."

"They're already on their way, Branwen called them as soon as she'd followed the car to this place. Thank the gods that Loki kept her as a back-stop watch. And told her there would be bodies around tonight if things went sour."

Achillea nodded, Loki had turned up trumps. His foresight had probably saved Igrat's life. Then, she turned to Igrat. "Iggie, can you hear me? Good. You're a mess but you know that don't you? Nothing fatal though and the Boss will get your nose fixed. Where else did they hit you?"

"Shest, with a shain." Igrat's voice was blurring.

"Stay with me Iggie. You're not in any danger unless you let go." Achillea ran her fingers down the sides of Igrat's chest. "Right, at least two ribs fractured probably on both sides and your tits are bruised. Tell Mike, you'll have to go on top for the next few months."

Igrat chuckled and erupted into a burst of coughing. "He won't like that. Very strictly brought-up Catholic he is." She lost control of her voice at the end. That, more than anything else showed how badly she was hurt.

"Well, he's going to have to make an exception or take Holy Orders. Keep coughing, I know it hurts but it will clear liquid out of your lungs and save you a bout of pneumonia."

"Achillea, look who we have here." McCarty was speaking, he'd finished looking at the bodies. "Our old friend from Casablanca."

Achillea looked down at the body of Frank Barnes. Two holes in his chest so close they touched; one between the eyes. The other man's wounds were identical. Six shots, no misses. From a moving man at moving targets in the darkness. There was nobody better with guns than Henry McCarty. She looked again at Barnes and spat on his body.

"You should have left him alive Henry. He wanted a lesson in knife fighting. I'd have given him a long one." The wreckage of the door to the room swung open as a group of men with a gurney hurried in.

"Please, sirs, you have a wounded person here?" It was a Swiss ambulance team.

"Over here." Igrat's voice was weak but steady. Quietly, Achillea was proud of her. She'd seen professional street-fighters making a worse fuss over lesser wounds. The ambulance men went quickly to work, getting Igrat on to the gurney and out of the door. As they left, three policemen, one in plain clothes, the other two in uniform came in. None of them saw Branwen quietly slip out to join Igrat.

"Mister Smith. Have we an explanation for this?" The implication that the detective didn't like foreigners shooting each other on his patch was quite clear.

"These two men abducted one of my associates, holding her for ransom. With the assistance of your department we traced their taxi to this building. We were working our way up here when we heard screaming. We couldn't wait for your men; my associate's life was in danger. One of the men, that one, was beating her with a chain. That chain." Henry pointed at the blood-stained links on the floor. "He would have killed her, already she was badly injured."

The detective picked up the chain and looked at it, thinking hard. He didn't like the gunplay and foreigners causing trouble but he also had a teenage daughter. The sight of the blood-stained chain decided him. "I think a man who would do such things to a woman is no loss. Very well, this is just for the young woman they brutalized. This one time only, I will write this up as self-defense against two hardened criminals."

Waiting Room, Geneva Hospital Emergency Ward, Geneva.

"Mr. Smith?" The doctor was looking around the waiting room.

"Doctor?"

"Ah Mister . . . . Smith. I'm pleased to tell you your associate is resting comfortably and is in no danger. We've reset her nose and splinted it but she will need some further attention to straighten it when she is stronger. You have good surgeons in America for such things I believe? Her face is badly bruised. There is also a possibility one of her eyes might be damaged. Her ribs are fractured; two of them on one side, one on the other, but we have taped these up and this is easing her discomfort. She also received at least two very heavy blows to the kidneys. There is blood in her urine but they are functioning. She is a strong woman. She will recover unless something unexpected happens."

"Can she travel?"

The doctor was indignant. "Of course not. Did you not listen? She was treated with sadistic cruelty and received serious injuries. She must not travel; not for a week, perhaps ten days. Then only with great care. But she will be as well-treated here as in any of your American hospitals."

"I have no doubt of that, Sir. And thank you for all your efforts." McCarty turned to Achillea. "Looks like she'll have to stay while we go ahead."

"Excuse me. Mister Smith?" The speaker was a man so tall he had to bend down to leave the elevator. "Hartzleff, from the German Embassy. The Cultural Department." There was an awkward silence. Everybody knew that the Cultural Department of the German Embassy meant Gestapo or Abwehr or both. "Perhaps we could speak privately?"

The two men drifted over to a deserted corner. Once there, Hartzleff resumed. "I have heard what has befallen your associate Mister Smith. I do not know who was responsible, but you have my word it was none of our work." McCarty did his best to look skeptical. "Mister Smith, if that it's your name which I doubt, I know you are a smuggler and a black marketeer. You bring women's stockings and other luxuries over from America and sell them in France and Germany for an enormous profit which is banked here because your IRS would catch you if you took it back with you.

"I tell you this because we do not care about your activities. If anything, they are helpful to us. A few luxuries keep many people

369

quiet. So, although our countries are at war, there is no quarrel between us and you have nothing to fear from us. You may be certain your associate may recover here in peace as far as we are concerned. I have posted two of my men downstairs. If you wish, they will remain here to help protect your associate. In case of misunderstandings. Or if you prefer, they will leave with me."

McCarty thought for a moment. He had little doubt that if Hartzleff had pulled Igrat in as part of his political or intelligence duties, she would have suffered just as badly and probably worse. It was the thought that something like this could be done unofficially, in the private sector as it were, that genuinely appalled the Gestapo officer. "All the evidence suggests that this was just some gangsters trying to muscle in on my operation. The responsible parties are dead; so I think this incident is concluded, Herr Hartzleff. But your reassurances are welcome and the assistance of your men also."

Hartzleff nodded brusquely and headed back out. McCarty shook his head and rejoined Achillea. "Well, the Gestapo have just denied responsibility, for what that's worth. There'll be two Gestapo men downstairs. They're going to be there anyway so I thought it better we know where they are than have them lurking around somewhere else."

"Good thinking. We knew they weren't involved anyway. The Boss is going to be really mad at Donovan for trying to pull this one."

"Yeah." McCarty shuddered slightly at the prospect of the news getting back to Washington. "He'd be really mad if it was any one of us. Since it's Igrat, he'll go completely ballistic."

United States Strategic Bombardment Commission, Blair House, Washington D.C. USA.

The Seer flipped through the code book, looking at some of the code-names assigned to people. He'd chosen his own, a name he'd won a long time before. Curtis LeMay was "The Diplomat," a reference to the time when a Canadian fighter squadron had brought their Sopwith Snipes down to the US. He'd taken one look at the antiquated aircraft and blurted out "Jeez, they're crap." Leslie Groves was "The Architect" after his construction of the Pentagon. Thomas Power was "The Butcher". On a whim he checked his own staff, Lillith

370

was "The Librarian" and Naamah "The Doctor." Igrat was "The Champ". It occurred to him that whoever awarded these names was a pretty fine judge of character.

"General LeMay is here, Boss."

"Thanks Lillith. Please find Sir Archibald McIndoe and get him ready to work on Igrat when she gets back. When are they due in?"

"Twenty four hours, Boss. Igrat sneaked out the hospital and joined Henry and Achillea. They're treating her like eggs. They've got what amounts to a complete hospital, complete with a bed, a doctor and a couple of nurses, in the front end of a Connie."

Stuyvesant nodded. C-69s were used to evacuate casualties from Russia. The experience had been put to use in getting Igrat back quickly and safely. "Good. Impress upon Sir Archibald that he's the finest plastic surgeon found practicing on the North American continent. If he doesn't fix Igrat's nose properly, he'll be the finest plastic surgeon found floating in the Potomac." He hesitated slightly and controlled his temper. "No, he's a good man, you don't need to say that. Just tell him a pretty girl has placed her trust in him. That'll work a lot better. "

Lillith nodded and went out. A few seconds later, Curtis LeMay entered

"Curt, good to see you. How did the strike go?"

"Helsinki? So-so. One of the three groups hit the wrong target. They missed the main marshalling yards and hit a smaller set further south. Radar pictures look similar. I'm going to speak to Tommy about that. He can do better. We burned out most of the southern part of the city. It would have been less if the 7th had hit their assigned target. We lost 17 aircraft. Nine B-29s, five F-61s and three F-65s. In exchange we got around a dozen Heinkel 219 and Me-110s."

"110s? I didn't know they had any of those left."

"Finnish. We lucked out. Next time the low-level flak will be waiting."

"We're leaking out that the purpose of the raid is to force the Nazis to pull back low-level flak from the front line and ease the pressure on the fighter-bombers. They won't believe it, of course. They'll see it for what it is, a one-shot trick pony we can't repeat. They'll also see it as desperation on our part; a last-ditch attempt to find some way to use all the bombers we've bought. Tomorrow the papers will be running the story about how Tommy Power has cracked the way to destroy cities. Low and fast, over the rooftops with incendiaries."

"Once more with the low altitude and over-the-rooftops. God help us if we really had to do it that way." LeMay rubbed his eyes. "You wanted to set up a meeting?"

"Yes, with you, General Groves and the supervisory committee. We've got some paperwork arriving that everybody needs to consider. It got held up a little but its safely on its way over. We'll invite Major General Donovan as well, but I don't think he'll be able to attend."

CHAPTER TWELVE
RESTORING ORDER

South Helsinki, Finland

It was a strange thing. In the soft gray light of dawn, the damage to the city didn't seem to be all that bad. The shells of the buildings were still standing. Their glass was gone and the area of wall around the windows was stained black certainly, but the outer stone shells were still there. It was only from the air that the devastation was truly apparent. From above it could be seen that the buildings were indeed shells, their insides gutted by fire. The incendiaries had landed on roofs already damaged by one hundred pound bombs mixed in with the incendiaries and set the wooden inside structure ablaze. That might have been controllable but for the two thousand pound bombs that the B-29s had dropped right at the start of the attack. They had blown the windows in. The fires on the top floors had drawn air in through the base of the buildings and up. That turned controllable fires into infernos. The same suction effect drew burning embers from adjacent fires in and they had completed the process. South Helsinki had been burned out. It just didn't look like it. Not quite.

Marshal Carl Gustaf Emil Mannerheim looked at the ruined buildings. Outwardly dispassionate, inwardly despair tore at him. Under his leadership the Finnish Army had fought the Soviet Army to a standstill in the Winter War. He believed that achievement had saved Finland from Soviet occupation. Then the damned fool politicians had started the Continuation War in the hope of recovering the territory lost in 1940 and bringing about the dream of a Greater Finland covering the whole of the Kola Peninsula. Being charitable, they couldn't have known then that doing so would bring them into conflict with the Americans. At that time Russia had been alone and it had seemed certain Germany would win that war as well. But the Americans had come in with their endless cornucopia of weapons and their ruthless determination to win, at all costs. Mannerheim looked around. Obviously one of the costs had been South Helsinki. At 78 years old, he didn't need this. Nor would he need what was obviously to come. The same destruction would be methodically meted out to every city and town in Finland. Starting with the bits of Helsinki still standing.

In the back of the car with him, President Risto Heikki Ryti was looking at the people, not at the burned-out buildings. Rather, he was looking at their remains; shrunken, blackened husks that the fires had left behind. The car was in a small square, just off the Mannerheiminte. It had been one where people had gathered in vain hope of shelter. There had been one exit out of the square when the fires had closed in, a narrow street. The entrance to it was blocked by a pile of charred bodies, ten or twenty high and five times that number deep. For a second, he wondered what the last minutes of those people had been like, fighting desperately to escape while the flames closed in.

"Why did they do it to us? What did we ever do to them?" Ryti's voice was cracking with emotion and bewilderment.

"What did we do to them?" Mannerheim could hardly believe the question. "We sank their ships. We shot down their aircraft. We killed their soldiers. We attacked them when we had led them to believe that a truce existed along our front. I think that was enough."

"But we didn't attack them. We have never fought Americans."

"We fought their allies. That's enough. And their aircraft fight over Kola and that too is enough. We had fair warning. The Americans told us that how we would be treated would depend on how much or little activity we undertook. You have seen the word from Sweden?"
"Of course. We cannot accept such terms."

"We cannot not accept them. They are the best we will get. If we do not accept them, and make the allies believe that we have accepted them, we will look back and see these terms as generosity incarnate. If anybody is left in our burned-out cities to look back of course."

"The Germans say they will prevent more such attacks. They are moving additional fighters and low-level anti-aircraft guns around our cities. They say any more such raids will be too costly for the Americans to contemplate."

"Perhaps. Although I do not think the Germans understand what the Americans are prepared to pay yet. Or what prices they will charge."

There was a silence as the open-topped touring car left the square that stank of roasted flesh and returned to the Mannerheiminte. The bodies here were more spaced out, spread evenly rather than piled up. Mannerheim looked at the carnage wanting to weep but unable to do so. One thing caught his eye. A couple, charred husks now like all the rest, but holding each other. Between them was the burned remains of a potted plant. Incredibly one of its leaves was green. Somehow, that leaf had escaped the fires and the heat. "Mister President, do me a personal favor and have this street renamed. I do not care to have such a scene bearing my name."

Ryti nodded wordlessly, looking at the scene unrolling as the car eased down the street. From the roadside the rescue workers stopped their efforts when they recognized the tall figure in the back of the car and their voices carried across the empty space.

"It's the Marshal."

"He'll save us."

"The Marshal will help us."

Once again, Mannerheim wanted to weep; the necessity of maintaining the staunch appearance prevented him. While the man who occupied the car was still President, there was nothing he could do. He could stop armies but not the bombers that flew overhead. While Ryti remained President, the bombers would return. Suddenly a deep chill racked Mannerheim's body and soul. For one horrible

375

moment he believed he was looking at the future, not just of Finland but of all Europe.

"So I must accept these terms?" Ryti asked the question. In his heart he knew the answer that was coming.

"No, you must not. You cannot, because nobody will believe you. We have accepted a truce once, unofficial certainly but real for all of that. You gave orders to break it. You took German bribes to break it. Now, you will send your acceptance of these terms to the Americans and they will wipe their asses with it."

The sudden, uncharacteristic coarseness shocked Ryti but he knew what the words meant. His term as President was finished. It had just ended, here on the street he would rename as his last official act. In that moment, he knew that he would rename the street after himself. The burned-out, corpse-covered street was a scene that should bear his name. It was his fault this had happened.

"Marshal, it is obvious that I can no longer lead Finland under these circumstances. Will you become Prime Minister and accept the allied terms on Finland's behalf?" His voice was hopeless, despairing.

Mannerheim stared at Ryti and measured the situation. "No. I am too old and I lack knowledge of the detailed techniques of government to take on such a role. Nor would the allies accept it. There must be a clean break with the past."

Ryti sighed. Again, he had expected the answer. "Then I must resign from the office of president, and ask parliament to elect you as Regent. At a time such as this, it is necessary that civil and military authority be combined in one person so that there is no doubt over who carries the right authority."

In the back of the car, Mannerheim weighed the situation then decided on the course that had to be followed. He would have to send word via Sweden that the new terms would be accepted, that the Finnish Army would never again attack allied positions. "The Americans do not like the position of Regent. They think it sounds like a cinema. I will have to be elected as President to avoid any misconceptions about the nature of my office. The Americans understand Presidents." Ryti nodded. It was not as if he had much choice in the matter, not surrounded by the stench of burned-out city and the heat from the incinerated buildings. "We must hope that the Swedes can make the allies believe that."

Mannerheim nodded. It all depended on the Swedes and their strange friends in Switzerland. Once again, he looked at the burned-out city and shuddered. The feeling he was looking at Europe's grave still lingered within him.

Mechanized Column, 71st Infantry Division, Kola Peninsula

The scouts had spotted the train as soon as dawn had broken. Then, they had worked their way back to where the rest of the column had set up its positions. They had skied back with the word that the officers needed to know, past the long lines of ripped-up track that would stop the single surviving great gun. The gun couldn't pass the blockage. The railwaymen couldn't repair the tracks under fire. They were all trapped. Ahead of them, the glow in the sky showed where the sun would soon rise. Overhead, the clouds were turning dark, angry red. An old saying rolled through the corporal's mind.

Red sky at night, soldier's delight.
Red sky in the morning, soldier's warning.

An old verse, almost a child's saying but with truth behind it. There was another storm coming. Probably not as severe as the great storm that had started this whole offensive. It would be a bad one none the less. The corporal guessed that the Army would be using that storm to break off and retreat. The offensive had failed. Everybody knew it. Only this long contest between the mechanized column and the American Navy gun was still going on. It had become almost a private war in itself.

The treeline was ahead and the scouts planed into it. They sought out their commander in the prepared positions. Asbach had seen them come in and was hurrying out to meet them. His snow-shoes eased his passage across the packed ground.

"Report corporal?"

"The train has stopped. Some eight kilometers behind that ridge. We saw men dismounting from it. We think they are the railway engineers and the sailors. Perhaps they are moving up to attack."

"If we are lucky, perhaps. Corporal, take your men back. There is fresh coffee made and some stew. You have done well." Asbach turned around and thought. *Why had the train stopped so far back?* "One moment Corporal, did you see the Siberians?"

"No, no sign of them."

That was bad. *They were up to something but what?* They were only a depleted platoon in strength. Even Siberians couldn't attack a reinforced unit like this, not one that was dug in and waiting. Not unless they got some help.

"Lang, we have flank guards out."

"Yes Asbach, a light platoon each side. And I sent a squad to watch our rear as well."

"Good, take as many men as we have left and form a reserve. Form it around a couple of half-tracks for support. If we get attacked, move to reinforce wherever the attack is coming from."

"Very good Asbach. I'll have two good squads each in a 'track."

Asbach nodded and returned to his thoughts. There was one source of manpower that the train could access. Partisans. They were all around him. He always knew that. Now they were closing in to help the train. *That damned train.*

He shook himself. It was as if that hell-spawned train was alive, that it was fighting him all by itself. It had sucked him and all the other forces around him into a private little war. One that had little to do with the greater war that was going on around them. *Had the devil himself possessed that great gun and was using it for his own plans?* Asbach hadn't been a religious man since his youth. He'd lost his faith in God during the stone-by-stone fighting for Moscow. But he believed in the devil and now he was getting a growing feeling that the devil was becoming inordinately interested in him.

Behind him, the sun started to edge over the horizon, the dark of the night turning into royal blue. And that's when Asbach heard the sound of aircraft engines.

F-61D "Evil Dreams" Over Letnerechenskiy, Kola Peninsula

It had been a hard night. First of all, two hours over Helsinki being buffeted by the rising air currents from the growing fires down below. They had hunted the anti-aircraft guns that threatened the B-29s. They'd got most of them, or at least the ones that opened fire. Sometimes they'd been too late. They still remembered the sight of one B-29 with its port engines on fire. It had folded up in mid-air and crashed on to the city beneath. And another just exploded, sending fire and fragments in great arcs downwards. Then, they had landed at their home base, to be hurriedly reloaded with bombs and rockets. All so they could go and support the train that was trying to get through to safety in the north.

Lieutenant Quayle thought that it was only fair. He had been the one who had shot up the trains in the first place. But he didn't like being out this close to dawn. *No, that wasn't quite right, it was at dawn and the sun was already showing its tip over the horizon. Wasn't there a legend that witches melted in the sunlight if they were caught out after daybreak? Or was that vampires?*

Evil Dreams headed south, looking down at the rails in the dawn twilight. Their shine was a faint but ghostly trail that reminded him of a snail moving. His first job was to find the train. Apparently only a single gun survived, and he had to ensure it was clear of the battle area. Then he had to track the rails back and try and work out where the German force was hiding. Word was they were hidden in the woods. That was bad news. His favorite anti-personnel weapon, napalm, wasn't that effective against targets hidden in dense trees. The fire tended to run through the tree tops and miss the troops underneath. So he had one thousand pound bombs and five inch rockets. Plus his cannon and machine guns of course.

"I've got the train Boss." Sergeant James Morton's eyes were hurting and he had a bad headache. Too much work, too many searchlights, not enough sleep. Helsinki had been the added bit of strain on the Black Widow crews that had pushed them over the edge. They needed rest, needed it very badly.

Evil Dreams orbited over the train, recognizing the gun in the dim light. Then, the crew set off north again and tried to work out where the German ambush unit was situated. The railway skirted the ridgeline, curved around a mound and then set off across the shallow valley. Then it curved away around another gentle rise. Quayle looked down at the track in the valley. Somehow it looked wrong.

"Donnie, look at that track. It seem wrong to you?"

Phelan looked hard, cupping his eyes and trying to focus on the track. Even with binoculars specially designed for low-light conditions, it was hard to make out but . . . . Then as the light strengthened he realized what he was looking at.

"Got it, Boss. The tracks been torn up. Rails are off to the sides. The sleepers have been pulled away. Shadows make it look like the bed has a couple of holes in it as well." That could be a mistake, the shallow-incidence light made every slight bump or dip look like a mountain or a yawning chasm.

Quayle circled around again. *Now, if the track was torn up here, then the best place to cover it would be over there wouldn't it?* He looked down hoping for a flash of light as an incautious officer watched him with binoculars but no such luck. Too much to hope for. "Donnie, get on the radio and call our friends over. We'll need some help for this." And better to have four Black Widows than one if enemy fighters turned up. As soon as the light grew better, they would be replaced by Thunderbolts or Thunderstorms and that would make life a lot more comfortable.

Right, it was time to start. He had to make a choice and Quayle picked a point that looked as if it would give a good field of fire for the hidden German force. *Evil Dreams* angled over and started her run towards the selected piece of pine forest. Quayle leveled the aircraft out and let fly with all twelve of his five inch rockets. Below him, the wood line erupted into explosions as the salvo struck home.

Mechanized Column, 71st Infantry Division, Kola Peninsula

The American Night Witch pilot was good, very good. Even in the deceptive light of early dawn he had searched out his target and selected the likely position of his prey. He'd got damned close as well, the rocket salvo had punched into the treeline barely 100 meters from his position, close enough for some of the rockets to land amongst his men. Asbach had held his breath, hoping that none of them would open fire and reveal his true position. Doing that would bring down accurate fire from the Night Witch overhead. Discipline held, and the Night

Witch climbed away, resuming its circling and waiting for something to break cover. Asbach guessed that the big twin-engined jabo wouldn't be on its own much longer, it had probably called in its friends and reinforcements would be on the way.

Then Asbach heard the sound he had been expecting, hoping that he wouldn't hear it but expecting it nevertheless. The crash of light mortar rounds, the rattle of machine guns and the baying 'urrah, urrah' of Russian infantry. Asbach listened carefully, for sounds could tell him what eyes could not. *Was the rhythmic thumping of StG-44s, the German rear-guard? Or partisans with captured weapons?* The ripping sound of the German MG-42s and MG-45s were already dominating the symphony. That meant the attack had to be developing fast. Mixed up with the sound of the German weapons was another tearing noise, one so fast that individual shots were indistinguishable. *That had to be the PPS-45.* And finally, a slow, dull, thumping, richer and heavier than the rest. The American .45 machine pistols they handed out with such largess. A crude, clumsy weapon but one that was accurate and fired a crippling bullet.

Asbach held his breath. It was a partisan attack for sure. But if Lang moved his two half tracks to support the tiny force at the rear of the formation, he would reveal the position of the unit to the Night Witches overhead. Even as he thought the situation through, a runner slid in the snow beside him.

"Captain's compliments and he's leading his reaction force in on foot, doesn't want to move his vehicles. Says the enemy is attacking in at least battalion strength and there are ski-troops mixed in with Partisans. They have mortars, machine guns and our rifles."

Asbach nodded. "Tell Lang to drive the enemy back. Keep them away from our main position. If those Partisans have a radio and they report where we are, our friends up there will be having a field day." The runner nodded and slid off to rejoin his units.

Asbach sighed gently. This was likely to be the final confrontation between him and the men on that accursed train. Once, in Monte Carlo, before the war, he had seen the combination of hope and despair on the face of a man who had placed his last few chips on a single number on the roulette wheel. He had watched that wheel spin with hope despite the odds against him. Against all common sense, he had been shocked when the turn went against him and he lost the last of his small wealth. Now, Asbach knew just how that man had felt.

Top Floor, Bank de Commerce et Industrie, Geneva, Switzerland.

"Any word from the Finns, Tage?"

"Much news, it will be public soon but we have had warning first. Helsinki, what's left of it, told Stockholm less than an hour ago and they told me. Risto Heikki Ryti has resigned as President and Marshal Mannerheim is being elected to take his place. Ryti had to go, nobody would believe him, even if he did declare peace. The message from the Marshal is that Finland will accept the Russian peace terms as laid down in our last meeting, harsh though they are. He believes German troops in the north of the country will retreat to Norway but it will be necessary for the Canadians and Russians to deal with those in the South."

"I am surprised, I'd thought the Finns were certain to reject those terms." Loki relaxed in his chair, spinning it slightly from side to side as he absorbed the news. "And Finland is out completely?"

"Completely." Tage Erlander had also found it hard to believe that Finland would collapse. "It was the bombing that did it, that and the way their Motti tactics failed against the Canadians. Their success against the Russians and the lack of any real strikes against the homeland had persuaded Ryti that carrying on the war was risk-free. As he saw it, Finland had everything to gain by carrying on and nothing to lose. Then, the Canadians cut up the Finnish Army and the Americans burned Helsinki down. Win or lose, Finland was going to get hurt and hurt badly."

"How many died in Helsinki? Anybody know yet?"

"Final total? No, nobody will know for days or weeks. The estimates are rising every hour. It was 10,000 at dawn, now it is 20,000 and still it rises. The Finns had no real air raid precautions in place, not against the sort of raid the Americans launched. Oh, they had anti-aircraft guns, searchlights, all those things and sirens to warn people. But all they'd experienced before was some Russian planes scattering a few light bombs. Their buildings had strong cellars and, as usual, people went there to hide from the bombs. They died there, roasted by the fires. The only ones who lived were the ones who started to run early and kept running. It is rumored the American had night fighters over the city and they strafed the refugees as they ran."

Loki snorted. "Not likely. I'd guess they were attacking the anti-aircraft guns to protect the bombers." *And I know the mind behind this* thought Loki, not knowing how completely wrong his belief was. "Doesn't matter though. Finland's out, that's what matters. Tage, we need to get this through to Washington and Moscow as quickly as possible. Does your embassy still have its circuits open?"

"Of course."

"Good, and I will tell the Swiss government."

Haven't I just done that? thought Erlander then dismissed the idea as unfair. *The banks weren't the same thing as the Swiss Government, not even this one. Not quite anyway.* "Well, we wanted the Americans to intervene and they did. Just not the way we thought."

"True Tage. But we wanted them to secure a less severe peace for the Finns, not force the original down their throats. You know, when this is all over, all of the Nordic countries are going to have to think about this very carefully. If the Russian Bear is on the move up your way and the Americans will back those moves, it doesn't look very good. If you don't hang together."

"We will all hang separately." Erlander half-chuckled at the quotation. "But Danes, Norwegians, Swedes hanging together? That would be a first time. And to have the Finland in there as well. Or what is left of Finland. It will not be a happy or comfortable alliance."

"So much worse than being Russian provinces?" Loki was irritated. The petty quarrels of his original homeland in the face of impending disaster rankled him. "Look, Tage, we all share much more than our differences suggest, you know that. Scandinavia has to put up a united face when this damned war ends or it'll get eaten alive. You know that as well."

Tage Erlander sighed, this strange Swiss banker was right, the times when Scandinavia could remain absorbed in its own petty affairs while the rest of the world ignored it were fading fast. This war would end and Sweden had better be prepared for it. Otherwise, the fate of Helsinki could be repeated many, many times. Then, he asked himself the one question that he had always been afraid to ask. *Just how far would the Americans go to bring Nazi Germany down?*

Watching him, Loki saw the message sink home. He had tried before to bring Scandinavia to the center of the world stage. His efforts had been a disaster. *Because Stuyvesant had played his own game as usual and wrecked everything.* The thought seethed through Loki's mind and made him want to slam his fist down on his desk. *It had so nearly worked before* . . . . Then he forced himself to calm down. This time it would be different, this time Stuyvesant owed him for all the intelligence material he was relaying back. This time Stuyvesant was in a war that he couldn't win without Loki's help. Now, when Loki tried to get Scandinavia united again, it would work. Because that was the price of his aid to the Americans.

Mechanized Column, 71st Infantry Division, Kola Peninsula

There had been a time when artillerists had fought their guns to the barrel. Gunners would fight cavalry and infantry hand-to-hand around their guns to prevent the disgrace of the artillery pieces being lost. When indirect fire had become the normal way of doing things and the guns had been positioned miles behind friendly lines, it had seemed those days were gone. Russia had quickly dispelled that idea. First tank thrusts that penetrated the defenses and suddenly emerged kilometers behind friendly lines had brought the guns back into the front line. Then had come the partisans whose sudden strikes could turn a safe haven into a battlefield without warning. Gunners had had to fight their guns to the barrel again and know how to use the weapons that kind of fighting required.

Sergeant Heim had been in Russia since the heady days of 1941. Then, the Heer had driven through western Russia, scattering the Soviet Army before them. For a while the huge encirclements brought in prisoners by the tens or hundreds of thousands and cities had fallen with the regularity of a ticking clock. It had seemed like the war really would be over by Christmas. But the Heer hadn't made it to Moscow by the time the winter arrived. In the snows of that first winter, the Soviet counter-offensive had driven the Germans from the gates of Moscow. That's when Heim had learned that artillerymen still had to fight like infantry sometimes. The lesson had stayed with him in the years that came next, the fall of Moscow in 1942, the last German drive forward, the arrival of the Americans, the descent of the war into a bloody, futile deadlock. As every year rolled by, the gunners had had to protect their guns. Now they had to do it again.

The perimeter of the defensive position had been weak. Just a squad of panzergrenadiers. A total of eight men with two machine guns and four rifles. One of the machine gun teams had gone in the first second of the attack, a grenade thrown out of the trees had landed in the pit beside them, killing both men instantly. Then there had been the roar of rifle, machine gun and machine-pistol fire. It had been followed by the sight of the white-clad partisans and ski-troops slipping through the trees to assault the paper-thin defense line.

Both sides had been blasting off ammunition at each other. That was something else that had changed since 1941. Now virtually every soldier had an automatic, or at least semi-automatic, weapon. Attacks tended to be concentrations of automatic fire poured at the other side. The hope was to pin them down until the artillery got them. Only, there was no artillery in this battle. The partisans had light mortars only, weapons that were of little use in the dense trees. Their rounds exploded in the treetops, scattering down light fragments but without the power to do crippling damage. The German unit had Heim's four surviving 150mm self-propelled guns but they had been lined up on where the train would have to appear and men would have to work on the torn-up tracks. The gun was in a limited-traverse housing. Turning the whole vehicle around just wasn't going to be possible.

So, this battle was infantryman against infantryman and would be decided by the weapons they carried. And the numbers on each side of course. There, the partisans had an advantage. They had struck the weakest part of the German position. Already they were wearing the defenses down. The partisans themselves weren't normally the best of soldiers. Today, the Siberians were mixed in with them and they could stand toe-to-toe with the best Germany had to offer. The squad guarding the rear wasn't going to last much longer. Then, Heim knew he would be fighting as an infantryman again.

"Pass word out, all the gun crews, get ready. Man the machine gun with two men per gun. The rest of you, get rifles and get between the vehicles." Each one of the self-propelled guns had an MG-45 machine gun mounted on the gun casement for exactly this emergency. They would act as pillboxes while the rest of the crews prevented the enemy getting too close.

385

A single figure dressed in white suddenly backed out of the woods. He was firing his rifle from the hip, short bursts ripping out at an unseen enemy following him. "Kameraden!" The word rang through the waiting guns. The man turned and ran for the guns. He dived into cover as he reached the illusion of protection offered by their steel shapes.

"Come here." Heim's voice was sharp and insistent. The man quickly mounted the self-propelled gun and dropped into the fighting compartment. "What is happening."

"Partisans. And ski troops. They have chewed us up, I am the only one left. There are hundreds of them."

Heim shook his head. There weren't, it just seemed like that. His mind flipped back to that winter offensive of 1941/42 and the Siberians sliding through the snow. They had harried their enemies the way wolves brought down their prey. "We'll hold them here. Join the men by the guns."

The MG-45 was already loaded and waiting. Heim pulled back the charging lever and nestled down behind the gun. It wouldn't be long now. His eyes ran along the nearest group of trees, *was there movement already from behind them?* The butt of the machine gun fitted neatly into his shoulder and he squeezed the trigger gently. The movement sent a short burst into the suspect trees. That broke the brief silence that had descended on the battlefield. A hail of return fire ricocheted off the armor of his self-propelled gun. Heim briefly thanked the gods of war that the fire was from rifles only. The self-propelled guns only had armor to protect them against rifle-caliber weapons. Anything more would go through and bounce around inside.

His men were returning fire. Their StG-44s cracked out quick bursts as the gunners tried to spot the muzzle flashes of the approaching Russians and pin them down. Firing was spreading quickly along the line of self-propelled guns. The machine guns laced the treeline with tracers, the riflemen filled in the gaps. On the other side, the automatic weapons carried by the partisans returned a growing volume of fire. Heim noted that for all the sound and fury of the fire exchange, nobody actually seemed to get hit. Idly the mathematician's part of his mind, the part no artilleryman could do without, wondered just how many rounds got fired from these assault rifles and machine pistols to get a kill, and how that compared with the old bolt-action weapons. *It sometimes seemed as if we have replaced one round that hits with a lot that don't.*

That idle speculation didn't last long. Nor did it stop Heim from raking the woodline with his machine gun. The problem now wasn't ammunition, it was heat build-up on the barrel. *Carry on like this and the barrel will burn out.* Over on the left, the gun at the extreme end of the line stopped firing. Either the gunner inside had been hit or his weapon had jammed. Almost at once, the weight of Russian fire shifted to that section. Heim saw more white-clad figures moving through the snow towards the silent vehicle. Their fire was pinning down the men next to the vehicle. Soon, they would be close enough to blast them out with hand grenades. Heim switched his fire to the new threat. He saw his burst of fire tumble down three or four of the ghostly figures. Then he had to duck as almost every gun the Russians had concentrated on him. He hadn't heard such a concentration of ringing since the church bells at his wedding. His wife's family had been overjoyed at the ceremony. That hadn't surprised Heim, their first baby had been born seven months later.

He shook his head, clearing the memory out and peeked over the edge of the armor. He was just in time to see a gray-black cloud of smoke flash from the ground. A rolling explosion enveloped the side of the gun. Either an RPG-1 or a captured Panzerfaust he thought. He'd heard the Americans had copied the Panzerfaust and were building them in a new factory in Siberia. Rumor had it they were building so many that every Russian soldier would carry one. That was only fair, the Germans had copied the American Bazooka as their Panzerschreck. The stricken self-propelled gun was already starting to burn. The petrol engine used by the British tank that served as its chassis would see the fire quickly become terminal.

That didn't take long at all. The fire took hold and reached the ammunition store. The gun exploded in a brilliant white flash that scattered great burning trails across the snow. *Three guns left and the Russians were closing in fast.* It hadn't taken long for them to exploit the destruction of the gun. They used the cloud of black smoke from the burning vehicle to cover their approach. Heim thought quickly. *The Panzerfaust has a range of around 30 – 60 meters depending on the version the Russians had captured. If they seized the position around the burning gun, they could open fire on the next vehicle and roll the whole artillery position up. It was time to do something about that.*

"Take over the machine gun!" He snapped the words at the nearest soldier on the ground beside his vehicle and jumped down. Then he pointed at two men from the crew. "You and you. Follow me."

He repeated the same process with the three surviving gun crews. That gave him seven men including himself, all armed with assault rifles. A dozen men were left to man the remaining artillery positions. It was thin but he hoped it would be enough. Then, he took his squad behind the parked guns and worked his way towards the burning gun. A quick burst of fire from right next to it showed him that his fears were already well on the way to being realized. The Russians had taken the position and were holding it, positioning themselves dangerously close to the destroyed self propelled gun in order to take advantage from the smoke. That could work against them as well, they had to be ducking to avoid the wreckage being flung around by the secondary explosions.

He took aim and his seven men raked the position with fire from their rifles. Then, they ran forward, their snow shoes helping them glide over the piles of frozen snow and ice that lay between them and the Russians. Two of his men went down. One collapsed in a bloody heap as a PPS-45 burst ripped him up. The other, Heim couldn't see. *A grenade fragment? Or a rifle bullet. It didn't matter.* He and the four others jumped into the Russian troops. They flailed with their rifle butts and stabbed out with bayonets. A frantic, chaotic slaughter that Heim couldn't understand or follow. He beat one Russian down, bayoneted him, then fired his rifle so that the recoil jerked the bayonet out of the body. When he ducked, he felt a slam on his side. A butt strike from a Russian who held an StG-44 identical to Heim's own. The blow took his breath away but the Russian fell also, shot down by the one surviving man who was with Heim.

There were five dead Russians in the pit by the burning self-propelled gun and three more dead Germans. Heim looked across, another group of partisans were already approaching, attempting to regain the self-propelled gun position. Heim did a quick count. *Eighteen, perhaps twenty?*

"How many rounds have you got?"

"One magazine. And Shultzie has two. Here."

The soldier handed the extra magazine over to Heim. With two magazines each, the two of them couldn't hold this position. The best they could do was hope that they could delay the Russian assault long enough for somebody to think of something. He took aim at one group and squeezed off a quick burst. They scattered, leaving a figure laying still on the ground. That was good, but the burst of return fire wasn't. It seemed as though every gun in the Russian army was firing on his little position.

Across from the cover, another group of partisans rushed forward. Suddenly, they were intercepted by a burst of fire that felled four of them and sent the remainder scuttling back to cover. Heim looked over to his left. A group of German troops, almost twenty of them were moving in to the gun positions and along the line. A part of them were heading this way. Heim watched them, with shock recognizing the figure that led the section.

"Sergeant, your men told me you were here. Situation?"

"Enemy in the woods over there and around our flank. They got this gun but we pushed them out again. There's a lot of them, a hundred or more. All with a automatic weapons and there's ski-troops mixed in with them." Heim looked at Captain Lang with amazement. Despite everything, the man's silk scarf was still snowy, unstained white.

"Well done. I've got 22 men with me. I'll leave six with you and disperse the rest between the remaining guns. That should hold this position."

There was a note of query in Lang's voice, as if he was expecting approval. Heim appreciated it. "That's good, but there's our friend overhead to worry about."

"Ah yes, the Night Witches. We've run out of our Fliegerschrecks. We will have to hope that they will not do us too much harm. Hope is about all we have left right now."

Heim nodded. The reinforcements Captain Lang had brought would help hold the area here. *But what was happening on the flanks? And how long would it be before the Ami Jabos turned up in strength.*

Heim got one answer to that question almost immediately, the sight of a blue flare that turned red streaking up from the Russian positions.

F-61D "Evil Dreams" Over Letnerechenskiy, Kola Peninsula

The flares arched up, out of the pine forest and down, changing from blue to red as they burned. They formed a box, defining three of the edges with the front edge of the trees making the fourth. In between them was their target. Its location was marked by a plume of black smoke rising from the trees. That could only be a vehicle burning and the vehicles down there were all German. Lieutenant Quayle swung *Evil Dreams* around and headed for the defined area. He'd already fired his rockets but he still had six five hundred pound bombs and his guns.

"We're coming in from the east." That made sense, if any of the bombs hung up on the racks, they'd land clear of the Russians closing in on the German unit. Bombs often hung up and released late, Quayle had never known one release prematurely. "Donnie, the turret guns are yours, open up on anything that fires on us. Be generous guys, we're going home soon and we don't want to take anything back with us."

"Situation *Evil Dreams*?" The voice crackled over the radio unexpectedly. "This is *Night Mare*."

"Welcome to the party *Night Mare*. Watch our run, that'll mark position for you. You have rockets?"

"Sure have *Evil Dreams*. And thousand pounders."

That was a problem, thousand pounders were all very well when the Night Witches were behind enemy lines with nothing friendly around but they were too big for this situation. "Hold off on the bombs *Night Mare*, we're hitting a confined area here."

"Roger. Watching your run now."

Evil Dreams had finished her long turn and started her run towards the area of pine forest marked by the flares. Quayle added power to the engines and started the Black Widow in a shallow dive, her nose pointing straight at the edge of the pine forest. The black stain of the burning vehicle was on the left as she swept down and released her bombs into the treeline framed by the box. Behind her, *Night Mare* followed the same path. She released her bombs a fraction of a second later. They exploded in the open, a few meters beyond the edge of the pine trees.

"Neat job *Night Mare*." The explosions from the smaller bombs had raked the trees with fragments but the blast from the thousand pounders had leveled the tree edge. "And what do we see down there?"

The explosions from the big bombs hadn't just knocked the trees down. It had exposed at least one German vehicle. It was an eight-wheeled armored car with a large gun fitted. One of the 75mm-armed tank killers. Quayle brought *Evil Dreams* around and swept down again. He'd selected his 23mm cannon this time. He walked the burst along the ruined treeline until the armor-piercing shots tore into the armored car. The 23mm V-Ya wasn't much good against tanks, unless the crew were lucky. It was very good against thinly armored vehicles. What had once been an armored car tank destroyer was now a burning pile of wreckage.

Mechanized Column, 71st Infantry Division, Kola Peninsula

Lieutenant Kolchek pulled himself out of the debris thrown around by the bombs. Through the blast-induced confusion he tried to get a grasp on what was happening around him. The rising sun was warming the ground and trees, causing threads of mist to form. He knew what would happen over the next few minutes, as the sun rose further, the mist would grow, the threads would coalesce into a ground fog that would last until the sun grew hot enough to burn it off. Before then, visibility limited by the trees would shrink to a few meters. That loaded the dice in favor of the attackers.

As if to confirm his opinion, a barrage of shots rang out. A few rifles but mostly the ripping noise of the PPS-45s and the slow, heavy thud of the American M-3s. The bullets ricocheted off the tree stumps and tore through the piles of broken branches that now covered his front. The partisans had taken the opportunity of the disruption caused by the airstrike to push forward until they were within almost touching distance of the German positions. The rattle of gunfire was joined by the heavier thud of grenades, Kolchak guessed what was happening now, the partisans had closed up to the point where the sub-machine gunners were keeping a foxhole pinned down while the grenadiers tossed their weapons into it. His positions had been mutually supporting but the combination of the strike and the mist was interrupting those plans.

"Sergeant, send a runner back to Colonel Asbach. Tell him we're falling back, trying to establish a new perimeter. Everybody else, drop back, at least 50 meters. Try and get some separation from the Ivans."

Kolchek started to scramble backwards. If he could get his men back, they could set up a new line. It would be better-placed that the compromised position he was being forced to abandon. He had in a position in mind. It was where a shallow depression ran through the pine trees. *Probably the remnant of a path or game trail.* Once his men were set up there, they could establish a front line that could hold. The problem was that this would leave the rearguard and artillery positions hanging. *Well, that was for them to worry about, the Colonel would have to warn them.*

Floundering through the snow, Kolchek saw the depression ahead of him. He also saw something else, sets of long parallel lines in the snow. He looked at them for a second before the significance of them sunk in. That was just a second too long. As he realized he was looking at ski-tracks, the Siberians in the ditch he was relying on opened fire on the men retreating towards them. Kolchek was one of the first to go down, hit over a dozen times by the spraying burst from a PPS-45. As he bled out on the ground he saw his men being cut down by the Siberians to their rear and the partisans closing in from the front.

1st Platoon, Ski Group, 78th Siberian Infantry Division, Kola Peninsula

Knyaz watched the Hitlerites being shot down with grim glee. As the two American sturmoviks had swept overhead, he had lead a group of his ski-troops through a small gap that existed between the fascist flank and rear positions. They had been screened by the trees, the developing mist, the blast from the bombs and the raking bursts of gunfire from the air. His men had moved in behind the fascists and occupied a good position. Then the Hitlerites had disengaged and tried to set up a new defense line. Knyaz and his men had held their fire to the last second before opening up with a withering barrage of automatic fire. Instinctively, the fascists who had survived that first blast of gunfire had recoiled from it and fallen back. Straight into another burst of gunfire from the partisans following up the fascist retreat.

Knyaz had done the same thing before, many times since the grim days before Moscow in the winter of 1941. The fascists hadn't understood what fighting Siberians had meant back then. Now they knew. They rued the day the Siberian divisions had arrived on the European front. Today was another, and the Hitlerite bodies covering the ground in front of his position were proof of that.

"Bratishka, we have much more to do." Knyaz thought quickly. The whole German rear was hanging in the air with nothing between his troops and the German command post in the center. "Now, we must help the partisans fighting the fascist artillery. Let us take their gun positions from the rear and show them what it means to fight with the bayonet!"

It sounded good but Knyaz knew it wouldn't come to that. This battle was being fought with grenades and sub-machine guns and they would clear the fascist artillery out of their positions.

Mechanized Column, 71st Infantry Division, Kola Peninsula

Captain Lang heard the gunfire erupting from the trees behind him. A novice he might be, he was grimly aware now of how little he really knew of warfare. The thought of his behavior when he had first arrived made his stomach cramp with humiliation. *Yes, a novice I might be but I can tell that the gunfire and the grenade blasts were indeed behind me. Quite a long way behind me, tens of meters at a guess.* He closed his eyes for a second and thought. *What would he do if he was the Ivan?* He knew the answer because it was straight out of the book. *Swing around, pivot his advance and take the gun positions from the rear.* With infantry in front and behind, the gunners would be cut down and the pieces would be taken. That could not be.

"Sergeant, get the men together. We'll cover you while your crews start up the guns. They'll have to break out, try to join the Colonel in the center. He'll know what to do. Hurry up man, the Ivans are closing in on us."

Sergeant Heim needed no encouragement to hurry. Unlike Lang, he was a veteran and he knew that the Ivan ski-troops would be on him very soon. To emphasize that message, a Panzerfaust flew out of the mist and trees. It exploded on the ground, a few meters short of one of the three remaining self-propelled guns. That enthused the crew far more than any verbal exhortations could have done and the gun started to move out. As it did so, a second Panzerfaust exploded in the mud where it had been just a few second earlier. Heim watched the other guns starting to back up while Lang's handful of infantrymen tried to pin down the partisans advancing from the front.

The gunners were doing their best, Heim knew it, Lang knew it, but time was critically short and conditions were not good. One thing saved the guns, they had been positioned to fire on where the train would be arriving and that was the direction they had to go. So, the drivers were in a better position to move their vehicles, they could see where they were going. And their vehicles were faster going forward. And old joke ran through Heim's mind but he dismissed it with irritation. *Who knew how Italian tanks would perform? They'd never been seen on the Russian Front.*

1st Platoon, Ski Group, 78th Siberian Infantry Division, Kola Peninsula

Russian was a remarkably good language for cursing and Knyaz used the available vocabulary to the full. The Hitlerites had guessed his move and were pulling their guns out. The whole rear of the German position was crumbling. The guns and their infantry cover were retreating away from his men and the partisans. The latter were doing their best, they fired their captured Panzerfausts with abandon. The explosions flowered all over the positions the fascists had been holding. But they were missed the guns. That wasn't surprising, the Panzerfaust was an abominably inaccurate and short-ranged weapon. Knyaz waved his arm and his men started to shift diagonally backwards. They were trying to close in on the gun positions before they could be evacuated. His men fired on the fascists, sending them tumbling down but too few. The guns were getting clear.

Two of the three survivors did. The third, the last to get moving, couldn't quite get out of range fast enough. One Panzerfaust hit it in the tracks. The rocket blew off the forward idler and a road wheel. The track broke and the self-propelled gun spun around and stopped. A second Panzerfaust hit the side of the boxy gun compartment and sent steel fragments howling around inside the structure. Knyaz saw the surviving crew abandon the vehicle. Almost without thinking he and his men opened fire, cutting them down in a hail of sub-machine gun fire.

The self-propelled gun was already starting to burn when a series of blasts turned it into an inferno. The partisans were close enough to throw anti-tank grenades at it. For a brief second, Knyaz actually felt sorry for the gun. *It had been stolen from its original owners and brought so far to die in the pine forests of Russia.* Then his mind snapped back to more important things. With the fascist flank and rear caving in, the battle was moving into end game. Crushing the fascist pocket completely. The fascists had also come a long way to die in the forests of Russia. Knyaz didn't feel sorry for them at all.

Mechanized Column, 71st Infantry Division, Kola Peninsula

It was an odd thing, Asbach mused, that the Night Witches overhead didn't seem nearly so deadly in daylight. He'd never actually seen one before. All he'd seen were dark shadows flashing overhead or bursts of fire from the darkness. To see the grey jabos circle his position and occasionally dive down to deliver bursts of gunfire, somehow took the mystery away from the feared intruders.

"Colonel, our right flank has caved in, Kolchek tried to disengage but the Siberians had got behind him. There's only one survivor, a runner he sent out. Captain Lang reports he's had to disengage from the rear, he was outflanked and had the enemy behind him. Siberians again."

Siberians, Asbach thought, *always the Siberians.* "Is Lang still alive?"

"Yes Colonel. He and the two surviving guns are heading here."

That was it, Asbach saw that the game was over. His command was being squeezed back and would soon be overrun. That would be the end for nobody took prisoners on the Russian Front. Even the Canadians and Americans had given up that custom. Asbach shuddered slightly, in one way it was lucky they were fighting Siberians. Some of the American units had whole battalions recruited from the American Indian tribes, Sioux, Apache, Comanche. The SS had tried to demoralize some of the Apache troops. They had taken a

395

few prisoners in night raids then left their mutilated bodies for the Apache soldiers to find. Only, it hadn't worked. The Apache had buried their dead and then replied in kind. When the SS had found what had been done to the bodies of the victims, even the hardest of the SS men had vomited in horror. No, it was better to be fighting the Siberians.

Asbach stared at his map. He had one option left. He still had his three Pumas although the 75mm tank destroyers were both gone. He had nine surviving half tracks and the two self propelled guns. Any hope of catching or destroying the last railway gun was gone but he could save what was left of his command. He'd make a panzerkeil, an armored wedge that would drive through the Russian force on his left flank. The Pumas and self-propelled guns would lead All the surviving men would be in the half-tracks behind. They'd just crash through and keep going. There was a road a little to the south, the one that they'd come in on. Once on that, they'd just keep heading south until they ran out of fuel or they reached safety.

He rapped out the necessary orders, watching the men pull back from the forward positions he'd set up so carefully to stop the train. The devil's train, he was certain that gun was possessed by the very devil himself. It had won, it had won the battle that it shouldn't even have fought. Asbach shook his head. *There was no way that gun should have survived. It had to be the devil's own work.* Halfway through the hasty preparations, Lang and his guns arrived. Asbach repeated the plan, such as it was, for him.

The partisans and Siberians were already closing in when Asbach's force launched its attack. There was no pretext of holding ground or seizing anything. This was a breakout and that was all it was. The three Pumas started off the assault. They firedg their 50mm cannon at the suspected partisan positions in the woods. Lang's two remaining 150mm guns joined in and lobbed shells over open sights into the trees. They killed the partisans hidden there and opened the way for the armored vehicles. Then, the armored cars and half-tracks surged forward and sprayed gunfire wildly into the trees.

Surprise, the sudden gunfire and the violence of the attack pulled it off. One of the Pumas blew up when it was hit by a Panzerfaust. A half-track got hung up on a treestump and was grenaded to death but the other vehicles got out. They headed south in a straggling column, determined only to get clear of the death trap that had destroyed their unit.

Behind them, ski-troops and partisans watched them burst out of the trees and run. Some felt tempted to cheer but it was neither the time nor the place. The partisans had lost a lot of their people in this battle. The rest of the bands would have to disperse and hide for the Germans would surely want revenge.

F-61D "Evil Dreams" Over Letnerechenskiy, Kola Peninsula

Circling overhead, Quayle saw the flurry of explosions. The German column erupted from the woods and headed for the road leading south. *Night Mare* had already set off back to base, her guns almost empty and her fuel tanks running dry. Quayle reckoned he had enough 23mm ammunition left for one quick pass then he too would have to head home. It was broad daylight and no time for Black Widows to be up. He swung the big fighter over, dropped the nose and made his run. The vehicles filled his gunsight and he pressed the firing button, seeing the red-orange tracers streak out to hit the center half-track. Then, his guns ran dry and he pulled out of the dive, setting course for home. It was definitely past his bed-time.

Mechanized Column, 71st Infantry Division, Kola Peninsula

Captain Lang saw the half-track lurch off the dirt track and topple into a ditch. It was already burning, its engine compartment gouted black smoke. In a few seconds, the fire would spread and the vehicle would explode.

"Stop! Now!" His command was definitive, unanswerable and the driver of the self-propelled gun responded instantly. The gun stopped dead, rocking on its suspension, so sharply that the gun behind was barely able to avoid colliding with it. By the time the column had stopped, Lang had grabbed a pry-bar and was running over to the ditched vehicle. He didn't bother with the driver's compartment. It was already shot up and on fire. There was no hope for the driver. But there was hope for the men in the back.

The door in the rear was jammed. Lang had expected that. He rammed the pry-bar into the crack between the frame and the door and started to heave. He felt his face reddening from the heat, could smell his eyebrows singing but the door would not shift. Then, another man added his weight to the bar and the door finally sprung open. Lang jumped inside, the smoke making his eyes water. A man was sprawled on the floor by the rear hatch. Lang seized him under the arms and dragged him out. It was Sergeant Heim, burned, unconscious and hit by fragments from the armor but still alive. The other men threw snow over him to put out the smoldering greatcoat wrapped around him.

Lang heard the whumph behind him as the fuel tank on the half-track exploded. The whole vehicle burned, an orange ball spread underneath it as the blazing fuel ran aft. He didn't think, he didn't even wonder what to do. He ignored a cry of 'stop' from somebody and plunged back into the burning rear compartment of the wrecked half-track. He had his arm up to give his eyes some protection, but he could feel his skin tightening and cracking as the fire started to do its work. In his mind was the picture of a pig roasting on a spit at one of the staff college rides and in his mind, the pig had his face. He stumbled over the other figure in the back of the half-track, and reached out with one hand to grab Colonel Asbach by the collar.

He didn't know how he did it, he just kept dragged Asbach backwards until the heat stopped and he could feel the blessed cold of the snow. Then he passed out.

Asbach was already being loaded on to an improvised stretcher, ready for the run home. The men had concluded that their colonel might have a chance, if they could drive him home. Around Lang, men peeled the charred greatcoat off his body, wincing at the sight of his burns. He also might stand a chance, if they could get him home again fast enough. Then one of them snorted and pointed out a miracle. Surrounded by the charred remains of his greatcoat and the burned rags of his uniform, Captain Lang's white silk scarf was still untouched and pristine.

United States Strategic Bombardment Commission, Blair House, Washington D.C. USA.

"The paperwork is here." Lillith walked in with a pile of papers in her hands and put them on The Seer's desk. He picked the top one up. His imagination told him that it still smelled slightly of cheese and salami. When he read the synopsis his eyebrows raised slightly.

"This is gold. Important things first. How's Igrat?"

"In Bethesda. Her nose is very bad, broken in a lot of places. Sir Archibald is looking at it now. She's very sick, she took a big chance in getting here and now she's paying for it. Mike Collins is with her, holding her hand and crying. I don't think anybody has ever seen the Big Fella crying before."

"Might do him some good. Snap him out of it; he's been moping around doing nothing in particular ever since he arrived here. Looking after Igrat might give him an aim in life." He paused for a second, not noting that Lillith's eyes had narrowed suspiciously. "As for Igrat, as long as she's still breathing, she'll be all right."

"It's not surviving that will be worrying her Seer. It's her looks. She doesn't want to spend the rest of her life with a crushed and twisted nose."

"And she won't. Sir Archibald will see to that. He's the best there is. Now, the microdots, they got through as well?"

"Sure did. We fished the plastic packet they were in out of the cheese and salami, ran them through the machine and we're printing them out now. They'll be ready for your three o'clock."

"Good. Schedule. I'll be at the Intelligence Committee until 11. Then we all go over to Bethesda and see Igrat. Anybody who wants to go, gets time off to do it. I have to be back for the Dropshot Supervisory Committee at three. Please call Naamah and tell her I need to see her urgently.

Intelligence Supervisory Committee, Senate Conference Room, Washington D.C.

"Gentlemen, the room is secured and no unauthorized personnel are in attendance. The meeting may now proceed. Firstly I'd......"

"We have an important matter to discuss." Brigadier-General Donovan cut straight across the President, an act that got him a furious glance from President Dewey. Donovan had been one of Roosevelt's favorites but that state of grace had not transferred to the Dewey Administration. There was no love lost between the two men. "I have been increasingly concerned with the security of intelligence information being brought back from Sweden. The precautions taken in carrying it have been negligent in the extreme. This vital data was entrusted to the carriage of two young woman, both of doubtful character, and an old man. We feared it could have been taken from them at any time. With this last shipment, our fears were justified. The couriers, if they can be called that, were intercepted and the product stolen by German agents. It was only through the efforts of two of my men that it was recovered and it is now on its way back here."

"Is this true, Stuyvesant?" Dewey stared hard at The Seer.

"No, Sir. It is not." A gasp ran around the conference room. It wasn't often that somebody got openly called a liar in this kind of meeting.

Donovan got angrily to his feet waving his hand at the Seer. "I've said for years that we should have a centralized intelligence system. Now everybody can see why we need it. You. . . . ."

"Sit down Donovan." Dewey's voice cracked across the room. "Stuyvesant, what's your side of this?"

"Sir. We have been aware for some time that the OSS was unhealthily interested in the pipeline from Geneva. I say unhealthily because it could have attracted attention we didn't need. On the trip before this one, an OSS man actually tried to harass our people. General Donovan, I believe these are the two men you claim retrieved the allegedly lost information?" The Seer slid two pictures across the table. One was of Frank Barnes, the other of William Schwartz.

"That's them. How dare you expose their identit. . . ."

"Be quiet Donovan. Carry on please Stuyvesant."

"Well, in that incident, our courier removed the wallet from the man harassing our operation. General Donovan's description is quite correct Sir, our courier is indeed a young woman of poor character. Sneaky, devious, underhanded, conniving and rather sly."

"In that work, those sounds like qualifications." Dewey was beginning to be amused and he could already begin to see where this was going.

"That's my opinion too, Sir. She's also utterly reliable and absolutely loyal." The Seer didn't add 'to me' although he should have done. "She's also a first-class, highly skilled thief. She stole this from the OSS man."

He slid Frank Barnes' wallet over the table. President Dewey took a glance at the picture in it, then looked very hard at Donovan. "I see. Carry on Stuyvesant."

"Anyway, this latest trip, our team were aware of the fact they were being followed from early on. They lost the initial tail in a hotel of dubious repute. I'm afraid dubious reputations are rather prominent in this story Sir. That allowed them to make the pick-up. However, they guessed that they would be intercepted on the way out. There are only two ways out of Geneva, one is by train and the other by aircraft. So they broke the usual schedule. Our courier, her name is Igrat Shafrid by the way, acted as a decoy while the intelligence package left another way. When we were speaking of character, did I also mention Miss Shafrid is extremely courageous? She took her part in this knowing full well the risk she was running.

"Anyway, as expected, she was picked up at the train station. Not be the Gestapo or the Abwehr but by General Donovan's agents from the OSS."

"That's a lie!" Donovan was outraged.

"Can you prove that Stuyvesant?" President Dewey was also outraged but for different reasons. He had a sense of when things were right or not and Stuyvesant's story was ringing true.

"Sir, I can. Miss Shafrid was picked up by two of Donovan's men as I said. Fortunately, we had preparations in place and she and her abductors were followed from the moment they left the station. The precautions taken by our team left Donovan's men with a problem. The intelligence package wasn't on her and they didn't know where she had got it. So they tried to beat the truth out of her. This is what they did to her." The Seer laid pictures taken in Geneva's emergency ward, ones taken before the blood had been cleaned off her and where her nose was still crushed and flattened to one side. "In addition to the injuries you can see here, she was also sexually assaulted."

"What?" Dewey's voice was outraged.

401

"Mister President, I must protest at these allegation..."

"Shut up, Donovan. Stuyvesant, carry on please."

"Sir, the other two members of the team had followed the abductors to their refuge and, with the assistance of the Swiss Police raided it. In the process of this, the two OSS men who were torturing Miss Shafrid, were both shot dead. You see, Sir, that 'old man' is probably the best pistol-fighter I have ever met. The third member of the team is a skilled street-fighter and an artiste with a knife. Anyway, these are official Swiss Police photographs of the bodies." He reached into his file and laid the two pictures of Frank Barnes and William Schwartz on the conference table. The bullet hole in each forehead showed up clearly. The Seer had thought of bringing the severed heads up to the conference room. Loki had sent them over in a box of ice and there had been a time when The Seer would have produced them. But now, pictures told the story well enough.

"And that's more or less it Sir. Except, two things. One is General Donovan said our intelligence packet was being brought over by his two men. Well, that isn't true. I have it here. And he doesn't know where it came from. Our source is still secure despite his blundering."

"That is some comfort Stuyvesant. General Donovan, I must say I am outraged at the story that has unfolded here today. I have no doubt that you acted as you though best but your methods are completely unacceptable. Stuyvesant, this young woman, she is receiving the best possible treatment?"

"Indeed Sir, Sir Archibald MacIndoe is treating her himself."

"Good. She deserves some recognition for her bravery in this affair. I'll consult with the appropriate authorities and decide upon a suitable award. Stuyvesant, before we go any further, what is your opinion on the proposal for a unified intelligence service?"

"Sir, I can think of no greater domestic threat to democracy. We have seen one reason here today. Another is that if there is one centralized source for intelligence, there is only one opinion on that intelligence. Decisions are controlled in part by the information on which those decisions are based. If the information is controlled by a small group, so is the decision. We need to have conflicting opinions so those who make decisions can choose the interpretation for themselves."

"Checks and balances. Sounds familiar. I agree Stuyvesant. General Donovan, your plans to form a single centralized intelligence service are rejected. I do not wish to see them raised again. Also, you will attend a meeting with the Strategic Bombing Commission to determine which of the operations run by your OSS will be better placed in their custody. With that decision, I call this meeting to a close. May I say I hope never to have to deal with a matter of this character again."

Corrective Surgery Ward, Bethesda Hospital, Bethesda, Maryland

"How is she Doctor?"

"Much better than expected. She is a very strong young woman and her constitution is remarkable. Do you know the fractures in her ribs are already beginning to knit? Quite remarkable. That's not so good in one respect, her nose was also beginning to knit so I had to rebreak some of the bones. The damage is quite severe, there's no hope of returning her nose to its original shape but we spent the morning going through some pictures and Miss Shafrid has picked a new nose she rather likes. I think she'll be very happy with it."

"Thank you Doctor. Send the account to me personally, it will be paid by return."

"Paid? My dear young man." *That was a joke* thought Stuyvesant though he was still slightly pleased by the phrase. "If you wish to pay me, send a donation to my institute for burn patients up in Canada. So many young men are being so badly burned in this war. To help a young woman this way has been a blessed relief. She will fully recover, most of those poor young men will bear their scars until their deaths."

"Can we see her?" Inanna broke across the Doctor MacIndoe's obvious distress.

"Of course, her young man is away for the moment, but you can all go in. I must caution you, she looks very bad at the moment, the original injuries plus the bruising from the surgery. So, it's important you don't show shock. But otherwise, she is recovering very well.

403

Quite remarkable." Sir Archibald, went off, down the corridor to where some other patients were awaiting their turn for his services.

"Well, I don't need make-up to play a clown do I?" Igrat was laying on her bed, surrounded by flowers, chocolates and fresh fruit.

"Mike?" The Seer spoke drily.

"Mike. How he got all this stuff I do not know. The black market must have done well. I've given some of it away already and I bet he'll have more when he gets back." Igrat tried to smile then winced at the effort. "Everything OK?"

"Everything's fine honey. Donovan's crashed and burned. So badly he'll never be a threat to us again. That centralized intelligence idea of his could have been bad for us."

"What?" Lillith's voice was sharp, questioning.

"Can you imagine a greater danger to us that a centralized intelligence service with all the national records available to it? At best, hiding would become really hard, at worst impossible. So it had to be stopped."

"You. You had the whole thing planned didn't you? You sent Iggie into a meat grinder knowing what would happen." Lillith's face had changed completely, her skin had drawn back, outlining her bones in sharp relief and her eyes stood out. At this point she looked more like a vulture that anything else. "You played your games and Iggie got beaten into a pulp and you never even warned her. In the name of all the gods, she's your daughter!"

"Uh-oh." Naamah's voice came quietly from the back of the room.

"Lillith, NO!" Igrat's voice, blurred as it was cut right across the outburst. "Phillip did tell me. I knew the whole plan right from the start and I volunteered for it. It was OK with me. He explained why we had to do it and I agreed with him. I knew the risks, but I believed in Henry and Achillea. We just didn't believe Donovan would go this far. Right? Now don't make me talk too much again, it hurts."

Lillith relaxed, her face returning to normal. "Sorry, Phillip. I didn't mean to . . . . . ."

"Don't worry about it. Everything worked out in the end, that's all that mattered."

The party left, but Naamah remained behind for a moment. She sat quietly beside Igrat's bed. "That was a lie wasn't it. You didn't know what was going to happen. Or what the plan was."

"I didn't. Oh I guessed some of it, but Phillip didn't tell me and I didn't volunteer. I just trusted him. But remember what happened when Lillith last went into vengeful harpy mode? Our family almost broke up forever and I couldn't stand that. So the truth remains buried. Right? Because if you tell anybody, I'll throttle you."

Naamah chuckled. "Right, and I stand warned. You just get well. I can't stay, I've got a one o'clock with General Donovan."

Hospitality Suite, United States Strategic Bombardment Commission, Blair House, Washington D.C. USA.

"Why isn't Stuyvesant here himself?" Donovan sounded aggrieved and put out.

"He's got other business. In Bethseda. But I have full authority to act on his behalf. Tell me General, how was your steak?"

"Delicious, I thought steaks like this were unobtainable except on the black market?"

"My family has a farm in Kansas. They keep us supplied with striploins."

Donovan spooned up the rest of the mushroom sauce with the last piece of steak. "This was excellent, thank you for cooking it. You're not eating any?"

"I'm a vegetarian. Don't eat meat. Anyway, cheese salad does well for my lunch, I have to watch my figure."

"So, where do we go from here?" Donovan was back to being testy. In addition to the humiliation this morning, he wasn't feeling very well. Overeating probably.

"Well, we need to have unrestricted access to all intelligence data on German industry. Of course we already have most of it but if there is any we don't have, we need it. And we need to know our courier system won't be compromised again. Other than that...."

Donovan leaned back. If that was all he was going to lose, things weren't too bad. "Nothing else?"

Naamah looked at the clock. Over 45 minutes since Donovan had started eating. "Just one thing, you really shouldn't have had Igrat beaten like that. She's a nice girl. She sleeps around a bit, well a lot really, but she never did any harm to anybody who wasn't threatening her. There was no need to do all that to her."

"So what are you going to do, kill me?" Donovan's face was split with a grin, one that quickly changed to a grimace as his stomach cramped. He gasped and doubled up, slumping over the table.

"I already have, General." Naamah picked up his fork and pushed a tiny fragment of mushroom left on his plate. "Have you ever heard of death cap mushrooms?"

United States Strategic Bombardment Commission, Blair House, Washington D.C. USA.

"Warning Boss, Mike's on his way up."

"Right Lillith, action stations."

The Seer sat back and relaxed, he'd been expecting this. He'd reckoned it would take the morning for Mike Collins to get over his grief and work up a head of steam. Then, he'd be coming this way. Well, it looked like he'd got here. The door suddenly hurtled open, bounced off its hinges and almost laid out the man storming through.

"You bastard Stuyvesant."

"Actually no, Mike, my mother and father were married when I was born."

Collins blinked, then set out again. "You sent a wee girl to do a job rather than risk your own cowardly hide. And she got smashed up because of you. So get out from behind that desk and fight like a man."

Styvesant grinned. "Mike, look behind you."

"You'll not fool me with that old trick."

"Just humor me, look on it as respect for tradition if you wish."

Collins glanced behind him. Then turned his head a little more carefully. While he'd been shouting, Lillith and Naamah had quietly entered the office and were pointing M3 sub-machine guns at him. They were carefully positioned so they could kill him without endangering anybody else.

"Hiding behind women again?"

"If necessary Mike. Won't be the first time. I do what's necessary to win Mike. Whatever is necessary. Always remember that."

"And you've not the courage to fight fair like a man."

"Mike, I've always believed if I get into a fair fight, it's because I made a mistake. I never fight fair. I never have and hopefully I never will. Just remember, if you're within ten feet of me, you can be sure there's a gun pointing at your back somehow. Now calm down. Igrat's going to be all right, it's just you'll have to look after her for a while."

"And then you'll send her on a courier mission again."

"Of course, it's something she's superbly good at. Don't try and take that away from her, Mike, not unless you want to lose her. Iggie's a free spirit, try and protect her with cotton wool and she'll smother. Just settle down with her and go along with the ride."

"So send me along with her." Collins was calming down and Stuyvesant waved Lillith and Naamah away.

"Mike, I can't do that. Her safety depends on her own abilities and those of her bodyguards. You're a lightweight, a playboy.

407

Ask yourself, if she was going out again with somebody like you protecting her, would you be happy about it?"

Michael Collins thought about that for a long moment. "No, I would not."

"I thought not. Want a drink? I've got some Irish whiskey."

"I'll not say no, though drinking with you is not what I thought of doing when I came here."

Stuyvesant poured out two shot glasses of whiskey and added a drop of water to each. Collins took one and sipped it gently. "Good stuff. I've not had this good in many a year. Will Ireland ever recover?"

Stuyvesant drank down his own glass and looked at the drop left in the bottom. "Recover? Perhaps. They're a tough people but they've never had it this bad. They have a chance, I'll say that."

"They'll have a chance and you'll not say more than that. You're a heartless, cold, man Stuyvesant. I would not want to be you."

"You don't have to be. But just ask yourself what you do want. Holiday's over, Mike. You've had your party and you've had a vacation. Now decide what you want to do with your life. Winter's passing, spring is on its way and this war will be over one day. Just try and work out what you and Igrat want to do in the spring."

United States Strategic Bombardment Commission, Blair House, Washington D.C. USA.

"Gentlemen, the room is secured and no unauthorized personnel are in attendance. The meeting may now proceed. Firstly, although General Donovan was invited to attend this meeting, I regret to tell you that he was taken seriously ill this afternoon. He collapsed in the building and was rushed to Walter Reed Hospital. There, it was determined that he has suffered from complete renal collapse and advanced cirrhosis of the liver. He is currently in a coma and is not expected to recover consciousness. The prognosis is that his condition is terminal and he has two days, perhaps three before toxemia kills him. We will therefore proceed without him."

"No great loss." LeMay grunted from his seat.

"Curt, he won the Medal." General Groves was shocked at the attitude in the room to the news.

"I know, we honor him for what he did then, just as we condemn him for what he tried to do today. Philip, what he tried was beyond reason. I'm sorry Les, I can't find it in me to forgive that. Trying it was bad enough, trying it and fouling up was worse. I'm glad he's out of this meeting."

"I didn't even know he was cleared for 'Dropshot'." General Groves was curious.

"He was not. He would have been here for discussions related to conventional bombing only." The Seer passed around the packages of data received from Geneva. "Gentlemen, this information relates to the plans made by the Germans for countering the effects of a strategic bombing offensive against their industrial heartland. Naturally, they were preparing for conventional bombing only."

There was silence in the room for almost half an hour as the members of the Dropshot Supervisory Committee read through the translated German papers. Eventually, General LeMay put his pile down, shuffled them into a neat stack and spoke quietly past his pipe. "Well, that ends any thought of a precisely-targeted bombing offensive."

"I must agree General." The Seer also spoke quietly. "There's no point in trying to take out a key industrial sector. If we succeed, they'll just strip less essential sectors to repair the damage. There are no key sectors, not ones we can destroy anyway. If we try, it'll be a battle of attrition, trying to run them out of industry before we run out of bombers."

"You know what this means don't you?" Groves was also speaking quietly, the secrets of the B-36 and the atomic bomb were so huge that they made any attempt at drama look absurd. "Conventional strategic bombing was always doomed to fail. We can't do enough damage fast enough to take down a complete industrial infrastructure."

"I hate to say it Les, but you're right. Back in the 1930s, we were wrong. No other way to say it. We couldn't do it with B-29s, we

409

sure as hell couldn't do it with B-17s and we won't be able to do it with B-36s. It has to be nuclear."

"And I hate to say it Curt, but you and Stuyvesant were right. We can't just take down a portion of their industry and expect them to fold. These documents show they mean to keep fighting as long as they house a machine tool in a brick outhouse. For the record, I formally withdraw my reservations on waiting for The Big One. We have to take the whole lot out at once. The Little One and the interim variants cannot work."

Stuyvesant looked around at the room and the nodding heads. "Does anybody wish to maintain their reservations on the record?" The heads all shook. It was decided. It would be The Big One. Quietly he wondered if Loki would ever realize what decision the information he had provided had been responsible for.

Bridge, USS "Gettysburg" CVB-43, Flagship Task Force 58

"Captain, thank you for allowing me on your bridge."

"You're welcome Captain Lokken. We're just pulling into Churchill now." The exchange was interrupted by a blast on the ship's siren, one that was picked up by other ships in the formation. The dawn seascape seemed to reverberate with the sounds.

"What is happening Captain?"

"Nothing to worry about. Two of the light fleet carriers are leaving the Fast Carrier Force. They're on their way out to the Pacific Fleet. They're just getting their send-off. Look over to port, you can see their replacements, *Shiloh* and *Chickamauga*. Sister ships of *Gettysburg*."

"Two more great carriers like this one. It wouldn't have mattered if we'd won would it? You would have just built more ships and come right back."

"That's right, captain. And since we won, we're going to build more ships anyway. The Atlantic is our lake now, we're going to go boating."

Lokken nodded slowly, watching the long line of ships enter the huge natural harbor that was Churchill's reason for existence. "And so it will go on."

"Not for you Captain, as soon as our Doc releases you, you're off to a prisoner of war camp. An officer's only one of course."

"I would wish to stay with my men. What few there are left."

"I bet you would Captain, but its less trouble all around if we separate the officers from the enlisted men. So, it's an officer's camp for you. Don't sweat it, I'm told the conditions are quite good and the Red Cross has its representatives on site. So, don't worry, for you the war is over."

Military Hospital, 71st Infantry Division, Kola Peninsula

Lang woke up, carefully and uncertainly. The last thing he remembered was the flames scorching his skin. His men had been rolling him in the snow to put him out, He couldn't feel the burns now but that could just be anesthetic. In fact, he felt remarkably comfortable. He just lay on the bed, luxuriating in the feel of the soft mattress and the sheets.

"Comfortable are we, Major?" An acidic voice cut through his daze. Major-General Marcks was looking down at him.

"Sir, Sir?" Lang was flummoxed by the words but wasn't quite sure why.

"That's right Lang, its Major Lang now. And you have a piece of over-decorated tin to go with it. Also your friends on the General Staff want you back."

"General Sir, tell them to go to hell. I'll stay here, if you want me of course. And if I'm able"

"Asbach spoke quite highly of you. Thinks you have the makings of a good soldier. And your wounds are not severe, your greatcoat took most of the fire and your gloves protected your hands. You'll be happy to know your silk scarf survived intact, in fact your men have it under guard for you. They've already beaten up one man who tried to steal it. But I'm not supposed to know that."

411

"The men Sir? How many escaped?"

"Most who survived that last battle. We lost another half-track to a Grizzly but that was all, and the crew of that escaped. The battle's over Lang. We're back to where we were before it all started. Just there's a lot fewer of us. And the Finns are out of the war, they capitulated after the Amis burned Helsinki to the ground. This Winter War has not gone well. Asbach said it wouldn't and he was right. Fortunately, the Navy has taken the blame, we were all betrayed by them you know." Marcks was absent-mindedly rubbing his ear.

The way that Marcks spoke of Asbach suddenly sank in. "The Colonel Sir, how is he? How is Asbach?"

"Asbach is alive, although he was not as fortunate as you. Or perhaps more fortunate, depending on how one looks at it. His burns were much more severe. His injuries make him unfit for any kind of military service. He's going home. He left a message for you though, he says that when you get some leave, if you have nothing better to do, drop in and see him. The two of you can kill a bottle or three of his family brandy."

"I'll do that Sir and, Sir, may I . . . . . . "

"Stay with my division? I think so, I need somebody to replace Asbach. Yes, Lang, you can stay. Now, anything else?"

Lang thought for a second. "A bottle or three of brandy, that sounds good. Where does Asbach's family live Sir?"

"On the Rhine, the family business is making brandy. Their home is in one of the small towns there, place called Duren."

Marcks stomped out, swinging the door shut behind him. A sacrilegious thought entered Lang's mind. *At least out here I don't have to keep remembering whose ass to lick.* With that comfort, Lang relaxed on his pillows.

Curly, *Battery B, US Navy 5th Artillery Battalion, Kola Peninsula.*

"Well, we're nearly there. Knyaz, you'll be leaving us now?"

412

"No, Commander, my division is grouped around this railhead. If it is permissible, I'd like to stay with you until we're in."

"Knyaz, if I may make a suggestion, why don't you get your ski troops and go in ahead of us. That way you'll get your welcome before this gun grabs all the attention."

Knyaz nodded, that was a good idea. The escape of the railway guns had made headline news around the world, even if only one of the three had actually made it. There was even talk of making a Hollywood film about the exploit. *I would rather like to be played by Clark Gable.* Knyaz thought.

"Very well Commander, thank you. John, fly well and burn many fascists."

Marosy mouthed the word "Napalm" and got an appreciative laugh from the Russians. "Knyaz, thanks for everything. We'd never have got out if it hadn't been for you and your Siberians. They've got a new bird for us back at base. If you ever need anything, just get the word through. Anything bratischka, I mean that."

"And I will take you up on it. Now goodbye my friend."

After three days on the train, it felt good to be back on skis again. It had been a hard job repairing the tracks where the fascists had ripped them up. The engineers had settled for clearing the wreckage away and rebuilding the line by removing track from behind the train. Meanwhile, Knyaz and his men had kept guard but the fascists had gone. Once the work was done, it had been a gentle ride home. But it still felt good to be on skis again.

The cantonment started just as the railway like entered a marshalling yard. Knyaz had his surviving troops spread out on either side of the line, in echelons. He had to admit the arrowhead of ski-troops made a dashing figure as they entered the area occupied by the 78th Siberian Infantry Division. He could hear the watching men give the traditional 'Urrah! Urrah! He brought his men to a halt in what passed for the parade ground. Across to his left he could see Rifleman Kabanov receiving an enthusiastic 'welcome' from two of the canteen girls. *It was good to be young sometimes*, Knyaz thought, forgetting he was only 26.

"Knyaz. You have returned." It was his general, standing before him in the trampled snow. Knyaz frowned slightly. Things weren't quite normal. The General usually called him Tovarish Lieutenant.

"Sir. Regret to advise you that we have lost 22 men dead and fourteen wounded. But we have killed many fascists and captured much of their material. I will have a full report for you later Tovarish General."

"There is no hurry, you have a party to attend first, Tovarish *Senior* Lieutenant." The General was beaming at him and Knyaz closed his eyes to imagine himself with his new insignia. And his extra pay. That thought made him wonder. *Have I been around Americans too much?*

As if to confirm his belief, there was a deafening whistle from the approaching train. *Curly* edged into the marshalling yard, surrounded by cheering troops. They ran alongside the lines to welcome the gun back home. The General looked at the railway gun and shook his head. "You can't keep it you know."

Knyaz tried to look shocked. "Tovarish General, it is not our fault. He just followed us home."

EPILOGUE

C-99B "Arctic Express" Seattle, Washington, Ten Months Later

The rumble of the nose doors opening and the whine as the engines behind the wings spooled down were so familiar to Major Dedmon that he hardly noticed them. Around *Arctic Express*, trucks would be gathering to remove the cargo. It was mostly 20mm Shvak and 23mm V-YA cannon for aircraft. Built in Russian factories, the guns were reverse lend-lease. Their value was charged as a payment against Russia's account. Even in a world war, the accountants had to be kept happy. Around him, the flight deck crew finished their shut-down checks. Dedmon signed the chit that handed his aircraft over to its ground crew. That also was routine. He would leave his aircraft in their hands and they'd look after her before the next long haul to Russia.

Inside the terminal, Dedmon's crew, as usual, started to go their separate ways. This time, however, they were stopped by Colonel Sutherland. "You men, a moment please. I'm pleased to inform you that your tour of duty on the Air Bridge has been completed. I have your new assignments here. Some of you are going to the Pacific Coast to fly with the C-99 flights to Hawaii and Australia. Others will be going to other bases in the Zone of the Interior for other air transport duties." He handed out envelopes.

"You're breaking my crew up?" Dedmon was upset at the idea.

"I'm afraid so Bob. Needs must when the devil drives I'm afraid. There's too much expertise here to keep in one group. It needs to be shared out. You'd better hurry by the way. There's a C-69 Connie leaving in two hours. One of the seats has your name on it."

"Very good Sir." Dedmon went off to say his farewells to the crew that had been with him for nearly a year. If he moved fast, he would just have time for a quick wash, climb into a new uniform and collect up his property. Behind him Colonel Sutherland watched with a degree of sadness. It was hard to play the genial old man, put out to grass in a backwater assignment, while watching these young men and deciding when they were ready to go on to bigger and deadlier things. The crew of *Arctic Express*, formed a group, shaking hands and slapping backs. Doubtless they were promising to keep in touch. Those promises would almost certainly never be kept. Then, they finally went their separate ways.

C-69 Constellation "Queen of Naugatuck"

"Hi Sir, I think we're going to be neighbors for the next few hours." The young Captain managed to combine the right amount of respect for Dedmon's rank with friendliness and the camaraderie of pilots. Dedmon found himself instantly liking the man.

"Looks like it. I'm Bob Dedmon. Been flying C-99s for the last year or so."

"Andras Pico, co-pilot on C-99s for about the same length of time. My bird was *Snow Queen*."

"*Arctic Express*. The flight roster says we're heading for Fort Worth. That's Texas. My home state."

"Colorado is home for me. You get your bag lunch?"

Dedmon held up the brown paper bag he had been given. He'd already looked, it contained a cheese sandwich, a ham sandwich, an apple and a bottle of something labeled 'orange juice' although it didn't look like any juice Dedmon had ever seen before.

416

"Excuse me, Sirs, do we have to sign in? I've never ridden one of these before."

An Airman was looking down at the two men. Pico returned the gaze. "You reported at the desk? And they gave you a seat number?"

"Sir, yes sir."

"That's fine then. Just find your seat and strap in. What's your name son?"

"Martin Sir. John Paul Martin." The airman looked around and suddenly realized he had been standing right next to his assigned seat. He smiled sheepishly and sat down, nearly dropping his bag lunch in the process. "I've been a tail gunner on B-29s for the last six months."

Dedmon and Pico nodded respectfully. The B-29 crews had taken a ferocious battering. This young airman was lucky to be alive. Dedmon asked the inevitable question. "Many missions?"

"Not combat, no, Sir. Mostly training flights and ELINT missions around Japan. Saw quite a few Japanese fighters, mostly Army Ingas and Gails. A few Navy Zeros but we kept out of their way. I got lucky I guess. Never fired my guns."

Pico and Dedmon exchanged glances. Some airmen, speaking to officers informally like this, would have exaggerated their experience to gain favor. This young man was above that. They approved.

"Gentlemen, we are about to take off. Please ensure you are strapped in securely. In the event of this aircraft crashing, remember to eat your bag lunches before impact, we are not allowed to waste food." A groan went around the passenger cabin, the joke was an old one. "Personnel facilities are in the rear of the aircraft. We have no female passengers today so use of those facilities is unrestricted."

Pico smiled. "Did I ever tell you about the time we flew a group of Army nurses out? Hit bad turbulence, one of those times when a storm cut in and we didn't expect it. We were bouncing all over the place. Everybody on board was airsick but those nurses got to

417

work, passing out sick bags. They cleaned up after the ones who lost it, as cool as you like. Then, when we're out of it, one of them throws a hissy-fit because somebody had left the seat in the latrine up."

Dallas-Fort Worth, Texas

The flight down had taken six hours, most of which Dedmon had spent asleep. His companions had been considerate enough not to wake him, another point which had won them favor in his eyes. After landing, they had been herded into Air Force busses that had taken them for another two hour drive. Finally, their transport had pulled into a reception area that was indoors and lacked windows. The busses had dropped them and pulled out. A harassed-looking man with a clipboard had met them and taken them under his wing.

"I'm Colonel Lane. The General will speak to you in a few minutes. If you just come with me please."

He'd led them into a large briefing room, one without seats. Several additional groups of men arrived. Then an uneasy hush fell over the room. A stocky figure with a grim expression frozen on his face stepped out and stood behind the podium. A stir went around the room as the audience recognized General Curtis LeMay. They'd expected his voice to be a roar but in fact it was quiet, hard to hear.

"Gentlemen, you have been gathered here for the most important mission the USAF has ever flown. In addition, it is the most secret mission we have ever contemplated. There is a rule here you must never forget. What you see here, what you learn here, what you think here, must stay here. You must never, never breathe a word about your work to anybody. If you do, you will be in a military prison for so long you will forget what daylight looks like. Many people know parts of the story but very few know it all. If somebody uses a part of the story to persuade you to tell them the rest, you will terminate the conversation immediately and report the meeting to the Federal Bureau of Investigation. They will take it from there.

"When you fly, you will take off at night and you will land at night. If anybody asks you what you fly, you will reply that you are C-99 crews. Many of you, especially pilots and navigators are C-99 veterans. Feel free to bore any such audiences to death with stories about how you secure cargo and check weight balances." A stir of laughter ran around the room. "Now, the next step is to assemble crews.

Circulate amongst yourselves, try to form up into groups of about six you feel happy with. No more than three officers per group. We will assign anybody who isn't in a group after a reasonable time."

Dedmon looked at Pico and the two men nodded. Then they looked at Martin "Want in Martin?"

"Yes, SIR!" The pleasure was immediate and obvious.

"Bob, the guy over there, Sergeant King, knew him on the C-99 runs. He's the best mechanic I've ever known. Snag him?"

"Go for it."

Pico stepped away and a few seconds later brought a well-built, even overweight, Sergeant back with him. Dedmon stuck out a hand. "Sergeant King, want to join our happy band of brothers?"

The Sergeant looked cheerful. He'd been afraid his girth would put off potential crews. "Be happy to, Sirs."

Dedmon looked around again. Then he heard Martin's voice behind him. "Sir, the EW officer over there, Captain Mollins, knew him on the RB-29 flights around Japan. If we need an EW man, he's the best I saw while on the RBs."

Dedmon acknowledged the advice. A couple of minutes later, the EW officer was part of the crew. Meanwhile, Sergeant King had seen another flight engineer, Sergeant Gordon, he'd worked with and brought him over to join the group. Dedmon looked at the six men and felt a quiet satisfaction. These were good men, he had the makings of a fine crew here. Then his eye was caught by one last man, one who seemed left out by the rapidly coalescing groups around him.

"Anybody know that one?"

His crew shook their heads. "Offer him a home?"

There was a moment of thought, then a series of nods. Dedmon went over to the man. "I'm Major Dedmon, want to join my crew? We're over there."

419

The man looked at him then broke into an open, friendly smile. "That's right friendly of you Sir. I was feeling kind of left out here. I'm a bombardier, used to be on B-17s. If you'll have me, I'm in. Name's Crane. Sergeant Sammy Crane. Most people call me Argus."

Dedmon took his group up to the front where General LeMay was speaking quietly with Colonel Lane. The other groups were still speaking and getting to know each other. "Sir, our crew is ready, there's seven of us."

LeMay looked at them expressionlessly. "Not going to take time to get to know each other?"

"No Sir, we'll have time for that later. We'd just like to get started."

"I have no cause for complaint with that. Colonel Lane, take these men into the main hangar to choose their aircraft." LeMay turned and started inspecting a file. Dedmon got the distinct feeling he'd done the right thing at the right time.

Lane took his clipboard and noted the crew's names and expertise. "If you gentlemen will come with me."

The party went through the doors, down a corridor then through another door, this one guarded by two Air Force Police. Then he ushered the crew into the building beyond.

"Oh My God!" The chorus of comments was born of shock and surprise, shock at the sheer size of the hangar, stunned amazement at what it contained.

Lane looked slightly conceited. "They all say that when they come in here for the first time. That's why we call this the Ohmygod hangar. And those eight aircraft are called B-36s. The B-36H-30-FW Peacemaker to be precise. They're the month's production from this particular final assembly plant. Gentlemen, as the first registered crew of this intake, you get first choice. Take your pick. That aircraft will be yours for the indefinite future."

Dedmon looked at the aircraft, he recognized the wings as being those of the C-99 only they had jet pods mounted under the wings. Two jets per wing in addition to the six piston engines. The tail was similar to the C-99 but the fuselage was totally different. He looked underneath and saw the gaping, cavernous bomb bay. *Twice, three times the size of that on a B-29?* "I'd never guessed bombers like this existed."

"Tens of thousands of people in America know these aircraft exist, the people who build them, the people who assemble them, the people who fly them. They keep their mouths shut. I'll add something to what General LeMay said. You tell anybody about these aircraft, you're not just committing treason. You're breaking faith with everybody who has worked for six years to build up this force and to keep it secret. Now, which one would you like?"

The crew wandered around the eight aircraft in the hangar. Eventually, Dedmon found himself standing underneath one particular B-36. He couldn't understand why but he felt comfortable with this particular aircraft. It didn't make sense. They were all identical as far as he could see but this one seemed right somehow.

"What do you think guys?"

"She seems a real Lady, Bob." The rest of the group nodded.

"Colonel, could we have this one please?"

Lane looked up and read the tail number, then noted it against the crew list. "Right Major Dedmon, she's yours. What you going to call her?"

Dedmon looked up at the great silver bomber. "She is a real lady all right. In fact, she's a *Texan Lady.*"

THE END